"Could we talk?"

"About?" Every hair on Claire's arms stood up.

"Us?" he said simply.

Her chest tightened, and her palms got clammy. "What about us?"

She didn't want to hear that their kisses were only flirting and that he'd decided they should only be friends or maybe not even that. Or worse yet that an old girlfriend had popped back up in his life.

"I like you, Claire, and if you're living close by we could date, couldn't we?" he blurted out.

"Are you asking me for a date, but only if I live in Sunset? Is Randlett too far to drive?" She sewed up a couple more squares.

"If you lived on the moon and you said that you'd go out with me, I'd figure out a way to get there," he answered.

High Praise for Carolyn Brown

"Brown always gives the reader emotion, eternal love, and all the excitement you can handle."

—FreshFiction.com

COWBOY BOLD

"Western romance lovers are in for a treat. This wickedly saucy series is unputdownable. There's no one who creates a rancher with a heart of gold like Carolyn Brown."

—*RT Book Reviews*

"*Cowboy Bold* is the start of an amazing new series by an author who really knows how to hook her readers with sexy cowboys, strong women, a bunch of humor, and a stellar story...Everything about this book is a roaring good time."

—Harlequin Junkie, Top Pick

LUCKIEST COWBOY OF ALL

"Wonderfully charming characters...This sweet, heart-warming romance is sure to increase Brown's fan base."

—*Publishers Weekly*

"Carolyn Brown's cowboys are as real as they come...*Luckiest Cowboy of All* shows that there is always a second chance for true love, forgiveness, and a happily ever after. This series is fascinating, well developed, and satisfyingly sexy."

—*RT Book Reviews*

TOUGHEST COWBOY IN TEXAS

"One of the best feel good reads I've had the pleasure of reading yet this year! It tugged on your heart strings and had you cheering for true love."

—*OnceUponanAlpha.com*

"Top Pick! A beautiful second-chance love story that has humor, HOT cowboys, and an amazing HEA."

—*Harlequin Junkie*

"Terrific...an emotional star-crossed-lovers' tale with tangible depths and an attitude that's relatable to real life."

—*RT Book Reviews*

"The *Toughest Cowboy in Texas* is a delightful, fast-paced novel full of dynamic and lively characters and, more importantly, white-hot romance!"

—*Romance Reviews Today*

WICKED COWBOY CHARM

"A nice blend of warmth, down-home goodness, humor, and romance. Lively, flirty banter and genuine, down-to-earth characters are the highlights of this engaging story...The flirty banter between Deke and Josie is amusing and heart warming, and the chemistry between them sizzles."

—*RT Book Reviews*

MERRY COWBOY CHRISTMAS

"Top Pick! Carolyn Brown writes about everyday things that happen to all of us, and she does it with panache, class, empathy, and humor. 4½ stars."

—Night Owl Reviews

"A captivating cast of characters fills the pages of this sweet and funny novel."

—*Publishers Weekly*

"Brown's modern storytelling and fun-filled plot will engage readers and wrap them up in this sweet, Southern holiday romance."

—*RT Book Reviews*

HOT COWBOY NIGHTS

"Humorous storytelling, snappy dialogue, and colorful characters are the highlights of this story."

—*RT Book Reviews*

"Carolyn Brown manages to create a romance that's steamy, light, and fun, while also a relationship with substance and heart . . . a character-driven delight for romance fans."

—Fresh Fiction

WILD COWBOY WAYS

"With an irresistibly charismatic cowboy at the center of this story, Brown's latest is a sexy, fun read...The genuine, electric chemistry between Allie and Blake jumps off the page."

—*RT Book Reviews*

"A breathtaking romance filled with soul-sizzling passion and a heart-stealing plot. A five-star hit!"

—Romancing-the-Book.com

"Heartwarming and funny... *Wild Cowboy Ways* will pull you in and won't let you go until the end. I loved this book and recommend it to everyone. 5 stars."

—BookJunkiez.com

"A perfect read to just curl up with. The book is light, sweet, and just the right amount of humor and emotions to keep you reading along. Carolyn Brown will get you falling in love with the characters before you can blink...It made me feel like I was watching a classic Hallmark movie. *swoon*"

—OnceUponanAlpha.com

Also by Carolyn Brown

The Longhorn Canyon series

Cowboy Bold

The Happy, Texas series

Luckiest Cowboy of All
Long, Tall Cowboy Christmas
Toughest Cowboy in Texas

The Lucky Penny Ranch series

Wild Cowboy Ways
Hot Cowboy Nights
Merry Cowboy Christmas
Wicked Cowboy Charm

Cowboy Honor

A Longhorn Canyon Novel

Carolyn Brown

FOREVER

New York

Copyright © 2018 by Carolyn Brown
Preview from *Cowboy Brave* copyright © 2018 by Carolyn Brown
O Little Town of Bramble copyright © 2011 by Cathleen Smith
Compilation copyright © 2018 by Hachette Book Group, Inc.
Cover design by Elizabeth Turner Stokes
Cover copyright © 2018 by Hachette Book Group, Inc.

Forever
Hachette Book Group
1290 Avenue of the Americas, New York, NY 10104
forever-romance.com
twitter.com/foreverromance

First Edition: September 2018

Forever is an imprint of Grand Central Publishing. The Forever name and logo are trademarks of Hachette Book Group, Inc.

The publisher is not responsible for websites (or their content) that are not owned by the publisher.

The Hachette Speakers Bureau provides a wide range of authors for speaking events. To find out more, go to www.hachettespeakersbureau.com or call (866) 376-6591.

ISBNs: 978-1-5387-4488-8 (mass market), 978-1-5387-4490-1 (ebook)

Printed in the United States of America

OPM

10 9 8 7 6 5 4 3 2 1

This one is for my granddaughter, Kara Brown Dobbs. Thank you for all the support and love you give me and for loaning me Zaylie for this story!

Contents

Cowboy Honor

Carolyn Brown

Dear Reader,

It's a rare thing when I get to write a book in the season that it's actually set in. But this time I got to experience ice and snow, cold weather, and the Christmas holiday as I wrote *Cowboy Honor*. That means I didn't have to turn down the air-conditioning and put on the Christmas CDs to keep me in the right spirit.

And I loved it!

During the Christmas holiday, Mr. B and I rented ten condos and took the family to Florida. It was amazing, and one of the things that made it even more special was that I got to spend a week watching my great-grandchildren play in the heated pool and on the beach. Zaylie was the only girl, but she held her own with all those boys. It was so special to see her in action during that time, because she is the inspiration for the little girl named Zaylie in *Cowboy Honor*. She's tiny with wispy blond hair and big blue eyes—but beware! She could easily be the poster child for that saying about dynamite coming in small packages.

I have so many people to thank for helping me take an idea and turn it into the book you hold in your hands today. First of all, a huge thanks to my granddaughter, Kara Brown Dobbs, for letting me use Zaylie's name and her attitude in the book. And once again, many, many thanks to my editor, Leah Hultenschmidt. I gave her a manuscript and she waved this virtual magic wand over it, and it turned from a pumpkin to a glittery coach! Also to my whole Forever team. I'm truly blessed to have you all in my life.

Big hugs to Erin and the whole Folio Literary Management team. I'm grateful for everything y'all do so that I don't have to worry about anything but writing my stories.

And to Mr. B—my soul mate and best friend. Thank you for all you do and for understanding my passion. It takes a special person to live with an author who has voices in her head and cowboys in bed with her every night as she goes to sleep.

Don't put your boots and hats away when you finish Claire and Levi's story. Justin is about to meet his match in *Cowboy Brave,* which will arrive the first of 2019.

Happy Reading to all y'all.

Until next time,
Carolyn Brown

Chapter One

At the sound of heavy boots stomping across the wooden porch of the old cabin, Claire grabbed her purse, unzipped the side pocket, and brought out a small pistol. Her heart was in her throat, and her pulse raced so fast that she couldn't breathe, but she held the gun in both hands and pointed it straight at the door. A key rattled in the lock and the knob turned, but her hands were rock steady and the red laser dot was unwavering on the left side of the intruder's chest. What looked like the abominable snowman filled the space, and her four-year-old niece, Zaylie, squealed and dived beneath the quilt they were both huddling under.

With shoulders and a chest so broad that it obliterated the blowing snow, the man just stood there staring at her. After what seemed like forever but was probably less than a minute, he whipped off the black face mask and wiped snow from his thick eyelashes. Fear sent adrenaline rushing through Claire's body, but her brother had told her to never show that she was afraid—even if she was terrified.

"Who are you and what are you doin' here?" She kept the pistol aimed at his chest. If she missed a target that big, her brother would never let her live it down.

Both of his hands went up. "Don't shoot, lady. I'm Levi Jackson, the foreman of this ranch." He shut the door behind him with a heavy thud. "I'm not here to hurt anyone. My four-wheeler ran out of gas, and I need a place to hole up until this storm is over."

She lowered the gun but kept it in her lap. "Just don't get too close."

"Okay, I'll keep my distance. Take it easy." He kicked off his cowboy boots and bent forward to undo the short zippers on the legs of his coveralls and then the longer one down the front. He shrugged his wide shoulders out of the garment and hung it on a nail inside the door.

"What are y'all doin' here anyway?" he asked as he made his way across the room toward the kitchen area.

"My vehicle slid off the road in this awful snow storm and hit a tree. We saw this place. It was unlocked." She kept her finger on the trigger and her eyes on him. "We're not hurting anything, and we'll be gone as soon as it stops snowing."

He removed his cowboy hat and combed his light brown hair back with his fingers. "When did this happen? Were you injured?"

"It was last night. We're fine except for a few bruises. We slid off the road, went through a fence, and hit a tree. My van is down there not far off the road if you need proof. My cell phone battery had gone dead, and I left the charger at my brother's, and..." She shrugged.

"I'm glad you found shelter. It's nasty out there! I'm just going to get a fire started so we can warm this place up a bit." He kept one eye on her as he walked to a cabinet. "I'm going to get the matches. Don't shoot me."

Zaylie pushed the quilt back far enough to peek out with one blue eye, but she quickly dived back under when the man took a few more steps.

"It's okay." Claire hugged the child closer with her free hand. "He's going to start a fire so we can get warm."

The huge cowboy removed his gloves and stuck them in his pocket, then retrieved a box of matches from the top shelf. "I'd sure feel better if you put the safety back on that pistol and put it away." He strode back across the room and dropped to his knees in front of the old stone fireplace. "It won't take long to get this place warmed up."

"I wish I'd found those matches. I would've started that fire myself." She pushed the safety switch to the on position but kept her thumb on it.

"Seems like we might be here a while. Mind if I ask your names?" He dropped the match in the fireplace, and the kindling blazed.

"I'm Claire Mason. This is my niece, Zaylie. Sorry to be trespassin' like this."

"It's no problem. We never lock the door just in case someone needs to use the cabin." He sat down on the worn sofa facing the fire and removed his socks. Stretching his bare feet toward the fire to warm them, he glanced over his shoulder. "Sure y'all ain't hurt?"

Zaylie stopped shivering from under the quilt, and Claire slipped the pistol back into her purse. "We're fine. Thank you for starting a fire."

"If you'd come over here closer to it, you'd warm up quicker," he said. "Now, I'm going to reach in my hip pocket for my phone. I need to let the folks at the ranch know where I am."

Claire nodded but reached back into her purse, pulled out the pistol, and closed her fingers around the grip again. His angular face broke out into a smile when someone answered.

"Retta, I'm at the cabin. Four-wheeler is out of gas, and the battery on my phone is almost gone. Did Justin and Cade find that rangy old bull?"

He listened and then said, "That's great. No, we'll wait out the blizzard. There's food and plenty of wood." He drew his feet up on the sofa and tucked them under a blanket. "Okay, it's not a real blizzard, but for north central Texas it sure feels like one. My phone is starting to bleep so listen up." He told her about finding a half-frozen lady and a child in the cabin. Then he held the phone out and sighed before he laid it on an end table next to the sofa. "Well, that's the last of communication with the outside world. Last weather report I heard said the storm was going to hang around until tomorrow. Y'all hungry?"

Zaylie pushed back the blanket and nodded. "I'm hungry. Who is Retta?"

"You goin' to take your hand off that gun, ma'am, or do I need to verbalize every thing I'm doin' so you don't get trigger happy and shoot me? Justin and Cade Maguire own this ranch and Retta is Cade's wife. They can't come get us right now, but they'll be here soon as possible."

Levi didn't look afraid even when he tiptoed across the cold floor to the other side of the cabin. For that matter, he looked as if he knew the place very well, like he might really be the foreman of the ranch, just as he said.

Claire slipped the gun back in her purse, but she didn't zip the pocket. "Thank you for not throwing us out."

"What are you doing?" Zaylie pushed the covers back a little more.

"I'm going over here to this chest of drawers to get some dry socks, maybe two pair until this floor gets warmed up. And then I'm going to make hot soup for lunch," he answered as he dug around in a dresser drawer and brought out a pair of gray socks. "There's lots here. Y'all need some to keep your feet warm?"

"I brought our suitcases in with us." Claire nodded toward a couple of bags at the end of the bed.

In a few long strides he was back to the sofa, where he held the socks near the fire and then put them on his feet. "Ahh, that's much better. Now, let's get some food ready." He opened a cabinet and pulled out some cans of soup.

"That sounds good." She could be polite and appreciative, but that didn't mean he was luring her into trusting him—not even with food and a sexy grin.

*   *   *

Levi had a reputation on the Longhorn Canyon Ranch for bringing in strays, from dogs to turtles to a crippled miniature donkey. His experience had taught him to give an animal space and to let them come to him. No need to be in a rush anyway—the storm wouldn't let up until tomorrow morning at the earliest, and it might be a day past that before Cade or Justin could rescue them. He just hoped that she kept that cute little pistol tucked away and didn't point it at him again.

The tiny one-room cabin could sleep up to four people and was often rented out to hunters in the fall and spring. Two sets of bunk beds set end to end covered the south wall. A sofa with a couple of mismatched end tables faced the stone fireplace. Four chairs—no two alike—were pushed around a small kitchen table over in the far corner. Cupboards without doors hung above a wall-hung sink. A tiny two-burner stove and an apartment-size refrigerator were on one end of the kitchen area and a closet that had been converted into a pantry on the other.

"Where were y'all headed?" he asked as he turned the knob and struck a match to light one of the stove burners.

"My daddy went away again." Zaylie sighed. "But he'll be home for Christmas."

He didn't want to spook the child by looking right at her, so he stole sideways glances. She was a delicate-looking little girl with huge blue eyes and wispy blond hair falling to her shoulders.

"We were on our way home from San Antonio, Texas, to Randlett, Oklahoma, right across the Red River," Claire answered. She didn't look a thing like her niece, with her long brown hair twisted up on top of her head with some kind of big clip and light green eyes set in a round face.

"How did you get way back here?" He poured two cans of noodle soup into a pan and set it on the burner.

The electricity flickered, and Zaylie dived back under the quilt.

"Don't be afraid," Levi said. "We've got plenty of wood so we won't freeze, and the hurricane lamps you see scattered around aren't just for pretty."

"But you'll keep the monsters away if it gets dark, won't you?" Her blue eyes were huge.

"I promise." He nodded and turned his attention toward Claire. "How did you get this far off the highway going from San Antonio to Randlett?"

"There was an accident on the Interstate and the GPS on my phone rerouted me, but then I lost service, probably because of the storm," she explained. "When I got it back, I'd gotten off on the wrong road and the snow was coming down so hard I couldn't see more than a foot in front of the van. The battery in my phone played out, and I hit a really big pothole in the road and a slick spot at the same time." She talked fast and twisted the edge of the quilt, obviously more than a little nervous.

"The car went like this." Zaylie waved her arms around. "And then a tree was right there, and the car stopped with a big bump. And Aunt Claire said 'shit' and then she hit the steering wheel." Zaylie slung her legs off the bed and ventured over closer to the fire. Holding her little hands out to warm them, she looked so vulnerable that Levi wanted to hug her and reassure her that everything would be fine. Poor little thing had to have been scared out of her mind when the car was slipping and sliding all over the road.

"Zaylie Noelle Mason, little girls don't say that word," Claire scolded.

"I didn't say it, you did," Zaylie argued, and then turned her attention back to Levi. "I held Aunt Claire's hand real tight so I wouldn't get blowed away. Is the soup ready yet?"

"Almost. And I'm thinking I could make a hoecake too."

"Hoecake?" Claire eased off the bed and joined Zaylie at the fireplace.

"Something like a cornbread pancake. It'll take less fuel than firing up the oven, and it will cook faster."

"Sounds good," she said.

"Dejert?" Zaylie asked.

"Dessert," Claire translated.

He rustled around in the cabinet and found a can of peaches, powdered sugar, and pancake mix. "How about some peach fritters for dessert?"

"I like peaches. Is this like campin' out?" Zaylie left the fireplace, put her knees on the sofa, and peered over the back at him.

"Little bit," he answered with a smile.

Claire had the same look in her eye that the ranch's old mama cat, Gussie, did when someone got too close to her kittens as she made her way across the room and joined Zaylie on the sofa. Yep, he would have to go real slow to gain her trust.

"Looks like there's some blood on your forehead, Miz Claire. There's a first-aid kit in the bathroom if you want to clean it up." He wanted to offer to clean the wound and see just how deep it was, but his better judgment told him that wouldn't be wise. She looked like she might spook easier than a wild deer.

"Oh. Come on, Zaylie, you might need to help me." She took the little girl by the hand and led her to the bathroom.

Levi read the directions on the cornbread mix and stirred it up. When the oil in a cast iron skillet was hot, he poured the mixture in it and covered it with a heavy lid.

While that cooked, he whipped up some peach fritters to fry as soon as the bread was done. It took two things to get an animal to trust him—patience and food. He hoped it worked as well on humans.

"You didn't let me help." Zaylie was fussing when they came out of the bathroom.

"But you were there if I'd needed you," Claire told her.

Levi removed the lid from the skillet, flipped the hoecake over so it would brown on the other side, and carried the pot of soup to the table. "Did you hit your head on the steering wheel?"

Claire nodded.

"Airbags open?"

Another nod.

"Seat belt leave a bruise?"

"Yes, and it hurts," Zaylie said. "And Aunt Claire's got

one on her leg too. Want to know how we got from the tree to here?"

"I sure do," Levi answered.

"Aunt Claire got the suitcase and I got the tote bag," Zaylie said. "And the snow was in my face and I fell down three times." She held up the right amount of fingers. "And I cried because my face was cold."

"I would have cried too." Levi turned the cornbread out onto a plate and then made the fritters. "And you spent the night here in the cabin?"

"Yep, we did, and then you came." Zaylie crawled up into a kitchen chair. "How did you get in here? Aunt Claire locked the door."

"We keep a key under the mat just in case." Levi smiled.

"I'm glad." She made herself comfortable at the table. "I like chicken noodle soup."

"Me too." He finished putting the rest of the food on the table and held a chair for Claire.

She hesitated and glanced at her purse on the bunk bed, but finally sat down. "How long have you been foreman on this ranch?"

"Couple of years as foreman, but I've worked here since I was big enough to do a job. My dad was the foreman before me. Justin and Cade are more like my brothers than just friends since we were all three raised here on the ranch." He chose the chair across from Claire. "It's not my best cookin', but it's what I can do with what we've got to work with. Do you folks say grace?"

"I'll do it." Zaylie bowed her head. "Jesus, I'm a little mad at you for lettin' Aunt Claire get lost, but I'll forgive you since you sent someone to cook for us. Amen."

"Amen." Claire smiled.

"Amen." Levi grinned as he cut the hoecake into pie-shaped

wedges. "Don't know how good it'll all be, but it's fillin' and it's hot."

"Thank you," Claire said.

"So you lived in Randlett your whole life?" he asked.

"No, I moved there three years ago to take care of my grandmother after she fell and broke her hip," Claire answered as she filled three bowls.

"But Nanny died," Zaylie said. "They put her in a fancy pink box in a pink dress, and Daddy gave me a pink rose to put on the box after the preacher said a prayer."

"Six months ago," Claire said. "Cancer."

"I'm so sorry," Levi said. "So you work in Randlett? At the casino, maybe?"

"No." She shook her head. "I've run a little Etsy business for six years—homemade quilts. It lets me work at home and be flexible enough to take care of Zaylie when my brother is deployed or away on missions." Her voice had lost that high squeaky sound and settled into a husky tone that was downright sexy.

He wished his phone was working so he could research Etsy and see what kind of business that was. He'd never heard of it, but he'd bet dollars to cow patties that if it was like that Pinterest thing that Retta was always looking at on her phone that she could show him what Etsy was.

"I like this hoecake stuff," Zaylie declared after the first bite. "It's wondermous."

"I'm real glad that you like it, Zaylie. I'm not the cook that Retta is, but when we get back to the ranch house, I bet she'll make you a real good meal." Levi dipped up a second bowl of soup. "Anyone else?"

"Not yet. I'm goin' to save room for those fritter things. Never ate hoecake or them things before," Zaylie said. "Have you, Aunt Claire?"

Claire shook her head. "No, ma'am."

"Nanny didn't ever make them, did she?"

"Nanny wasn't much of a cook, remember?"

"But she could make real good hot chocolate when she didn't burn it," Zaylie said.

"Yes, she could," Claire agreed. "Nanny liked to cook until she broke her hip, and then things went downhill from there. We thought the hip problem brought on dementia, but it turned out to be a brain tumor. That's why I moved in with her. This is very good, and it warms from the inside out." She ladled out another bowl full.

He met her gaze across the table, but she quickly looked away. Levi recognized something in her expression like one of the abandoned animals he'd brought to the ranch through the years. The eyes did not lie, and they couldn't cover up deep pain. Regret, remorse, grief—there was something about her that needed rescuing.

*   *   *

"Read to me," Zaylie said as she yawned.

"She takes an hour nap after lunch each day," Claire explained to Levi. He'd been nothing but kind and hadn't done one thing that would cause her to feel threatened in any way, but she still needed to keep Zaylie close.

"I'm too big for naps," Zaylie declared. "Aunt Claire reads to me and sometimes I just doze off like Nanny used to do, but it's not a nap. Just restin' my eyes."

"She sure talks big for a four-year-old," Levi said.

"Been around adults her whole life." Claire removed her coat and hung it on the back of a chair. "I didn't think I'd ever be warm again, but I'm beginning to thaw out a little."

Zaylie followed her lead but covered up with a throw

when she reached the sofa. "My feet is still cold. Aunt Claire made me take off my shoes and socks when we got here 'cause they was wet. I put on dry socks, but they're still cold."

Levi went to the dresser and brought out a pair of thick gray socks and threw them across the room. "Put these on over your socks and pull them all the way up over the legs of your jeans. They've got wool in them, so they'll help."

"Can Aunt Claire have some too?" Zaylie asked.

"Sure thing." Levi tossed a pair toward Claire.

She caught them midair. "Thank you."

"Pretty good catch. You ever play baseball?"

"In high school, but that was a long time ago."

"Aunt Claire is old." Zaylie yawned again.

"Ouch!" Levi grinned.

"At that age, they don't have filters on their mouths." Claire blushed.

Zaylie threw both hands over her lips. "What is a filter? I don't want one of them things on my face."

"Don't worry, sweetheart, this cabin doesn't have any filters," Levi assured her. "You just rest your eyes. I'm going to do the same thing over there on that other bunk bed."

He crossed the floor, stretched out on the lower bed of the unused set of bunks, tucked his hands behind his head, and shut his eyes.

Claire settled down with Zaylie and made it through two pages of a children's book they'd brought before the child was asleep. She tucked the throw up around her and tiptoed over to the bed where she and Zaylie had slept the night before.

She sat down and stared at Levi. Long lashes rested on his high cheekbones. A little scruff on his face testified that he hadn't shaved that morning. His knit shirt hugged his chest like a glove, leaving little to the imagination. Her eyes traveled on down his body and stopped at a big silver belt buckle engraved with a bull rider. Was he a real cowboy or a wannabe who thought a belt buckle and boots would impress the women at the bars on Saturday nights?

She lay on her side so that she could keep an eye on both Zaylie and Levi. And that's when it hit her—she'd failed at several of the tests that her brother had taught her. She'd told Levi where she was from, that she had no relatives who would be looking for her, that she had no cell phone, and he already knew she was stranded.

If Levi wasn't really the foreman of the ranch, she and poor Zaylie might never be heard or seen again.

Chapter Two

Levi awoke to find Zaylie's big blue eyes boring holes into his face. She stood back a few feet, but she wasn't blinking as she cocked her head to one side and then the other as she studied him. It was even more unnerving than the hard north wind that rattled the windows. Who was she and how in the devil had she gotten into his bedroom? He glanced toward the ceiling, realized he was on a narrow bunk bed, and then it all came back to him in a flash. He shifted his eyes toward the window at the foot of the bed only to see nothing but blowing snow continuing to build up on the sash.

He bumped his head on the top bunk when he tried to sit up, but the little girl didn't budge from her spot or look away. It was as if she saw straight into his soul. Grabbing his head with both hands, he moaned as he eased his way to a standing position.

"That hurted, didn't it?" she said.

"Yes, it did," he answered.

"It's time for a snack," she told him. "We get a snack after we rest our eyes."

On a ranch the size of Longhorn Canyon, it wasn't uncommon to lose cell phone power at the end of a day, so he'd learned to carry a simple pocket watch. Glad that he had, he worked it up out of his pocket and checked the time.

"Three o'clock. You're probably right about snack time," he said.

Claire shot up like a wind-up doll and was on her feet in a split second. "I didn't mean to fall asleep."

Zaylie spun around and threw her arms around Claire's waist. "We all rested our eyes. It's snack time now. He said so."

"How about crackers with peanut butter and hot tea?" Levi asked.

Zaylie raised one shoulder slightly. "I like milk better."

"Sorry, princess, we don't have any milk in the cabin," he said. "But we do have tea bags and sugar."

Zaylie sighed. "Got any candy bars?"

"Zaylie Noelle Mason!" Claire scolded.

Levi put another log on the fire and then crossed the room. "I see there's a few cans of green beans if you'd rather have that for a snack."

Zaylie's nose curled as she shook her head from side to side. "Crackers and tea is fine."

"And?" Claire coaxed.

Zaylie sighed. "And thank you."

Levi brought an old blue granite coffeepot from the cabinet, filled it with water, and put it on the stove to heat. "I'm glad that we've still got runnin' water and the pipes haven't frozen. I can't remember the last time we had a snow storm this early in the fall and without much warning." He moved things around in the cabinets to see if there might be something Zaylie would like better than crackers and peanut butter. He almost shouted when he found a package of chocolate cookies and the expiration date was two weeks away. "Look what I found." He held them up.

"Yay!" Zaylie pumped her fist in the air. "My favorite. You sure there's not any milk up there?"

"Haven't found any yet," he said.

"Did you ride here?" Zaylie asked.

"I was on the four-wheeler tryin' to find a bull that got out of the corral. When I realized I didn't have enough gas to get back to the house, I decided to hole up here until the storm passed by."

It would sure help if Claire would either add to the conversation or else stop looking at him like that.

Like how is she lookin' at you? asked that aggravating voice in his head.

Like she's afraid I'm going to hurt her or Zaylie, he answered himself as he found the box of tea bags, and right beside them was instant hot chocolate.

"So how far is your ranch house from where we are right now?" Claire led Zaylie to the table.

"A couple of miles," he answered. "The Longhorn Canyon covers a pretty good chunk of land."

Zaylie crawled up into the pink chair. "Can this be my forever chair?"

"Of course it can. Pink is for a princess, right?" Levi asked.

Zaylie giggled. "It's my color, but I'm not a real princess. I'm just a little girl."

"So you have a color and it's pink. Do you like unicorns or dragons better?" Levi opened the package of cookies and set them in the middle of the table.

"Unicorns with pink wings and glitter on their horns." Zaylie picked up a cookie.

"I didn't find any milk, Miz Zaylie, but look at what was hiding at the back of the cabinet." Levi showed her the box of hot chocolate mix. "Would you rather have this than tea?"

"Yes!" Zaylie squealed. "I love hot chocolate, and Aunt Claire makes the bestest in the whole world."

"And it comes out of a package just like that." Claire finally smiled.

"I bet the unicorns put it here while we took a nap because I sure didn't see it when I was makin' hoecakes for dinner." Levi dumped a package into Zaylie's cup and then raised an eyebrow at Claire. "Tea or chocolate?"

"I'd rather have tea. No sugar though." Her eyes moved to the window. "It's hard to judge time when it's like this."

He pulled the pocket watch out and took a couple of steps toward the table to show her. "Three fifteen."

"Seems like it should be later. If I had my new fabric in here, I could at least be cutting out squares or patterns. I'm not used to being still," she said.

"What?" Levi raised an eyebrow.

"Aunt Claire makes quilts," Zaylie said. "And we got lots of stuff in the van."

"I was just thinkin' out loud," Claire said.

"So you do pretty good selling quilts?" Levi asked as he made a cup of tea for Claire and hot chocolate for himself.

"I make a living at it. I probably won't ever be a millionaire, but we pay the bills and have what we need," she answered. "They are custom designs and usually one of a kind."

"Do you have a store as well as this Etsy place?" He set Zaylie's hot chocolate in front of her. "Be careful now. It's really hot."

"No, I just sell online," Claire answered.

Her voice had a sweet Southern lilt to it that appealed to

him so much he could've listened to her read the entire dictionary and not gotten bored. Add that to the fact that she was so danged cute with those green eyes and delicate face, and he wanted to gather her up in his arms and protect her.

"I noticed that Benjy left one of his sketch pads on the top bunk. I guess you could design new patterns while we wait." He went back to the cabinet and picked up Claire's tea and his hot chocolate to carry to the table.

"That's a great idea." She took a sip of the tea. "You don't think he'd mind if I used a few pages?"

"Who's Benjy?" Zaylie reached for a second cookie.

"He's a young boy who is an amazing artist," Levi answered.

Zaylie took a sip. "Yep, just like Aunt Claire makes for me. Can I dip my cookie in it?"

"I always dip mine." Levi set the mugs down before he pulled out his chair. "But you better ask your aunt about that. She's the real boss."

Thank you, Claire mouthed toward Levi and then turned to Zaylie. "Yes, you may dip your cookies but only a couple more."

"Daddy is the real boss," Zaylie informed him seriously. "But when he's gone, he lets Aunt Claire be the boss." She dipped a third cookie into the hot chocolate and quickly put it into her mouth. "This is so good, and it's not cold."

Levi raised an eyebrow toward Claire, but before she could explain, Zaylie piped up again. "I'm glad that Levi found us and can cook."

"Hey, I can cook," Claire said.

"Yep, but he's not afraid to turn on the stove," Zaylie said.

"I've been replaced with nothing more than a cup of warm chocolate." Claire sighed.

Levi shook his head. "I could use some help in the kitchen. I've exhausted my knowledge in the make-it-out-of-what's-here department. The cabinets aren't well stocked this time of year, so if we're stuck here another couple of days feel free to help me out."

"And after we get rescued?" Claire asked.

"Then we'll take your car to a repair shop and you can stay on the ranch until it's fixed," he said.

"Oh no!" She held up a hand. "Thank you for the offer, but I can't impose on you and your friends like that. I'll just go to the nearest hotel until the weather lets up. I have another car in Randlett that I can drive for a while," she said.

"Not on these roads you won't. It's at least twenty miles to the nearest motel, and that's not a decent one. You've landed in the country, lady. Matter of fact, you've kind of landed in the backwoods of the country. We'd be glad to put you up until your van is fixed."

"What about turkey day and Miz Franny?" Zaylie groaned.

"Don't worry, sweet girl." Claire reached over and tucked a strand of hair behind Zaylie's ear. "That's not until the end of the week. The snow will all melt, and our van will be fixed; we'll be home long before that. We'll call Miz Franny as soon as I get my phone charged."

"Good," Zaylie said. "I don't want to eat soup on turkey day." She looked around the cabin. "We got to have chocolate pie and banana pudding."

Levi nodded. "I agree. And mashed potatoes and giblet gravy."

"And banana pudding." Zaylie made a motion with her hand to include everything they'd mentioned.

"What's your favorite side dish? Mine is sweet potato casserole," he answered.

"Macaroni and cheese is my favorite vegabull." Zaylie picked up another cookie.

"Mac and cheese is not a vegetable," Claire said.

"It is in my make-believe world," Zaylie declared.

"Mac and cheese is not a vegetable in any world," Claire informed her.

The woman might be small, but with her sass, Levi wouldn't argue with her, even if she didn't tote around a pistol in her purse.

"Uh-huh," Zaylie argued.

Claire rolled her eyes and then brought them to rest on Levi.

"Don't look at me. I thought it was too," he said with a big grin on his face. "And I love mac and cheese. Too bad we don't have the stuff to make it." It wouldn't take that child long to completely wrap him around her tiny pinky finger. "Anyone for more chocolate or tea?"

"No, but I'd sure like to see that sketchbook," Claire answered.

Zaylie clapped her hands. "Can I draw too?"

"Sure you can." Levi brought it down from the top bunk.

Expecting Claire to work on her designs at the table, he picked up a well-read Louis L'Amour novel from the fireplace mantel and sank down on the sofa to give her plenty of space. She fumbled around in a tote bag and found a couple of pencils and a small ruler. Then she sat down cross-legged on the floor between him and the fireplace. She tore one sheet from the book and gave it to Zaylie along with a pencil, and then she went to work.

Levi read a couple of pages, but he couldn't keep his attention on the book. He kept peeking over the top to see what Claire was doing. She'd measure and work, sigh and erase, and then repeat the same thing.

"What're you trying to draw?" he finally asked.

"This house to show my daddy," Zaylie said before Claire could answer. "Aunt Claire can't take a picture of it 'cause her phone ain't workin'."

"I see." Levi smiled and nodded toward Claire. "And what about you?"

"A log cabin pattern using yellows and blues. It will remind me of this experience."

"And how's that?" Levi asked.

"We're in a cabin," she answered shortly.

"I got that much," he shot back.

"Blue is a cold color and yellow is warm. So the blue is for the snow, and the yellow is the fire that keeps us warm," she explained.

"Why are you erasing so much?" he asked.

It looked like an abstract painting to him, done in black and white. He cocked his head to one side and frowned. Maybe it was more like a stained-glass window with no color. How on earth that could be a quilt someday was beyond his comprehension.

"I'm trying to decide how big it will be and where the colors will fit best. Do I want them to be a small size, like maybe for a throw instead of a full-size or king-size quilt or larger? And do I start with yellow in the middle to illustrate hope at the center or with the snow in the middle and then the fire like it really happened?"

"In our part of the world, this kind of weather won't last very long. Fire melts snow, so it could go either way you want to design it," he said.

"You aren't much help," she said.

"Well, darlin', designin' quilts ain't my expertise," he told her.

"Evidently not," she said.

He bit back the grin that tickled the corners of his mouth. "Sassy, ain't you?"

"Been accused of it a few times. I've decided that this should be a king-size quilt. Darker blue calico in the middle with the colors lightening by degrees out to a blue and yellow print just before a more solid yellow at the edges."

The only thing that Levi knew about quilts was that they kept him warm in the winter, and he knew even less about design and art. He went back to his book, but he still couldn't focus on it. Finally, he laid it on the end table.

"So do y'all live in town or out in the country?" he asked.

"In town." She didn't even look up from the sketch pad.

"We were up that way last year to a bull sale. Bought a big old Angus that's been a good breeder for us," Levi said.

Zaylie looked up from her drawing. "What's a breeder?"

"Well, that would be a—" He stammered trying to find a simple way to answer a four-year-old. With those big blue eyes staring at him, he couldn't begin to find the words to explain in simple terms. "Uh . . ."

"It's a bull or a boy cow," Claire explained simply.

"Okay." Zaylie went back to drawing.

"Thank you," Levi whispered.

"Always keep it simple when it comes to explainin' anything to a four-year-old." Claire nodded and turned her attention to Zaylie. "Are you going to put a sun in your picture?"

"Nope, there ain't no sun out there, so I can't draw it. And"—Zaylie frowned—"I'm almost five."

"Yes, you are," Claire said.

"I'm going to draw lots of snow, but now I'm going to turn it over and draw the inside of the cabin," Zaylie said.

"Great idea," Claire told her. "Do you plan on putting people in your picture?"

"Maybe," Zaylie answered.

"Then please don't make me shorter than you."

Zaylie giggled. "I drew that one for Daddy because I wanted him to see how much I growed."

"Did you say that he's coming home by Christmas?" Levi would never want a job that made him leave his child for weeks on end even if she was in amazingly good hands.

"Yep." Zaylie nodded.

"When did you draw the one where Claire was shorter than you?"

"Last time he went away. He was gone a long time." She sighed. "This time he's on a mission not a ployment. I like them better because they ain't as long."

"Does your mama go on missions too?" Levi asked.

"Nope, she went to heaven when I was a baby. She got a neurasm in her head and the angels took her away," Zaylie answered as she drew a fireplace.

"Aneurysm," Claire explained. "Zaylie was less than a year old."

"That's terrible." Levi could sympathize with Zaylie since his own mother had taken off with her new husband when Levi was only three years old. Since both Skip and Mavis worked at the Longhorn Canyon Ranch, he'd spent his days there with Cade and Justin even before they ever started to school. By the time he was thirteen, he was on the payroll. Even though Skip and Mavis had given him a wonderful life, there'd always been something missing that he couldn't put a finger on. Maybe it was because he was so close to Justin and Cade Maguire they were like brothers—and yet they weren't. If he'd had a sibling perhaps that would have filled the empty hole that he felt in his life but never talked about.

Zaylie's chin jacked up a couple of inches. "No, it's not. The angels love her. My daddy said so."

She was as full of sass as her aunt. Levi bit back a grin, not wanting her to think he was making fun of her. Being a big kid in school and not playing football or even basketball, he'd had his share of folks making fun of him, and he'd never do that to anyone.

"I meant that I'm sorry that she couldn't stay with you." Levi stumbled over the words.

"Someday Daddy is goin' to get me a new mommy. But I got a picture of my mommy so I don't forget her. I bring it with me when I stay with Aunt Claire," Zaylie said.

"I bet she was beautiful." Levi wanted to hug Zaylie but feared Claire might stab him with her pencil. Despite falling asleep earlier, she still hadn't relaxed around him. Hopefully, when she got to know him better, she'd see that he just wanted to help her, that he would protect her and Zaylie.

"Yep, she was." Zaylie jumped up and went to dig around in a tote bag. In a few seconds she was back with a box of crayons and a small, framed picture. "This is me and my mama." She handed the photo to him.

Levi held it up to get the glare off the glass. The woman had blond hair, big blue eyes, and delicate features. The woman in the picture gave off the same confidence as Claire had when she'd pointed that gun at him.

"You look a lot like her."

Zaylie's smile showed that she hadn't lost a single baby tooth yet. "That's what Aunt Claire says. Daddy likes for me to color my pictures. He says it makes them real."

"I agree with your daddy." Levi handed the picture back to her and watched her start to color the picture she'd drawn. "You color in the lines really well."

"I'm not a baby," she scolded as she chose yellow for the fire.

"That's a pretty sassy tone, young lady." Claire wrote something in the quilt square she'd made on the paper.

Levi held up a palm and chuckled. "It's okay. I kind of waded into that one."

Zaylie frowned. "I have to make it pretty for Daddy."

"Yes, you do," Levi agreed.

*   *   *

Claire shut her eyes and visualized the bolts of fabric she'd bought in San Antonio that were now stacked neatly in the back of the van. The colors would be perfect for the new project. She could get all the pieces cut, and when she got home, she'd be ready to start sewing the top together. If only the ladies in Randlett were interested in quilting, she wouldn't be looking around for a place to put in a small quilt shop. She'd tried twice in the past three years to start a quilting bee at her church, and once she'd bought an advertisement in the local paper offering quilting classes for free. Neither had worked—the women there just weren't interested.

Suddenly, the vision of a dozen bolts of fabric lining the shelves of her new shop faded and was replaced with one of Levi standing in the doorway earlier that day. She still wasn't ready to let her guard down completely, but it was nice to have an adult to talk to. She blinked away the picture in her head and opened her eyes. He'd gone back to reading, and Zaylie was busy coloring. If someone peeked in the window they'd think a young family had taken up residence in the cabin.

Are you going to trust him enough to get some sleep tonight? Her brother Grant's voice was clear in her head. *Who knows what he's capable of? And you've always been gullible.*

I am not gullible. I'm a grown woman who's vigilant,

and besides I have a gun. I'll keep it at my fingertips, and Zaylie will be right beside me in the bed. I'm a big girl. I can take care of us. Like always, arguing with her brother put a frown on her face.

She rolled her eyes toward the ceiling and noticed more than a dozen pictures lined up on the fireplace mantel. "Who are the people in those photos?" Ha! That was one way to find out if Levi really was who he said, and it would take her mind off her brother's smart-ass remarks.

She stood up and walked across the room to get a closer look herself. "This is you. Who are these other people?"

"That's Cade and Justin with me in that picture. The one next to it is Retta and Cade on their wedding day. The event was held outside in the front yard last month with the reception right here in the cabin."

"And this one?" She picked up a picture of Levi with a young boy. "How old is this boy?"

"He's twelve. That would be Benjy, the boy I told you about who can draw so well," Levi responded.

That much pride in his tone said that Benjy had to be his son. She slid a sideways look over at Levi and then back to the picture. The kid didn't look a thing like Levi, but maybe he got his looks from his mother. She set the picture back on the mantel.

Levi went on, "We open up the ranch every summer for about five or six weeks for city kids to get to experience ranch life. We always have four girls and four boys, and Benjy was here every summer for three years. Last summer his granny died and there was no one to take care of him, so my adoptive parents, Mavis and Skip, decided to take him in. The formal papers will be signed right after the new year if all goes well," he explained. "That will legally make him my little brother, even though we don't have an ounce of shared DNA."

She had no doubts now that he was telling the truth, but there was still something unsettling about the man. What kind of person offered to take in a complete stranger and a child? She might be there to rob him blind—not that she would, but he didn't know that, did he?

To take her mind off all the questions, she handed him the picture and said, "Tell me about this boy."

"Benjy is a really good kid, but he's what they call high-functioning autistic—" Levi touched the picture as if he were brushing back Benjy's hair. "He's great help on the ranch with small jobs, and he loves to be here. He remembers everything he reads and sometimes spouts it off at strange times, but he's got the sweetest nature of anybody in the whole state of Texas."

She decided that anyone who had that much compassion for a child couldn't be a bad person. She'd still keep her little gun handy, but she wasn't nearly as uneasy about spending the night in the cabin with Levi as she'd been a few hours earlier.

Chapter Three

Levi awoke the next morning to blaring sunshine reflecting off the pictures on the mantel straight into his eyes. He rolled out of the bottom bunk, stretched, and started for the kitchen area to make a pot of coffee, when he heard the familiar sound of a tractor. Forgetting about everything else, he hurriedly pulled on his coveralls and stomped his feet down into cowboy boots.

"What's that noise?" Claire sat up and covered her eyes with her hands. "Oh, the sun is out."

"Are we being rescued?" Zaylie knuckled her eyes and yawned.

Levi pulled the face mask over his head. "Yes, ma'am, we are. Y'all get dressed as warm as you can, and we'll have breakfast at the ranch house."

He had to push back several inches of snow to open the door, and a blast of icy wind hit him in the eyes, but he could see the tractor. He stepped outside, shut the door, and threw up a hand to wave.

Justin parked as close to the porch as he possibly could, and he hopped down out of the biggest tractor on the ranch. Levi and Justin had gone through school together, best friends since they were in the church nursery. But down deep Levi had always known that Justin and his brother Cade would someday be the owners of the Longhorn Canyon Ranch, and all he'd ever be was the foreman, just as Skip had been. Not that he was jealous of them or that they didn't treat him just like family. But Justin had always had the good looks, the confidence, and the swagger to get any girl he wanted.

He clamped a hand on Levi's shoulder. "I hear you've found a damsel in distress and don't have a white horse to bring her to the ranch." He motioned toward the four-wheeler. "Seriously, is everything all right? Is anybody hurt? Is she one of them tall blondes that me and you both like?"

"The woman's name is Claire, and her niece is Zaylie. They say they're fine, but I wouldn't call her a damsel in distress by any stretch of the imagination," Levi answered. "She carries a gun in her purse, and you've heard that dynamite comes in small packages. Well, she's living proof. So to answer your question, she's a short brunette, but with her attitude she could probably put out a forest fire by spittin' on it."

"Scared you, did she?" Justin's eyes twinkled.

"Let's just say, I'm real glad to see you and even happier that she didn't shoot first and ask questions later," Levi answered.

Justin had a way with women. They flocked to him like flies on honey. Cade was a big flirt, or at least he had been until last summer when Retta arrived. Justin went beyond that. He had a reputation around Montague County for bringing home a different woman every weekend for a one-night stand.

"I thought you were kiddin' me. A real gun?" Justin picked up two shovels from the trailer hitched to the back of the tractor and handed one to Levi.

Levi nodded. "A .38 pistol, looks like about a five shot, but the way she handled it I reckon she'd only need one to put a man down. And it's equipped with a laser sighting. That little red dot on my chest damn sure made me take notice. But you should know that she's definitely not your type. Short, not tall. Brunette, not blond. And real sassy."

"Sounds like she ain't a damsel in distress at all. And I like a sassy woman as much as a sweet tall gal," Justin said.

"I'm tellin' you, I wouldn't mess with her or her niece," Levi said.

"You already got a thing for her?" Justin teased.

"Nope, just givin' you some advice," Levi answered.

"Advice noted. Now, let's dig that four-wheeler out and get it loaded, and then we'll take y'all home. Retta's makin' a big breakfast, and she says we're supposed to be there soon as possible." Justin sank the blade of the shovel deep into the snow.

"Think this stuff will melt by Thanksgiving?" Levi asked as they worked on the snowdrift covering half the four-wheeler. He couldn't help noticing that Justin kept glancing back toward the cabin.

"Probably not. The weatherman says not to expect temperatures above freezin' for several days," Justin answered.

"If this is what the whole winter is going to be like, we're in for a cold one," Levi said. "I told Claire they could stay on the ranch until this stuff melts. You think Cade and Retta will have a problem with a couple of guests for a few days? I would've asked first, but we didn't have cell service."

"What are you so nervous about, Levi?" Justin asked. "We're family, and you know it. You've brought home strays all your life. You work as hard as we do. This ranch might belong to us on paper, but we couldn't run it without you."

"I've never brought home..."

"Bullshit! You and I both have brought home women for the night." Justin laughed. "And besides, Retta's got the girls' bunkhouse ready for them. Let's get a path cleared from here to the trailer so we can push this four-wheeler onto it."

Levi hefted the first shovel full of wet snow to the side. "You could have parked a little closer."

Justin was right—he and Justin hadn't spent many weekends in an empty bed. Saturday night was for beers and dancing at their favorite honky-tonk. Levi was no slouch when it came to sweet talking women, but Justin? That cowboy was a pro.

Snow flew to the side as Justin created a pathway. "This is hard work. You could've offered me a cup of coffee."

"Just got out of bed and haven't even made a pot yet," Levi said. "But if you want to suffer the wrath of Retta, I'll go inside and put it on to brew. Or the pretty boy prince of the Rusty Spur can keep workin' and stop whinin' so much."

"No, thank you. Retta's been a little touchy here this past week, so I'm not going to get on her bad side. But it looks to me like you've been lazy this mornin'. Next thing you know, you'll be wantin' to sleep in every morning until noon. And I don't see you sittin' in the corner at the honky-tonk all alone. It's a wonder they don't have to put in one of those machines for the ladies to take a number and wait," Justin said.

Levi stopped long enough to pack a snowball and aim it right at Justin's shoulder. "That machine would have your number on it, not mine. And the sun is barely up and it's not like there was anything to do. It was going to be a long day if you hadn't been able to rescue us, so why not sleep as long as possible?"

Justin sidestepped the snowball and packed one into his hands. He hit the mark right in Levi's chest. "It's seven o'clock, and the sun's been up for an hour. In my book that's lazy."

Levi grunted and shot a mean look toward Justin. "I'm not wastin' my time and energy on a snowball fight. Let's just get shovelin'."

"You started it," Justin reminded him.

"Well, I'm ending it because I'm hungry and I need caffeine." Levi put his shoulders into the digging.

"Five bucks says I get to the middle faster than you do," Justin said.

"Forget the money. If I get to the middle first, you do all my work today." Levi would have rather bet that Justin would be flirting with Claire by the time they got from the cabin to the house. He'd win that one for sure!

Justin shook his head. "Let's just get this done. Then we should turn off the water and drain the pipes. It could be a real mess if they froze and busted and flooded the place."

"We're lucky it hasn't already happened," Levi said.

"Yep." Justin kept digging. "So tell me more about these two."

"Who?" Levi leaned on the shovel a few minutes.

"The pistol-totin' lady and her niece," Justin answered.

"Zaylie is almost five years old. Cute as a button with

her blond hair and blue eyes. Claire's got these strange aqua eyes that lean more toward green than blue, kind of like the color of the water down in the gulf. Remember when your folks took us to the rodeo down there? Her eyes are that color. She barely comes to my shoulder."

Justin stopped and leaned on his shovel. "Is Claire young, old, or somewhere in between? Is she seriously out of our league?"

"She's about our age, I'd guess. Don't know if she's out of our league or not. I only met her yesterday, for God's sake." Levi cleared the last two feet and started slinging snow as he dug toward the well house. "This won't take long, and then I'll turn off the water so we can get out of here."

"I'll do that. You go on in and get the fire put out and make sure the pipes are drained soon as I turn off the water," Justin said.

Levi stomped the snow from his boots on the porch and shoved the door open to find Claire and Zaylie sitting on the sofa. They were both dressed, and their coats were on the top of the suitcase.

Zaylie's gaze darted around the cabin, and she moved closer to Claire, but when Levi removed his cowboy hat and face mask, she smiled up at him. "I didn't know if that was you. You look so big with all that stuff."

"It's me, and we're almost ready to go. Justin is..."

"Got it! Drain the pipes now," Justin yelled from outside. "I'll warm up the tractor."

Levi went to the bathroom, turned on all the water faucets, and then headed to the kitchen, where he caught the last of the water in a pitcher. Using that, he drowned the remaining embers in the fireplace while Claire and Zaylie bundled up.

"That's everything," he said. "The snow has drifted, so,

Miz Zaylie, may I carry you to the tractor? It's pretty slick out there."

Zaylie lifted her arms. "You going to carry Aunt Claire?"

He picked up the little girl with one arm and the suitcase with the other hand. "I'll come back for her as soon as I get you up in the tractor with Justin."

"Oh look!" she exclaimed when Levi carried her outside. "It's all shiny and white and pretty like in *Frozen*."

Levi glanced over his shoulder.

"It's one of her favorite movies," Claire explained.

He could feel Claire's eyes boring into his back as he waded through snowdrifts halfway up his knees to the tractor. She should be putting a little faith in him by now. After all, they'd spent the night together, and he'd been a perfect gentleman.

He dropped the suitcase on the trailer beside the four-wheeler and put Zaylie in the passenger's seat. It would be a tight fit for all of them, but it was only a couple of miles.

When he reached the cabin the second time, Claire was waiting with the tote bag in her hand and her purse over her shoulder. He scooped her up like a bride and pulled the door shut.

"Put me down. I can walk." She squirmed. "My shoes might get wet, but they'll dry."

"As short as you are, you'd sink up to your butt in that drift." He nodded toward the place where the snow had blown against the porch. "Drop the tote bag between the suitcase and the four-wheeler. It'll ride fine there. We'll come back soon as we can and get the rest of your stuff and haul your van to the repair shop."

"You can take me to a hotel, and I'll get in touch with a tow company and..." she started.

He interrupted. "Honey, we aren't going to be able to get

off this ranch until this stuff melts. I've only ever seen snow before Thanksgiving in this area one time in my whole life, and this kind of thing cripples us."

The door swung open from the inside, and he settled Claire on the seat beside Zaylie, then climbed in behind her. She shifted over to the side and put Zaylie in her lap, but there still wasn't enough room for Levi. So he picked both of them up and set Claire in his lap.

Justin stuck out a hand. "Hello, Claire. I'm Justin Maguire. Welcome to the Longhorn Canyon Ranch."

She shook it. "Thank you for rescuing us."

"You're very welcome." Justin put the tractor in gear. "It's a tight fit, but we're only fifteen minutes from the house."

"We appreciate your hospitality."

"Oh, we've got plenty of room. And from what the weatherman says, we can't expect to do much until after next weekend. Then the cold front will move out. But right now Retta has the girls' bunkhouse warmed up and ready for you," Justin said as he expertly turned the tractor around and started back toward the ranch.

Levi couldn't believe his ears or his eyes. Justin hadn't put on his pickup drawl or flirted. Did Claire intimidate him, or had he finally found a woman that just flat didn't set his vibes to quivering?

*   *   *

Thanksgiving with strangers—not exactly what Claire had envisioned for the holiday, but it didn't seem like she had a lot of choice. She'd thought she and Zaylie would be back home by now, sharing their dinner with Franny, their sweet little elderly neighbor.

She bit back a sigh. Things could be far worse. She and Zaylie could have been hurt too badly to get to the cabin or stranded in a place where there was no shelter. There was no sense in asking why they'd been put in this situation. She'd learned from past experience asking that question seldom got any kind of answer. Otherwise, she'd know why she was always the one everyone turned to for help, but when she needed something, she was the last in line to get it. Not that she was whining about her lot in life—she loved her brother and Zaylie. And she'd adored her grandmother.

Her thoughts were interrupted when Zaylie reached out to warm her hands by the tractor's heater vent. "Feels good. Almost like the fire Levi made for us."

"Didn't you bring gloves?" Justin asked.

"They're at our house in Randlett," Claire answered.

"Know what works pretty good for gloves? Big old thick socks," he said.

"Levi gave me socks in the cabin when my toes was cold." Zaylie picked up Claire's hands and held them toward the vent.

"Did you count all your toes before you put your shoes on?" Levi asked.

Zaylie's brows drew down over her blue eyes. "Why?"

"Some of your toes might have frozen plumb off," he teased.

"Uh-uh," she argued.

"You better count them tonight to be sure," Levi told her.

"I will. I can count to a hundred," Zaylie informed him.

"Do you have a hundred toes?" Justin asked.

"No, silly. I gots ten toes and ten fingers."

Claire stretched her fingers toward the heat vent, but sitting in a stranger's lap was truly heating her up a lot more than the warm air. Levi's warm breath tickled the soft skin on her neck, sending tingles down her spine. A woman would have to be stone-cold dead not to be affected by a cowboy as sexy as Levi Jackson.

"Just look at all the snow, Aunt Claire." Zaylie waved her hand around the cab. "It's everywhere. Can we build a snowman? We gots to take a picture to show Daddy."

"Yes, darlin' girl, we can, but first we'll have to borrow a phone charger." If she could get her phone up and running she could call Franny, tell her the predicament she was in, and that it would be a few days before she could get home.

"Little problem there," Justin said. "The wind has knocked out our cell phone service, and internet will be out for several days. But we've got electricity, and you're welcome to make calls on our landline."

"We lose any cattle?" Levi asked.

"None yet. We've moved most of them into the pasture around the barn. Still got a couple of stragglers that we're planning on rounding up soon as breakfast is over and we get the four-wheelers refueled," Justin answered. "We got the bull in a stall in the barn. He's not real happy, but he'll get over it."

"Why is he sad?" Zaylie asked. "Me and Aunt Claire was glad to get out of the cold."

"Yes, we were." Claire tucked a strand of wispy blond hair under the edge of Zaylie's stocking hat and studied Justin with a sideways look.

His black felt cowboy hat was crammed down over his brown hair, and his square face was a study in angles. He was one of those cowboys who could walk into a bar and every woman in the place would turn and stare. But when his hand brushed hers she didn't get a single vibe from him—not like all the sparks flitting around her and Levi.

Sweet Lord! I've already got Stockholm syndrome. He cooks a couple of meals for us and I think he's wonderful.

For heaven's sake, the man's not kidnapping you. You don't have any kind of syndrome. The voice in her head belonged to Franny, an eighty-year-old outspoken old girl who'd been her grandmother's best friend and was still Claire's neighbor. *Be thankful that the good Lord sent help to you and that precious baby, or you might be frozen to death.*

Yes, ma'am, Claire mouthed, and then cut her eyes around to make sure that she hadn't said the words out loud.

"Moses doesn't want to be in that stall because, Miz Zaylie, he doesn't like Gussie, the cat, and she hates him. I imagine it's because she has a litter of kittens in the barn, and she's afraid something as big as Moses might hurt them," Justin explained.

His drawl wasn't nearly as deep as Levi's, and although she hadn't seen them standing together, she'd bet that Levi was a lot taller. She blushed when she found herself looking at his big, square hands and his feet.

Dammit! What's wrong with me? she thought.

You're just wondering what all women would. Franny was giggling so hard that had Levi been clairvoyant, he could have heard the cackling.

Zaylie's light blue eyes popped wide open. "Moses got lost in the snow too?"

"Not the real Moses in the Bible. Our bull is named Moses. So you know about Moses in the Bible?" Justin asked.

"I'm almost five, and next year I go to school, and I go to church, and I know about Moses and Joshua and even Nomie." She squared her shoulders and looked him right in the eye. "And Moses is a crazy name for a boy cow. Why'd you name him that?"

"We didn't," Levi said. "The people we bought him from did, and he won't answer to anything else."

"Why'd them people name him Moses?" Zaylie persisted.

"We didn't think to ask them," Justin answered. "Who's Nomie?"

"Naomi," Claire answered.

"Can I pet Gussie?" Zaylie changed the subject. "That's a funny name for a cat."

"Gussie is real friendly and likes to be petted. She's named after Levi's first girlfriend." Justin chuckled.

"I was in the third grade, and she had pretty blue eyes," Levi said quickly.

So the girls had chased after him even when he was a little boy. That sure enough wasn't hard to imagine. Had one caught him? He didn't wear a wedding ring. But that could have been because of the ranch work he did all the time.

"I wanted a kitten my whole life." Zaylie sighed.

"Well, since you've wanted a kitten for so long and since Gussie don't like Moses in the barn, we might even bring them in the house. Would you like that?" Levi asked.

Zaylie clapped her hands. "Yes. And I can pet them and Gussie won't bite me?"

"Naw, she's a sweetheart." Levi grinned.

"Franny's got a cat and his name is Willie, but he don't like kids," Zaylie said, and then her finger shot past Levi's nose to point out the window. "Look, I see a house."

"Franny is our neighbor in Randlett," Claire explained. "She and my grandmother were best friends. I'll need to call her and ask if she'll keep a watch on things until we get home."

Justin stopped the tractor as close to the yard fence as possible. "Cade has shoveled a path to the back gate. It's still pretty slick since we got the layer of ice before the snow started, so be careful."

Levi opened the door, slid out from under Claire and Zaylie, and held up his arms. "Zaylie first. You want me to carry you inside or you reckon you can walk?"

A dog ran out from the porch to greet them, and Zaylie wiggled out of his arms as soon as she could. "Can I pet that dog? He won't bite me will he?"

Thank goodness Cade had shoveled the walk because Zaylie dropped down on her knees to wrap her arms around the dog's neck. He licked her on the chin, and her giggles rang out across the fields. If the snow had still been there, she would've been buried up to her neck.

"His name is Beau, and he won't hurt you." Levi knelt down beside her. "He loves kids, and pettin' is right down his alley just like it is Gussie's. Looks like you two are goin' to get along real good."

A kid and a dog tell the character of a man. If either one is afraid of him, then you'd better be scared too. Franny's advice came back to Claire's mind.

If that was the case, then she had nothing to fear, because Zaylie wasn't a bit afraid of Levi anymore. The dog's tail wagged so fast that it was a blur, and Levi's grin was so big that it lit up the gray skies.

Levi straightened up. "Old Beau missed me. Had to stop and let him know that I missed him too." He scooped Claire out of the seat as effortlessly as if he were picking up a feather pillow. When he set her down, her feet almost went out from under her, so he picked her up again.

"I'll carry you inside," he said.

Claire did not like being helpless. She'd taken care of herself most of her life. But before she could protest, she was in his arms again, her ear pressed against his chest. His heartbeat seemed a little fast, but then so was hers.

Zaylie followed along behind them. "Can the dog come in the house?"

"If he wants to," Justin answered.

Zaylie picked her way slowly toward the house with Beau right behind her and Levi and Claire bringing up the rear. When the door opened, she and the dog rushed inside. The woman holding the door for them was fairly tall, but then everyone looked tall to Claire. Skinny jeans and a sweatshirt showed that she was curvy like Claire instead of model thin. Dark hair was pulled up into a ponytail, and her big brown eyes looked kind and sweet.

"Hello, I'm Retta. Welcome to Longhorn Canyon," she said. "Levi told us no one was hurt. Is that right?"

"Pleased to meet you." Claire wiggled, and Levi set her down. "And thank you for the offer to stay here."

There had to be a way to get to Bowie. If a tow truck could rescue a pickup that had slid off the road, then it could come out to the ranch and take her and Zaylie to a hotel.

"No one is hurt. But she could have been if she'd tried to walk on that ice in the shoes she's wearin'," Levi said. "This must be heaven. I smell coffee and bacon."

Zaylie slipped out of her jacket, handed it to Claire, and sniffed the air. "And cimamum. I love cimamum!"

Claire chalked up the antsy feeling making her nervous to hunger and relief. A cup of coffee and maybe whatever smelled like cinnamon should put her to rights, and then she'd call someone to give them a ride, even if it was in a tow truck.

Retta laid a hand on her shoulder. "You've met Justin and Levi. My husband, Cade, is out in the barn, but he'll be in pretty soon. Take off your coats and have a seat."

She motioned toward the table where breakfast was already waiting.

Claire nodded. "Thank you for going to so much trouble. It smells delicious. By the way, I'm Claire..."

Zaylie butted in. "I'm Zaylie. Are the kittens in the house?"

"You are very welcome, Claire. And, Miz Zaylie, the kittens aren't here yet, but Cade is going to bring them from the barn this morning." Retta poured mugs of coffee and carried them to the table. "Moses doesn't like to be penned up, and the cats are making him nervous. Do you like kittens, Zaylie?"

"Yep, I do, but we can't have pets 'cause Daddy goes on ployments and missions too much."

Claire was surprised she felt at ease with these people. Growing up she'd lived in so many places that most of the time she barely had time to make a friend, but that was the way of the military life. Move in. Get everything put away. Orders arrived. It was time to pack again. And from the time that Claire was ten years old, she did a lot of the organization of getting things ready to move—again.

"Well, how would you like to keep a watch on Gussie and her three babies in the bunkhouse where you and Claire will be stayin' while you are here?" Retta asked.

"For real?" Zaylie's sudden intake of breath said that she couldn't believe her ears. "Aunt Claire, can we do that?"

"If Gussie don't mind, I sure don't." Claire hung her jacket and Zaylie's on a hook beside the coveralls that Levi had removed. "Is this the right place to put these?"

"That's just fine. And it'll be great to have some girl company while we're snowed in," Retta answered.

Zaylie danced around the table. "I get to have a pet," she sing-songed and then stopped to hug the dog again. "Can Beau come in our new house too?"

Levi pulled out a chair for Claire and then one for Zaylie. "Gussie loves Beau, and yes, he can go inside the bunkhouse."

"It's like Christmas and my birthday," she said.

"Your birthday *is* Christmas." Claire laughed.

"For real? You were born on Christmas Day?" Retta asked.

"Yep. Daddy says it's double special 'cause me and Jesus gots the same birthday," Zaylie said.

"I agree with him," Retta told her.

Justin sat down in one of the remaining chairs and picked up a mug of coffee. "As soon as I finish this, I'll take the tractor out to the barn. Cade might need some help herdin' them cats."

"I'll go with you," Levi said.

Retta slapped a hand on his shoulder. "I don't think so. You haven't had breakfast yet. If two big old strappin' Maguire men can't catch a cat and three kittens, then I've misjudged them. And besides, Mavis is worried about you, so you are going to call her as soon as you get through eating."

"Who's Mavis?" Zaylie asked.

"That's my mother," Levi answered.

"Can I see her sometime?" Zaylie asked.

"Of course you can," Levi said. "Now let's dig into this good food. I'm starving."

"Me too," Zaylie chimed in.

"Good, because I made a lot of food," Retta said. "Now, Miz Zaylie, would you like chocolate or white milk?"

"White, please. We didn't have milk at the cabin. But Levi cooked us some homey cakes and they was good." Zaylie held her plate out toward Claire. "Biscuits and gravy and then I'll have some of them cimamum rolls."

Retta glanced over at Levi. "Homey cakes?"

"Cornbread hoecakes," he explained.

Retta set a glass of milk beside Zaylie's plate, and then she took a place across the table from her. Claire kept a close watch on everyone. Justin was staring at the Band-Aid on her forehead. Was he waiting for her to explain how it got there? Retta couldn't wipe the smile off her face or blink as she watched Zaylie.

"There's enough food here for an army," Claire said as she covered a biscuit with gravy for Zaylie.

"Air Force," Zaylie corrected her with a frown. "I will say the prayer?"

Levi grinned and bowed his head. Claire did the same. You never knew what would come out of Zaylie's mouth when she said the prayer, but it always came straight from her heart.

Her little head dropped to her chest, and she shut her eyes. "Thank you, Jesus, for everything but 'specially for this milk. Amen."

Retta stifled a giggle, and she winked at Claire. "She gets right to the point, doesn't she?"

"Oh yeah," Claire said. "Always has."

"When y'all get done with breakfast, Levi can go on out and help with the chores, and I'll take you down to the girls' bunkhouse. There's a huge bathtub in there, and I bet you'd both love a long, hot bath," Retta said.

"That sounds heavenly," Claire said. "We were grateful that the cabin was there, and we had hot water in the kitchen, but I didn't want to take a shower or let Zaylie have one and then get out in the cold. But if I can use the house phone, surely a tow truck or someone can come and get me and Zaylie. We can go to a hotel and call for someone from Randlett to come get us."

"Nonsense," Retta said. "It's no trouble at all to have you here, and we've got plenty of room."

"I want to stay here and play with the kitties and pet Beau," Zaylie chimed in. "Don't make me go to a hotel, Aunt Claire." Tears ran down her cheeks. "Please don't make me go to a hotel. What if they don't even have matches and we freeze."

Claire wiped Zaylie's cheeks with her napkin. It was rare to see her niece so distraught, and this spoke to just how frightened she must have been after their accident. "Okay, okay, but only for a day or two until the snow melts and our preacher can drive down here and get us."

"Thank you, Aunt Claire." Zaylie sniffled. "Did I ruin my makeup?"

Retta giggled, and both cowboys chuckled.

"What?" Zaylie sighed loudly. "That's what Aunt Claire says when she cries. She almost ruined her makeup when we got so cold before Levi rescued us."

"She couldn't find the matches," Levi explained as he passed the food.

"Oh my!" Retta gasped. "It's a wonder you didn't freeze. They should be kept on the mantel from now on, Levi."

"Already taken care of." He set about eating breakfast. "This is a whole lot better than what I stirred up yesterday morning."

"Y'all are all welcome. Excuse me, please." She hurriedly pushed her chair back and practically ran from the room.

When she returned she was slightly green around the mouth, and her eyes were watery. Bless her heart. She'd cooked breakfast when the smell of food gagged her. Now that was a good hostess. There was no way that Claire's sister-in-law, Haley, would have cooked anything at all when she was pregnant. She barely came out of her bedroom that first three months. Claire had carried crackers and warm tea to her every morning just so she could get out of bed. Retta couldn't be very far along. She wasn't showing yet, and usually morning sickness was over after the first trimester.

Retta went to the cabinet and brought down a box of chamomile tea. "Would anyone like a cup of tea?"

"Not me." Justin finished his coffee and pushed back his chair. "You okay, Retta?"

"I'm fine. Just a little stomach bug." Retta smiled.

"Well, keep it to yourself. We don't need it on Thanksgiving," Justin teased. "I'm going to shove off now and get the tractor back to the barn. I've got to go hunt down a couple more cows, so if you'll give me the keys to your van, I'll bring the rest of your things to the bunkhouse, Miz Claire."

"It's not locked and thank you." It would be great to have more than what she'd packed in the small suitcase. Good old organized Claire—that's what her mother called her from the time she was a little girl. Well, by golly, no one fussed when she made her lists and things went like clockwork. She always packed big suitcases full of Zaylie's clothing and toys and one small just-in-case suitcase for emergencies. It held a change of clothing, nightshirts, and toiletries in case they had to stop in a hotel.

"You're welcome." Justin nodded and disappeared out the back door.

"So your daddy's in the Air Force?" Retta asked Zaylie. "I bet you miss him when he's gone."

Zaylie nodded. "I stay with Aunt Claire when Daddy is ployed or on a mission."

"We live in Randlett, just over the line into Oklahoma." Claire reached for a cinnamon roll. "These look delicious.

Before my grandmother took sick, she used to make them often."

"Aha! So you are an Okie!" Retta's smile got bigger. "I'll have an ally for a few days in this land of Texas Longhorns. I've felt like the only chicken at a coyote convention and with the bowl games coming up? Well…" Retta threw up her palms defensively.

"Bless. Your. Heart," Claire said seriously. "And I mean that in a good way. Are they all enemies of our precious Boomer Sooners?"

"Hey, now!" Levi exclaimed. "Way I see it is that y'all are enemies of our precious Longhorns."

Claire shot a look across the table at him. "All depends on which side of the Red River you are from."

"All these cowboys are Longhorns," Retta told her. "It was the one thing that almost kept me from marryin' Cade."

"Well, honey, I haven't always lived in Oklahoma, but I'm a Boomer Sooner now and you've got a friend," Claire said.

Even if she hadn't been an OU fan, she would have joined Retta. Three against one was horrible odds, and the woman had made breakfast for her. They might never see each other again after the snow melted, but Claire had always had a soft heart for the underdog. Not that the Sooners could ever be called the underdogs, but Retta deserved her allegiance.

"Am I a Bloomer?" Zaylie asked.

"That's Boomer, baby girl, and yes you are when you live with me, which is a lot of the time," Claire answered. "That makes three against three. Those are a little better odds, right Retta?"

Levi groaned as he took a second cinnamon roll from the platter. "Sassy women against us cowboys."

"You ain't got a chance," Retta told him.

"I don't think Zaylie is a Sooner. She lives in Texas, right? That makes her a Longhorn," Levi argued.

"She lives with me part of the time." Claire was enjoying the bantering. It had been a very long time since she'd spent more than an hour around people her own age—and that was at church where she didn't argue about what state had the best football team.

Levi tilted his chin up a few notches. "Don't you think we should let her grow up and make up her own mind?"

"She might change when she's grown, but right now she's a Sooner." Claire accentuated every word with a shake of her forefinger. He leaned back like he was afraid she'd put his eye out. Hadn't a woman ever argued with him? Well, he was in for a surprise while she was there because she spoke her mind and stood up for herself. If he didn't like it, he could get out a snowplow and figure out a way to get her to a hotel—even if Zaylie did throw a bawlin' fit.

Zaylie reached for a second cinnamon roll. "I like red and white pom-poms. What color is your team?"

"Ugly old orange," Retta answered for him.

"I like red better." Zaylie bit into the roll. "Mmm, just like you made for me and Nanny."

"Out of the mouths of babes. Even a four-year-old knows that red is better than orange." Retta patted her on the shoulder.

"Y'all are ganging up on me, so I'm going to the barn." Levi finished the last bite of his roll and pushed back the chair. "Thanks for breakfast, Retta. There's no way the hired hands can get here today, so we'll have to double up on the work." He leaned forward and whispered in Claire's ear. "This ain't over. I'll convince her that orange is beautiful before she leaves."

"What are you whisperin' about?" Zaylie asked, suddenly fidgety.

"Big people stuff," Claire answered.

"You'll come back, won't you, Levi? You didn't tell her that you were going away forever, did you? You ain't goin' to call that towin' truck to come and get us and take us to the hotel, are you?" Zaylie asked.

"Of course I'll be back. I live here on the ranch, and besides, I'll have to see if you have a favorite kitten and if you're makin' friends with Gussie," Levi answered. "I wouldn't leave you all alone or call the tow truck. What if you couldn't find the matches?"

Zaylie cut her eyes toward Claire.

"Hey, don't look at me like that," Claire said. "How was I to know they were behind the cereal on a shelf so high I couldn't see them?"

Zaylie turned back toward Levi. "Don't forget."

"I won't." He patted her on the head. "You get all settled in, and I'll be there before lunchtime. I promise."

"Okay." Zaylie nodded, seriously.

"See y'all later." He carried his plate to the sink. "Breakfast was delicious, Retta."

"Don't forget to call Mavis, or wc'll both be in trouble," Retta reminded him, then turned back to Claire. "I lived in the bunkhouse until Cade and I got married." She talked as shc cleared the table. "I went down there last night and got it warmed up and checked the cabinets. There are still a few things from when I was there, but we'll need to take milk and snacks down there. You and Zaylie can come up here to eat your regular meals. What do you like, Zaylie? Bananas or apples?"

"Is a bunkhouse bigger than the cabin?" Zaylie asked. "And I like apples better. Bananas are squishy."

"Thank you," Claire said softly. "This has been pretty traumatic. She's always sad when her dad has to leave for a while, and then she's sad when I take her home and I leave. It's a tough life for a little girl with no mama."

"I can only imagine." Retta nodded. "What happened to her mother?"

"She died when Zaylie was just a baby."

"I'm so sorry." Retta's eyes filled with tears. "I can't imagine the turmoil in her little heart and life. She's lucky to have you."

"Thank you," Claire said.

It had definitely been hard on Zaylie, but then it hadn't been easy on Claire either. She'd been on standby for five years—make that six because she'd helped take care of Haley until the baby was born. That wasn't right either. It seemed like she'd been on standby her whole life. Not that she was complaining. Someone had to do the jobs that she'd taken on.

"We gotted really cold before Levi came. He will come back, won't he?" Zaylie was saying when Claire tuned back in to the conversation.

"Well, honey," Retta said, "there are plenty of work coats around here. That jacket you were wearing is way too thin to keep you warm. Benjy left a coat here last time he was on the ranch too. It'll be miles too big, but we can roll up the sleeves, and yes, Levi will come back. He lives here."

A weak smile barely turned up the corners of Claire's mouth. Zaylie didn't put much trust in the fact that someone lived there. Her daddy lived in base housing, but when he left, he didn't come back in a few hours. Her Nanny lived in the house in Randlett, and she left to never come back.

Claire made herself think of something else. "If I'd known about all this, I would've packed warmer things, like gloves and coats instead of jackets. They would have sure come in handy when we were trudging through the snow to the cabin."

"Aunt Claire was bleedin' when the car hit the tree," Zaylie said. "We had to walk, and my feet got wet."

"We made it though didn't we?" Claire was determined to banish wandering thoughts and pay attention to the conversation. "All I could think about was making it to that cabin. I had a suitcase in one hand and held on to Zaylie with the other. I was so glad to get inside and under the quilts on the bunk bed so we could stop shivering."

"Did all the airbags pop open?" Retta loaded food into a couple of brown grocery bags.

"Every one of them. When the front end hit the tree it felt like we were bein' invaded inside as well as outside with all that white," Claire answered.

"You realize you might have totaled that vehicle, don't you?" Retta asked.

"I'm pretty sure it is, but I keep hoping that it can be repaired. Tell me what I can do to help you."

"Not a thing." Retta headed toward the back door. "I've got it ready now. Y'all ready to go to the bunkhouse? We have a spare bedroom here in the big house, but you'd have to share, and I thought you'd be happier in the bunkhouse where you'll have more privacy."

"Thank you. The bunkhouse sounds great. And yes, I'm ready to go. I'd really like a bath and a long nap. I didn't sleep well either night," Claire admitted. "We'll be out of your way as soon as possible."

"I wouldn't have slept in that situation either. You wouldn't have known it, but Levi has a heart of gold. He would have protected you against anything, not harmed you." Retta handed them each a warmer coat. "Is being away from your job going to create a problem?"

"I work at home. I make and sell quilts on Etsy," Claire answered. She started to tell her that on the way down to

San Antonio, she'd spotted a small, empty building in Sunset where she'd love to put in a quilting shop. But there was no need talking about it when the place might not even be available.

"I love Pinterest and Etsy so much. We'll have to compare notes when you get settled," Retta said.

"We gots 'terio in the van," Zaylie said.

"What?" Retta slipped her arms into a warmly lined jacket and handed one to Claire and to Zaylie.

"Material in the van," Claire translated. "I bought several bolts of fabric in San Antonio. Levi offered to bring it to the bunkhouse so I can cut the pieces for several quilt tops while we're waiting to get home," Claire answered. "I'll try to stay out of everyone's way and not be an imposition."

Retta laid a hand on her shoulder. "I'm sorry that all this happened, but I'm a firm believer that things happen for a reason. In a few weeks or months, we'll look back and see why it all went down this way. When I came to the ranch in June, I figured it was for five weeks, but lookin' back, I can see the plan in it all."

"I hope you're right."

A picture of Levi popped into Claire's mind, and she wondered what kind of plan this was for him. Common sense said that he had a girlfriend or maybe even a fiancée in the wings. No man that was as kind and sweet, plus as handsome, as Levi Jackson was single. It just wasn't possible.

*   *   *

The first thing that Zaylie saw when Retta opened the bunkhouse door was a big fluffy yellow cat in a basket with three little black kittens curled up against her belly. Zaylie immediately dropped to her knees and began talking to them in the high-pitched tone she used when she was playing with her baby dolls.

"Looks like she's going to spoil those cats," a man commented as he stood up from the sofa. He towered over Claire, even more than Levi did, but he wasn't as stocky.

Retta went to him, and he draped an arm around her shoulders. "I'm Cade Maguire. You must be Claire."

She moved forward and stuck out a hand. "I'm pleased to meet you, and thank you for your hospitality."

They shook, and then he kissed Retta on the forehead. "I've got more work to do. I'll see you at noon."

"And I'm Zaylie, and thank you for bringing me the kitties." Zaylie waved from the basket.

"You are very welcome. I'm sure Gussie will enjoy being in the house." Cade smiled.

While Zaylie was busy getting acquainted with the cat and kittens, Retta showed Claire the rest of the cabin—four small bedrooms, one large one, a tiny kitchenette, complete with a washer and dryer.

"And now I'll let y'all get settled in. See you at noon," Retta said.

"Thanks again," Claire said.

She took care of herself, her family, and a booming quilting business, but suddenly Claire was completely overwhelmed. Everything had happened in a whirlwind, and she was used to order and schedules. And she did not like the feeling one bit. She grabbed the telephone, sank down on the sofa, and dialed Franny's phone number.

"Hello," she answered cautiously.

"Franny, it's Claire."

"Well, praise the Lord! I didn't recognize the number and thought it might be one of them guys tryin' to sell me more insurance," she said. "Where are you? Are you and that baby girl all right? I've been worried. You should have been home. Did you get stuck down there in the snow?"

When Franny stopped for a breath of air, Claire started answering questions before Franny could fire off more. Claire told her about getting lost and wrecking the van and the rest of the story. When she finished she felt as if a weight had been lifted. Now someone knew where she was and that she and Zaylie were alive.

"Franny, I really don't like this feeling of dependence. It doesn't set well with me." Claire sighed.

"You're in good hands. Don't worry. The sun will come out and melt the snow. You'll be home before long, and this will be just a story that you and Zaylie tell Grant when he comes home," Franny said.

"How do you know I'm in good hands?" Claire asked.

"When me and my late husband lived on the ranch between here and the Red River, we knew the old Maguire couple. They were fine folks, and I wouldn't expect a bit less from their offspring. This would be their grandsons runnin' the place now, I'm sure," Franny answered.

"I guess so, but it was the foreman of the ranch, Levi Jackson, who rescued us. How do you know the Maguires?"

Franny giggled. "Honey, it's not that far from where you are to Randlett. We were pretty often at the same ranch sales that they were. Lizzy Maguire and I both had a little taste for a shot of Jack Daniel's whiskey and gossip. I always looked forward to catchin' up with her even if she was a dyed-in-the-wool, hardheaded Longhorn fan. And little Levi is the foreman on that big ranch, you say? That means his dad, Skip, has stepped down. Is Mavis still alive?"

"Yes, he is, and I overheard them talking about Levi calling Mavis, so I'd guess she's still living. But Levi is not little," Claire answered.

"I guess I should've said young Levi. That boy was always big for his age, but he had a gentle way about him. How old is he now?"

Claire's brow wrinkled as she tried to guess Levi's age. "I'd guess somewhere near my age, maybe a little older."

"That's what I'd think. I remember them being kids back when you and Grant were visiting your grandmother, and y'all were about the same age as those boys. And, Claire, everything happens for a reason," Franny said.

"You're the second person who's said that to me today." Claire wondered what reason there could be for her vehicle being totaled, for her having to spend the holiday with strangers, or why her life had gone completely sideways. None of it made a bit of sense to her.

"Well, whoever said it first is a smart cookie," Franny said. "Call me every day, and don't worry about your place up here. I'll keep a close eye on it. The storm went to the east of us. We got about half an inch of snow, and it's already melted, but they're sayin' that down around Bowie and Nocona, it might take several days to get back to normal."

Claire groaned. Two days had just stretched into the better part of a week.

"When life gives you lemons, throw them in the trash and make a chocolate cake. It tastes better." Franny's giggles were high pitched enough that Claire held the phone out from her ear.

"You are crazy." Claire laughed with her.

"Yep, I am. I've got your number. If you don't call me by nine tomorrow night, I'll call you," Franny said.

"I'll keep you posted each evening. You stay warm. Bye now," Claire said.

The moment she put the receiver back on the stand,

Gussie hopped up in her lap, turned around a couple of times, and curled up into a ball. Looking up with big eyes, she started to purr.

"You're a whole lot friendlier than Franny's cat, Willie. Is Zaylie babysitting for you so you can have some time away from those kitties?" she crooned.

The cat purred even louder.

"I wish you could talk. I'd like to know if Levi has a significant other in his life, but I don't want to ask Retta."

"What's a giftother?" Zaylie sat down on the floor beside her with three squirmy kittens in her arms.

"Significant other is a girlfriend," Claire changed the subject. "Let's put all these cats back in the basket and take a bath in that enormous tub. You want to go first or should I?"

"Me!" Zaylie carefully carried the kittens back to the basket.

"You drop all your clothes by the washing machine, and I'll start a bath for you. We've each got a change of clothes and pajamas in that suitcase. That'll do until Levi brings the rest of our stuff."

"Why didn't you put more in the suitcase like my toys?" Zaylie asked.

"Because I packed it that way in case we got tired and had to stop at a hotel. You didn't need your toys until we get home to Randlett."

"Okay." Zaylie bounced and twirled like a ballerina all the way to the washer where she stripped down to nothing and then ran to the bathroom ahead of Claire. She played in the water until it was lukewarm and then Claire shampooed her hair. When she got out and was dressed in fresh clothing, she wanted to know if she could rest her eyes in the bed in her room.

"Which one is yours?" Claire asked.

She yawned. "The one right next to yours, just like at home."

"I saw lots of little girl books on the case in the living area. You want to take one with you to look at?" Claire brushed the tangles from her hair.

"Nope. I just want to rest my eyes, and then I'll read a story to the kittens." Her tiny hands knotted into fists, and she rubbed her eyes with them.

She was sound asleep before Claire got the washer loaded and headed toward the bathroom for her turn in the big tub. She ran the tub full of water and sighed as she sank down into it. She'd never take warm water or a bathtub for granted again. She leaned her head back and shut her eyes. A series of pictures of Levi flashed through her mind— standing in the cabin door, covered with snow and looking like he was really ten feet tall, and probably even bullet-proof, then one of him smiling at Zaylie's prayers, and an up close and personal one as he carried her into the house.

He'd sure enough proved what Franny said about him having a gentle way about him.

Chapter Four

Instead of calling Mavis right away, Levi went out to the barn to check on Little Bit, the crippled miniature donkey he'd taken in over the summer. He slipped his hand between the rails and scratched the animal's ears.

"Be glad you ain't a human, Little Bit. Mamas always want to meddle in your life when it comes to women." He sighed. "Guess I'd better face the music."

He used the phone in the tack room, and Mavis answered on the first ring. "I've been worried sick about you gettin' stuck in that cabin with a woman and a child. What's her name and where's she from? What do you know about her?"

"Well, hello to you too. And I'm fine, thanks for asking."

Mavis chuckled. "Sarcasm does not fit you, my son."

"Prying fits you real good," he shot back. "But to answer your question, her name is Claire Mason, and her four-year-old niece is Zaylie. She's from Randlett and…"

Mavis butted in before he could say another word. "I'll

call you back in a few minutes. You stay right there beside whatever phone you are talkin' from, and don't leave."

He heard the click when she hung up and laid the old corded receiver back on the base. While he waited, he hefted the saddles over to the sawhorses lined up against the wall and did some general straightening. Even though he was expecting it, the phone startled him when it rang.

"Hello," he said.

"Okay, I called Frances Crocker up in Randlett. She's an old friend who used to raise Angus cattle and went to a few sales with us back when the old folks were runnin' the Longhorn Canyon. And she says that Claire is Pauline Mason's granddaughter. There weren't no finer woman than Pauline, so I'm sure Claire is a decent woman."

"Yep," Levi said, and changed the subject. "How's Benjy doin'? I miss that boy."

"He loves the snow. He and Skip have made three snowmen, and now he's sitting beside the window with his sketch pad drawin' them." Mavis went into a long-winded description of each snowman.

"Man, since I've got that younger brother, I don't matter no more," Levi teased.

"Honey, no one could ever replace you. We had you from the time you were a little thing, but Benjy is sure filling a void in our lives. I won't keep you from your work any longer, but I'll expect a call every day until I can get out there and meet this woman."

"She'll be gone before then, I'm sure," Levi told her.

"Well, if she's still here Sunday and the roads are clear, I'll expect to see her in church with all y'all. Bye now."

Justin stuck his head in the door and said, "Hey, if you're done in here, you could take a four-wheeler and a little trailer out to the old cabin and get Claire's van unloaded.

And on the way, you can make sure there's not a stray cow standing out there udder deep in a snow drift."

"Are we missin' a cow?" Levi asked.

"Haven't actually called roll, but Cade thinks maybe we're still half a dozen short, so keep your eyes open. Mavis give you a talkin' to?"

Levi pulled his gloves from his coat pocket. "Oh yeah, what about your mama? Did you get a call from her?"

Justin nodded. "She called and said that I was to be careful until we got to know this woman better. I told her Claire just ain't my type, but she was definitely yours."

Levi frowned. "Thanks for that. Now she'll talk to Mavis and they'll nag me to death over the whole thing."

Justin chuckled. "I was savin' my own butt. What else did Mavis say?"

"Mavis called a friend of hers in Randlett. There's not a detective in Texas who can do the job of a couple of mamas who are worried about a strange woman living close to their boys, even if we're looking thirty in the eye."

"Hey now!" Justin threw up his hands. "Speak for yourself. I'm not going to think about that thirtieth birthday for two more years."

"By then your mama might be payin' women to get stranded on the ranch just so you'll settle down." Levi grinned.

"By then maybe Retta and Cade will have a kid or two, and that will take her attention away from me." Justin followed him out into the barn where the four-wheelers were located.

"Don't bet on it." Levi pulled a trailer over and hooked it up.

"Why?" Justin asked.

"Benjy's not keeping Mavis and Skip from nosin' around

in my business." He settled into the seat and started up the engine.

"Guess we're doomed." In a few long strides, Justin crossed the floor and opened the barn door for him.

"If women start dropping out of the sky with parachutes, I make a motion that we run like the devil is chasin' us." Levi chuckled and waved over his shoulder.

*   *   *

Claire was folding laundry when Levi poked his head inside and whispered, "Ready for me to unload your things?"

"Of course." Claire blushed as she quickly covered her folded underpants with a shirt. "I'll get my coat and shoes on and help you."

He stepped inside the house with an armload of fabric bolts. "I've got all the stuff from your van out here, but I can take care of it."

She put on the coat Retta had loaned her and slipped her feet into her shoes.

"Where do you want this?" he asked.

"In any of the bedrooms except the one right there. Zaylie is in it." She headed outside and brought in a suitcase.

"I said I could do this," he said.

"I'm not used to people waiting on me. I'll help," she said.

He shrugged and picked up another four bolts of fabric. "Sorry to say it looks like the vehicle's totaled."

She bit back a groan. She could afford to get another good used vehicle, but it would cut into the money she had saved to put in a quilting store.

Levi laid the rest of the bolts on the bed.

"Looks to me like you've got enough stuff to start a store here. Did you buy out Walmart or something?" he asked.

"No, I did not buy out Walmart," she answered honestly. He didn't need to know that she had gotten it on a clearance sale that a fabric store was having. Or that she'd gotten the complete twenty-yard bolts at seventy-five percent off, and had hopes that they would be the first inventory in her new store.

"Well, you must make a helluva lot of quilts. Where's Zaylie?"

"Resting her eyes," Claire answered. "She'll be disappointed that she missed you."

"I can stay a few minutes." He removed his cowboy hat and laid it on the small table. "I told her that I'd come see her before noon. Got to keep my word."

"Then take off your coat, and have a seat. You want something to drink?" she asked. "Coffee is already made, but I'll be glad to fix you a cup of hot chocolate."

"Coffee is fine."

"Want some cookies?"

He hung his denim work coat on the back of a kitchen chair and kicked back in a recliner. "Just coffee. First to warm my freezing hands and then to heat up my insides."

*   *   *

Not that he needed it so much for his insides. Every time that he looked into Claire's gorgeous eyes and heard her sexy voice, warmth spread through his whole body.

Claire handed him a mug of steaming coffee and carried hers to the sofa. Her long hair was still slightly damp, and she didn't have a bit of makeup on, but she was still beautiful. She'd changed into a pair of gray sweatpants with a matching shirt, and she looked fabulous even in that. Gussie hopped up on the sofa and curled up beside her.

"Looks like Gussie is making herself right at home."

"Yes, she is, and Zaylie loves having her and the kittens to fuss over. Thank you again for bringing all my stuff from the van and for taking us in like this," Claire said.

"You're not used to folks helpin' you, are you?"

"Why would you ask that?" Claire asked.

"I could have brought everything inside," he said.

"I'm perfectly able of doing that myself. Been doin' a pretty good job of it for the past twenty-eight years with nothin' more than a temper and a pistol." She paused long enough to take a drink of her coffee. "Does your girlfriend lean on you for every little thing?"

"Never have been married, and most of my relationships lasted a weekend at the longest," he answered.

"Not a very honorable cowboy then, are you?" she asked.

"Hey," he argued. "I never lie, never promise what I'm not willin' to deliver, and never, ever give my word unless I mean to keep it. I live by the cowboy honor code."

"And that is?" she asked.

"There's ten of them. You want me to say them all right now?"

"Got somewhere you need to be?" She kicked off her shoes and pulled her feet up on the sofa.

"Okay then." He raised one finger. "Live each day with courage. Take pride in your work. Finish what you start." He set the coffee on the end table so he could use the other hand, raising a finger for each statement. "Be tough but fair. Do what has to be done. When you make a promise keep it. Ride for the brand. Talk less, say more. Remember some things aren't for sale, and last, know where to draw the line." He finished and picked up the mug again.

"I saw that on a plaque one time at Cracker Barrel. Is that where you got them?"

"Nope." Levi shook his head. "My dad made me memorize them when I was a kid. He said that he lived by them and that if I wanted to be a good cowboy, then I would do the same."

"He sounds like a good father," she said.

"The best." Levi finished off his coffee and went to the kitchen for a refill. "You want more?"

She nodded and handed him her cup.

"Did you call your folks and let them know that you are okay?"

She shrugged. "My mother is in Italy, and my father is in Hawaii. I wouldn't call them for anything less than a death in the family. And I can't get in touch with my brother. He calls me when he can."

Good grief! No wonder she was so independent. She had to be.

She went on, "But I did call my neighbor, Franny. She and my grandmother were good friends, and we kind of watch out for each other. She said that she knew Cade and Justin's grandparents and Mavis and Skip back in the day," she said.

"Mavis said that she called someone named Frances to check up on you. Would that be Franny?" he asked.

"It would." She nodded. "I expect that she'll call me later to tell me that she talked to your..." She paused.

"Mother does fine even if I call her Mavis."

"Small world when your mother knows my neighbor," she said.

They were silent for so long that he thought about pouring the rest of the coffee down the drain and making an excuse to leave. That he needed to get back to work wouldn't be a lie. Then Zaylie came out of one of the bedrooms rubbing sleep from her eyes. When she saw him, she squealed and ran across the room to stand at the end of the recliner and put her hand on his shoulder.

"You came." She sighed. "You said you would and you did."

"I always keep my word," he told her with a sideways look at Claire. "Do you like this bunkhouse all right? Will it do until you can get back home?"

"I like it better than Aunt Claire's house," she answered.

"Why's that?"

She pointed to the basket in the corner. "I've got kittens and Gussie, but I miss Franny because she brings me chocolate chip cookies," Zaylie said.

"Zaylie!" Claire scolded. "You shouldn't just miss Franny because of her cookies. She's a sweet lady who loves you."

Zaylie shrugged. "Can I have a snack now?"

"Yes, you may. What do you want? An apple? Cookies and milk?"

"Cookies and milk and then an apple," she said.

Levi stood up. "I'd be glad to pour some milk and get you some cookies. I'm sure they won't be as good as Franny's, but they might do."

"Chocolate milk, please, and three cookies." Zaylie held up the right number of fingers. "And it's okay if they ain't as good as Franny's because you smell better." She clapped her hands on her cheeks and ran across the room. "I forgot to see if my kitties are still resting their eyes."

Levi raised an eyebrow at Claire as he headed toward the kitchen.

"Arthritis cream with lots of menthol in it," she whispered.

He shot a sly wink across the room. Someday he wanted a daughter just like Zaylie, but first he'd have to find a wife.

*   *   *

All that sass about how independent she was melted like ice cubes in July when one of his eyelids closed in a slow wink. Then as if nothing had happened, he put three cookies on a plate and squirted chocolate syrup into a glass of milk. Worn work jeans hugged his thighs and butt, and ripped abs showed through a snug-fitting knit shirt. His boots were scuffed, and his belt buckle testified that he either rode bulls now or had in the past.

Her chest tightened and her pulse raced. She could almost feel the sparks dancing around her, and it was pure insanity. She'd never been attracted to cowboys—not even with their sexy swagger, big belt buckles, and all that self-confidence. She'd always leaned toward the preppy type, like Mark, who'd been a lawyer in Wichita Falls. Italian loafers, nice suits, and an expensive haircut—that was her type.

And look what that got you, the aggravating voice in her head said loudly. *Nothing but heartache and bad memories.*

She wanted to argue with the voice, but it was useless to do battle with the truth. Mark had been a mistake from the beginning with his desire to be in control. Telling her that she should get a "real" job, even if it was going back to being a schoolteacher, or that she should get a better car. Or worse yet, getting angry at her for keeping Zaylie when Grant had to be away. That was the straw that broke the old proverbial camel's back.

Levi brought the milk and cookies to the coffee table that took up space between the sofa and the two recliners. "Here you go, Miz Zaylie."

"Thank you." She tiptoed across the room with a sleeping kitten draped over her arm. "Shhh. We have to be quiet so she don't wake up." She picked up the milk and drank enough to leave a chocolate mustache on her upper lip.

"I understand. If she wakes up she'll whine," he whispered. "I've got to get back to work, but I'll close the door real easy. And Claire, I'm leaving the old ranch work truck out in front of the bunkhouse. Keys are in it so you can go back and forth to the house."

"It's not that far. We can walk," she argued.

"That's your choice, but if you don't drive, then you'll be wading in snow up to your butt and to Zaylie's waist." Levi put on his coat and hat and waved over his shoulder as he left.

Zaylie finished her milk and two cookies, leaving one on the plate. No need in letting it sit there alone and it was still two hours before lunch, so Claire ate it. While she was swallowing the last bite the phone rang. She grabbed it on the fourth ring.

"Hello," she said.

"Claire," came Grant's voice through the static. "I've been worried. I tried to call your cell phone and finally called Franny, who told me what happened and gave me this number. Thank God y'all are all right."

She quickly put it on speaker mode and called Zaylie. She came from the bedroom carrying one of the kittens and started talking the moment she heard her father's voice. "Guess what, Daddy? I've got a mama cat and three kittens, and we got a bunkhouse, and there's snow everywhere."

"That's wonderful, princess, but don't you give away all my hugs to your new friends," Grant said.

"I save a gazillion just for you all the time," she said, and giggled.

"Zaylie, tell him about Retta and Levi," Claire said.

"Levi is a hero," she said as the kitten wiggled free and

made a mad dash under the sofa. "He made a fire, and he cooked. And Retta is real nice and guess what? We got a big bathtub, and we got our own washin' 'chine, and guess what else? There's a pet donkey that I get to go see when the snow melts. Can I have cowboy boots for Christmas?"

Grant's laughter sounded relieved as much as amused. "Why would you want cowboy boots?"

"Levi has them and 'cause my feet got cold."

"Then you definitely have to ask Santa for them. It looks like we'll have this mission wrapped up by Christmas, so I should be home," Grant said. "But right now I've got to go. Be good, buttercup."

"I will, Daddy. I love you." She made kissing noises toward the phone.

Claire took it off speaker and put it to her ear. "We're fine, Grant. Don't worry about us. These are good people."

"I hope so. Franny vouched for them, so that makes me feel a lot better," he said. "I'll call again when I get the chance."

"Be careful, and know we love you," she said.

"Rightbackatcha," he replied. "And if they're givin' away kittens, I might consider letting Zaylie have two."

"You're kiddin' me," Claire gasped.

"Don't tell her just yet. Kittens and boots might be a pretty good Christmas present."

The phone went dead, and Claire stared at it for a long time before she set it back on the stand. Was her brother getting out of the service? Was he taking a different job—one that wouldn't involve leaving home again? Those were the only two things that would make pets a possibility.

Either of those two decisions would definitely change Claire's life. She'd been a caregiver for years, staying with Haley through the morning sickness while Grant was on a mission that lasted several weeks of the first trimester. Then right after that Grant was deployed for six months. He'd asked Claire to stay so Haley wouldn't be alone through the pregnancy, and he hadn't arrived back on base until one day before Zaylie was born on Christmas morning. By New Year's Claire was in Randlett to help with her grandmother, and now she kept Zaylie for Grant. If her brother was making a life change, then it would impact her world as well, and she wasn't sure how she felt about it.

She went to the bedroom and opened the suitcase that contained her quilt cutting tools and was on her way to the kitchen table when the phone rang again.

"Hey, Zaylie, can you answer that?" she asked.

"Hello," she said. "Guess what. I named the kittens. They are Grumpy, Happy, and Sleepy. Here's Aunt Claire."

Claire laid her supplies down and took the phone, expecting it to be Franny. "Hello. Evidently she's seen Snow White too often."

"Claire, could you possibly come up here to the house and help me get dinner ready for the guys and maybe do the baking for Thanksgiving dinner? I feel awful asking for your help, but I can't stand the smell of food," Retta said.

"Be there in five minutes." Claire carried the phone back to the base and turned to Zaylie. "Gussie is going to have to take care of the babies for a while. Retta needs us. You ready to do some baking?"

"Yes!" Zaylie squealed. "I like to cook. Are we going to walk in the snow?"

"No, darlin' girl. Levi left a truck for us." Claire pulled on her shoes and tied them before she helped Zaylie.

Remembering that a path had been cleared from the backyard fence to the house, Claire drove around to that spot and parked the truck. Before she could even open the door, Zaylie had bailed out and was sliding down the path. Claire had a hand up to knock on the door, when it flew open, and Retta motioned them inside.

"Thank you so much for doing this," she said.

Claire hung up her jacket and then Zaylie's. "You are so welcome. I'm glad to help, especially with all you're doing for us. How far along are you?"

"How did you know?" Retta asked.

"Zaylie's mama, Haley, had a terrible time with it the first trimester, so I went to stay with her while my brother was on a mission. Then when it was about over, Grant got deployed, so I stayed on with her the next six months. I'm pretty familiar with all the symptoms," she answered.

"I'm six weeks, and we'd planned to tell the guys on Thanksgiving. But we told them an hour ago because I can't stand the smell of food, and I'm hoping you can cook." Retta threw a hand over her mouth and headed toward the bathroom.

"Zaylie, pick out an apron." Claire pointed toward the hooks and then followed Retta. She held Retta's hair back and then washed her face with a cold rag. "Saltine crackers and sweet tea will help. And yes, I can cook. What did you plan for the noon meal today? I see you've got a chicken in the slow cooker."

"Dumplings." Retta gagged on the answer.

"I can do that, but first let's get you some crackers and tea and let you lie on the sofa with this cool rag on your head," Claire told her.

"You are a lifesaver," Retta said.

Claire followed her into the living room. "How long are you suffering from it each day?"

Retta stretched out on the sofa. "From the time I get up until about two o'clock in the afternoon. After that I'm not throwing up, but I still feel slightly queasy."

Claire covered her with a throw and then laid the cool rag on her forehead. "You'll need to stay hydrated, and before you get out of bed in the morning, you should eat crackers and have a glass or cup of tea. Zaylie and I will come up here and make breakfast and dinner for the guys, and we can help with supper. Don't worry about Thanksgiving dinner. I can take care of that."

She went to the kitchen and filled a glass with sweet tea from the gallon jug in the refrigerator, put half a dozen crackers on a plate, and carried them to the living room. Zaylie was right behind her, carrying a colorful bibbed apron.

"Is Retta going to die?" Zaylie asked. "I don't want her to die and have to be put into the ground like Nanny."

"No, she's just got a tummy ache. So you and I are going to do the cookin'. Do you think you are big enough to help me with that job like you do at home?" Claire asked.

"Aunt Claire!" Zaylie rolled her blue eyes. "I'm almost five years old. I'm a big girl."

Claire set the plate and glass on the end table and hugged her niece. "I knew I could count on you." Then she turned to Retta. "Eat one cracker slowly and sip the tea; don't gulp it. Let that settle and then repeat the process. You might even feel like eating a little dinner once you get that down. You might want to call your mom to come stay with you until this is over."

"My mother passed away years ago, and my dad's been gone for nearly a year. They would have made wonderful grandparents, and it makes me sad that my baby will never know them. They were good people." Retta cautiously nibbled on a cracker.

"A sister then?" Claire asked. "You'll need help for a few weeks."

"I'm an only child, and before you ask, I'm not comfortable enough around Cade's mama to ever ask for her help. I can call Mavis, I guess." Retta took a sip of tea.

"Well, you definitely need someone," Claire said. "Now tell me what you were going to do this afternoon."

"I was going to make a banana nut cake today. It's better if it ages a couple of days, and it's Cade's favorite." Retta lay back on the sofa.

"I'm glad to help out while I'm here. It makes me feel like I'm less of a bother." Claire laid the cold cloth over Retta's eyes. "Right now I'd better get busy. If these guys are like my brother, they get real cranky when they are hungry."

"Are we going to live here?" Zaylie asked on the way back to the kitchen.

"We have to until the snow melts." Claire slipped the bibbed apron over Zaylie's head.

"If Santa knows where this house is, I hope the snow don't never melt. I like it here, Aunt Claire. But I wouldn't want Santa to leave my boots in the wrong place." She dragged a chair over to the bar that separated the kitchen and the small nook where the family ate.

Claire turned off the cooker and removed the chicken. "Santa knows where every little boy or girl is at Christmas."

Dammit! I shouldn't have said that. Claire frowned. *That could have been my ace in the hole if she fusses when we have to leave, and now I've thrown it away.*

Zaylie crawled up on the chair. "Good! I don't want somebody else to get my boots. When's Levi comin' home?"

"In a little while," Claire muttered.

"Hey, hey, did I hear my name?" Levi sniffed the air as he entered the kitchen. "Do I smell dumplin's? That's one of my favorite meals. Do you like them, Zaylie?"

"I love 'em. I'm glad you came home," Zaylie said. "Do you like my apron?"

"Yes, I do. I bet you're a wonderful cook." He grinned.

"Yes, I am. Aunt Claire teached me to cook, and she's the best."

"I can believe that," he said.

He talked to Zaylie, but his gaze had locked with Claire's. There was something about his mossy green eyes that seemed to be looking right into her soul. Was he flirting? She finally blinked, but that shiver dancing down her spine said that she'd felt something brand-new and more than a little bit exciting.

Later that night back at the bunkhouse, she wondered whether Levi had felt the same little tingle of chemistry. But before she could analyze what it even meant, Zaylie skipped over and piled all three kittens in her lap. Then she cuddled her tiny body up against Claire's side.

"Can we live here forever? Or at least until Daddy comes home?" she asked.

"No, we have to go home when we can. Franny misses us." Claire brushed Zaylie's wispy hair out of her eyes.

Zaylie's chin quivered. "But Aunt Claire, the babies need me."

Lord, let the snow melt fast, Claire sent up a silent prayer. *Every day that we stay will just make it harder for her to leave.*

Chapter Five

Levi heard Cade's deep voice, patient and reassuring, through the bathroom door the next morning. Even though comforting a sick and cranky wife couldn't be fun, Levi envied him. A wife who adored him, a new baby on the way—Cade had it all.

Levi continued on to the kitchen, poured himself a cup of coffee, and stared out the kitchen window. What did he have to offer a woman? He didn't have a square foot of land that belonged to him or even a house. He had a good job and a few dollars in his savings account, but...

"Dammit!" he swore under his breath, and then a movement caught his attention.

The old work truck, once a shiny orange and now faded with age, was coming to a stop right outside the gate. He couldn't take his eyes off Claire and Zaylie as they made their way to the house with Beau right behind them. Had she felt that little spark the day before when they'd locked eyes? Was it too soon to even feel like that?

She was downright cute in that old coat hanging down to her knees and rolled up at the sleeves, and a ponytail swinging back and forth with each step. He waited until they were on the porch before he left the window and filled a mug of coffee for her. When she had hung up her coat and Zaylie's, he handed it to her.

"Something to warm the hands," he said.

"Thank you." She smiled. "Bad morning for Retta?"

"Oh yeah. What can I do to help with breakfast?" Levi asked.

"No, I can take care of it. We'll have bacon, eggs, biscuits, and pancakes this morning. I'm pretty organized, so I'll have it ready in less than thirty minutes," she said.

He got out a skillet and set it on the stove. "I can fry bacon while you do biscuits and pancakes."

"I really don't need..." she started.

"I want to help," Levi said. "We're grateful that you are here for Retta. We're all so excited that we're going to have a baby on the ranch, but we feel so sorry for what she's having to go through right now."

"Baby? Who's getting a baby?" Zaylie slapped hands on her cheeks. "Aunt Claire, are you havin' a baby for me? I want a sister and we can name her Cinderella and she can play with the kittens with me..." She stopped to suck in more air.

Claire took advantage of the timing and said, "Retta is going to have a baby, but I don't think she's going to name her Cinderella."

Zaylie picked up the biscuit cutter and pushed it down in the dough. "We'll just see about that."

Levi chuckled. "I bet she's heard that from you and in that tone, right?"

"More than once." Claire nodded.

"Mavis and Skip said that pretty often when I was a kid." He laid several strips of bacon in the frying pan.

"So how old were you when they adopted you?" she asked.

"Somewhere around three. I don't remember much about my mother, other than the pretty lady who came to see me on Christmas a few times. She was more like a distant cousin than a mom," he said.

* * *

With military parents, Claire could relate to that. When she and Grant were growing up, one or the other of her parents was pretty often sent to posts where the family couldn't go. She and her brother seldom had two parents at home at the same time. And when they were home together, it was more like two strangers lived in the house with Grant and Claire. It wasn't that the children weren't loved, or that they wanted for anything, but it wasn't a warm family.

She carried the pan of biscuits to the stove, and Levi stepped to one side to allow her to get them into the oven. When she straightened up, their noses were only inches apart, and their gazes locked. Neither of them blinked for several seconds.

"Aunt Claire, can we have Easter eggs?" Zaylie's voice jerked her back to the present, and she quickly took two steps back.

"Easter eggs?" Levi's drawl was even deeper than normal as he went back to frying bacon.

A blush crept up into her cheeks. "Hard-boiled eggs."

"Well, I'd like some Easter eggs too, Miz Zaylie, so I'll put some on to boil. Do you like them better than scrambled eggs?" Levi asked.

"I like all eggs, and I like bacon, and I like pancakes," she answered. "Can I crack the eggs, Aunt Claire? I like this kitchen better than the one at your house."

"I thought you wanted Easter eggs," Claire said.

"I do, and Levi does, but we need ramblin' eggs for everyone else," she said.

Levi raised an eyebrow.

"Scrambled eggs," Claire translated. "And yes, you can crack the eggs. That would be a big help while I make pancakes." Claire kept her back to Levi until the heat left her face. She couldn't stay on the ranch a day longer than was necessary—she'd almost kissed Levi right there in front of Zaylie. And the bad thing is that she wished that she had so she'd know if it was as good as she'd imagined.

Cade made it into the kitchen. "Retta is on the sofa with a cool rag on her eyes. Claire, thank you so much for your help. As soon as this mess clears up, Mavis will come out and help us, but you are a godsend right now. All three of us can run a ranch with a hand tied behind our backs, but we hate to cook."

"Amen to that. I can grill a mean steak or make a pot of chili that's fit to eat, but that's the limit of my cooking ability," Justin said as he joined them in the kitchen. "I called the body shop that we've used for years and told him what your van looks like, Claire. He says that it's totaled for sure, and he'll buy it from you for parts after you talk to your insurance company."

Cade started back toward the living room. "Justin's right. We'd survive on our cookin', but that's about the extent of it. I hate that your van is wrecked, but if it had to happen, I'm glad it was on this ranch."

"I'll stay and help," Zaylie said seriously. "I'm a big girl and I can make bickets."

Cade stopped long enough to pat her on the cheek. "Thank you, sweetheart. I bet you make wonderful biscuits."

"Yes, I do," she said.

Justin went straight for the coffeepot and picked it up. "Has Retta got crackers and tea? If not I'll take some in for her. She said your suggestion helped a lot yesterday."

"She's got both, but she might like the company," Cade answered.

Levi moved to the bar where Claire was making pancakes on an electric griddle. "We all love Retta so much, and it's tough to see her so sick. She told us last night that just having you here helps as much as your cracker and tea remedy."

"I'm thankful that it's helping her. Zaylie's mama was miserable for three whole months with morning sickness. Nanny told us about tea and crackers, and it sure helped her," Claire said.

"Know what I'm thankful for?" Zaylie asked. "For my kittens and for bacon."

"Bacon!" Levi slapped his forehead and rushed to the stove. "Thank goodness it didn't burn. That's all we need— the smell of burning food would sure make Retta sick."

When the bacon was finished, Levi got down six plates, just in case Retta could eat a little something, and started to set the table.

"I can do that," Claire said.

"It's tough for you to accept help, isn't it?" Levi went on about what he was doing.

"What makes you think that?" Claire asked.

"No thinkin' to it. You prove it every time you turn around."

"Sorry. Force of habit," Claire said.

"Why?" Levi asked.

"Well, someone had to be the planner in our family, and that job fell on me at a young age. My parents were busy with their careers and didn't have a lot of time for two kids."

"You the oldest, then?" Levi removed milk from the fridge when he'd finished setting the table.

"No, I'm the youngest by two years. Story is that I was an accident. They'd only planned to have one child," she said.

"Well, you are sure enough a pretty accident," he said, and grinned.

Heat started on her neck and crept up to her cheeks. There was no doubt that he was flirting now, and she liked it.

"Call Cade and Justin to breakfast while I get the biscuits from the oven," she said.

"Aha! You're letting me do something. Progress is made." He chuckled.

*   *   *

Levi got finished with the feeding chores and planned to do some maintenance work on the tractors that afternoon. But he had to wait for Justin to finish what he was doing to help out, which left him with an hour in the middle of the morning with nothing to do. He checked on Little Bit, the donkey. Poor little thing looked up at him with big brown eyes like he was begging to be let out.

"I know you don't like to be cooped up. How would you like some kid company?" he asked as he tugged on his gloves. "You wait right here and I'll be back in a few minutes."

He'd barely made it inside the house when Zaylie came running to greet him. "I told Aunt Claire you was home."

"How did you know?" Levi asked.

"I heard your boots on the porch. I'm getting boots for Christmas." Zaylie took him by the hand and led him into the kitchen.

She stopped in the middle of the floor. "Want to go to the bunkhouse and see the kittens?"

"She's been worrying about those cats all morning." Claire smiled.

Levi let go of Zaylie's hand and brushed flour from Claire's hair. Then he picked up a wet cloth and wiped it off her nose. "Been makin' bread have you?"

"No, a banana nut cake and the recipe said to sift the flour three times," she answered.

"It ought to be a good one with all that much work. I wondered if maybe you and Zaylie might like to ride out to the barn with me to see Little Bit, the miniature donkey."

Zaylie's blue eyes got wide. "Can I pet him?"

Levi nodded. "Sure you can. He loves kids."

She danced and twirled around several times across the floor to grab Claire's hand. "Please, please, please."

"Cade is with Retta, and there's nothing that has to be done right now," Claire agreed.

Zaylie headed toward the back door in a run, but Claire caught her by the shirttail as she ran past her.

"But first you need your coat and stocking hat, young lady," Claire told her.

"I'll help with hers while you put yours on," Levi offered.

"I can..." Claire started but stopped. "Thank you. That would be nice."

The icy pathway was still frozen solid, so Zaylie slid to the truck, part of the time on her feet, the rest on her butt, giggling the whole time.

Levi tucked Claire's hand into the crook of his arm and

covered it with his. "Is this her first time to see this much snow and ice?"

"We had a pretty good snow a couple of years ago, and I took pictures of her, but I don't think she remembers it too well." Claire shivered.

Levi wanted to let go of her hand and draw her close to his side, but he didn't. He didn't want the disappointment when she pulled away from him.

"I left the truck engine runnin'. It'll be warm in there."

He settled Zaylie into the backseat and fastened the seat belt. When he turned around, Claire was struggling to get up into the truck. He put a hand on each side of Claire's slim waist and lifted her into the passenger's seat. "Guess I should get a runner put on the truck for short folks."

"We do have our challenges. I've never seen a truck that high off the ground," she said.

"It's so I can drive it all over the pasture without gettin' stuck," he explained. "And tall folks have challenges too. Cade is six feet four inches, and if he's wearin' his cowboy hat he has to duck when he passes through doors. I'm only six feet tall, so I don't have that problem."

But I liked the way you felt in my arms, so I'll procrastinate about that runner business, he thought.

"My daddy is tall. I miss him." Zaylie sighed.

"But it's not long until Christmas," Claire reminded her.

"Really? Is it the day after Thanksgiving?"

"No, it's about thirty days after Thanksgiving," Claire said.

"That's for . . . ever." Another long sigh.

"It really is forever to her," Levi said. "When you compare her almost five years to our almost thirty, then it's like six months to her."

"Who says I'm almost thirty?" Claire protested.

"I figured it out from things you said. So how old are you?"

"I was twenty-eight last May," she answered.

"So was I, only in April, so I'm older than you." Levi parked the truck beside the barn.

Zaylie undid her seat belt. "Y'all are old."

"Relatively speakin'." Levi grinned. "But someday you'll be twenty-eight and you'll think it's young."

"Was Nanny twenty-eight when she died?" Zaylie asked.

"No, she was eighty-eight." Claire unfastened her seat belt.

"Wait for me to come around and help you both," Levi said as he got out of the truck.

"Eighty-eight!" Zaylie squeaked. "That's a lot."

"Yes, it is, and I can only hope I live that long so I can watch you grow up and have a wonderful life." Claire put her hands on Levi's shoulders, and his went around her waist again. When she was on the ground and headed into the barn, he picked up Zaylie and slung her up on his shoulders.

"Look, Aunt Claire, I'm a hundred feet tall," she squealed.

There was no way she'd hit her head on the tall door frame, but Levi said, "Duck, Miz Zaylie, or you might get knocked off."

With a loud giggle, she bent her head forward until her wispy blond hair tickled him on the forehead. He carried her to the stall and eased her down onto the barn floor. The little donkey came over to the rails and stuck part of his head out, his big brown eyes begging Zaylie to pet him.

"Can I go in there with him, please, Aunt Claire, can I?" she begged.

Claire turned to Levi. "Is it safe?"

The donkey was adorable. Just one more animal that Zaylie

would fall in love with. And when it was time to leave, she would cry for days about having to leave him and her kittens. Life would have been so much easier if she hadn't even thought about driving through Bowie and Sunset to scout out a place for a quilt shop.

"Look over there in the corner." Levi pointed to a cotton-tailed rabbit.

"A bunny too? Can I pet it?" Zaylie whispered in awe.

"His name is Hopalong and yes, you can pet him. If you sit down, he'll come and get in your lap," Levi answered, and turned to Claire. "Is it all right if I open the gate and let her inside?"

Claire nodded, and Zaylie put her hands on each side of Little Bit's head and kissed him on the forehead before making her way to the corner and sitting down in the straw. Sure enough Hopalong came right over to her and inched his way into her lap. Then Little Bit nudged her on the shoulder, wanting his share of the attention.

"She's in heaven," Claire whispered.

Levi leaned on the top rail of the stall. He was close enough that he caught a whiff of her perfume with every breath. She stepped up on the bottom rail so she could see better, and her arm brushed against his. Even through his coat and her jacket, he could feel the sparks.

"She's going to be sad for weeks when she has to leave. She is already attached to Beau and the cats and now a little donkey and a bunny." Claire rested her elbows on the top rail. "I may have to wait until she's asleep and get her a few miles down the road before she wakes up."

"But just think of all the memories she'll have," Levi said. "Has she ever lived on a ranch?"

"She's lived in military housing and my place her whole life. This is a brand-new experience for her as well as for me," Claire admitted. "My brother and I went to two different boarding schools and stayed a year with our grandmother. That was the closest we ever got to country living, and her house, which is where I live now, is right in the middle of Randlett. And I talk too much and too fast when I'm nervous," she said.

"So what are you nervous about?" Levi moved over a little closer so he could nudge her with his shoulder.

"I've been thinkin' of takin' my quilting business a step further and putting in a store. It'd have fabric for folks who want to quilt. I'd have my sewing machines there, and maybe I'd even invest in a quilting machine so I don't have to pay someone to do that for me. And I'd give lessons and…" She stopped. "I'm talking too much. You aren't interested in this."

"Yes, I am. Mavis goes to a quilting bee at the church twice a month. They make quilts and raffle them off for the missionary fund," he said.

"So there might be a little interest in this area?" she asked.

"You could talk to Mavis, and she'd tell you, but I'd guess there would be." His heart threw in an extra beat at the thought of her living close by.

"I saw an empty house right on the highway in Sunset. It has a FOR SALE BY OWNER sign in the front yard. It looked like a perfect place," she said.

He couldn't wipe the smile off his face. "That would be the old Harris home. I've been in that house. It's got three bedrooms, a single bathroom, and a small kitchen. The folks moved down to Waco to be near their son."

"A room for my sewing machine, one for my quilting machine, and the living room could be my store front. And I could live in the third bedroom," she said.

"Sounds like it'd be perfect." He almost groaned. There she was, a successful entrepreneur looking to expand and make more money, whereas his assets were a four-year-old pickup truck that was paid off and ten head of prime heifers. "So what makes you nervous about it?"

"Change, again. Moving, again. Having a store instead of a house for Zaylie when she needs to stay with me." She named off her concerns fast enough that he had no doubt she'd been arguing with herself for a long time about this idea.

"You seem like the type to take the bull by the horns and spit in his eye," Levi said.

"Or look him in the eye and then take a step back and shoot him," she said. "That doesn't mean I like decidin' whether to shoot or spit."

"Aunt Claire, look at Hopalong. He likes me," Zaylie said just above a whisper.

"And so does Little Bit. If Hard Times was here, I bet he'd like you too," Levi said.

"Hard Times?" Zaylie frowned.

"He's the turtle. Remember the picture in the dining room?" Levi asked.

"On the wall with the ones of Gussie and Beau?" Claire reminded her.

"Oh yeah. When is the turtle comin' home so I can see him too?"

"In the springtime when the leaves are green," Levi said.

"Is that when Benjy comes home too?" Zaylie asked.

"No, Benjy will probably be here just as soon as the weather clears up," Levi told her. "But you"—he turned his attention toward Claire—"can call and talk to Mavis about that quiltin' stuff this evening if you want to."

"Maybe I'll just wait until she and Benjy come out here.

Talkin' about those drawings, I thought they were reprints from a famous artist," Claire said.

"Someday Benjy might be famous, but right now he's just our resident artist," Levi said. "I sure hope they get out here before you leave, and if not, I can bet that Mavis will be one of the first people in your new store."

"I want to see Benjy," Zaylie said. "He can draw my kittens. Aunt Claire, can I have a bunny and a donkey for Christmas?"

"I don't think so. Remember, you asked for kittens, and Santa's going to have a hard enough time gettin' squirmy cats down the chimney. And remember you asked for cowboy boots too," she answered.

"That child belongs on a ranch," Levi whispered.

"They don't put Air Force bases on ranches," Claire told him. "And my brother has a few more years before he can retire."

"Miracles happen during the Christmas season," Levi said. "Miz Zaylie, we should be going back to the house now."

"Can I come back tomorrow?" Zaylie asked.

"You can come back every day you're here if you want," Levi said.

"Okay." She kissed Hopalong on the nose and then did the same to Little Bit.

"Thank you, Levi," Claire said softly.

"Seeing the animals through a child's eyes—that makes me so happy." He opened the gate for Zaylie, and she waved at the donkey and bunny until she couldn't see them anymore.

Retta was in the kitchen when they got back to the house. "I'm feelin' better so I thought I'd help with dinner. That pot roast you've got in the oven sure smells good. Oh, Mavis called and you are supposed to call her back as soon as you get here," Retta told Levi. "She's offered to help out until after Christmas. Soon as the roads are fit, she'll be here before breakfast and stay until after supper like she used to do before we got married."

"I got to pet the donkey and the bunny, and I wish I could live here forever..." Zaylie was telling Retta all about her two new friends when Levi slipped out and went to the living room to call Mavis.

She picked up on the first ring. "Why didn't you call me immediately when you found out Retta was pregnant? She needs my help."

"Yes, she does, and we'll be glad to have you back on the ranch until she feels better," Levi said. "I'm sorry that I didn't call you. I was so shocked and excited and she's been so sick that—"

"And you've got company," Mavis butted in. "Tell me about them so I won't be surprised when I get there."

"She and Retta hit it off from the beginning, and she's very good in the kitchen as well as keeping Retta calm. It seems like the morning sickness is worse if she's all stressed out. And Claire does quilting. She sells them on something called Retsy."

"You mean Etsy?" Mavis asked.

"That's it," Levi said. "And she's kind of, sort of, interested in the old Harris place to put in a little shop. She'd like to talk to you about it."

"Put her on the phone," Mavis said.

"She's fixin' dinner right now."

"I'll only talk a minute or two," Mavis told him.

"Hey, Claire, Mavis wants to talk to you," he yelled as he carried the phone to the kitchen.

She took it from him and said, "Hello, Miz Mavis. I'm Claire Mason."

"So glad you're there to help Retta out while she's been sick. Levi tells me you sell quilts on Etsy and are looking for a shop?"

"Yes, and I hear that you've got a quilting bee at the church."

"We do, and we've got quite a bunch of quilters in our area who would be happy to have a local place. Come to church with me, and I'll introduce you around so you can get to know everyone."

"That'd be so nice of you."

"And I know the lady who has the key to the Harris house anytime you want to look at it. Well, I know you're in the middle of fixin' dinner and I don't mean to keep you, so we'll talk more about this when I get there."

"Thank you." Claire was smiling like she'd just won the lottery when she got off the phone.

And Levi felt like he'd given her the winning ticket.

Chapter Six

"Guess what, Retta?" Zaylie did her usual twists and turns into the house on Thanksgiving morning. "Aunt Claire says that she might buy a store."

"Oh really? What kind of store?" Retta bent to hug Claire.

"A quiltin' one," Zaylie said.

"Would you like that?" Retta asked.

"Yep, because it's not far from this ranch, and maybe I can come back and see my kittens and Little Bit sometime..." She paused and bit her fingernail.

"If?" Claire prompted.

"If it's all right with you," Zaylie finished.

"Of course it's all right with me," Retta said.

Claire slipped an apron over her head and started a pot of coffee. "I talked to Mavis yesterday, and it seems like there's enough interest in this area that a store might work."

"There's not in Randlett?" Retta asked.

Claire shook her head. "Nope, I tried but couldn't attract anyone, not even with newspaper ads offering free classes. I figure if it was meant for me to stay in Randlett, then something would have happened. And my grandmother left her house and car and all her possessions to me and Grant. Someday he's going to need a house to move into and..." She paused. "I'd like to be completely set up before that time comes."

"Sounds like you've thought this out," Retta said.

"It's been on my mind for more than a year. Now what would you like me to fix for breakfast?"

"I'd thought about omelets with peppers and onions, but..." Her expression said that even the thought of something spicy might send her to the bathroom.

Claire patted her on the shoulder. "Not ready for spicy yet, are you?"

"Might not ever be again," Retta answered.

"Good mornin' and happy Thanksgiving." Levi wore faded jeans and a denim shirt with the sleeves rolled up. "What can I do to help with breakfast?"

"Aunt Claire is going to buy a store, and Retta says that I can come see you and the animals!" Zaylie ran to him and wrapped her arms around his legs.

Levi picked her up and swung her around until they were both dizzy. "Wouldn't that be wonderful?"

Zaylie was giggling when he set her down. "We're havin' special thanks this mornin'."

Levi smiled at Claire and met her eyes in the middle of the room, holding the gaze for several seconds. Warmth spread through her like a cup of hot chocolate on a bitter-cold day. After talking to Mavis, she felt like looking at the house was the right decision. Maybe, just maybe, all this happened to steer her toward settling in Sunset.

"What's this about a special Thanksgiving?" Justin came into the kitchen.

"Well, if it's all right with you guys"—Claire glanced at Retta—"we'll do a brunch now and dinner in the middle of the afternoon."

"That sounds great," Retta agreed.

"I'm game for whatever makes my beautiful wife happy." Cade came up behind Retta and slipped his arms around her waist.

The way they looked at each other—that's what Claire wanted someday. It didn't really matter if it was a military guy or someone who sold used cars. Money, power, or prestige could never buy the kind of love that Retta and Cade had, and if Claire couldn't have that, then she'd simply be Zaylie's old maid aunt who made quilts.

"Okay, then, y'all clear out of the kitchen and let Claire have some room." Retta tiptoed slightly and kissed Cade on the cheek. "Go take care of the chores so that we can all have the rest of the day to enjoy the holiday."

"Zaylie and I'll have it on the table in an hour," Claire said.

"Breakfast and then parade," Cade said.

Zaylie pumped her fist in the air. "And then the football game."

Claire wished that she had a camera to capture the three cowboys when they whipped around to stare at her with stunned expressions. It was as if they thought little girls only played with dolls and didn't know how to throw a football.

"What'd I do?" Zaylie asked.

"Nothing, princess," Levi said. "Do you really like to watch football?"

"Yep, I do." Zaylie nodded. "Am I really a princess?"

"Of course you are," Levi answered.

"She likes football, but it's the cheerleaders that take her eye," Claire explained.

"Who are you rootin' for?" Levi asked.

"The Dallas Cowboys," Zaylie said. "I'm goin' to cheer for the Sooners someday." She showed off with a couple of snappy little arm movements.

Cade, Justin, and Levi all groaned in unison.

"You think you'd ever be a cheerleader for the Longhorns?" Levi asked.

"Why would I do that?" She pulled a chair up to the bar. "Them Longhorns don't like my Boomers."

"Smart girl you're raisin'." Retta hugged Claire again. "I've enjoyed havin' y'all here, but I feel a little like I've...well, like..." she stammered.

"You were good to take us in. This won't begin to pay for what you've done for us," Claire said.

The three guys were talkin' about the fastest way to get the cattle feed out as they slipped out the back door, but Levi turned around and smiled at Retta. *Thank you,* he mouthed.

Retta swiped at a tear. "I'm overwhelmed right now with this pregnancy coming along so soon, and having another woman in the house has helped so much."

Claire hugged Retta and asked, "Why?"

"Cade and I've only been married a month, and I'm six weeks pregnant. I was terrified for him to tell his folks."

"So you're worried that his folks will think you were a gold digger and got pregnant just to get your hooks into this ranch?" Claire asked.

Retta nodded. "I would never do that to Cade, and it wasn't on purpose. We'd actually thought we might wait a year before even trying."

"Don't you know that first babies are not bound by the nine-month law? First babies can come anytime from before the wedding to six months after or just whenever they want to arrive. All the rest take nine months," Claire teased.

"Here's hoping that Cade's mama thinks that way. See you at breakfast."

"Here's hopin' you can eat and it will stay down."

"Amen," Retta said as she left the room.

Claire laid a hand on her stomach. What would it be like to be pregnant? Would she have morning sickness or sail through the pregnancy without a single symptom? Would the baby look like Levi?

"Whoa!" she said abruptly.

"What?" Zaylie asked.

"I was talkin' to myself." Claire almost blushed at the vision of Levi holding a tiny baby in his arms. She blinked away the picture and vowed that she wouldn't go there again.

*   *   *

Levi hefted a fifty-pound bag of feed onto each shoulder and carried them from the barn out to the pasture. Using his pocketknife, he split the first bag and dumped it into the feeder, then did the same with the second as the cows gathered around him.

When he finished that, he went back into the barn to find Moses bellowing loud enough that Claire could probably hear him in the house. Justin was busy in the tack room, and Cade had tossed a bag of feed into a wheelbarrow and pushed it toward his stall. Levi picked up a flat-edge shovel and threw a bale of hay onto a second wheelbarrow.

Cade slung open the gate to Moses's stall and slipped a rope around the bull's neck. "Come on, you big baby. I'll be glad when this stuff melts so you can go back outside."

"Amen to that." Levi went right to work with the shovel.

"Have you got a thing for Claire?" he asked bluntly.

Levi stopped and propped his arm on the top of the shovel. "Where did that come from, and why would you ask such a thing?"

"She seems to be a great person," Cade said. "And there's just something in the way you look at her."

"Claire has a prosperous business, and she's about to expand." Levi told him about her idea for buying the old Harris house. "What have I got to offer a woman like that?"

"We might not be kin by blood, but you've always been as close as a brother to me and Justin, and you know it. And speakin' from that standpoint, you've got a lot to offer a woman. First of all you've got your heart to give her."

Levi rolled the filled wheelbarrow out of the stall. "Don't seem like a lot from my standpoint."

"Hey, you two lazybones got your jobs done?" Justin called out. "Cattle out in the side pasture is fed and watered. I called Mama from the tack room. She says that they're comin' for Christmas and wants to know if Levi has a thing for Claire."

"Good Lord!" Levi threw up his hands. "How come it's me everyone is worried about and not you, Justin? You're the next in line to settle down. I'm the youngest one of us three."

"Because you've been flirtin' with her, not me," Justin said.

"And if she puts in a quiltin' shop in Sunset, she'll be just down the road from the ranch," Cade commented.

"Lucky you." Justin grinned.

"Gangin' up on me ain't fair, especially when I'm starving," Levi muttered as they all headed for the door.

*   *   *

Brunch was served buffet-style on the coffee table so no one had to miss a single float or band in Macy's parade. Retta slathered two pumpkin muffins with butter and added a small vegetarian quiche tart to her plate. "I swear this baby is going to love pumpkin."

"Give it a couple of days. Tomorrow you might be craving pot roast and hating pumpkin," Claire said.

"Or craving watermelons right here in the middle of winter," Justin said.

"Or strawberries," Levi chimed in.

"Stop it!" Retta covered her ears. "Now I want both of those things."

"So do I, and I'm not even pregnant," Claire said.

"Me either and a good cold watermelon does sound good," Levi said.

Claire tilted her head to the side so she could see him. "Well, I sure hope you aren't pregnant. Do you think we should get a test for you to take?"

"Shhh…" He put his fingers on his lips. "What goes on in the cabin stays in the cabin."

"If you are, I want a DNA test to prove I'm the mother," Claire declared.

"I think you've met your match, Levi." Justin chuckled.

"That's just kickoff. We've still got lots of game," Levi said.

"The parade is still on." Zaylie frowned. "The game ain't even started."

"That's right, baby girl." Claire started to gather up the dirty dishes. "I'll leave the leftovers in case you guys want something to nibble on during the game. If Levi gets to craving pickles and ice cream, y'all might want to see if his belt is gettin' too tight."

Justin laughed out loud. "If he and Retta start racing to

the bathroom first thing in the morning, will you bring him tea and crackers?"

"We'll see when it happens," Claire said.

Retta carried the rest of the dishes and followed her to the kitchen. "I can help with this cleanup and whatever else you need me to do. I'm a lot less nauseated today." She lowered her voice. "These guys are smothering me to death. So help me get them out the door in the mornings, please."

"You got it. Together we can conquer the world." Claire smiled. "Now shoo. Get on out of here and go protect your interests in there when the ball game starts. I heard you make that bet with Cade about your team winning." Claire motioned toward the living room with her hand.

As she was leaving, Levi came in and opened the fridge. "Just gettin' us guys a beer and Zaylie a glass of chocolate milk. You want anything, Claire?"

"Not a thing," she answered.

"How about some strawberries, picked fresh from the garden?" He took out a gallon of milk and the chocolate syrup.

"Why don't you go bring in a couple of quarts for Thanksgiving dinner?" she smarted off.

"I would if I could," he said.

The serious look on his face said that he wasn't joking. He would actually go to the garden and pick strawberries if it were possible. Something pinged in her heart—kind of like an internal text message saying that this really was an honorable cowboy. But what kind of message did she send back? That she was self-reliant and she'd always picked her own strawberries or that she would love for him to do something so sweet for her.

He stirred the syrup into the milk. "Dark enough?"

"Not nearly. She likes chocolate." She reached for the bottle of chocolate and accidentally knocked it to the floor.

They both grabbed for it at the same time and bumped heads as they fell to their knees. His hand closed over hers when she picked up the syrup. His free hand tipped up her chin, and she barely had time to moisten her lips before he brushed a sweet kiss across them. Her first thought when the kiss ended was that she'd gladly let him pick strawberries for her.

"Why, Claire Mason, you're on your knees. Does that mean you're proposing to me?" he teased.

"I reckon I could ask you the same thing," she shot back. "But if you were, the answer would be no. I don't marry a man just because he's pregnant and craving strawberries in the winter."

He straightened up and pulled her with him. "Rejected, again. Some of us old cowboys just can't win."

She squirted more chocolate into the milk. *"C'est la vie."*

"Did you just cuss at me in a foreign language? I don't understand anything but English and redneck. Remember, I'm just a ranch foreman who's only got two pairs of boots. One for work and one for Sunday. I don't wear them fancy shoes like men do who spout off things like say-la-vee."

"It means 'such is life,' and you don't fool me with that poor old country boy line, Levi Jackson." She put her hands on his chest and gave him a push. "You'd better get on out of here before they come lookin' for beer and find that you've got lipstick smeared on your mouth."

"Are you serious?" He ran the back of his hand across his lips.

"Nope, I didn't even put lipstick on this mornin'," she answered.

"That was evil."

She patted him on the cheek, and sparks flew when her palm touched his face. "What? The kiss or the teasing?"

"The kiss was wonderful." He picked up a six-pack of beer from the fridge in one hand and the glass of milk in the other. "I've wanted to taste your lips all day."

"And how did they taste?" She was surprised that her voice wasn't high and squeaky.

"Like what I imagine heaven will be like," he whispered as he left the room.

She opened her mouth to smart off, but not a single word would come out.

*   *   *

While Cade gave thanks for the Thanksgiving meal, Levi opened one eye enough to glance down the length of the table. It was a fine spread with a golden brown turkey taking center stage. His eyes strayed to Claire sitting across the table from him. Both she and Zaylie had their eyes shut, and they were holding hands. On the last Thanksgiving before his mother married and left Texas with her new husband, they had sat across the table. He'd been between Mavis and Skip, and it had been Mavis who'd helped cut up his turkey that day and who had held his hand while Skip said grace.

Suck it up, cowboy, that irritating voice in his head said. *Mavis didn't give birth to you, but you couldn't ask for better parents than what you had, or friends either. You are a blessed man.*

"Amen," Cade said. "We have a Maguire family tradition that says before we start carving up that beautiful bird that we express something that we're thankful for. I'll go first this year. I'm thankful for my wife, Retta, and that by this time next year, we'll have a new baby sitting at this table with us."

Justin raised his hand. "I'm grateful for the Longhorn Canyon Ranch and all the sacrifices that went on even before our time that has kept it running."

Retta wiped one lonesome tear from her cheek. "I'm thankful that Cade hired me to supervise a cabin full of little girls back in the summer. I'm not sure I ever believed in fate, but I do now because it's brought me love and happiness."

"My cats and that Aunt Claire can't drive too good on ice," Zaylie piped up when the adults looked at her.

All eyes went to Levi.

"Family, friends, and tastes of heaven," he said.

Then everyone shifted their gaze to Claire.

Two dots of color flushed her cheeks. "That Levi rescued us."

"We've got a lot to be thankful for." Cade pushed back his chair and picked up the carving knife. "And we want to thank you, Claire, for all you've done today to make this a great Thanksgiving."

"Amen!" voices said, blending together in agreement.

Zaylie held up her plate. "I want one of them legs."

"And I'll share it with her," Claire said.

After dinner, everyone helped with cleanup and then went right back to the living room to watch another ball game. Retta curled up next to Cade on the sofa and fell asleep. Zaylie stretched out on the floor with her arm around Beau, and they had a kid and dog snoring contest. Justin leaned his head back in a recliner during a commercial, and before it ended he was napping.

Claire had kicked off her shoes and had drawn her feet up under her on the love seat. She looked downright cute in those tight jeans and an orange T-shirt with HAPPY FALL Y'ALL embroidered across the front.

"Looks like we're the only ones awake. You've traveled

a lot, different countries as well as states. Of all the places you've ever lived, which was your favorite?" Levi asked.

"The little house in Randlett with Nanny," she answered without a second's pause.

"Why?" He was shocked at her answer.

"It was more like a home instead of a house," she answered.

"What's the difference in the two?"

"I like to think of home as a feeling, not a place. It's where a person feels loved and, well, words don't actually describe what it's like to feel like you are home," she answered.

"I felt all that at Mavis and Skip's place. I was born in Bowie and my mama brought me home to their house. Other than this ranch, that's the only place I ever lived," he said.

"Your mama must have loved you very much," Claire said.

Levi felt his jaw drop. "Why would you say that? She abandoned me."

"No, she saw that you had a home and chose to leave you in it." Claire's dark brows knit together. "I lived with a mother and father both, at least most of the time. This is hard to explain, but feeling like you're a nuisance..." She paused as if searching for the right word and then went on. "Did you ever think that maybe she loved the new husband, but she wasn't sure how you'd feel about being uprooted from the only home you'd ever known? She had to have known that Mavis and Skip loved you and were willing to raise you in a wonderful home. From what little y'all have told me about them this week, I'd say they are amazing people," Claire answered.

Home—she'd said home, not house. And Levi had surely had that his whole life. First in his growing-up years. And then when he'd graduated from high school and the Maguires gave him a job and a room in their home—there was that word again—as part of his benefit package to help Justin on the ranch until Cade could finish his degree. Then they'd given the ranch to the boys, and he'd been made foreman. So yes, he'd always had a stable home.

"I never looked at it like that," Levi said. "If Randlett is the place you liked best, then why are you leaving?"

"I want to expand my business, and there's no opportunity there." She went on to tell him that the house had been left for her and Grant together.

"Have you always thought about everyone but yourself?" Levi asked.

"I'd say that moving to a new place and starting up a business is thinking about myself," she told him.

"Not really," Levi argued. "It's thinking about your brother needing a place to live when he needs it."

"Then why do I feel guilty about it?" she asked.

"Why should you feel like that? Sounds to me like you've pretty much taken care of folks your whole life. It's time for you to do something that you want to do," Levi answered.

"Who's winnin'?" Cade yawned and pointed toward the television.

Levi quickly glanced that way and rattled off the scores. "Looks like you might owe Retta another five bucks if your team don't get their heads together and start playin' some offensive ball."

"Did I hear my name?" Retta asked. "And is there any more of that pecan pie?"

"Yes you did, and yes there was one more slice when I checked last time," Levi said. "Want me to get you a slice? I'm on my way to the kitchen for a beer."

"Love it," Retta said.

Justin awoke, stood up, and rolled the kinks from his

neck. "I'll go with you. I'm thinkin' about a piece of that banana nut cake."

"You could bring me a cold beer," Cade yelled as Justin and Levi made their way toward the kitchen.

"I was awake for part of that conversation," Justin confessed. "Claire is a smart woman, and I can tell that you are definitely interested in her."

"And you aren't even a little bit interested?" Levi asked.

Justin had far more to offer a woman than he did—place, prestige, all of it. He was half owner of the Longhorn Canyon Ranch. He was a good-lookin' cowboy with maybe even more swagger than Levi.

"No sparks. She's cute, but..." Justin's shoulders raised slightly in half a shrug.

"But?" Levi asked.

"Just that. Cute, smart, and funny, but no sparks. If I can't have the whole package I'll be the bachelor uncle to Cade and Retta's kids. I want what they've got, and I'm not going to settle for anything else."

Levi nodded. "Don't we all?"

Chapter Seven

Claire knew from past experience with Zaylie's mother that one good day in the first trimester did not mean that morning sickness was completely over. So it wasn't a surprise when she found Retta in the bathroom on Friday morning. Or that she could hear Cade in there with her. Claire hadn't even gotten her coat hung on the hall tree in the foyer when Cade carried Retta out of the bathroom and laid her on the sofa.

"I know it will be worth it in the end," Retta said. "But I hate being sick."

"I know, darlin'. I'm so sorry that you have to go through this." Cade washed her face with a wet cloth.

Claire slipped away into the kitchen where Zaylie was already on a chair on the other side of the bar with a biscuit cutter in her hand. "Is today Christmas tree day?"

"I don't know, sweetheart. If we were home in Randlett it would be, but this isn't our house. I'm not sure when Retta and Cade start decorating, but we can ask them," Claire answered. "Well, would you look at that?"

"What?" Zaylie's eyes darted around the room.

"The roof is dripping. The snow and ice is starting to thaw. We might be able to go home day after tomorrow," Claire said.

"I'll be glad to drive you." Levi entered the kitchen.

He was dressed in faded jeans and a long-sleeved knit shirt, but his hair still looked like he'd combed it with a hay rake. When he caught her staring at it, he ran his fingers through it.

"Yes!" Zaylie pumped her little fist in the air. "I want Levi to drive us. Oh no!" Her hands went to her cheeks, and her eyes got huge. "That's tomorrow and then the next day, and we'll leave. What about my kittens?" Tears welled up in her eyes and began to run down her cheeks and drip on her shirt. "And Beau?" She sobbed and moved her little hands up to cover her eyes. "And Little Bit?" She sat down on the floor and got the hiccups. "Oh, we can't leave, Aunt Claire. We just can't."

Levi sat down beside the little girl and pulled her onto his lap. "Well, you could stay a few more days." He patted her back and looked up at Claire. "I just talked to Mavis, and she's called the Harris family. They can't get up here until Wednesday for you to see the house, and they would rather be the ones to show you around. If you just stay on a bit longer, it would save you a trip back down here."

No matter when they left, there would be a scene, so Claire figured she might as well get it over with in a couple of days rather than prolonging the issue. But when Zaylie's blue eyes begged her to say yes, she simply couldn't say no.

"Okay, but only until Wednesday, and then we're leaving," Claire said.

"Yay!" She jumped up out of Levi's lap and wrapped her arms around Claire. "I love you to the moon and back. Can we put up a Christmas tree here?"

"Yes, you can, princess." Levi got to his feet. "We put up the tree and decorate the Saturday after Thanksgiving, which is tomorrow."

"And we'd love to have your help, Zaylie." Justin yawned as he crossed the floor and poured a cup of coffee.

"*Princess* Zaylie. Levi said so." She grinned.

"Pardon me." Justin bent at the waist and kissed her hand. "My mistake. It won't happen again."

Zaylie giggled. "Will you marry me when I get old, Justin? You can be the prince like in Cinderella."

"Oh, honey, when you get to the age that you're thinkin' about boys, I'll be old and gray haired. Besides, I figured you'd want to marry Levi since he rescued you," Justin teased.

"That's in *Snow White* and I'm Cinderella," she said. "I can't marry Levi because Aunt Claire is going to do that."

Instantly, heat flushed into Claire's cheeks, and she looked up to see Levi staring right at her.

"Zaylie Noelle Mason! Why would you say that?" she gasped.

"Because you are Snow White and I'm Cinderella. Remember?" Zaylie put up her palms in frustration.

"You are so right." Claire quickly explained, "On Halloween, I dressed up like Snow White and she was Cinderella."

"So you think I'm the prince that wakes Snow White with a kiss?" Levi asked.

"Yep, and then you'll live happy ever after." Zaylie nodded. "Come on, Justin, let's go see if Retta is feelin' better." She grabbed his hand and pulled him toward the living room. "I sure wish she'd have that baby today so I could hold it."

Claire whipped around to stir up the biscuit dough and hoped that her beet-red face didn't cook the dough right there in the bowl. She felt Levi's presence before he spoke, his warm breath warming her neck. "You think that the princess is clairvoyant?"

"No, sir, I do not!" Her tone was so squeaky that she didn't even recognize it as her own voice. "And if a witch shows up at the back door with a pretty apple, I'll be sure to shoot her sorry ass."

"Well, in case you are hungry and eat the apple, I'll do my best to wake you with a kiss," he whispered, and was gone before she could smart off an answer.

*   *   *

The rest of the day Levi was in and out of the house for meals, but there were no more little moments when Claire was alone with him. Mavis called right after breakfast to tell her that the Harrises would be ready to show her the house at four o'clock on Wednesday afternoon. She fretted all day about whether to take Zaylie with her or to ask Retta if she would babysit for a couple of hours. If she took her, then Zaylie would tell Grant, and she'd like to have everything set in stone before she said a word to her brother.

Maybe it was so that he couldn't talk her out of her decision to leave Randlett. To him, it would be downright crazy to sink the majority of her savings account into a house when she already had one for free. He'd try to talk her out of it, and down deep in her heart, she felt like she was doing the right thing.

That night she tossed and turned, had trouble getting to sleep and then woke up every two hours. She'd settled into a pretty routine life years ago, and now everything was changing; it was exciting and scary at the same time.

The next morning the roads had cleared enough that the hired hands could get to the ranch, so Justin and Cade took a lunch with them, and Levi was sent to Wichita Falls for a big load of some kind of special feed.

She'd gotten the kitchen put back to rights and was thinking about what to have for lunch since the guys wouldn't be there, when the phone rang.

"Can you get that?" Retta called from the living room. "I don't want to move an inch."

"Longhorn Canyon," Claire answered.

"Hey, it's Levi. I'm passing the old Harris place right now and thought I'd give you a call and tell you what I see, now that you're interested in this place. The roof looks solid, but the house could use a coat of paint come spring. I'd be glad to help. Bet between the two of us we could get it done in a weekend," he said.

Immediately her I-can-do-it-myself attitude rose up, and she opened her mouth to tell him as much, but then she remembered the strawberries. "I haven't even bought the place yet, but thank you for the offer."

"Sure thing. You want me to watch Zaylie while you go look at the place? We should be able to let Little Bit out into the corral by then, and she can play with him," Levi said. "It'd be hard to talk business with her running from room to room and asking a million questions."

Claire swallowed a ton of pride. "She'd love that, and I appreciate you thinking of it." She took a deep breath. Asking for a favor wasn't easy, but there was no way around it. "Would it be all right if I drive the work truck that day?"

"Not a problem, or you can borrow my truck, either one.

Your choice," Levi said. "Is Zaylie getting excited about putting up the tree?"

"Oh yes! She's boring Retta to tears talking about it," Claire answered. "I should go in there and give Retta some relief, but thanks again for the help."

"I'm here for you. See you later," he said.

"Bye." She put the house phone back on the base.

By evening Retta was feeling well enough to help put up the Christmas tree. As they waited for the guys to come back with the tree and all the trimmings, she told Claire, "I just want you to know that I like having you and Zaylie here, and you two are welcome to stay as long as you like. You should definitely come for our big ranch party here before Christmas."

"When is this party?" Claire asked.

"It's always the first Saturday in December," she said. "If you want to stay until then, you'd be right here close to Sunset. That's sayin' that you like the Harris place and decide to put in a business there."

Zaylie whipped around from the window where she'd been watching for the guys to bring in the tree and decorations. "A party! Right here! Can I go to it?"

Retta pulled her close for a hug. "You are sure enough invited. There will be lots of little kids there. According to the guys, it's a family affair, and we get to dress up."

Zaylie's eyes almost popped right out of her head. "For real. Like Cinderella."

"Maybe not that dressed up but in a pretty Sunday school dress," Retta answered.

"And you, Miz Zaylie"—Levi entered the living room with a long box on his shoulder—"would look like a princess even if you just wore your jeans. Reckon you could hold the door open for Justin and Cade? They're right behind me with all the boxes of decorations."

"Yep, I can." Zaylie ran that way.

Children usually adapted better than adults, but Claire was still amazed that Zaylie had fit right into the ranch so quickly.

So did you, the pesky little voice in her head said. *Other than that little bout of fear in the cabin, it's like you're visiting your closest friends or family.*

I'm just making the best out of a bad situation, she argued.

"So do y'all have a big tree at your house or just a little one?" Levi glanced at Claire as he put the box on the floor.

"We have a four-foot one. The house is small, so that pretty much fills up the living room," Claire answered.

"When will you put yours up?" Retta asked.

Claire wasn't sure how to answer that. With this new idea thrown out concerning her staying two more weeks—well, she'd have to think long and hard about that. "Probably when we get back to Randlett. It looks like Grant will be finished in time for the holidays, and I want to have things ready."

Zaylie hopped around on one foot. "I get two trees this year!"

"Sounds like it." Levi followed Justin and Cade inside. Each of them had a box or two on his shoulders. "That's all of the tree stuff. Y'all ready to get this show on the road?"

Cade opened the big box with a Christmas tree on the front and got busy putting the tree branches on the tall center section. "I keep tellin' the guys that we need one of those things that you just pop out of the box and it already has the lights on it."

"But what's the fun in that?" Justin chuckled. "Dad always fussed about havin' to get all the branches perfect so that Mama would be happy. And Mama griped because he thought his work was done when he got the tree positioned according to Mama's instruction. This brings back memories."

"What are your memories?" Levi bumped a shoulder against Claire's.

"The lady who cleaned our house usually put up the tree about a week before the holiday," Claire answered. "When we were growing up, holidays meant work-related parties. But Grant and I have tried to make our Christmas a lot more personal." Claire turned to Retta. "How about your traditions before you came to the ranch?"

"My folks loved Christmas. We had a party every year for the neighbors and their church family and went to several just like it. Mama loved a real tree, so we'd go to the woods and Daddy would cut it down, and then we'd decorate it." She opened a box and began to lay the ornaments out on the coffee table. "It's my first Christmas on the ranch, and my holiday season as Mrs. Cade Maguire, and I'm looking forward to some new traditions too—like hanging the ornament Benjy gave us for our wedding gift."

"What does it look like?" Zaylie asked.

"He drew a picture of wedding bells on a pretty white ball and put our date on it," Retta answered.

Levi pulled out strands of lights wrapped around cardboard. "I'm a real good pack mule with these things, but I'm not worth much when it comes to gettin' them positioned on the tree. We usually get Mavis and Skip to do this part, but maybe you could help me, Claire?"

"Be glad to," Claire agreed.

"Why do you call them Mavis and Skip?" Zaylie frowned.

"Because I lived with them from just about the time I

was born and that's what my mother called them. Mama and Daddy just didn't sound right even after they adopted me," Levi explained as simply as he could.

"Am I 'dopted, Aunt Claire?"

Claire clipped the first light onto the tree. "No, you aren't."

"Well, rats! I can't call my daddy Grant then?"

"I don't think so," Claire answered. "Why would you want to do that?"

"'Cause Levi did," she said, and then the ornaments caught her attention. "Ohhh, look at that pretty blue one. It's like Cinderella's dress."

Levi carefully unwound two feet of lights and handed them to Claire. "You work your magic, and I'll just follow around behind you," he said.

Even though it was a big tree, there was no way for them to do the job without their shoulders and hands continually touching. She tried to follow the conversation between Retta and Zaylie, who were talking about the different ornaments, to keep her mind from thinking about the effect that his touch had on her.

It didn't work.

Justin was untangling the garland and doing some creative cussin', as Franny called it when she didn't want to say swear words in front of Zaylie. "Dratted, blasted stuff. I don't know why we don't throw it in the danged trash and buy new every year."

It was amusing, but not so much that Claire couldn't still feel the sparks flying around the room every time Claire looked up into Levi's eyes.

Why this cowboy? And are you letting your heart lead you to this area more than your common sense? Are you aware that Sunset is a tiny place with few businesses? Grant had popped back into her head.

"I don't know," she said out loud.

"Me either," Justin said. "It seems like the smart thing to do."

"Were you really talkin' to him?" Levi whispered.

She shook her head.

"Want to tell me who you were arguing with?"

"Nope, let's just get these lights on here," she answered.

"Okay folks, that's the first string of lights," Levi said when they finished. "Retta, you and Cade want to do the next round?"

Yes, please say yes, Claire thought as she touched her shoulder to see if it was on fire. Then suddenly she changed her mind. *No, let us do another strand.*

"Looks to me like y'all are doin' a good job, so keep it up," Retta answered. "This is my first time to see all these pretty ornaments, and Cade is telling me what he remembers about each one."

"Okay, then." Levi picked up a second cardboard and slipped the string of lights onto his arms. "We'll be doing a duck walk by the time we get to the bottom of the tree."

"You will," Claire said. "I barely have to even bend. That's one of the advantages of being short."

"Something that runs in your family?" Levi asked.

"My granny was barely five feet tall, and they say I got her temper as well," she answered.

"Oh really? I've seen some sass but not so much temper," Levi said.

"You haven't made me mad—yet." She gave him a sideways look that said if he did he'd better watch out.

"What's that supposed to mean—yet?"

"Just what it says." She looked over her shoulder to find him grinning.

"It means that you should never light the fuse on a stick of dynamite unless you are ready to run." Cade laughed.

After a few more turns around the tree, Levi plugged in the lights and Zaylie clapped her hands. "Looks like we're ready for Retta and Cade to get the garland on the tree."

"And then the ornaments?" Zaylie asked.

"That's right, ladybug. Then all of us will put them on," Justin said.

"I'm not a ladybug. I'm a princess," Zaylie said with a giggle.

"Princess Ladybug," Justin teased.

When everything was all finished, Levi held Zaylie up high so she could slide the star down on top of the tree, and then Cade plugged it in. It was by far the prettiest tree that Claire had ever seen. But then she'd always loved the big antique lights and ornaments. Zaylie's little blue eyes sparkled as much as the tree did, then her energy played out. She was talking about showing her kittens the tree one minute, and the next she'd leaned over on the arm of the sofa and was sound asleep.

"Looks like it's time to take Princess Ladybug to the bunkhouse. She's had so much excitement, and there's even more on the way tomorrow," Claire whispered.

"Don't wake her," Levi said. "I'll just wrap her in a throw and carry her to the bunkhouse for you."

"I'll get our coats," Claire said.

I can't believe you're letting that cowboy do something for you. Grant was back in her head.

Would you leave it alone? It's only carrying Zaylie to the bunkhouse. It's not like I'm going into a partnership with him on my new business, she argued.

"Would you look at that moon?" Levi whispered when they were outside.

"Gorgeous, isn't it?" she said softly, as she went ahead of him and opened the bunkhouse door.

Levi carried Zaylie straight to the bedroom and gently laid her on the bed. "She's like a little rag doll. She really is worn out."

Zaylie scarcely even wiggled as Claire removed her shoes and jacket, and got her into flannel pajamas.

"I've only seen her this tired a couple of times. Last Christmas was one of them. So far her dad has been able to spend the holiday with her. That's unusual to get time off four years in a row," Claire whispered, and tiptoed out of the room.

"I don't know why you're talking so quiet," Levi said. "I don't think a sonic boom would wake her."

"I'm not taking any chances. If she wakes up now, she'll be wired until midnight or after and then be cranky for church tomorrow. Seems like a decade ago that we went to chapel with Grant, and it was only last week." Claire removed her coat and sat down on the sofa. "Would you like something to drink? Tea? Coffee? I can make a pot."

"Not this late or I'll never get to sleep, and then I'll be the one who's snorin' in church tomorrow." Levi shed his coat and sat down on the other end of the sofa. "You'd planned to go to Randlett tomorrow, but now that you're stayin' until Wednesday, is there a reason you should go twice?"

"I have several quilts I need to mail, but they can wait until Wednesday or Thursday," she said.

"I've been thinkin' that maybe you should go tomorrow."

"Oh really?" Claire's heart dropped. After that kiss and the offer to keep Zaylie, she'd thought maybe he wanted her to stay a while longer.

"It's like this," he explained. "If Zaylie spends a few hours there, it won't be as tough on her when you leave on Wednesday. We could pick up those quilts you need to mail and kind of make it a road trip. I don't have anything to do tomorrow afternoon after church, and I'm glad to drive y'all up there." He paused and went on. "And I bet they've got cell service up there, so maybe Zaylie could have some FaceTime with her dad. That would help with the transition from here to there. She just about broke my heart today when she cried. I don't think I could stand it if she sobbed like that when y'all leave."

Claire felt a little better after he'd explained. "That sounds like a good idea. I could bring the boxes that need mailing down here and get them out on Monday. And it might help with leaving. If I send Grant an email he might be able to arrange things so he can talk to her while we're there."

"Has your brother ever thought of remarrying?" Levi asked.

She shook her head. "He loved Haley so much that I've always thought he'd never even date again, but…"

"But what?" Levi asked.

"There was something about him this time when I was down there in San Antonio, and when he called last time, he said that Zaylie might have two of the kittens if y'all were giving them away." She turned around to face him and drew her legs up on the sofa to sit cross-legged.

"Why would that be different?" Levi asked.

"His voice sounded happier this time, and he's never even considered pets for Zaylie," she answered. "I'm wondering if there might be a woman in his life."

"Hmmm—Haley, Zaylie. Was that by chance or on purpose?"

"On purpose. My brother is Grant Zane so they combined the two names," she said. "What's your full name?"

"Levi Robert Jackson. Robert is Skip's real name. And yours?"

"Claire Amanda," she said. "Nanny's name was Amanda Pauline."

"How is it going to affect you if your brother does remarry?"

"I'd be happy for him, but by damn, the new wife better be good to Zaylie, or I'll yank all her hair out and then shoot her," Claire said without a moment's hesitation.

"I've only known that little girl less than a week and I'd be right behind you." Levi yawned. "Guess that's my cue to go home. It's been a long day for all of us."

They stood to their feet at the same time. He picked up his coat, and she walked him to the door.

He slipped his arms into his coat and zipped it up.

"You've never had girlfriends, as in friends, not romantically involved?" she asked.

"Nope, is that what we are? Just friends?" He bent slightly and brushed a sweet kiss across her lips.

She'd been kissed before—she'd been in a relationship that lasted almost a year. But there was something about Levi's kisses that made her imagine tangled sheets and sweaty bodies.

"I think when kisses are involved, it's called friends with benefits." She smiled up at him.

"And I thought when used that way you spelled benefits S-E-X." He kissed her on the forehead.

She shoved him toward the door. "You need to go outside and cool off."

"Good night, Claire." He chuckled.

"Good night, Levi." She shut the door and slid down the backside of it.

He'd said that her kiss was like a taste of heaven. She felt like maybe his was more like dragging her down into the sinful pits of hell.

Chapter Eight

"But Aunt Claire, they got to go to church. What if they die and they ain't even heard preachin'? Will they go to heaven so Nanny can see them?" Zaylie whined.

Claire twisted Zaylie's thin hair up into a ponytail and clipped on an oversized bow that matched her cute little navy blue dress and leggings. "Cats do not go to church."

"They ain't cats. They are kittens, and they can go to children's church with me," she argued.

"And what if they got hungry. Gussie won't be there to feed them." Claire was glad to hear the hard rap on the door and see Levi stick his head inside the bunkhouse.

Zaylie crossed her arms over her chest and looked up at him with begging eyes. "Levi, my kitties want to go to church with me."

"Sorry, princess, Gussie would cry if we took the babies away right now. In a couple of weeks, she'll tell me that she wants me to find good homes for them, but today she wants them to stay with her. Besides they might get hungry," Levi said.

"Big people make me so mad!" She stomped her foot.

"Well, little lady, you can get glad in the same boots," Claire said. "Now, let's get your jacket on. We don't want to be late for church."

Claire buttoned Zaylie's jacket and reached for her own only to find that Levi was holding it out for her.

"You ladies both look lovely today," he said.

"Thank you." Claire slipped her arms into the jacket and was only mildly surprised at the sparks dancing around the room at his touch on her neck as he straightened the collar.

Zaylie skipped over to the basket where Gussie and the kittens were sleeping. She picked each one up and kissed it on the nose. "I'll pray for you."

"Why would you do that?" Levi asked.

"If you don't go to church, you go to hell," she answered seriously.

"Who told you that?" Claire gasped.

"Teresa did," she said with a shrug.

"Teresa?" Levi whispered.

"Her best friend," Claire said out the side of her mouth.

Teresa's mother, Angela, was a single mom who was in the Air Force with Grant. They were on the same team that got sent out on missions they weren't allowed to talk about, and at least twice they'd been deployed together. When Angela was gone, then her mother stepped in and took care of Teresa. With her dark hair, light coffee-colored skin, Teresa was Zaylie's exact opposite. But they were like two little peas in a pod when they were together, and it had always been that way.

Zaylie kissed Gussie one more time and then held up her arms for Levi to pick her up. "I'm ready now. Can I sit with you, Levi?" Zaylie laid her head on his shoulder.

"Of course you can, if it's all right with Claire," Levi answered.

"Yes, you can sit by Levi," Claire agreed. "But you have to be quiet."

"I promise." Zaylie flashed her sweetest little grin.

Claire stole sideways looks at Levi the whole way from the ranch to the little white church where the parking lot was full. His jeans and shirt had been ironed, and his black boots were shined to a gloss. His cowboy hat lay on the console between them.

Levi parked beside a van, waved at the folks inside, and settled his hat on his head. He was a fine-looking cowboy in that hat and denim jacket. He got out and rounded the front of the truck to open the doors for Claire and Zaylie. By the time she was out of the vehicle, there were two adults and a red-haired boy in front of her.

"Good mornin'. This is Claire and Zaylie," Levi made introductions. "Claire, this is Mavis, Skip, and Benjy."

The lady who was no taller than Claire stuck out her hand. She wore a bright red coat that reached her ankles. Kinky gray hair peeked out from the hood. Her red lipstick had run a little into the wrinkles around her mouth, but her smile was genuine and warm. "I'm pleased to meet you. Our little quilting circle is so excited that you might be putting in a shop. And there's at least two churches in Bowie that have quilting bees and one in Montague, so we'll keep you busy."

Claire shook hands with the lady. "I'm so glad to meet all y'all. I've heard so many good things about you that I feel that I already know you."

As tall as Levi, Skip looked like he needed to stuff his coat pockets with rocks to keep the brisk wind from blowing him away. His angular face was lined with wrinkles, but his eyes twinkled when he squatted down so he was on Zaylie's level. "I understand that you are takin' care of Gussie and the new batch of kittens."

"Yes, I am, but they couldn't come to church. If they go to hell, it's Aunt Claire and Levi's fault." She looked up at Benjy. "I like your pictures. Will you teach me to draw like that?"

"Yes, I will. You have blue eyes. Only eight percent of the people in the world have blue eyes. Cade has blue eyes, but they're different than yours," Benjy said.

Levi held out a hand toward Skip to help him up and then drew him close for a man hug. "I missed seein' y'all this week."

"She's cute," Skip whispered.

"Which one?"

"Both," he answered.

"Don't I get a hug?" Mavis opened her arms.

"Of course you do." Levi wrapped her up in his arms and squeezed until she squealed before he let go. "I expect we'd better go inside or else we'll be sittin' on the front row. Looks like the parking lot is already pretty full."

"Don't Benjy get a hug?" Zaylie asked.

Levi laid a hand on Benjy's shoulder, but he shrugged it away.

"I'll give him a hug." Zaylie wrapped her arms around the boy.

To everyone's surprise, he hugged her back. Then she took him by the hand and pulled him toward the church. "Come on, Benjy. You can sit with me."

"You have to be quiet," Benjy said. "The preacher talks for thirty minutes, but if you aren't quiet, he thinks you aren't listening so he just keeps on goin'. Mavis's roast beef will burn if church lasts too long. I have a little sketch pad in my backpack. I'll draw pictures for you."

*   *   *

"Well, that's a surprise," Skip whispered as he fell in beside Levi.

"What? Benjy takin' up with Zaylie, or Mavis and Claire talkin' a mile a minute about quiltin'?" Levi nodded toward Claire and Mavis walking ahead of them. They were the same height, so it was easy for them to put their heads together and whisper.

"Both," Skip answered as he rushed ahead to open the door for the women.

The minute they were inside, Levi saw Cade motioning to them to join him, Retta, and Justin on a pew up near the front of the church. Skip nodded, but Zaylie and Benjy had already headed that way. When they were all squeezed together in the old oak pew, Levi was on the end with Claire beside him. Zaylie was wedged in between her aunt and Benjy.

"I want to sit by Levi," Zaylie whispered loudly.

He leaned around Claire and said, "How about next week?"

She nodded and put a finger to her lips. "Benjy says we have to be very quiet or the roast beast at his house will burn up."

Thank you, Claire mouthed toward Levi.

You're welcome. Levi removed his denim coat and draped it over the back of the pew. He never remembered the church being so warm before. Claire unbuttoned her jacket, and he helped her out of it.

Then they both settled back in their space, shoulders and thighs both pressed firmly together. The song leader took her place behind the podium and called out a number for congregational singing. Claire picked up a hymnal and opened to the page and then realized that she'd gotten the last one, so she shared it with Levi.

When their hands brushed against each other the sanctuary got even hotter. Folks who saw them sharing a hymnbook would think they were a couple, and rumors would spread like wild fire that week.

Levi and Claire harmonized through all four verses of the hymn, but he didn't pay much attention to the words. He couldn't stop thinking about that dang hymnal and the repercussions that it would bring about—especially with Mavis. Then the preacher took the podium and read a few verses in Psalm 37 about not fretting.

"Are you a worrier?" Levi whispered softly into Claire's ear.

She nodded. "Can't lie in church, so sometimes. You?"

"Shhh . . . roast beast will burn," Zaylie scolded them.

Levi winked at Claire and tried to pay attention to the sermon, but his mind kept wandering back to what Claire had told him about her parents. One with a new wife in Hawaii. The other in Italy with friends. Both he and Claire were kind of like orphans, only he'd had roots and Mavis and Skip. Suddenly, he didn't feel abandoned but blessed.

He was sure glad that the preacher asked Justin to deliver the benediction because if he'd been called upon, he would have stuttered and stammered through it that morning. As soon as the last amen was said and the people began to move toward the doors, he picked up Claire's jacket and helped her into it.

Zaylie tucked her hand back into Benjy's and looked up at him adoringly. "Can you come see us at the ranch next week?"

"If it doesn't snow anymore. I like the snow, but I miss the ranch. Snow is precipitation in the form of ice crystals, and no two snow flakes are alike," Benjy answered.

"You are very smart," Zaylie said.

"Yes, I am." Benjy nodded. "But now I have to go home and eat, and then I have to do my homework for school. I'll see you when I come to the ranch."

Zaylie let go of his hand. "And I will show you the new kittens."

"It's amazing," Levi whispered to Claire as they made their way out to the center aisle.

"I agree. I didn't think she'd be that good especially after that pouting fit over the cats," she said.

"No, I mean that Benjy lets her hold his hand. He usually doesn't like anyone to touch him," Levi explained.

Mavis turned around and said, "I doubt he's ever been around someone as little as she is. He probably sees her like he would a baby kitten. Why don't y'all come home with us for Sunday dinner? I'd like to show Claire a new quilt pattern I got last week. If the committee approves, we'll probably make it for the next quilting bee."

"We're going to drive up to Randlett to get some stuff that Claire needs to mail, and"—he lowered his voice—"Zaylie is going to have a hard time leaving the ranch, so we're trying to smooth the pathway. Maybe next Sunday?"

"I'll probably be gone by then, but I understand you're coming to the ranch tomorrow to help Retta. Maybe you could bring it then?" Claire asked.

"I sure will," Mavis said. "I'll get Skip to bring Benjy out to the ranch after school. I'd like to see him spend some more time with Zaylie."

"That would be great. She misses her little friend Teresa, especially since we haven't had cell service. When their parents are out on a mission, they usually have some FaceTime every day," Claire said.

"Sounds great." Mavis drew her coat tightly around her body and stepped out into the weather.

"So you and Mavis hit it off pretty good, huh?" Levi asked as he and Claire each held one of Zaylie's hands and bent against the north wind.

"Sure," Claire said. "She's a sweetheart, and we speak the language of quilts."

"Bye, Benjy!" Zaylie yelled when they were outside and in the truck.

He waved at her through the van window.

"He uses them big words I don't know. Am I ever going to be that smart?" Zaylie asked.

"Of course you are," Levi said as he lifted Zaylie into the backseat of his truck. "Are you hungry?"

"Yes, and I want a hamburger with pickies and no onions," she said.

"Pickles, right?" Levi asked Claire.

"You're beginning to understand her." She smiled.

"Retta told me that she invited you to stay longer. I might not even need a translator if you stick around the ranch until after the party," he whispered.

"And tator tots and chocolate milk," Zaylie said from the backseat. "And then an ice cream cone."

"You're makin' me hungry just talking about all that food." Levi chuckled.

"Me too," Claire said. "But save some room for a snack because Franny says she's made cookies and we have to visit her before we leave town." It was her turn to whisper. "It makes sense if I buy the house to be closer, but I've imposed on y'all's hospitality too long."

"No, you haven't," Levi said. "We love having you both."

"I'll think about it," she said. "But right now, we're on our own mission, aren't we? I'm hoping that seeing Franny will make Zaylie remember how much she loves staying in Nanny's house."

Suddenly, it got as warm in the truck as it had been in the church. From what Claire had said, Franny was pretty much a surrogate grandmother, and meeting her made him more than a little bit nervous.

Chapter Nine

How many more miles? Are we nearly there?" Zaylie asked from the backseat as they went through Wichita Falls.

"Not much longer," Claire answered. "Why don't you read two more books?"

"I'm tired of reading. How many more songs is it?"

"Six or maybe five if there's advertising," Claire answered.

"I might can make it that far." Zaylie sighed.

"Songs?" Levi raised a dark eyebrow.

Claire pointed toward the radio. "We measure distance by songs, and it teaches her to count."

"Smart." Levi nodded.

At the same time the radio DJ announced that he would be playing five in a row, Claire noticed that Levi had reset the cruise to add a few more miles an hour.

"I can't wait to see Franny. I haven't seen her in forever," Zaylie said after the fifth song. "Just one more and oh, oh, there's the church."

"Forever is last summer when she came to stay with me for a week," Claire explained to Levi. "Turn left at the next stop sign."

Zaylie pointed at both. "I can see Nanny's house. We are here. And there's Franny's."

"Just pull up under the carport," Claire said. "We'll bring my stuff out the back door."

She'd barely slid out of the seat when her cell phone rang. It startled her so badly that she dropped her purse on the driveway, and then when she and Levi both bent at the same time to get it, they bumped heads.

"We've got to stop meeting like this," he joked.

"Answer it!" Zaylie dropped to her knees and fished it out of the purse. "It might be Daddy."

Claire recognized her brother's picture and was glad that she'd recharged the phone before leaving the ranch. "Why don't you answer it?"

"Hello," Zaylie said, and then squealed when she heard her dad's voice and saw his face. "Daddy, it's you. It's been forever."

"Yes, it has," Grant said. "So are y'all home now?"

Claire unlocked the kitchen door of her grandmother's house. Oddly, she didn't think of it as "home."

Zaylie ran in first and headed back to her room. "We just now got here, Daddy, and guess what? Levi brought us up here to get some quilt stuff and we get to stay longer at the ranch, and I don't have to leave my kittens."

"Guess I just lost my place," Levi said.

"So do I when Grant calls. And you can bet she's going to want some FaceTime with Teresa before we leave," Claire told him. "Follow me and we'll load up the boxes while she's talking."

His cell phone pinged in his pocket before they made it

across the kitchen floor and to the living room. He fished it out and then hit a button.

"Hey Retta, what's up?" he asked. "She wants to talk to you." He handed the phone to Claire.

"I have an enormous favor to ask," Retta said.

"Tell me." Claire sat down on the sofa.

"Cade's mother, Gloria, has given me and Cade a honeymoon trip to Florida as an early Christmas present. I don't want to hurt her feelings, but..."

"But what? That's an amazing present," Claire said.

"We've got the ranch party and— Just a minute. Cade is right here and holding out his hand. He wants to talk to Levi," Retta said.

"Putting this on speaker," Levi said as he took the phone. "Just me and Claire here. What's going on? Is everyone all right?"

"We're fine," Cade said. "Mama has given Retta and me a little vacation in Florida, but we have to go this next week. That's the only time she could book a condo. I want to go, but Retta is worried about leaving the ranch right now."

"Go on. We can take care of it, and I bet Mavis would come help out," Levi said.

"She's got Benjy to take care of," Retta said.

"I'll help," Claire said. "This would be great for you. Might even take care of that morning sickness if you're less stressed. I'll be glad to stay on another week and help."

"You know Mavis won't be able to keep her nose out of the party planning, so she'll be there part of the day to help out too," Levi said. "Pack your bags and get going."

"When are you leaving?" Claire asked.

"Today. Are you sure about this, Claire?" Retta's voice sounded both excited and apprehensive.

"Of course I am," Claire said. "Go on and have a fabulous late honeymoon. Don't forget your tea and crackers," Claire said.

"Okay," Retta said.

"Hallelujah! And thank you both," Cade said.

"Hey, you're not foolin' me one bit, Cade," Levi chuckled. "You hate putting up outside decorations, and this way you get out of it."

"And in addition to that, I get to spend a week with my lovely wife all alone. We're on our way to get out the suitcases right now. See y'all later." The phone went dark.

"Well, welcome to Longhorn Canyon for another week," Levi said.

"Thank you," Claire said. "We need to take my sewing machine back with us too since I'm staying a little longer."

"Just show me what you want loaded, and I'll get after it." Levi grinned.

"But we have to come back here in only two more days," Zaylie was saying when they passed by her bedroom door. "And Daddy, I just can't leave my kittens."

"It's okay, baby girl. Maybe Santa will bring you some kittens," Grant said.

"You tell Aunt Claire that." Zaylie came out of the room and handed the phone to Claire.

"Take me off speaker," Grant said.

"Okay. But before you start, I want you to know I've agreed to stay on for another week to help out at the ranch," Claire said.

"We're stayin' longer!" Zaylie danced around the bedroom. "Did you hear that, Daddy? I don't have to leave my babies."

"I'm so glad," Grant said. "It sounds like Zaylie is so happy there. Do you know when you'll be getting cell service back?"

She turned to Levi. "Got any idea when we get service back at home?"

"Justin said he called them and they said by tomorrow morning it should be up and going," Levi answered.

Claire relayed the info to Grant.

"Good. I need to talk to you when you're alone."

A chill ran down her spine. "You're scaring me, brother."

"I'm fine. I'm healthy, and it's not bad news. I just want to run something by you," he said, and chuckled.

"Well, I need to run something by you too but not right now," she said.

"Then we'll talk tomorrow night?"

She nodded. "I'll look forward to it."

They ended the call while Zaylie continued to dance. "Can we tell Franny that we get to stay at the ranch?"

The back door hinges squeaked, and Franny's voice drifted down the hallway. "Hey, is my precious little girl here? I brought cookies."

Franny was a tall, lanky woman with an angular face, a sharp nose, and gray hair that she pulled up on top of her head in a tight little bun. She set the plate of cookies on the coffee table and opened up her arms.

Zaylie ran into them. "Guess what, Franny. We get to stay at the ranch more days and I got kittens there and there's a dog and a donkey and I love it and do you want to come with us?" She finally stopped for a breath and grabbed a cookie.

"I can't leave Randlett, darlin'." Franny laughed. "This town would just plumb blow away if I wasn't here to hold it down."

Zaylie backed away from the hug and sighed, but she didn't cry. "Okay, but I wanted you to see my kitties."

"Show them to me on the phone when you get service

back in that area," Franny said, and then shifted her gaze to Levi. "You were just a little boy last time I saw you. Don't reckon you'd even remember me, but I'm Franny."

He shook hands with her and gave her a brilliant smile. "Of course I remember you. Your husband taught me how to whittle when we were at a cattle sale one summer."

"Nice that you remembered that. He liked kids," Franny said. "Now, let's have some cookies, and y'all can tell me about this adventure you're having."

Levi waited until the ladies sat down on the sofa before he took a seat in a rocking chair and reached for a cookie. His phone rang before he took the first bite.

"Hello, Retta," he said, and then handed it off to Claire. "It's for you again."

"Are you okay? Is something wrong?" Claire asked.

"No, I'm already packing and Cade is making the flight arrangements. Oh, and we have cell service back on now. But," Retta's voice cracked. "Dammit! I'm all emotional. I feel like I'm putting a burden on you."

"Too late to back out now…Zaylie knows." Claire laughed.

"Well, then thank you from the bottom of my heart for everything," Retta said. "God sure knew what he was doing when he dropped you into our laps."

"You sure it was God?" Claire giggled.

"Yes, ma'am. Bye now," Retta said.

"I'm glad you're stayin' a little longer. Fresh air and sunshine and animals is good for Zaylie," Franny said.

"And cats and a bunny rabbit." Zaylie nodded seriously. "Can we take the rest of the cookies home with us?"

"Of course you can," Franny told her. "And now I've got to be going. Got a meeting at the church to discuss the Christmas dinner. Y'all drive real safe on the way home.

And don't worry about a thing. I'll keep a good watch on the house for you."

"Thanks for everything," Claire said.

"No thanks necessary. You'd do the same for me." Franny bent to hug her and whispered softly, "He's one sexy cowboy, and I like the way he looks at you."

She was gone before Claire could respond, but that didn't stop the blush making her cheeks fiery red. To cover her embarrassment, she pointed down the hall. "Zaylie, go see if there's anything in your room that you want to take to the ranch. Levi, there's six boxes in that room that need to be loaded. They've got a blue sticky note on them with tomorrow's date. I'll get my sewing machine in the case and ready to go."

"Yes, yes, yes," Zaylie sing-songed as she danced down the hall. "We're going home to the ranch to see my kitties and Little Bit and Hopalong."

Home to the ranch—the words echoed in Claire's head.

Levi draped an arm around her shoulders. "She said home."

"I heard." Claire sighed. "It's goin' to be chaotic when we leave."

"What about you, Claire? Will it be hard for you?" he asked.

"Don't know until the time gets here," she said, knowing fully well that she'd probably be crying every bit as hard as Zaylie all the way from the ranch to Randlett. But until then, she planned on enjoying every day that she spent in the wide-open spaces of the Longhorn Canyon Ranch.

"Right now I'd like to see if Nanny's car will start. If it will, I'll drive it back to the ranch, and then we'll have a way to get home after the party is done."

She headed toward the door leading out into the garage

with him right behind her. Together they removed the canvas tarp covering an old boat of a car, and Levi whistled through his teeth. "Do you even know what this is?"

"It's the last brand-new car that my grandpa bought for my Nanny. A 1978 Lincoln, and it drinks gas like a thirsty camel suckin' down water after a two-week trek through the desert. That's what Nanny said when gas got so expensive, but she wouldn't trade it in," Claire answered.

"Buddy would drool over this." He brushed a layer of dust from the top of the shiny white vehicle.

"Who's Buddy?" she asked as she got inside the driver's seat.

"The guy who is going to tow your van to his repair shop. Remember I told you about him fixin' up old cars." He opened the passenger door and slid into the soft leather passenger seat. "This is in mint condition. You could get a fortune for it if you want to sell it."

"No, thank you. I'll just drive it until I find something more economical." She turned the key and nothing happened; tried three times and still nothing.

"Probably a dead battery. We can come back next Sunday and bring one with us if you want to take this to the ranch, but honestly, Claire, I wouldn't advise it. We don't have a garage to park it in, and it would be a shame to leave this beauty out in the weather even for a few weeks," he said.

"All right." She didn't put up an argument because what he said made sense, and besides she kind of liked driving the old pickup truck.

Chapter Ten

Zaylie awoke in a whiny mood the next morning, and wasn't her usual zippy self, eager to drag the kittens out of the basket and kiss them.

"I want my daddy." She sighed. "When is he going to call me?"

Claire sat down on the sofa and pulled Zaylie into her lap. "He will call as soon as he can. How about if after breakfast you call Teresa? We've got cell phone service back up. I bet she's missin' her mommy as much as you are your daddy."

"I miss Retta too. Can we call her?" Zaylie asked.

"Let's wait and let her call us. She might not be feeling too good this early in the morning," Claire said. "But we might ask Levi if it's all right for us to go see Little Bit and Hopalong after breakfast."

Another long sigh and she crawled off Claire's lap. "Can Levi go with us?"

"If he's not too busy, maybe he can. You like him, don't

you?" Claire followed her into the bedroom and got out a hot pink sweat suit for her to wear that day.

"I wish my daddy was like him." Zaylie lifted her arms so Claire could remove her pajamas.

"How's that?" Claire frowned.

"I wish my daddy was home all the time like Levi is," Zaylie said. "I wish he didn't have to go away no more. It hurts me right here." She pointed to her chest.

"I know, baby girl. Maybe someday he can stay home all the time," Claire said.

"After Christmas?" Zaylie pushed.

"I don't know about that, but you can ask him when he calls," Claire answered.

"Can Santa bring him home and make it so he never has to go away?"

Tears welled up in Claire's eyes as she remembered wishing the same thing when she was about five years old. "I don't think he'll fit in Santa's bag with those cowboy boots and kittens that you've ordered."

"What if Santa takes out everything but my daddy?" Zaylie asked.

Claire turned around and grabbed a tissue. If and when she ever settled into a permanent relationship, it was going to be with a man whose job did not take him away from home, not even for a few days. She dabbed her eyes, and when she turned around, Zaylie had left her bedroom.

She was sitting on the floor in front of the kitten basket petting Gussie. "You are a good mommy. I had a mommy, but the angels took her away."

Claire reached for another tissue. If there was a Santa and if he could grant wishes, then she wouldn't ask for anything for herself—she'd ask him to bring Grant home for good so that Zaylie could have at least one full-time parent.

*   *   *

Levi had already made coffee when Claire and Zaylie reached the ranch house that morning. He poured a cup and handed it to Claire, then ran a hand through his unruly hair. The thought of touching it herself, combined with the sparkle of mischief in his green eyes, put a little extra speed in her pulse.

"So how's the princess this morning?" he asked.

"Whiny, but we'll get through it," Claire whispered.

Just then Beau barked at the kitchen door. Zaylie ran to let him and Mavis in. "I remember you. You're Benjy's mama."

"Yes, I am, and you are Zaylie. We're going to get to know each other real good this next little while. You think you can help me cook and do some cleanin'?" Mavis asked.

"Yes, I can." She nodded seriously. "But I have to talk to my friend Teresa too. And right now I need to tell Beau all about my friend." She followed the dog out of the kitchen.

"I reckon that would be fine." Mavis hung up her coat. "You boys haven't started breakfast?"

"Naw, we was waitin' on you." Levi crossed the room and hugged her. "Want me to get the cast iron skillets out?"

"That's a start." Mavis put a bibbed apron over her red sweat suit. "Heard from Cade and Retta?"

Levi nodded. "He called last night. They'd checked in at the hotel in Dallas and would be flying out about noon today."

"Shall I make biscuits, Mavis?" Claire offered.

"That would be great," Mavis said. "Is this little friend of Zaylie's got a daddy that's in the service too?"

"No, a mama. And she's on the same team as Zaylie's dad," Levi answered.

"No wonder Zaylie and Teresa are such good friends. Did you ever have a friend like that, Claire?" Mavis asked.

Claire shrugged. "Not really. My situation was different. We weren't at one post as long as Grant has been. I keep thinking that they'll move him, but so far they've kept him and Angela, that's Teresa's mother, in the same place for four years."

"I can't even imagine moving around so much. I wouldn't like it at all," Levi said.

"Me either. I was born in Sunset and will probably die there," Mavis said.

"Good mornin'." Justin came into the kitchen with water droplets from his shower still hanging on his dark hair.

"Mornin'," Claire and Levi said at the same time.

Levi poured a cup of coffee and handed it off to him. "I'm going to see if I can cheer her up a little. I don't suppose she even knows just how dangerous some of those missions her daddy goes on are, does she?"

Claire shook her head. "And I hope that he retires before she gets old enough to realize."

He shook his head slowly. "I can't imagine the worry that you have when he leaves, him bein' your only sibling and you havin' the responsibilities that you do."

She smiled up at him. "Appreciate the roots that you have. Don't ever take them for granted."

"Listen to her, son," Mavis said. "That's good advice."

The noise of a chair dragged across the floor startled her. She whipped around to see Zaylie crawling up in it and reaching for the carton of eggs. "Is it time to crack the eggs?"

"I think it just might be, and I thought that we'd show Mavis the quilt top we designed in the cabin after we eat. Would you like that?"

"Okay." She sighed. "Maybe Daddy will call and I can show him the colors."

"I'm sure he would like that," Claire said around the lump in her throat.

*   *   *

Levi got out to the cabin where Claire and Zaylie had taken shelter and surveyed the damage to her van. There was no way the thing was worth fixing. He folded his arms over his chest and leaned against the other side of the big scrub oak tree Claire had crashed into. He played the old "what if" game while he waited on Buddy to arrive with his tow truck.

What if Claire did buy the Harris house? That would mean she'd be close by, and he could ask her out.

What if he did ask her on a real date? What if she'd rather just be friends?

What if she said yes? Would that lead to a real relationship?

What if he had to give up his Saturday-night partying with Justin? It hadn't been so hard to be a man down when Cade fell in love with Retta, but that would leave poor old Justin all alone for the bar hopping.

What if he fell in love with Claire? She was a successful businesswoman and might think a fling was all right, but anything long term with a ranch foreman—well that might be another matter.

He was so deep in thought that he didn't even hear Buddy's truck until the man leaned on the horn and startled him.

"I thought you might be frozen to death." Buddy laughed as he got out of the truck. "You wasn't movin' a muscle."

A short, round guy with close-cut hair and wearing mustard yellow coveralls, Buddy was always happy and had a smile that covered his round face. He'd been like that in high school, and folks thought he'd go on to college to play football like Cade had since he had speed and power in spite of his height. But his father died right before graduation, and Buddy settled into the auto repair business like it was what he'd always wanted to do.

"Hey, are you as ready to see the last of this snow as I am?" Buddy waved as he got out. "Man, alive! Was anyone hurt in this wreck?"

"Just some bruises, and if another snowflake don't fall this whole winter, I'm good with that. I'm not dreamin' of a white Christmas," Levi said.

"Me either." Buddy walked around the van, shaking his head the whole time. "That was one lucky lady drivin' this thing. If she'd been goin' any faster, that engine would have wound up in her lap. Talk has it that y'all were sharing a hymnbook at church. Has the lady caught your eye?"

Levi clamped a hand on Buddy's shoulder. "You know how old men and women love to gossip."

Buddy chuckled. "Yep, I do. They have to be inside durin' this kind of weather, so they keep the phone lines hot. I had to go take care of a wreck yesterday mornin', so I missed church, but my aunt was there, and she said that Claire is real cute. She thought that we'd make a real sweet little couple and I should ask her out. You know Aunt Maribeth. She's always tryin' to get me to settle down. But I don't want to get in the way of something you got goin'. But then again, if you ain't got an eye for her, you should ask me to dinner today so I can meet her. I'm tired of Saturday-night bar dates. I want someone permanent in my life." In addition to his ready smile, Buddy loved to talk, and it was hard to get a word in edgewise when he got started on something.

When Buddy finally stopped to draw in another breath, Levi said, "Okay, okay, I might have some chemistry with her, but that's confidential. I don't want to jinx it by sayin' too much."

"Your secret's safe with me, but if you change your mind, I expect a phone call invitin' me to stop by for dinner. I'll get all cleaned up in my Sunday best and bring her roses and champagne," Buddy said.

"You got it." Levi had never had a jealous streak until that moment. Just thinking of Claire with Buddy or anyone else made him feel like he was turning bullfrog green. "Now let's get this van hooked up so you can haul it away."

"Sounds good to me." Buddy got back into the tow truck and backed it up to the tail end of the van.

In only a few minutes, he'd pulled the vehicle away from the tree and was on his way back toward Sunset with it. He waved out the window at Levi and was gone, leaving only a scar on the old scrub oak tree and a bushel of unanswered questions in Levi's mind.

It was close enough to noon that he went on back to the house to find Zaylie waving at him through the window and holding up a rag of some kind.

"Levi!" She ran to him as he hung up his coat. "Look at the quilt I'm makin' for the kitties. Me and Mavis done dusted the livin' room and she said I'm a good duster and that my quilt is pretty." She held up the colorful rag she'd been waving.

He squatted down to her level and eyed them carefully. "I'd say that those little black kittens are really lucky to have you as their friend."

She threw her arms around his neck and hugged him tightly. "Aunt Claire says we can go see Little Bit and Hopa-long after we eat. Can you go with us?"

"You bet I can, and they'll be so happy to see you. I was thinkin' that today we might turn Little Bit out into the corral," Levi told her, and looked up at Claire who was putting the last touches on dinner.

"Y'all need to wash up while I get dinner on the table," she said.

"Where's Mavis?"

"Right here." She came out of the pantry with a jar of home-canned peaches in her hand. "Did Buddy come get that wrecked car?"

"Yep, he did. And he agrees with me that it's totaled. He also does a little resell business on the side. Fixes up cars, both newer ones and vintage ones. We could go there one evening if you're interested."

"I'm not interested in buying a car right now. I can drive Nanny's Lincoln until I decide what I want to buy next," Claire said.

Zaylie grabbed Levi by the hand and pulled him toward the bathroom. "We can wash our hands together. Mavis made nooels and I love 'em."

"Chicken and noodles," Claire translated. "With leftover sweet potato casserole and cranberry sauce from Thanksgiving."

He couldn't remember ever sitting at the table on the ranch without either or both of the Maguire brothers being there, so he stopped in his tracks when he and Zaylie reentered the kitchen. Should he take a place at one end or the other or sit in his customary spot? Finally, he pulled out a chair for Claire and took his normal seat across the table from her.

"It's good to have you at the table with us, Mavis. I've missed you," Levi said.

"Mavis used to eat here?" Zaylie asked.

"She took care of the cookin' until this past summer. And

she supervised the housekeeper that comes in every week. When Skip was on the ranch he ate with us too. Want me to dip up the noodles?"

"To tell the truth I missed bein' here, but Benjy needs me, and I can't be in two places at once. And yes, son, you can dip the noodles for us." Mavis passed Zaylie's bowl to him.

"Where's Justin?"

"Right here." He rushed in and sat in his normal place, leaving Cade's spot empty.

"I will say the blessin'." Zaylie bowed her head. "Jesus, will you tell Santa Claus to bring my daddy home forever? That's what I want more than cowboy boots. And thank you for the noonels. Amen."

Levi caught Claire's gaze when he looked up, and the tears in her eyes mirrored his. If it were in his power to answer Zaylie's prayer, he would have done it in a heartbeat.

"How much do you want, Miz Zaylie?" he managed to say around the lemon-size lump in his throat.

"Half a bowl please," Claire answered for her.

Levi dipped it up and thought that maybe he should say the prayer at the next meal. He could ask Jesus to tell Santa Claus to bring him a woman who'd be happy with being only a ranch foreman's wife.

Chapter Eleven

For Claire, quilting was a great stress reliever. That evening after Mavis went home she went straight to the bunkhouse and started to sew pieces together, making perfect little six-inch squares. As she stacked them up beside the machine, she counted off all the stressful things in her life, and one by one put them in a mental box. It was a coping mechanism—once they were inside the box, then she wouldn't think about them anymore.

Number one was the heightened feeling of chemistry when Levi was around or even when she thought about him. The electricity between them couldn't be denied, and she wouldn't mind exploring it further. Levi was everything she liked in a man. He was kind, trustworthy, honest, and honorable. He liked kids and animals, and he treated a woman with respect. It didn't matter what a man did for a living if he had all that going for him. But did he feel the same way about her? Until she was sure, she folded those feelings and put them inside the box.

Number two was dreading the day she had to leave the ranch with Zaylie. She couldn't bear to see the child weep, and yet it would be unavoidable. Until then, she shouldn't worry so much about it. Into the box all that went as the pile of quilt squares grew to Claire's right.

Three—the insurance company was sending an adjuster to Buddy's auto shop tomorrow. They'd only give her what it was worth in today's market. Since it was six years old, she doubted that it would even bring enough to put a down payment on another vehicle.

Four—she worried about Grant every day. About whether he'd come home this time and how she'd deal with Zaylie if she lost her last remaining parent.

Five—had she made the right decision in staying on at the ranch for another week? Retta had been so good to take her and Zaylie in that she couldn't refuse to help her, and yet if she'd turned her down, her mental box wouldn't be nearly as full.

A rap on the door sent Zaylie running to open it and throw herself into Levi's arms. "I'm so glad you came to see me."

He hugged her tightly, then set her down and brought out a candy bar from his coat pocket. "I think any little girl who helped Mavis all day should have a treat."

"Thank you! Snickers. It's my favorite kind. How did you know?" She held it to her heart dramatically.

"I just guessed," Levi said with a big smile.

She turned toward Claire. "Can I eat it right now, Aunt Claire?"

"Yes, you can." Claire's eyes went to Levi's. Suddenly the mental box flew open, and things began to surface. "Want a cup of coffee or a glass of tea?" She tried to look away, but his eyes held hers.

"Love one but don't let me keep you from working. I'll make a pot and bring you a cup." He removed his coat and hung it over the back of a kitchen chair as he crossed the floor. "Are you working on the quilt that you designed in the cabin?"

"Yep." She kept sewing even though her hands were trembling slightly.

"How much does one sell for like what you are making?"

"Depends on whether I have it machine quilted or if I get down the frames and quilt it by hand. Machine quilted will go for about six hundred dollars. If I hand quilt it maybe two to three thousand."

He stopped in his tracks on the way to the coffeepot. "And how many of these do you sell a week?"

"Two to four," she answered. "I can top out three a week, but I only hand quilt one or two a year. Most of them are machine quilted."

"Holy shhh—smoke! You do pretty good at that business," he said.

"I make about twice what I did when I taught school." She stopped the machine and cocked her head to one side. "Zaylie, darlin', will you get the phone. It's on the dresser in my bedroom."

As always she took off in a dead run, and then her squeal could have been heard halfway to the Red River. "Daddy, is it really you? Guess what? I'm home on the ranch."

Levi readied the coffee and sat down at the table across from Claire. "Could we talk?"

"About?" Every hair on Claire's arms stood up.

"Us?" he said simply.

Her chest tightened, and her palms got clammy. "What about us?"

She didn't want to hear that their kisses were only flirting and that he'd decided they should only be friends or maybe not even that. Or worse yet that an old girlfriend had popped back up in his life.

"I like you, Claire, and if you're living close by we could date, couldn't we?" he blurted out.

"Are you asking me for a date, but only if I live in Sunset? Is Randlett too far to drive?" She sewed up a couple more squares.

"If you lived on the moon and you said that you'd go out with me, I'd figure out a way to get there," he answered.

His tone said he was serious. The way her heart did a double beat said that she believed him.

"I'd love to take you and Zaylie for ice cream after Sunday dinner this next weekend. If it's a decent day we could take her to the park afterward to play for a little while. But I really want a real date, as in just me and you, like dinner and a movie." He picked up a quilt square and studied it.

"I'd like that too Levi." She pushed her chair back.

A date with Levi, a real one—she wanted to tell someone, but her mother wouldn't understand, her father was too busy with his new life to talk to her, and she didn't have a friend that close other than Retta. And there was no way she was calling Retta on the first night of her honeymoon.

"How do you get the corners so even?" Levi picked up a completed square.

"Lots of practice." How could he be interested in quilt squares when her pulse was racing and she wanted to talk about the date?

He put the piece down and laid a hand over hers. "Claire, will you be my date for the Christmas party?"

She felt like the quarterback of the football team had just asked her to the prom. "I'd love to."

He did a fist pump with his free hand, and then his cheeks

turned slightly red. The pulse in his neck quickened, and he squeezed her hand. "I was afraid you'd say no."

"Why?" Heat from his hand filled her whole body.

"You don't know how hard it is for someone like me to ask a girl like you out," he answered.

"What do you mean, like me?" She moved closer and looked up into his eyes.

"There's something between us for sure, and I don't want to let it slip away, but what you see is what you get," he answered. "I'm not poor, but I'm not rich either and probably won't ever be. But I like my job and love the Longhorn."

Before Claire could answer, Zaylie ran out of the bedroom and handed the phone to Claire. "Daddy wants to talk to you. Come on, Levi, you got to see Grumpy. He likes to play now."

Claire was more than a little disappointed when Levi removed his hand and followed Zaylie to the other side of the room and sat down cross-legged on the floor with her. She dangled a scrap of fabric down the side of the basket, and all three kittens attacked it.

"Take the phone off speaker," Grant said.

"Yes, sir!" Claire snapped a salute and then hit the right button before she put the phone to her ear.

"I'm sorry. I didn't mean to be so bossy, but Zaylie just told me that she wants a daddy like Levi for Christmas. When I asked her what she meant, she said one who stayed home and played with kittens with her. That stung, but I shouldn't have taken it out on you," he said.

"Forgiven," she told him. "Every time you leave she misses you more."

"She told me she'd rather that Santa Claus brought me home for good as getting new boots or even kittens." Grant sighed. "Are you sitting down?"

"Yes, but please don't tell me you're going to get deployed for a year," she said.

"Nothing that drastic. I've been seeing Angela for the past six months. In fact, I proposed on Thanksgiving, and she said yes."

"And you didn't tell me? Congratulations, brother. I'm so happy for you."

"We're looking to turn in our papers and retire after Christmas. I've got a job offer at the casino in Randlett as the security supervisor."

"Are you kiddin' me?" Claire gasped. "Why aren't y'all telling Zaylie and Teresa?"

"We want to tell them in person at Christmas. We should be home on the twenty-third if all goes well here. If we do this, we'll need a place in Randlett, so could you be on a lookout for us?" Grant said.

Now it was official. Her life was about to turn completely around in this new phase, and it scared the bejesus right out of her.

"There's no need to look for a place in Randlett," she told him. "You can have Nanny's place. It was left to us jointly. I've been holding out on you too." Claire told him about her plans and that she was going to see a house in Sunset the day after tomorrow. "There's one hitch about Nanny's house though. We were left everything jointly. I get the car."

"You drive a hard bargain. You know I love that old Lincoln," he groaned.

"It's a fair trade. You get a fully furnished house. I get the car that she drove us to school in the year we lived with her, back before she broke her hip and got dementia. Besides you were ashamed of it back then," she reminded him.

"That's before I knew what a gem it was," he said.

"Your choice." She'd believe that he was actually going to quit the Air Force when she saw the paperwork.

"You win. You get the car. I'll take the house," he agreed. "Just don't tell Zaylie. I want to be right there when she finds out."

"You got my word," she said.

"Word about what?" Zaylie looked up from the corner.

Grant laughed. "I guess we were lucky to get it talked through before she caught on."

"It's a miracle," Claire said. "I miss you, brother. Be safe."

"You too, and I'll try to call in a couple of days to hear more about this new venture. Good luck with it, sis. You deserve a life of your own," Grant said. "Love you."

"Love you more," she said, and hit the end button.

"What did you give your word about?"

"That I wouldn't let it slip what you are getting for Christmas from your dad," Claire answered honestly. She would tell Retta about this new turn of events as well as the date when she talked to her again.

Zaylie cut her eyes around at Claire. "Do you know what Santa is bringing me too?"

"Nope. That's between you and Santa," Claire said.

Levi moved to the sofa. "And Santa never tells us anything about what you ask him for because it's a secret."

Claire joined him, glad to sit down. She needed to process everything—date, Grant's engagement, Christmas. It was too much too fast. She took a deep breath and let it out very slowly.

Zaylie sucked in a lung full of air. "Are we going to be here for Christmas? Will Santa bring my boots here?"

Presents? What on earth would Claire get for her new friends?

"Sure, he will," Levi said.

Zaylie's blue eyes twinkled. "I want the kittens from you, Levi, and you have to talk my daddy into letting me have them, Aunt Claire. That's what I want from y'all."

When Levi winked at Claire she was reminded of that old country song that talked about with one little wink the troubles all took a hike. That's the way Claire felt that night. Levi had winked at her, and half her troubles had disappeared. Grant was coming home. He and Angela would live close enough that she could see them often. Zaylie could have her precious kittens, and she wouldn't throw nearly as big a hissy fit if she got to live with Teresa. Now if she could just figure out what to do about Christmas presents for the folks on the ranch.

*   *   *

Levi would gladly give all three of the kittens to Zaylie and go round up another dozen if he could. If her daddy said no, he'd buy her three matching little stuffed toy black cats that she could name Grumpy, Sleepy, and Happy.

"Read me a story, Levi." She tugged him toward the bookcase. "You pick it out. My daddy reads to me."

"I don't mean to..." he started to say to Claire.

"It's all right." She held up a hand. "Grant understands."

"Okay." He nodded. "But you have to pick the book out."

"This one." She carried *Oh, the Places You'll Go!* by Dr. Seuss over to him and crawled up into his lap. "If you read loud enough my kitties will hear."

He read the first two pages and she sighed. "I really miss my daddy."

"He'll be home soon," Levi said.

"Don't read no more." She shut the book. "I'll put it back

and get one about kitties, and I'll read it to Grumpy, Sleepy, and Happy."

She slid off his knees and picked out a favorite. In a few seconds she was sitting by the basket and reading the pictures however she saw them.

"My heart hurts for her," Levi whispered as he watched her pick up the kittens and put them in her lap so they could see the pictures.

"Mine too," Claire said. "I know exactly how she feels. I always wanted a father that came home every night for supper."

"Now I'm ready for my bath, Aunt Claire." Zaylie laid the book aside and put the kittens back in the basket.

"I should go," Levi said.

"Stay a while. I'd like to talk to you, if you have the time." Claire got up and headed toward the bathroom to run water in the tub.

He stood up and paced around the perimeter of the room half a dozen times. What if she said she wanted to back out of the date after all, that she couldn't commit to even that when Zaylie needed her? He wouldn't blame her if she did—the child needed at least one stable adult in her life, one who was always there for her and had nothing else in her life. It wasn't fair to Claire, but then life didn't come with a written guarantee that it would all be a bed of roses.

Claire was back in a few minutes. She led him to the sofa with her small hand in his. She sat down on the sofa and pulled him down beside her. "Please don't give those kittens to anyone else. Grant is probably going to get out of the service..." She went on to tell him the rest of the news in a voice barely above a whisper.

"Looks like that little girl has a lot of pull with Santa

Claus." Levi was so relieved that she hadn't called off their date that he shut his eyes and said a quick prayer.

"Put your worries in my pockets," Zaylie's little voice floated out of the bathroom.

"Is she singing Conway?" Levi's eyes popped open.

Claire nodded. "Grant and I love old country music. Probably because Nanny listened to it all the time when we were living with her that year, and we associate it with good times. That's what I learned, anyway, when I took psychology for my degree."

"Do you miss teaching?"

She scooted over and laid her head on his shoulder. "Not a bit. Can I put my worries in your pocket, Levi?"

"Anytime, dawlin'," he drawled.

"Seven 'Panish angels done took my mommy home," Zaylie sang out loud and clear.

Levi picked Claire up and sat her in his lap and drew her cheek to his chest. "This is going to change your world for sure. Are you going to be all right?" He tipped up her chin with his thumb and softly kissed her lips.

"Sweet as 'trawberry wine," Zaylie sang to the top of her lungs.

"Well, that song is sure appropriate right now after that kiss," he said with a grin. "I thought you said she liked old music. I believe that's Chris Stapleton."

"We listen to something other than Conway, Willie, and George Jones occasionally," she said.

Zaylie was singing, "I wanna rust you with my heart."

"I'm hoping that she means trust." Levi laughed out loud and then got serious. "Can I trust you with my heart?"

Claire leaned back slightly and locked eyes with his. "I'll take good care of it. I promise."

His lips found hers in a long, hot, lingering kiss that left

them both breathless, and then Zaylie sang a line or two of
"Jesus Loves Me."

"She only knows a few words of each song, but she covers what she knows when she's happy," Claire whispered.

Levi kept Claire in his arms as he stood up. They swayed
together as he hummed parts of several country songs.
Claire might be short, but she was just the right height for
him to rest his chin on the top of her head and breathe in the
remnants of the vanilla scent of her shampoo.

"Aunt Claire, the water is cold," Zaylie yelled.

Claire kissed Levi with so much heat and passion that it
took his breath away again. "Thank you for listening and for
the dance. It's been a long time since…"

Their eyes locked again, and she didn't need to finish
the sentence because he felt the same way. "I know…" he
whispered without blinking.

"Aunt Claire," Zaylie hollered again.

"On my way, baby girl. Pull the plug," Claire said.

"I done did," she said.

"I should be going now. Tell Zaylie good night for me.
I'll see you in the morning," Levi said. "And thank you for
the dance."

"Night," she whispered.

He crammed his hat down on his head and hunched his
shoulders against the bitter cold wind, but his heart was so
warm he didn't notice it nearly as much as he had earlier on
his way to the bunkhouse. He hummed-whistled the tune to
the song about trusting and hoped that he really could trust
Claire with his heart.

Chapter Twelve

After a night of tossing and turning, Levi found Justin in the kitchen the next morning before daylight. He'd already started the coffee and was leaning against the cabinet waiting for it to finish brewing. Levi pulled out a kitchen chair and sank into it.

"You look like you got something on your mind," Justin said.

"So do you," Levi fired back.

Justin poured two cups of coffee and carried them to the table. "It's been weeks since we've been out. Let's go to the Rusty Spur and see if we can't dance about a year's worth of leather off our boots on Friday night. Lettin' off a little steam might be good for both of us."

"You go on and have a good time. I'll hold down the fort." Levi sipped the strong, hot brew. He'd rather stay home and watch Claire sew up quilt squares than go out to a bar.

"It's Claire, ain't it?" Justin toyed with the handle of his mug.

Levi nodded. "I asked her to be my date at the Christmas party."

"Good for you, but that don't mean you can't go be my wingman on Friday. You don't have to bring a woman home or come draggin' in here at daylight either one. You can be my designated driver," Justin said.

Levi chuckled. "And ruin your best pickup line." He lowered his voice to a deep Texas drawl. "'Darlin', I'm way too wasted to get home on my own. I'll cook breakfast for you if you'll drive me.'"

A wide grin spread over Justin's face. "You know me way too well."

"Yep," Levi said again.

"I smell coffee." Zaylie twirled into the room like a ballet dancer. "Someday when I'm a big girl I'm going to drink coffee."

Before she could shed her coat, Levi was there to hang it up for her. "What else are you goin' to do when you are a big girl?"

"Be the boss," Zaylie answered. "Aunt Claire, can we have waffles for breakfast?"

"Sure if that's what you want. Mavis called, and she isn't going to come in until after she gets Benjy off to school each morning. Skip burned the bacon yesterday." Claire's shoulder brushed against Levi's when she passed him in the kitchen. He locked his little finger with hers for a second and squeezed it gently.

"Good mornin', ladies," Justin said from the table.

Levi got out the cast iron skillet and put it on the stove. "Want me to start fryin' some sausage to go with those waffles?"

"We got it." Claire smiled up at him. "Go on and finish your coffee before it gets cold."

His phone rang and he fished it out of his hip pocket. "Good mornin', Mavis. What's goin' on?" He took the conversation to the living room where he sank down on the sofa.

"Just checkin' in to see if any of y'all need anything from here before I come that way this mornin'?"

"You got a blackberry cobbler in the freezer?" he said.

"I'm sure I do," she answered. "Where's Claire?"

"Right here," he answered.

"Then go to the living room," Mavis said.

"I'm already here. What's on your mind, Mavis?"

"I heard that you told Buddy you might be interested in Claire."

"Gossip don't take long, does it?" He didn't want to have this conversation, but there didn't seem to be a way around it, so he blurted out, "I asked her to be my date to the Christmas party. She was invited to go to it anyway, but I want her to be there with me."

"You better dig in and get ready for a battle," Mavis told him.

"Does that mean you're goin' to fight me on this?" Levi asked.

"No, son, not me. I like Claire a lot."

"Then who?"

"I heard that Buddy says that even though he said he'd back down, he's going to make a play for her if she's as pretty as everyone is saying," Mavis said. "If you need me to run a little interference, you just let me know."

"Thanks, Mavis, but I can handle Buddy," he said.

"I hope so. See you in an hour or so, and I'll bring a cobbler with me. Bye now." The phone went dead before he could even say good-bye.

"Can you eat a gazillion waffles?" Zaylie hopped onto the sofa beside him.

Levi laid the phone on the end table. "Oh yeah, maybe two gazillion."

She giggled. "That's funny. Nobody, not even my daddy, can eat that many."

An ache hit him in the heart as usual when he thought of his biological father. The kid who'd gotten Levi's mother pregnant had only been seventeen. The night she told him about the baby, he took a curve too fast on the way home from her place. He'd died instantly when his car hit a big scrub oak tree, not totally unlike the one that Claire had plowed into.

Levi hoped that Grant did come home to stay at Christmas because all kids needed a father. "Well, princess, if your daddy can't eat that many, I'm sure I couldn't either." He picked her up and carried her back to the kitchen. "Look what I found in the living room. Does anyone know this kid, or should I throw her out the back door?"

"No, no, no!" Zaylie giggled. "Aunt Claire, tell him who I am."

"Let me look at her," Claire said in mock seriousness. "Are her eyes blue and does she have blond hair?"

Levi held her out toward Claire. "Why, I believe that might be Zaylie Mason."

"You think we should keep her?" Levi teased

"Maybe so since I made all these waffles and she ordered a gazillion," Claire said.

Zaylie wiggled free and ran to her chair at the table.

Just to get to touch her, Levi tucked a strand of hair behind Claire's ear. "Don't want one of those to fall out and get in the waffle batter."

"Thanks." She smiled.

* * *

Justin and Levi had both eaten breakfast and headed to the barn. Mavis wasn't there yet, and Zaylie was in the living room talking to Teresa. Claire stopped loading the dishwasher and watched a couple of bunnies hopping across the backyard. Had they been out to the barn to visit with Hopalong about boy bunny stuff, or were they girl bunnies out looking for a good time?

She caught bits and pieces of Zaylie's conversation with Teresa in the living room. But most of her focus was centered on the bunnies as they hopped out of sight. The ranch was so peaceful and quiet, even when it was bustling with activity like it had been the night they'd decorated the tree. She'd never found such tranquility anywhere she'd lived before. No wonder Zaylie loved it so much.

Levi startled her when he dashed in the back door and grabbed his gloves. "Forgot a couple of things."

"Gloves and what else?" she asked.

"This." He wrapped her up in his arms in a fierce embrace.

She could sure get used to a boyfriend like Levi who wasn't only just the sexiest cowboy in Texas but the most thoughtful one too.

With his rough knuckles he tipped up her chin, and his mouth moved toward hers. She didn't want to close her eyes, but the passion in his eyes drew her into the kiss. His lips touched hers, and she tiptoed as her hands found their way under his open jacket to splay out on his chest. His heart thumped against her palm, but it wasn't beating nearly as fast as hers. The tip of his tongue grazed her mouth, and a shiver of desire danced down her spine when she opened slightly. The taste of sweet maple syrup mixed with strong black coffee teased her senses, and she pressed her body closer to his.

And then, just like that, it was over and he took a step back, leaving her weak kneed and wanting more. "I've wanted to do that all morning. See you at noon." He was gone before she could say a word.

With weak knees, she quickly turned around to look out the kitchen window. He turned around and waved just before he got into his truck and drove off toward the barn. She held up a hand and was startled again when Zaylie tugged on the tail of her T-shirt.

"Aunt Claire, Franny wants to talk to you." Zaylie held up the phone.

"I thought you were talking to Teresa," Claire said.

"I was but we hanged up and Franny called."

"Hello," Claire said.

"You are out of breath. Were you busy?" Franny asked.

Define busy, Claire thought for a split second before she answered.

"I was but I'm finished. How're things in Randlett?" Claire glanced out the window, but Levi's truck was completely out of sight.

"Boring as usual. I miss having you and Zaylie next door."

"Well," Claire drew out the word as she checked to see where Zaylie was. She was sitting on the sofa watching cartoons on television. "I've got news but it's a big secret until Christmas. You may have more than one little girl living next door to you." She went on to tell Franny about Angela and Grant.

"Well, that house ain't big enough for you and them both. My renter is moving out next week. That'll give me time to get it repainted and the carpets cleaned, and then you can move in. It's just a little two-bedroom, one-bath house, but it'll be perfect for you," Franny said.

"I didn't know you had rental property," Claire said.

"Just the one place. It belonged to my aunt, and I inherited it when she died forty years ago. Now what's goin' on with you and the cowboy?"

"Thank you for the offer, but there's more news." Claire went on to tell Franny about moving to Sunset and opening a quilting shop.

"Follow your dreams, or you'll regret it," Franny said. "I'm going to miss you, but you've got to do what your heart tells you. Now tell me, did you sleep with the cowboy?"

"No," Claire gasped. "But I've got a problem. I feel like I should have a Christmas present ready for each one of them for being so good to us and..." She hesitated again.

Franny giggled. "You must like that cowboy for him to rattle you so much that you can't think. What do you do for a living?"

"Make quilts," Claire answered.

"What do you bet that those tall cowboys don't have a single throw that can reach to their toes on a cold night when they're watchin' television?"

"Franny, you are a genius," Claire squealed.

"And make one for Retta and the new baby while you're at it."

"Great idea. That takes a load off my mind." Claire felt a hundred percent better now that she had a plan.

"Good. I've got to go down to the church to help plan for our Christmas potluck. We always have it right after services on the second Sunday in December, and I'll expect you and Zaylie to be there." Her tone didn't leave a bit of wiggle room.

"We'll plan on it. Tell everyone hello for me."

"I'll do that. Bye now," Franny said, and the call ended.

She was about to text Levi, when he called. "Would you

and Zaylie like to get out a little while this mornin'? I need some supplies in Bowie."

"Hey." Mavis came through the kitchen door.

Claire waved. "Levi is going to Bowie. Do you need anything from there?"

"I'll make a list. Why don't you and Zaylie go with him? You'll do a better job of filling my list than he will. Men can take all day to find a can of baking powder."

"Are you sure you don't need my help?" Claire asked her.

Mavis made a motion of shooing her away.

"How about I pick you up in ten minutes?" Levi said. "There's a really good Tex-Mex place in Bowie. We could get some lunch there."

"Love to." She hoped that her breath didn't sound as breathy in Levi's ears as it did in hers.

Chapter Thirteen

Levi was getting into his truck when Justin drove up in a tractor and honked. He slung his long legs out of the big green tractor. "I thought you'd already left, and I was about to call you. I checked and we're out of hydraulic fluid, so would you pick up a couple of buckets? And Buddy called a few minutes ago. Said that your phone was busy, so he called me. Take Claire by there so they can make a deal about her van. The insurance adjustor just left and said that it was totaled. I would think that they called her soon as they left his place."

"Oil. Buddy's. Anything else?"

"Buddy's got about a dozen vehicles for sale. She might find something that she likes if y'all take time to look at them," Justin told him.

"Will do, but she doesn't seem to be in a hurry to buy anything right now," Levi said.

"Don't hurt for her to take a look." Justin waved over his shoulder as he disappeared into the barn.

Zaylie met Levi at the back door with her coat in her hands. "Guess what? My daddy is comin' home at Christmas, and me and Teresa get to see each other."

"That's all wonderful news." Levi's eyes traveled across the room to Claire.

"It's going to be a Merry Christmas, isn't it, Zaylie?" Claire said.

Levi winked, knowing that she was preparing the child for the time when she'd have to leave the ranch. He helped Zaylie get into her coat and held the door for Claire.

"Did the insurance agent call?" He'd have rather been talking about how beautiful she was even in jeans and a sweatshirt than cars. Or maybe how he loved the way her green eyes sparkled that morning or even that he'd like to kiss her until they were both breathless again. But not in front of Zaylie.

"Yes and they'll be sending a check. After the deductible it's not going to amount to a lot, but money isn't everything, and I'm so thankful that Zaylie wasn't hurt."

"Amen to that," Levi responded.

Zaylie skipped across the yard singing "'Smooth as 'ennessie whiskey, sweet as 'trawberry wine.'"

"You might want to let her listen to a lot of kiddy songs before she starts to school next year," Levi said. "Her kindergarten teacher might not like the class to hear 'Tennessee Whiskcy.'"

"You got a point." Claire nodded.

The radio was already on when he started the engine and "Love Can Build a Bridge" was playing. Zaylie came in loudly on the first line of the chorus every time. Levi kept time on the steering wheel with his thumb and hummed along, wondering if there was a bridge strong enough to bridge the gap between him and Claire. She made more money than he did, had a college degree, which proved she was a hell of a lot smarter than him, and God only knew that she could probably have any man that she set her sights on.

He stole a long, sideways look her way to find her mouthing the words saying that she'd swim out to save him in his sea of broken dreams. He hoped that she was thinking of him and the lyrics were sinking into her heart like they did his.

The song had ended and several more had played when he parked in front of the Walmart store and helped them out of the vehicle. "I should be back in half an hour, but don't rush. I'll come inside and find you when I get back, so take all the time you need. I saw that list Mavis gave you, and it will take a while to get it done."

"Thanks." Claire laid a hand on his arm.

Claire really was as warm as Tennessee whiskey. She definitely wasn't like what Levi called a sissy drink, those fruity things made with barely a shot of liquor. No, sir, his Claire was a good stiff shot of whiskey—something with strength that warmed the heart and soul as well as the body.

His phone rang before he got out of the parking lot, so he pulled off to the side and answered it. "Hello, Justin. I haven't talked to you in weeks," he teased.

"Well, you're certainly in a good mood." Justin chuckled. "Been to Buddy's yet?"

"Nope, that's our next stop after Claire gets her shopping done. I'm on my way to get our supplies."

"I'm glad I caught you. Will you run by the vet's place? I called in for some vaccinations. Allison will have it ready for you," Justin said.

"Will do. Just call if you think of anything else." Levi

tossed the phone onto the passenger's seat and pulled out onto the road.

The vet's office was on the way to the supply store, so he stopped there first, told the receptionist, Allison, what he needed, and waited for her to get the order from the back room.

"You sick, cowboy?" She smiled at him when she returned.

She was a short brunette, maybe not as curvy as Claire, and her voice didn't have that little raspy quality in it that Claire's did.

"No, why?"

"I haven't seen you at the Rusty Spur in weeks, and you're all business this mornin' instead of flirtin' like you usually do. I thought something might be the matter." Her hand lingered on his when she handed him the invoice for the medicine.

He wiggled it free and scrawled his name on the line. "Guess I've got other things on my mind."

"Save me a dance if you show up this weekend. I'll be there with my red cowboy boots on, ready to two-step some leather off. And, honey, whatever is ailin' you, I can make it all better by the end of the weekend," she said.

"Sorry, darlin', I got plans for the weekend," he said.

"Too bad. You'll be missin' a good time." Allison grinned. "Maybe Justin will save me a dance."

"I wouldn't be a bit surprised," he said.

He went from there to the tractor supply place to get what they needed, and as he rounded the end of an aisle there was another short brunette, this one a little heavier than Claire. When she felt his presence, she turned and smiled. Her eyes were green but not that clear aqua shade that Claire's were, and her lips weren't as full and kissable.

He returned the smile, picked up what he needed, and headed for the checkout counter.

As he was leaving, he remembered that he hadn't gotten a single Christmas present, so he drove over to the western wear store located across the lot from the tractor supply place. He picked up three pairs of warm gloves for the guys on his list, and then remembered Benjy and added a fourth. On his way to the checkout counter, he passed a display case filled with jewelry and stopped to look at a necklace. No, that wouldn't do for Retta—too personal. He should get her gloves or maybe a warm sweater. An older lady peeked around from the back side where she'd been arranging things and asked if she could help him.

But there was something about that necklace that reminded him of Claire. "That one right there with little things on that circle."

"That's sure to be our best seller this year. You can choose the charms you want on the basic necklace. Right now I've got it arranged for Christmas with a candle, a star, and a tiny little tree, but I can put whatever you want on it. For your mother?" she asked.

"No, ma'am. Maybe for a lady I know," he said. "Could I look at the charms?"

She pulled out a box and set it on the counter. "You get three with the necklace, but it will hold a dozen."

He picked out a snowflake, a longhorn symbol, and a tiny open heart. "Could you wrap that up for me?" Maybe if things went from a date to a relationship he would add a charm each year, but right now that said it all.

"Give me five minutes," she answered.

He walked around the counter and found a whole basket full of stuffed animals, and right there on top was a little donkey that looked like Little Bit. He picked it up and noticed a yellow cat right under it. He carried them to the counter and asked the lady if she'd wrap them up also.

"One box or two for them?" she asked.

"Just one will do," he answered, hoping that both gifts reminded Claire and Zaylie of the time they'd spent at the ranch.

*   *   *

Claire looked at several bolts of good quality fabric. The shades of green and golds reminded her of Levi's eyes. Statistics said that truly green eyes were the rarest of all the colors, but his went beyond that. They were sprinkled with gold flecks and had a darker green circle around the outer edge. And his brown lashes were so thick that it should have been a sin to put them on a cowboy, especially on one as masculine and sexy as Levi Jackson.

She added half a yard to each cutting so that she could make the quilted throws extra long like Franny had suggested. She was picking out thread when she saw Levi coming her way. "I'm about done here. One more spool of thread will do it." She motioned toward a full basket. "And that takes care of Mavis's list."

"You are really good," Levi said. "That would have taken me hours, and even then I probably wouldn't have gotten it all right."

"Organization is the key." His compliment warmed Claire's heart. She could get used to having someone in her life who was as kind and sweet as Levi.

"Guess what, Levi?" Zaylie stood on the front of the loaded cart. "Santa Claus is goin' to be right here in the store pretty soon. Can we come and see him?"

"Of course we can. Are you going to sit on his lap this year and not be afraid?" Claire picked out one piece of fabric from the limited supply. If this was all that could be found in the area, then her store might do really well.

"Yep, and I'm goin' to tell him to bring me some boots," Zaylie said seriously.

Levi stooped to her level. "I thought you were going to ask him to bring your daddy home forever."

"That's what I'm askin' Daddy for. Santa can bring me boots. And you can give me the kittens," she said. "Is it time to eat? I'm hungry."

"We've got one more stop, and then we'll eat. After that maybe we'll go to the park for half an hour and let you swing," he said.

She frowned. "Let's just go home and see about my kittens and Little Bit and Hopalong."

Go home.

They'd been at the ranch ten days and she called it home, and yet Claire had been thinking the same thing. That she'd rather go home as go to the park. For that matter she'd just as soon go back to the ranch and spend time alone with Levi even if she had to eat peanut butter sandwiches rather than go to a café.

"Where do we gots to go before we eat?" Zaylie sighed.

"Buddy's shop so he and your aunt Claire can make a deal about the wrecked van. He wants to buy it for parts." Levi straightened up.

"That won't take long, and then we can go home after we finish eating." She meant to say back to the ranch, not home, but once it was out of her mouth, there was no way to recall the words and put them back. Was her subconscious telling her that's the way she really felt about the Longhorn Canyon, or had it just slipped out because Zaylie had said it?

She was still thinking about that when they reached a place with a big sign above a metal building announcing that it was PARRISH AUTO. "I thought we were going to Buddy's shop."

"Buddy Parrish owns it now, but before he inherited the place, it was his dad's place. Ezra Parrish died right before we graduated, and Buddy took over. How do you like that little '67 Mustang over there?" He pointed to a row of vintage cars.

"Cute. I've always liked red cars. But I'm pretty practical—except where Nanny's car is concerned, and that's only because it has sentimental value. When I buy another vehicle it will be a pickup or another van," she said.

"Hey!" Buddy came out of the shop with a smile on his face. "I get to finally meet the beautiful Claire Mason. Buddy Parrish at your service, ma'am." He opened the truck door for her and held out his hand.

Claire put hers in his, but there was no instant vibes or sparks in spite of the brilliant smile. When she was on the ground, he held her hand a moment longer and then brought it to his lips to kiss the knuckles. "What folks have said about you don't begin to do you justice, darlin'."

"Oh really?" She raised an eyebrow.

"Gospel truth, cross my heart." He made the sign over his heart.

Levi rounded the back of the truck and took Zaylie out of the backseat. "We'll take a look at the old cars while you two do business."

Buddy turned his attention to Claire. "Let's go into my office and get out of this cold wind. Can I get you a cup of coffee or a cold soft drink while we talk?"

"No, thanks. We're in a bit of a hurry. Just quote me a price, and I'll sell it to you for the parts. I'll pick up the title when I'm back in Randlett on Sunday and get it to you next week," she said.

He rubbed a hand over his chin and gave her a price. "A thousand dollars is what I've got in mind for the vehicle."

"I really wasn't expecting that much, so thank you," she said.

"I was also thinkin': Will you go out with me this weekend? I know this sweet little bar that plays country music good for dancin'."

"I've got plans for the weekend, and—"

"How about next weekend?" he cut in. "I bet we'd have a real good time, darlin'."

"No, thank you. The truth is that I'm kind of involved with someone else. But I'll bring the title next week and you can pay me then," she said in her best phone voice that she reserved for business.

"Can't blame a guy for tryin'," Buddy said with a smile. "And I do a fair business here. When you get ready to buy something, holler at me; I'll try to find whatever you want."

"Thanks for that," Claire replied.

"Can we go eat now?" Zaylie yelled from halfway down the car lot.

"Cute kid," Buddy said.

"She can also be a handful." Claire rolled her eyes. "See you next week."

"Y'all get it settled?" Levi asked as Claire returned to the truck.

"We did," she answered as Levi finished buckling in Zaylie, then helped her into the truck and shut the door.

The two men said a few more words to each other that she couldn't hear, but Levi was whistling all the way around the back side of the truck.

"Buddy might look like a grease monkey, but he could buy half the state of Texas if he wanted it. I've partied with

him. He was probably givin' you some of his best flirting,"
Levi said as he started the engine.

"Honey, I can smell bullshit pickup lines from a mile
away, and they don't impress me at all," she said.

*But if you kissed my knuckles like he did, my legs would
probably buckle at the knees,* she thought.

Chapter Fourteen

The next day Mavis pulled off her apron in the middle of the afternoon and hung it on a nail. "I know that Levi offered to keep Zaylie for you this afternoon. But I was wondering if you'd let me take her back to the house?"

"Please," Zaylie begged. "Mavis said we could get Benjy and I can see where he goes to school and then we go to her house and have ice cream for a snack and you can get me after that."

"What about Levi? Think he might be disappointed?" Claire asked.

Zaylie drew in a breath and let it out in a whoosh. "Well, you can take him with you, can't you? That way he won't cry. Where are you goin' anyway? Is it for my Christmas?"

"Yes, it is," Claire answered without a moment's hesitation.

Mavis chuckled. "So what do you think, Claire? Maybe you really should take Levi with you so that he doesn't cry."

"What am I going to cry about?" Levi entered the kitchen by the back door.

"I'm going to Mavis's to see Benjy," Zaylie said. "But Aunt Claire's going to take you with her, so don't cry about bein' all lonely."

"I'll do my best not to." Levi grinned. "But it'll be tough. You reckon tomorrow you could go with me to the corral to see Little Bit? Maybe if you'll promise, I won't cry."

Zaylie ran across the floor to him and held up her arms. He picked her up, and she laid her head on his shoulder. "I promise."

For just a split second, Claire wished that she was in Zaylie's place—that she could lay her head on Levi's shoulder, right there in front of Mavis.

"Okay, we'd better get going," Mavis said. "Benjy gets nervous if me or Skip ain't right there waiting when he comes out of the building. We'll talk when you pick her up, Claire. I sure hope that you like the Harris house."

"Me too." Zaylie went straight for her coat when Levi put her down. "Do I get a hinch?"

"No, little girl, you don't." Claire laughed.

"Hint?" Levi whispered as he helped Claire into her coat.

"Yep," Claire said, and then pointed at Zaylie. "And you be nice."

"Yes, ma'am." Zaylie came to attention and saluted.

"Military brat for you," Claire said.

"From princess to general in the blink of an eye." With his hand on the small of her back, he escorted her out to his truck. "Getting to go with you is quite a treat." As usual, he picked her up and set her in the passenger seat.

"Well, I wouldn't want you to cry," she teased.

"I'm going to miss Zaylie so much when she's gone," Levi said as he drove off the ranch.

"Going to miss me when I'm gone?" she asked.

"Oh, honey, that's the day I might really cry," he said.

She didn't know if it was a pickup line or if he was sincere, but she didn't push the issue. Instead she enjoyed it the whole way to the Harris place.

The Harrises were waiting for her in their car. Mr. Harris got out of the driver's seat and waved across the top of the vehicle. He was a middle-aged guy with thinning gray hair and a round face. He opened the back door of the SUV, and an elderly woman's cane preceded her. Once it was firmly on the ground, he slipped a hand under her elbow and assisted her. A tiny lady even shorter than Claire, she had a few streaks of gray in her black hair and dark eyes.

Then to Claire's surprise another person came out of the vehicle, an older version of the first guy. So he must be the son and these were his parents.

"Hello," the lady said as she crossed the lawn. "I'm Delores Harris. This is my husband, Frank, and my son, Joe. You must be Claire. We're glad to meet you."

"It's a pleasure to meet all of you," Claire said.

"We already know that cowboy with you." Frank smiled. "My son, here, was his high school business teacher."

Joe stuck out a hand. "How you doin', Levi?"

"Great and you?" Levi asked.

"Just fine. I'm guessin' y'all already looked at the outside of the place." Joe removed a key from his pocket, unlocked the door, and stood back to let Claire go inside first.

"I understand you're interested in putting a quilting store in here," Joe said.

"That's right." Claire fell in love with the place from the first step she took inside. "I love the nine-foot ceilings. Are all the bedrooms this big?"

"Oh yeah," Joe said. "When they built these old houses they didn't scrimp on size because the furniture in those days was so big. I'm going to go sit on the porch with Mom and Dad and let y'all look without us interrupting you. If you like it, we'll talk business."

"It's perfect," Claire said to Levi a few minutes later. "I can see racks for my fabric lining the walls in this room, maybe a cutting table right there." She pointed to one side and whipped around. "And a desk right here instead of a checkout counter to keep it homey."

She wandered back through the wide hallway. "And a new quilting machine would go in this room. And my sewing machine in this one with my quilting rack suspended from the ceiling."

"Why would you need both?" Levi asked.

"One is to quilt by machine. The other is to keep the quilt tight so I can do it by hand. And my bedroom can be in this room." She grabbed his hand. "Let's go look at the kitchen."

"It's plenty big enough for a dozen women to gather around for a quilting lesson. Oh, Levi." She slung her arms around his neck and hugged him tightly. "I want it."

He tipped up her chin and she tiptoed. "Shall we celebrate with a kiss?"

"Yes," she whispered.

The kiss started out soft and sweet, but it soon developed heat. Claire leaned into him, feeling the hardness of his chest and body against hers. One of his arms wrapped around her, pulling her tighter into his embrace. His other hand moved from her chin to her cheek with his thumb making lazy circles on the tender spot right under her ear. When it ended they were both panting, and she was holding his hand against her cheek.

"I'm surprised we didn't burn down the house with that kiss," she whispered.

"What kind of celebration are we going to have when the deal is sealed and signed?" he asked hoarsely.

"Whew!" She shook her head.

"Amen!" he declared.

"We'd better get out of here." She slipped her hand in his.

"Reckon it's the house that caused such heat between us?" he asked.

She stopped in the middle of the living room. "If it is, maybe I'd do better to turn it into a dating service."

He laughed out loud. "I'll be your first client, but only if I can date the boss."

Claire started to say something, but Joe popped his head in the door. "Mom and Dad got cold, and it's not a bit warmer inside, so I put them back in the car. You reckon you could meet us at Dairy Queen in Bowie to talk?"

"No problem. We were just on our way out," Claire said.

"Great. See you there."

*   *   *

"Are you going to haggle with them or give them their asking price?" Levi asked as they drove south.

"We'll see what they've got in mind, but Levi, I really, really like that house and the location," she answered.

So do I, he thought. *You'll be within five miles of the ranch, and I can see you every day.*

"But Sunset is such a tiny place, less than four hundred people," he said.

"It's close to Bowie and only a little way from Nocona, and there's no quilting shops in between either of those places. I'm not lookin' to make a million bucks. I'm just wanting to expand my business outside of Etsy," she said. "And Mavis assures me that there are several quilting bees held in this area. I'm hoping to draw those ladies into my business."

When they arrived at the Dairy Queen less than ten minutes later, the Harrises were already seated at a table in a back corner.

"I'll be glad to wait outside. I promise I won't cry," he said once they were inside. "This is your business."

"Come with me," she answered. "And kick me under the table if I start to make a big mistake."

"Not you, darlin'. You got your head on so straight that you'll get it right," he told her.

"Thanks for the vote of confidence." She marched straight to the table and seated herself. "I don't like haggling, so here's what I'm willing to give." She quoted them a price.

Levi hadn't thought for a minute that Claire couldn't do business, but he hadn't expected she'd wade right into a negotiation like that. No sweet talkin' about the weather or hum-hawing that the house did need a coat of paint and a little cosmetic help on the inside.

Joe looked at his parents.

"That's less than what we had in mind," Delores said.

"I'm paying in cash. That means you don't have to have inspections done to meet a bank's standards, and since it's a cash deal the closing costs will be minimal," Claire said.

Frank ran a hand over his chin. "Inspections are expensive."

Joe must've been figuring in his head because he gave his parents a nod. "When you figure in all that and the closing costs, I believe we'll come out even."

Claire pulled out her checkbook. "So we've got a deal?"

"I believe we do," Delores said.

"Will a twenty percent down payment hold it in escrow until we see a lawyer? And do you have one who can work this out for us?" Claire held her pen above the check.

"Yes, we do, and twenty percent is fine. Just meet us a week from next Monday here in Bowie at Langston's Law Firm, and we'll do the deal then," she said. "We'd do it earlier, but me and Frank has got a whole round of doctor visits between now and then. Joe is going to give you the keys right now, so you can start measuring and getting things settled about how you want to fix things."

"Oh my," Claire gasped. "That's awfully generous, but…"

Joe slid a set of keys across the table.

Claire didn't touch them. "Are you sure about this?"

"Honey, I've known Mavis and the Maguires my whole life," Delores said. "You ain't got no better folks to vouch for you. If they trust you, so do I; now let's have some of those Blizzard things to celebrate. I'm right partial to the one with chocolate cookies in it, but Joe here likes the sea salt and caramel."

Claire made out the check, handed it to Delores, and then put the new key, along with her checkbook, back in her purse. Levi was both excited for her and yet worried at the same time. If she could pay cash for that house and still have enough left to start a business—well, to say the least, she sure enough was out of his league.

Chapter Fifteen

Claire went through the next day and Friday in a bit of a daze. One minute she'd wonder if she'd really made a deal to buy a house. The next she'd want to go look at it again and rethink about where she'd put things. She wanted a homey look to her store, not a formal one. The customers should be able to talk patterns and visit about colors, not feel like they were no more than a sale.

She looked down at the intricate pieces of the design that she'd created when they were stuck in the cabin, and thought seriously about making it a nice long throw size for Levi's Christmas. But did it look too girly for a big, rough cowboy? She was trying to make up her mind when Zaylie tugged on her shirttail that Friday evening.

"Aunt Claire, can we make Angela and Teresa one of them little quilts for Christmas?" Zaylie tugged on her hand.

"What a wonderful idea," Claire answered.

"Look at that moon." Zaylie pointed to the sky outside. "What happened to the other half?"

"We just can't see it right now."

"Can you make a quilt like that?" Zaylie asked.

"Don't know, but I bet we could come up with a pattern if we tried," Claire answered.

That moon is like life, the pesky voice in her head whispered. *You can see what lies behind in the past, but the future is hidden.*

"Okay, can we go see Little Bit?" Zaylie sighed. "I think he needs me to come and see him."

"Right now?" Claire asked.

Zaylie nodded. "He's lonesome."

"Okay but just for a few minutes."

"I love watching the stars pop out," Zaylie said with a sigh as they walked to the corral. "I wish Teresa could see Little Bit and Hopalong and Gussie and the kittens."

Claire tucked Zaylie's hand into hers. "Let's take pictures of you and the animals and you can send them to Teresa, and y'all can talk about them when you call her tonight."

"Yay!" Zaylie squealed. "And maybe she can come see them someday."

They'd gone about halfway across the pasture when Claire heard a truck speeding from around the back side of the barn. A second later she saw the headlights and recognized Levi's silhouette as he jumped from the driver's side, left the door hanging wide open, and raced around to the back. He threw the tailgate down and hefted what looked like a black calf onto his shoulders and carried it inside.

"What's he got?" Zaylie tugged at her hand, urging her to pick up her step.

"I'm not sure," Claire said.

"Run, Aunt Claire. It might be another little donkey."

Claire jogged along beside Zaylie across the pasture. She

stopped long enough to turn off the headlights and slam the door shut as she passed the truck. Zaylie ran on ahead, yelling at Levi.

"Where are you? Do you gots a new donkey?"

"What's going on?" Claire raised her voice.

He hollered back, "Thank God y'all are here. Go to the tack room, Claire, and bring towels and a blanket."

"Where's the tack room and do I need to keep Zaylie away?" She raised her voice.

"No, send her this way. I'm in the stall where we keep Little Bit when it's cold." His tone was desperate, so she ran down the long hallway. "Tack room is second door on your right."

She slung it open and gathered up three horse blankets, the fluffy throw on the back of the sofa, and a stack of towels from the cabinet beneath the sink.

"Are you hurt?" she called out as she crossed the huge center of the barn.

"No, I'm fine. I'm in the first stall on your left," he answered.

She dropped everything in her arms when she saw the black, newborn calf lying on the straw floor. "What can I do? Is it dead?"

"Grab a towel and start rubbing her down. She's still alive, but she's almost frozen. It's unusual to get a calf this late in the year. We've got to get the circulation going and get her on her feet." He tossed a towel to Zaylie and one to Claire.

"Where?" Zaylie asked.

"Anywhere," Levi answered.

Claire started at the middle of the calf's back and worked toward the tail. Zaylie cradled the animal's head in her lap and rubbed its ears and head. Levi worked on its legs and belly section.

"Jesus loves you, this I know." Zaylie sang through the children's hymn several times before she finally leaned forward and yelled at the calf. "Open your eyes and get up on your feet. If you don't Santa Claus ain't goin' to bring you a damn thing."

"Zaylie Noelle!" Claire scolded.

"Well, he ain't," Zaylie said.

The calf opened her eyes and shivered.

"Don't scold her. Whatever she's tellin' her is workin'," Levi said.

Zaylie started rubbing again. "You're sweet as 'ennessee whiskey and warm as a cup of 'trawberry wine." She grabbed the calf by the ears and looked right into its eyes. "You're goin' to do what I tell you to do."

"Little bossy, aren't you?" Claire was suddenly reminded of the Christmas story about Jesus being born in a barn with animals all around. She cocked her head to one side and imagined Levi as a shepherd standing beside the baby in a manger. "Maybe in another life," she said softly.

"Another life?" Levi asked.

"I was thinking out loud," Claire said.

Zaylie popped her hands on her hips. "Daddy says I get bossy from you."

Levi chuckled.

Zaylie turned toward him. "This baby cow can't do nothin' if we don't tell her." Then she whipped around toward the calf. "Get up! Right now!"

The calf rolled its big brown eyes and quivered from head to toe.

Zaylie tossed the towel aside and covered the calf with all three horse blankets, then laid the throw over the top of those. Then she crawled under the blankets, curled up against its back and wrapped her arms around it. "When

I get cold, Daddy wraps his arms around me to get me warm."

Levi stuck his hand under the blankets and smiled. "She's got a steady heartbeat. She'll get up in a little while. I'll make her a bottle of special milk. She'll need to be fed about every two hours all night. Looks like I'll be sleeping in the barn."

"Me too," Zaylie said. "She needs me. She ain't got a mama, and she might want me to sing to her."

Zaylie would fret all night if Claire made her leave, which meant she would be staying in the barn too. And that didn't sound nearly as ridiculous as it would have a month ago.

Levi whispered, "Let her stay, please. When she goes to sleep, I'll carry her to the bunkhouse for you."

"And leave that precious calf all alone? If Zaylie woke up in her bed she'd throw a fit. We'll all stay until you are sure it'll be okay." Claire settled into the corner of the stall. She'd never been that close to a newborn calf before, and there was something adventurous, downright exciting to think of spending a whole night with Levi.

"What's its name?" Zaylie asked.

"That's up to you. You're the one who's a calf whisperer," Levi said as he headed toward the tack room. "Be back in a few minutes."

Claire peeked through the rails and watched him. He damn sure wasn't one of those wannabe cowboys that she'd run into—the kind who probably spent hours in the gym to get their muscles and had never gotten dirty and sweaty working on a ranch in their lives. No, sir! Levi was the real thing. Those biceps came from lifting hay bales and putting up fence, from carrying heavy loads of feed—not from pumping iron.

"What's a whisperer?" Zaylie asked.

"That's someone who can talk to a baby calf and the animal knows what you are sayin'," Claire explained. Levi was more than just a calf whisperer. He was the total package when it came to caring for animals. Anyone who could rescue a turtle and a wild cottontail rabbit, well, that man had a heart of gold.

"Why wouldn't it know? It's got ears, don't it?" Zaylie asked. "Whoa! It's standin' up."

"Man, alive!" Levi exclaimed from the gate. "Zaylie, you've sure got a way with animals. You should be a rancher when you grow up."

"Nope, I'm goin' to be a movie star," Zaylie said. "Can I feed it that bottle?"

Levi groaned. "How about an animal doctor?"

Zaylie shook her head and reached for the bottle. "Are you goin' to put on your 'jamas, Levi?"

"Nope." He sat down beside Claire in the corner.

"Then I don't need mine." Zaylie touched the calf's nose with the nipple, and she turned her head away. "It ain't hungry."

"She has to eat," Levi said.

"It's a girl?" Zaylie asked.

"Yes, ma'am."

Zaylie stuck her finger inside the calf's mouth. When it started sucking, she put the bottle in its mouth and removed her finger.

"I tell you, she's a natural," Levi said. "I'd give your brother a job on the ranch just to get to keep her here."

"You're funny, Levi." Zaylie giggled.

"How's that?" he asked.

"My daddy is a soldier. He knows about missions and ployments, but he don't know about animals. Look, she's likin' this stuff. Her tail is waggin'."

Claire checked the time on her phone. Eight thirty and getting close to Zaylie's bedtime.

Levi stood up and extended a hand to Claire. "Let's move over into the next stall. I'll get a couple more blankets from the tack room."

"She won't go to sleep for a while," Claire said.

"We'll have things ready for when she does."

"I'll stay right here with Nomie," Zaylie said. "She wants me to sing to her some more."

"Nomie?" Levi raised an eyebrow.

"Nomie is in the Bible just like Moses. So that's her name."

"Naomi," Claire translated.

"Sounds like a right fine name to me," Levi said, and grinned.

The calf settled back down and laid its head in Zaylie's lap. "There we go. Hopalong might come see about you, but Gussie don't like cows so she won't be here."

Levi spread out three blankets in the next stall, creating a king-size bed. "When she falls asleep, I'll bring her over here to you and then I'll take Zaylie's place. I didn't think there was a chance of saving that baby calf, but I've got hope now."

"What happened to the mama? Did she die?" Claire sat down with her back against the solid barn wall.

"Don't know. I couldn't find her, but I imagine that it's her first and she rejected it. It happens sometimes. We keep good records, but somehow one of the young heifers must've gotten bred without us knowing. This is absolutely the wrong time of year for a cow to throw a calf. If Beau hadn't thrown a fit for me to follow him I wouldn't have found her, and she'd have frozen to death in another hour." He eased down next to Claire. "Are you warm enough? Want my coat?"

"I'm just fine," she answered. "If we ever get Zaylie out of that stall and over here, we might need another blanket to cover her with."

Nomie took right to the bottle at ten thirty, and not long after that Zaylie fell asleep curled up behind the calf. Levi eased her away and slipped a rolled-up blanket in her place and then carried the child over to the next stall. Claire pulled her close to her body and covered both of them with a blanket.

"Might as well sleep a couple of hours, and then I'll see if the new baby needs another bottle," Levi whispered.

"How long do you keep this up?" Claire asked.

"Just tonight. Tomorrow she'll get fed three times, and then we'll step it back to twice a day after that. She just needs a good start," he answered as he started to make his way back to the other stall.

She hesitated for a second and then said, "No sense in you gettin' awake every time Nomie wiggles. This is one giant bed. Catch a couple of hours right here."

"Thank you." He kicked off his boots and curled up on the far side of the blanket with his face toward the other stall.

Had someone told her six months ago that she'd be sleeping in a barn with a cowboy, she would have wondered what they'd been smoking or drinking.

In seconds his steady breath said that he was asleep, but Claire kept analyzing everything that had happened since she wrecked the van. Franny said one time that fate was a bitch on steroids, and right then, with a sleeping child in her arms and a sexy cowboy not three feet from her, she understood exactly what that meant.

Sometime in the middle of the night, after the two-o'clock feeding, Claire flipped over to the other side and snuggled up to Levi's back. Zaylie did the same thing, and when Levi stirred a couple of hours later, they were all three spooned up together sharing a single cover.

Levi slipped his hand through the railing and checked the sleeping calf. "She's good. I'm waiting until six for the next bottle. Are you warm enough?"

"Oh yeah," she answered.

Warmth was not a problem at all, not when she was right up against Levi's back.

Chapter Sixteen

Claire reached for Levi, but all she got was a hand full of blanket. Her eyes popped open to see him leading the calf out of the stall toward the door. She sat up and wiped the sleep from her eyes. Levi returned without the calf and eased down beside her. "Don't know what happened with that calf, but her mama came to claim her. She's in the corral right now, and Nomie is having breakfast."

"Does that happen often?" Claire asked.

"Never seen it before. When they reject them, we have to raise them on the bottle," he answered.

Zaylie sat up and yawned. "Where's Nomie?"

"Her mama came back to get her."

"Okay." Zaylie raised her arms and stretched. "But can we still go see her sometimes?"

"Of course you can," Levi assured her. "Nomie will be in the corral for several days or maybe longer. She and Little Bit will probably become good friends, and you can come and see both of them."

Zaylie kicked back the blanket. "I'm hungry, Aunt Claire. I want biscuits and gravy this mornin'."

"Oh, you do?" Claire raised an eyebrow.

"Please, Aunt Claire." Zaylie sighed. "Can we have biscuits and gravy? I'll help you make it."

Levi nudged her shoulder. "I'd be willin' to help too. But first I need a cup of good strong black coffee. How about you?"

"Yes." Claire got to her feet. "You goin' to drive us home?"

"For biscuits and gravy, I'll drive you anywhere you want to go, darlin'," he answered.

"Yay!" Zaylie was on her feet and running toward the barn doors. "And can we have banana muffins too?"

"Don't push your luck, young lady," Claire called after her.

"She's an amazing kid." Levi laid a hand on Claire's shoulder. "You and your brother have done a good job with her. Someday I want to have a whole house full of sassy little girls just like her."

"No sons?" Claire asked.

"Maybe half a dozen of each." He grinned.

"You better get a wife who don't mind bein' pregnant for about fifteen or twenty years," she said.

He opened the truck door for her. "Maybe we'll get lucky and have two at a time."

A cold shiver shot down her spine as she thought of someone as short as she was carrying twins. Lord, she'd look like she'd swallowed an elephant. She'd always been jealous of Grant for having a daughter and thought she'd like to have one of her own someday, but a dozen kids? She didn't know if she was up for that.

"Why would you want such a big family?" she asked when he was behind the wheel.

"I was an only child. Justin and Cade are like brothers,

but..." He paused. "We would have all been better off if we'd had a sister in the mix."

"How's that?" Claire pressed on.

"From guys who have sisters, I understand they can be a real pain in the butt, but in my opinion they teach a brother a lot," Levi said.

"And what if all you ever get is sons?" she asked.

"Then I'll be happy with them and beg Grant to let me borrow Zaylie once in a while to keep them in line." He parked outside the yard and hurried around to help her and Zaylie out of the truck.

That means he's plannin' on bein' in your life for a while. Franny's voice was clear in her head.

The smile that was so big it almost hurt her face said that she sure didn't mind that idea. Zaylie entered the house first, and Claire almost tripped over her when she went inside. Instead of hurrying over to the counter, she'd stopped at the doorway from the utility room into the kitchen and planted herself right there. Arms over her chest and head tilted to one side, she stared at the strange woman who was busy making breakfast.

"Well, hello, Levi." Allison looked up from the stove, and her eyes traveled from his boots to his hair. "Looks like you spent the night in the barn."

Justin's pearl snap shirt came almost to her knees. Her toenails were painted bright red, and her dark hair was pulled up in a messy bun on top of her head. "Y'all hungry? I made biscuits and gravy. Coffee is in the pot."

"Who is that, Aunt Claire?" Zaylie whispered loudly.

"I'm sorry," Levi apologized. "This is Allison Walker. Allison, this is Zaylie and her aunt Claire, who are helping us out until after Christmas."

Zaylie walked right up to her and stuck out her hand. "I'm almost five. How old are you?"

"More than five." Allison laughed. "Justin is in the shower. He'll be out in a few minutes, but I can put the food on the bar and everyone can eat when they're ready."

Claire stepped around Zaylie. "Pleased to meet you, Allison."

There was no doubt about what bed the woman had slept in the night before, not when she was wearing Justin's shirt. Or maybe that was using the term *sleeping* too loosely. A crazy surge of something akin to jealousy shot through Claire's body. Is this the lifestyle that Levi was used to? How many women had made him breakfast after a night in his bed? Had Allison been there? Had she worn his shirt when she cooked breakfast for him?

"Likewise." Allison nodded as she shook her hand. "Buddy was moanin' at the bar last night about how you turned him down." She reached out and plucked a piece of hay from Claire's hair. "Guess y'all all stayed in the barn last night?"

"Yep, we did," Zaylie said. "Nomie needed us to feed her all night long, but this mornin' she went back with her mama."

"Nomie?" Allison's eyes went back to Levi.

"A newborn calf that got separated from her mother. Zaylie named her Nomie," Levi explained.

"Moses is in the Bible and so is Nomie," Zaylie informed her as she got into her chair at the table. "Orange juice, please, and two biscuits with gravy on them."

"We have a bull named Moses," Levi explained. "So she named the new calf Naomi after someone in the Bible."

Allison bumped her hip against his. "Are you gettin' religious on me, Levi?"

"One never knows." Levi slipped an arm around Claire's shoulders.

"Good mornin', folks." Justin stopped in the doorway, and Claire swore that she could see a little bit of a blush on the big cowboy. Water droplets still hung on his brown hair, and his blue eyes scanned the room, taking in everyone and settling on Zaylie.

Before he could say anything else, the sound of the front door opening was followed by Benjy yelling for Levi. "Where are y'all?"

Mavis stopped as abruptly as Zaylie had, inhaled, and then let it out in a snort. "Justin Maguire, there's a little girl in the house."

"No, she's a big girl," Zaylie said. "She just looks like a little girl because she's short like Aunt Claire." She turned and frowned at Allison. "You've got on Justin's shirt. Why would you wear his shirt? Did you spill milk on yours?"

"Yes, I did." Two dots of high color turned Allison's cheeks crimson. "Breakfast is on the bar for anyone who wants to eat. I should be going now; let me get my things. Justin, walk me out to my car?"

"Sure thing." Justin looked eager to get away from the awkward situation.

"Y'all want to join us? Looks like there's plenty," Levi asked Mavis and Benjy.

"I do." Skip came through the back door. "We had pancakes and they were good, but man, this looks great. Good job, Claire."

"Aunt Claire didn't cook," Zaylie said.

"Justin's friend Allison did the cookin'." Claire was sure glad that she wasn't dressed in a man's shirt that barely reached her knees that morning. The way Mavis glared at Allison, it was a wonder that she wasn't anything but a greasy spot on the floor.

"Ohhh." Skip's eyes were suddenly as round as saucers,

and he turned toward Mavis. "Don't let it get your blood pressure up, darlin'. Boys been bein' boys since time began."

"But not with a little girl in the house," Mavis snorted.

Levi filled a plate with food and carried it to the table. "Benjy, you hungry?"

"I ate, but breakfast is the most important meal of the day, and it doesn't hurt to have two breakfasts so I'll eat again. Oranges are high in vitamin C, and that's good for the body. It protects against colds."

"Does all them freckles on your face make you smart?" Zaylie asked.

"I don't know. I'll have to read about freckles to find out. Did you really sleep in the barn with a new calf? Was it cold?" Benjy asked.

"We had a blanket to keep us from bein' cold," Zaylie said as she picked up her fork and began to eat.

Justin slipped back into the room and loaded a plate with food. "Well, that was embarrassing. I thought she was leavin'. Had no idea she was going to make breakfast. But Mavis, this isn't the first time..."

Mavis threw up a palm. "Things is different now. There's a little girl in the house who'll be askin' questions, and Benjy is here on Saturday mornin'. If you must bring home women, then do it on Saturday night and kick them out before breakfast on Sunday morning."

"Yes, ma'am," Justin said, and then picked up a plate.

"Are y'all talkin' big people stuff?" Zaylie frowned.

"Yep, we are," Justin answered. "So why did y'all sleep in the barn last night? Were you campin' out?"

"Nope," Zaylie answered. "We was savin' Nomie."

Levi told the story again of the poor little calf that had gotten separated from her mother. Claire watched his face as he talked. It lit up when he talked about how Zaylie was a calf whisperer. He really would make a good father to the dozen kids that he talked about.

"This is good breakfast," Zaylie declared. "Allison can come back and cook for us again when we sleep with Levi in the barn."

Justin's laughter echoed off the walls. "You goin' to yell at Levi, Mavis?" He wiped at his eyes with a napkin.

Claire bit the inside of her lip to keep from giggling. It was a double standard all right. She'd spent the night with Levi out in the barn, and no one was throwing a fit about that. But Justin bringing a woman home after the bar closed down was evidently a major sin.

"They were sleeping," Mavis said.

"Not all the time," Zaylie piped up. "We was feedin' Nomie when she was hungry."

"Okay, enough about last night," Claire said. "Let's talk about Retta and Cade coming home on Monday."

Claire let the conversation float around her as she drifted off to her own thoughts. If she inhaled deeply she could still get a whiff of the hay in the stall, and by shutting her eyes she could pretend that she was back there, curled up against Levi's broad back. To anyone else, it might seem like a strange night, but to her it had been a night in paradise.

Chapter Seventeen

Zaylie stomped her foot and crossed her arms over her chest. "Benjy gets to go to the barn, and he's not a big person."

"Benjy is going to work, not to play." Claire picked two pieces of straw from Zaylie's tangled hair. "Besides, I'm sure your kittens are wondering where you are. They haven't seen you since before supper yesterday."

The arms slowly uncrossed and she smiled. "I need to tell them all about Nomie. We need to go to the bunkhouse so I can see them."

"Maybe for an hour but then we should come back and help Miz Mavis and then get dinner ready," Claire said.

"Take all the time you need," Mavis said. "I'll put on a pot of beef stew for them. If you're back thirty minutes before time to eat to make a pan of cornbread, we'll be good. I bet both of you would like a nice long shower, or a bath after sleeping with the cows last night."

Claire draped an arm around Mavis's shoulders and gave her a sideways hug. "Thank you so much."

"I understand that deal you're workin' on is going to be finalized a week from Monday. You might as well stick around here until after that. You're welcome, and I can use the help for the ranch party. Besides, it'd be easier to be right here to run in and take a look at things as you change your mind about how you're goin' to do things," Mavis said.

Claire finished getting Zaylie's jacket on her and reached for hers. "Mavis, are you playin' matchmaker between me and Levi?"

Mavis tucked her chin down to her chest. "Looks like somebody needs to do something. I can see you're attracted to each other, and I like you, Claire. Don't sit on your hands and let him get away. He's a good man, but he's never been in a real serious relationship, so he might not know how to go about this courtin' business."

"What makes you even think we are anything other than friends?" Claire put on her jacket and laid a hand on Zaylie's shoulder to point her toward the front door.

"He's happy, and I've meddled enough. But I'd like for you to stay now that"—she nodded toward Zaylie and winked—"the deal is solid."

"Are y'all talkin' about my Christmas again?" Zaylie asked.

"Yes," they said in unison.

"You will be close by after the holidays anyway. Might as well just stick around and help me through then," Mavis said.

Zaylie ran on ahead of her as usual, giving Claire time to analyze what Mavis had told her. There was definitely chemistry between her and Levi—like nothing that she'd ever experienced before.

Zaylie hurried inside the bunkhouse, threw her jacket toward the sofa, and dropped down on her knees in front of the basket of kittens. "Did you miss me? I was helpin' Nomie." She went into a long narration about the new calf.

"I'm going to take a bath, sweetie." Claire's tone sounded strange in her own ears. "You stay right here until I get done, and then you can have one."

"'Kay." Zaylie nodded as she took all the kittens from the basket. "Where is Gussie?"

As if she knew her name, the cat pranced out of Claire's bedroom and went straight to the door and meowed. Claire opened it, and she darted outside.

"I'll take care of the babies," Zaylie said. "Levi says I'm good at ranchin'."

"You are good at everything you do," Claire agreed as she kicked off her shoes and undressed on the way to the bathroom.

When the tub was half full she added bath salts and then sank down into the warm water with a long sigh. She slid down on the sloped back and went over the last couple of days in her mind. Was Levi really the one?

She was jerked back to reality when her phone rang. "Zaylie, can you get that?"

"It's Daddy!" Zaylie squealed.

Claire quickly washed her hair, rinsed it, and pulled the plug on the tub. She wrapped herself in a big fluffy white robe and twisted a towel around her head. When she made it to the living room, Zaylie was holding up each kitten to show her dad. "I want all three of them for my Christmas present, Daddy. That's what I asked Levi to give me."

"Oh really?" Grant chuckled. "It's official, baby girl. I get to come home for Christmas and your birthday. You've told me what you want for Christmas, but I haven't heard a word about your birthday present."

"I want a mommy of my very own like Teresa has," Zaylie answered without a moment's hesitation.

"I don't think they sell mommies at the base store," he teased.

"Well, then go to the mommy store and get me one," Zaylie told him.

"I'll see what I can do, but what's your next idea just in case?"

"I'll take a ranch. Levi says I'll make a good rancher, but I need a ranch," she said.

"That might be harder to get than a mommy," Grant said. "Hey, do I see Claire back there with a towel on her head?"

"Yep, you do. Talk to her now, Daddy. Grumpy is cryin', and I need to tell him a story." Zaylie handed the phone off to Claire.

"Take it off video and speaker," he said.

"You don't like to see me wearing my towel turban?" she joked.

"That's part of it," he answered.

She hit a button and put the phone to her ear. "Okay, shoot. What's goin' on?"

"Angela and I are both so eager to start a life together, and with Zaylie asking for a mommy for her birthday, it seems like an omen." Grant's voice was more upbeat than it had been in years. "Things might be moving faster than we thought with this and with me coming home, but I don't want to jinx it too much. How's your new project going?"

"I'm signing the deal a week from Monday," she said. "And Mavis has asked me to stay another week."

"Pretty soon you're going to week-at-a-time it until you

just move in on that ranch for good." Grant laughed. "Got to go, but know I love and support you."

"Good-bye, and thanks," she said.

There was no doubt in Claire's mind that Angela would make a wonderful mother to Zaylie, but Claire felt that she was somehow still getting the short end of the stick.

Chapter Eighteen

You sick, son?" Skip asked at Sunday dinner.

"No, just not hungry. I hate to eat and run, but I need to check on the calf."

Skip raised his eyebrows. "Really? That calf seemed fine to me."

Levi sighed. "I reckon I just need some thinkin' time." He pushed back his chair.

"About a new calf or about a girl?" Skip asked.

"There is a fifty percent chance that a calf will be born a girl and the same for it to be a boy, just like human babies," Benjy said.

"You got that right, Benjy," Levi said. "And maybe both, Skip." He bent and gave Mavis a quick hug. "Thanks for a great dinner."

Levi waved one more time over his shoulder as he left and almost made it to his truck when Skip caught up with him. The north wind blew so hard they had to hold their cowboy hats down, or they would have ended up in the Gulf of Mexico.

"Get inside the truck," Skip yelled over the noise.

Skip asked, "Okay, kid, 'fess up. What's eatin' on you? You've never turned down dessert, especially when it was cobbler. So spit it out."

"Claire." He answered with one word.

"Go on." Skip removed his hat and held it on his knees.

"Kind of hard to explain. I asked her to the ranch party and she said yes, and we seemed to be gettin' along real well. But today she didn't want me to go to Randlett with her after church. She said she had to get some stuff for her quilts and asked if she could drive the work truck. I told her I'd go help, but she said she needed to get away and think about things," Levi told him.

Skip chuckled. "You're fallin' for that woman, son, and you want to spend time with her, but you can't smother her. From what your mother says, she's an independent woman, and she's got to have her own space."

"Kind of like that butterfly sayin' about not cagin' it up?" Levi asked. "I feel kind of stupid. I'm looking at thirty and acting like a lovesick teenager."

"Most of us have walked in your boots, son, and age don't have jack squat to do with it." Skip laid a hand on Levi's shoulder and squeezed.

"How do you know when it's the right one?" Levi asked.

"I don't know about all men, but I can tell you that when I met Mavis, my heart started skippin' around in my chest, and when I had to be away from her it was heavy like a stone. You don't always get to throw down a quilt in a clover field and hold hands and look into each other's eyes and fall in love. Where's the fun in that? You got to run the obstacle course like all of us did. That what comes easy ain't worth havin', and it won't last. You fight for something, and then you'll cherish it and hang on to it." He settled his hat back on his head and got out of the truck. "Good luck."

"Thanks, Skip." Levi started up the engine and headed toward the ranch.

When he arrived at the corral, Nomie was romping around with Little Bit. It was probably time to turn her and her mother back out into the pasture, but he hated to take the calf away from the donkey. He leaned on the railing and let his mind go back to what Levi had said about talking to Claire.

He usually turned to walking or working when he had something to mull over in his mind. That day he started walking with Beau at his heels. The wind had died down, but there was enough of a breeze to blow dead leaves across his feet. He kicked at them with the toe of his boot and drew his work coat tighter around his broad chest.

"Let's go home, old boy. We got us some thinkin' to do of our own. And the first thing we'd better be learning is how not to smother someone with too much attention. I should have known that from all the strays I've brought in. You've got to let them come to you—not rush them."

*   *   *

Claire made a cup of tea and curled up on the end of the sofa after she'd loaded the boxes of quilts that had sold on Etsy this week into the bed of the truck. She planned to ship them out tomorrow. Thank goodness, she still had plenty of stock, but she knew she needed to create many more with the new venture she was about to begin. She walked through her grandmother's house, making decisions about what she should take with her and what she should leave behind for Angela and Grant.

Her mind was racing with what-ifs. What if she went through with the deal, got everything in her shop up and running, and then things did not work out with Levi? What if Mavis thought Claire had done Levi wrong and ended their friendship? What if it ruined her business?

She shook her head to shake all the negative thoughts away. *Good glory, girl! It's not like he proposed to you. He asked you for a date, and you were already looking at that house before you had a wreck.*

"Anybody home?" Franny called out as she pushed her way into the living room. "I brought brownies and thumb print cookies. You got the coffeepot on? Don't answer that. I can smell it and I'll pour my own." She set the plate on the coffee table, went to the kitchen, and returned with a steaming mug in her hand. "Where is Zaylie?"

"In her room talking to Teresa on the phone." Claire reached for a brownie. "She'll be out soon. She can smell your brownies a mile away. Have a seat."

"Did you buy that old truck out there in the driveway?" Franny chose a rocking chair close to the end of the sofa where Claire was sitting.

"No, it's on loan from the ranch until I can decide what I want to buy, or if I want to drive Nanny's car," she answered.

"Honey, that old car eats gasoline worse than a young calf goin' after fresh green grass. It'll be fun to have, and to drive around town once in a while, but to drive it all the time would break you. Get something a little more economical," Franny said. "But that's not what's got your forehead in a frown today, is it?"

Claire slowly shook her head. "Not really. Franny, how long were you married?"

"Sixty years when my Joe died. Your Nanny and Poppa

weren't married quite that long, but we had good marriages," she answered.

"How'd you know that Joe was the one you wanted to share your life with?"

Franny leaned back in the rocking chair, and the expression on her face said that she'd left the present time and traveled back more than sixty years.

"It was a hot July day, the last Sunday in the month. He'd come to a church picnic with his cousin, and I took one look at that long, tall cowboy and decided I would marry him if I had to chase him all the way to the moon. Didn't have to do that because he said he felt the same way when he saw me across the lawn. I was seventeen that summer, and he was twenty. Mama hated him. Daddy threatened to shoot him." Franny smiled.

"Why?"

"Oh honey, that boy had a reputation with the women, and he didn't have jack squat. He'd worked on a ranch from the time he was fifteen, didn't finish school, and my folks said there wasn't no way I was going to even sit on the porch after church on Sunday and talk to him," Franny answered.

"But you did?"

"Oh no, we did not! We met in town behind the school on Sunday afternoons. Mama planned on me goin' to college and bein' a schoolteacher, but that was her dream, not mine..." She sipped her coffee before going on.

"The ranch owner offered him a job as foreman about that time and said if he'd sign on for five years he'd give him five acres and a little house. And when I say little, I mean it was one room," Franny said.

Claire immediately thought of the cabin. Could she live with Levi in that small space? Yes, her heart said before she could blink.

"So he proposed and we eloped. Daddy was so mad that he wouldn't even let me come home for a month, but hell, honey, we was in love so that month went fast," Franny said. "Mama finally drove out to see me and brought me a carload of my clothes and stuff, and we both cried because I wasn't goin' to be a teacher. Before she and Daddy both passed on they told me that they'd been wrong about Joe. Only regret I ever had after we married was not adoptin' a kid or two after we found out we couldn't have any of our own."

"How long did you date?" Claire asked.

"Two weeks." Franny giggled.

Claire gasped. It had been a little more than two weeks since she'd met Levi, and she was twenty-eight, not seventeen, but she couldn't fathom eloping with him tomorrow.

Not even if you could spend every night with him in that little cabin? the annoying voice inside her head asked. *Think of sharing one of those bunk beds with him.*

Or maybe replacing those with a nice big king-size bed. She felt the blush rising to her cheeks at the thought.

"And I ain't never looked back and wished I'd done something different with my life. Me and Joe added to that little parcel of land every year, and when he died we had three hundred acres. We'd built us another house, but on our anniversaries we still went back to our first house for a night or two." She finished off her coffee and set the mug on the coffee table. "Now let's talk about you."

She told Franny about all the doubts. "He's a good man, and he loves animals and kids. You should see him with Benjy and Zaylie."

"That's all good and fine, but what happens when he kisses you?" Franny asked.

"My knees go weak, and I don't want it to ever end," Claire said honestly.

"Then honey, that's worth givin' a chance. Has any other man ever made you all breathless like that?"

Claire shook her head. "No, ma'am."

"Then what are you waiting for?"

Claire sighed. "You know what kind of parents Grant and I came from. What happens if Levi and I get into a relationship, and I figure out I'm like my mother. That I'm more interested in my quilting business than I am in Levi, or being a wife and mother."

"The fact that you are worried about that says you're not a bit like your mother," Franny told her.

"How's that?"

"Think about it. Put your mom in your shoes. Would she be wastin' time thinkin' about whether she'd break a man's heart?" Franny scolded. "A relationship and a marriage is a partnership. You be honest with each other from the get-go, and ignore all those negative thoughts that the old devil sends to your head."

"Can't you just hear my mother if I told her that I'd eloped with a ranch foreman and we were going to live out on the boondocks in Texas? She'd have a heart attack. She went through the roof when I quit my teaching job and started quilting."

"And what did you do?"

"I told her that she'd lived her life the way she wanted and I would do the same," Claire answered.

"Then hold on to that, make your own decisions, and then stand by them," Franny said.

"Even when your parents were angry with you, did you really never have regrets?" Claire asked.

Franny shook her head. "Not one time. I'd made my bed and I was goin' to enjoy layin' in it."

"Is that brownies? I smell chocolate!" Zaylie yelled from

the bedroom door. She skipped into the room and picked up a brownie. "Guess what, Aunt Claire? Teresa wants a kitten for Christmas too."

"Is that right?" Claire acted surprised.

"Yep, and I told her that next time we got to do FaceTime I'd show her the three at our bunkhouse." Zaylie picked up a second brownie and ran back to her room.

"She's happier than I've ever seen her," Franny said. "I'm glad that y'all got stuck in Texas. It's been good for both of you."

Claire nodded, but wondered how could such turmoil in her life right then be good for her?

Because it dragged you out of that comfortable rut you've been in since Zaylie was born and has put some excitement in your life. The voice in her head was definitely her grandmother's.

But I liked my life. I knew exactly what was going on. Now I never know what emotion is going to float to the top at any minute, Claire argued.

She listened intently but her grandmother didn't have anything else to say.

*   *   *

Claire turned on the radio on the way back to the ranch that afternoon. One minute Zaylie was singing along with all the classic country songs. The next she'd leaned over against the door and was "resting her eyes." It seemed that the lyrics to every song that played spoke right to Claire, but when Chris Young began to sing "Chiseled in Stone," tears rolled down her cheeks.

It was from a man's point of view, but she could feel every sad emotion that he sang about. An old man was telling a younger one the story in song, saying that a person didn't know anything about how long the nights were or lonely life was until it was chiseled in stone. She thought about Franny losing her Joe and how sad her eyes had been when she talked about him. Then the lyrics talked about how the younger man should drop down on his knees and thank his lucky stars that he had someone to go home to.

Claire got the message.

The very next song was the one they'd played at Nanny's funeral, but that day as she drove through Wichita Falls and headed east toward the ranch, it had a whole new meaning. She didn't want to pray her final prayer with regrets that she didn't give whatever it was between her and Levi a chance. Maybe it would work. Maybe not. But she'd never know if she walked away without trying.

As if the songs were lined up just for her, the next one talked about putting her worries in his pocket and resting her head upon his shoulder. Levi would let her do just that, and she could rest her love on him.

"Cowboy honor," she muttered.

A vision of him naming off all the things in the cowboy's code of honor flashed through her mind. "Live each day with courage," she whispered. "Well, Levi Jackson, it's going to take all the courage and trust in me, but I'm willing to give us a try. Nanny used to say that if you try and fall on your butt, it's okay, but if you fail to try, then you are a loser."

Zaylie awoke somewhere between Nocona and the ranch, and the first words from her mouth were, "Are we home yet?"

"Not quite. Maybe another ten or fifteen minutes," Claire answered.

"How many songs is that?" Zaylie asked.

"Three or four."

"Okay." She started singing along with Randy Travis as he sang, "He Walked on Water." She'd come in behind the words, but somewhere in the middle of the song she stopped and asked, "Is he singin' about Levi, Aunt Claire?"

"No, he's talkin' about his grandpa," Claire answered around the lump forming in her throat. "What makes you think of Levi?"

"Levi's got a cowboy hat, and I bet he could walk on water," Zaylie answered.

"Only Jesus could do that," Claire told her.

"Well, if we was drownin' he'd walk on water and take us home," Zaylie said with conviction, and then sang with George Jones as he started, "A Picture of Me Without You."

Home.

Zaylie had used that word again. Claire had asked Franny if it made her sad to leave the ranch where she and Joe had lived their whole married life. She'd told her that home wasn't a place so much as it was a feeling of belonging.

Claire had barely gotten parked when she noticed Justin coming around the bunkhouse. In a few long strides he was at the truck, opening the doors for her and Zaylie.

When Zaylie was unbuckled and on the ground, she ran into the house. "I'm glad I'm home. I got to go see my little baby kitties."

He turned around to face Claire. "Want some help unloading all this?"

"Yes, thanks," she answered. "Where's Levi?"

"He's over at Mavis and Skip's."

She had a lot to say to Levi, but she sure didn't want to do it by phone. Hopefully, he'd be home before long.

Chapter Nineteen

Zaylie kept running to the living room window to see if Retta and Cade were home yet, then coming back to the kitchen or the guest room where Claire was sewing to ask how long it would be before they got home.

"Six o'clock," Claire told her for the hundredth time. "Their plane landed about four and it'll be near six when they get home."

"Is that forever from now?"

"It's two more hours. That's one movie and four songs." Claire finished machine quilting Retta's Christmas throw on her sewing machine. Small things she could manage, but even that would be easier with the big commercial-size quilter.

Zaylie sucked in a lung full of air and let it out with a long whoosh. "Okay." She stretched the one short word out into three syllables and sighed again. "I guess I'll watch *Cinderella*."

"Want me to put it in the DVD player for you?" Claire asked.

"I can do it myself." She left the room with her chin dragging on her chest and lower lip poked out in a pout.

Claire folded the quilt and put it into the box, taped it shut, and carried it out to the truck.

She was about to go back into the house when she heard a truck coming down the lane. She whipped around, hoping that maybe Retta and Cade had caught an earlier flight home, but it was Levi. Her first thought was to ignore him, like he'd done her all day. Oh, he'd said good morning and entered into the conversation about Retta and Cade's return during the noon meal. But there'd been no touching of any kind, not even an accidental brush of their hands as food was passed.

He rolled down the window and yelled, "Hey, you and Zaylie want to go out to the barn and see Little Bit and Nomie? I bet she's getting stir crazy."

It was on the tip of her tongue to tell him no, but she said, "Yes, give us two minutes to get our jackets, and we'll be right out."

She had some things to say, and the corral was a good place to get it out in the open. Zaylie would be romping around with the little donkey and calf, so she wouldn't be listening to a word they said.

Zaylie was sitting on the sofa in a pout and didn't even look up at Claire.

"Levi wants to know if we'd like to go see Little Bit and Nomie, but if you're busy..." Claire let the sentence hang.

"No! I want to go." Her expression changed instantly.

"You need to put on your shoes and your jacket." Claire held out both to her.

Zaylie's little hands were a blur as she tied her shoes.

"I'll tell Nomie all about Retta so she won't be afraid of her." She shoved her arms into her jacket and ran toward the door. "Levi, guess what? Nomie is goin' to love Retta."

Levi picked Zaylie up first, then put her into the backseat beside Beau and then opened the passenger door for Claire. "I figured she might be getting a little antsy. To tell the truth, Justin and I are ready for them to be home too."

For the first time, he didn't pick Claire up and set her in the seat, but waited for her to hoist herself into the truck. Tears stung her eyes as she fastened the seat belt, but she blinked them back.

When they reached the corral, Zaylie crawled through the two lower rails and then went back and forth from Nomie to Little Bit, hugging them and talking to them like they were human. Beau bounded out of the barn and sat down outside the corral as if he were guarding the little girl.

A cold north wind whipped Zaylie's wispy blond hair back and forth, but she just pushed it out of her face and kept telling the animals all about her plans when Retta got home.

"She sure does love the ranch life." Levi propped his elbows on the top rail.

Claire grabbed his shoulder and tugged at it to make him face her.

"What in the hell is going on, Levi?" she blurted out.

He turned to face her. "About Zaylie, Beau, or what?"

"About us?" She gazed into his eyes.

"Is there an us?" he asked.

"You tell me," she answered.

"Evidently, you don't like to be smothered, and you want to do things on your own. I have to fight you to give you any help at all. So this is me, backing off and giving you space," he said.

She blinked and let go of his shoulder. "I've had to take care of everything for so long that it's really hard for me to let go of the reins."

"I realize that, but if there's going to be an *us,* if we're going to go past a few kisses and into the dating phase, we're both going to have to compromise. I'm like a teenager that has a girlfriend and wants to spend every minute possible with her. You're like . . ." He inhaled deeply.

"I'm like trying to pet a porcupine?" she suggested.

"Something like that, or maybe like a porcupine that's stuck between a rock and a hard place and won't let me do a damn thing to help it get free," he said.

"So do you want to go past those hot kisses we've shared? Do you want us to be dating? If so, I'll try to shed a few prickly quills," she said.

"I'll try not to smother you." He nodded. "And yes, Claire, I want to date you. I want people to know that you're with me."

It was her turn to make a move or say something. Words didn't seem adequate for the way she felt. So she pushed herself between him and the fence, rested her palms on his chest, and pushed up to her tiptoes. Their lips met in a fiery kiss that told Claire that actions definitely spoke louder than words.

*   *   *

"Why are you kissin' Levi?" Zaylie reached through the railings and tugged on Claire's coattail.

Before Claire could answer, Levi's phone rang. He kissed her on the tip of the nose and took a couple of steps to the side.

"I kissed Levi because I wanted to," Claire said.

"Can I kiss a boy when I want to?" Zaylie asked.

"When you are twenty-eight," Claire told her.

"Thank God, I'm twenty-eight." Levi chuckled as he answered the phone.

"Is Retta home yet?" Mavis askcd. "We thought we'd give them a few minutes to get settled before we come out to the ranch."

"Nope, not for another hour or so."

"Are icicles still hangin' off you and Claire?"

"No, we've cleared the air," he answered.

"Well, praise the Lord. I didn't like the way things felt today."

"And you didn't talk to her about it?" Levi asked.

"God knows I wanted to, and it was almighty tough not to meddle. But something in my heart told me to let y'all work it out on your own. I can step in and help out when it comes to getting y'all some time together, but it's up to you what you do with it," Mavis answered. "So what's the verdict?"

"Isn't that meddling?" Levi teased.

"No, it's my reward for not meddling," she told him.

"Well, I think we're dating, but that sounds kind of juvenile, doesn't it?" he said.

"Not to me, it don't. But if you're dating, you should be talkin' to her, not me."

"I agree, but I'm also trying to not be a smothering boyfriend."

"That sounds mighty smart of you. Good luck, Levi."

"Bye now. See you later." He hit the end button and noticed Justin coming right toward him.

"Heard from Cade?" Justin asked.

"Nope. You?"

"Not yet. But when I talked to Cade this mornin' he said

that Retta was homesick. Who'd a thought that the woman he hired last summer who couldn't wait to get to the big city would learn to love this place the way she does."

"Claire and I are dating," Levi blurted out.

"That don't surprise me. Are you going to give her your class ring and go steady too?" Justin teased.

Levi slapped at Justin's arm.

"Been to bed with her?" Justin asked.

"No, and if I had I wouldn't be tellin' it around. She's a class act and deserves better," Levi said.

"I'm happy for you. Really, I am. Who knows, maybe someday another woman will get dropped on the ranch, and I'll find my soul mate," Justin said.

Soul mate? The words settled on Levi's heart and didn't sting a bit.

"Hey, now, dating doesn't mean the M word," Levi said.

Zaylie stuck her head out between two rails and yelled, "Hey, Justin, come see Nomie."

"I'm on my way." Justin started in that direction.

Claire turned away from the corral and drew her jacket across her chest. The wind whipped her ponytail around her face, but she kept walking toward him. As she got nearer and nearer, Levi didn't see her hair as much as the smile directed at him.

"So what did Mavis have to say when you told her about us?" Claire looped her arm into his.

"She's happy, but I'm wondering if your brother will try to talk you out of dating me." He laid a hand over hers.

"Honey, my brother has never run my life, and he damn sure ain't startin' now. I love him, and he's basically all the family I have, but I call the shots when it comes to my life." She poked him in the chest with a forefinger. "Besides, why would he be against someone who makes me happy?"

"Come on, Claire. I've got a good job and I'm not broke, but I sure don't bring home the kind of money you do," he said.

"Nanny always said that if you love what you do, whether you are the president of the United States of America or if you are a ditch digger for the county, then you are a success. Money doesn't make someone a success. Happiness does," she told him.

"Then by that definition, I'm a big success." He looked up in time for a huge raindrop to hit him right in the eye. He wiped it out and gathered Claire up in his arms, jogged to the other side of the truck, and settled her into the passenger's seat. "And on that note, I expect I'd better grab Zaylie and get her into the truck before she gets wet."

Justin passed him midway. "I'll be in the house right behind you. Snow and now a thunderstorm. Never a dull moment in Texas."

"You got that right." Levi opened the gate and picked up Zaylie.

They made it inside the truck before the sky opened up, and the wind blew great sheets of cold rain against the vehicle's windshield.

"I hope Cade and Retta aren't havin' to drive out of Dallas in this," Claire said.

"Can we call them?" Zaylie asked.

"Might not be a good idea if they're fighting their way through afternoon traffic in the rain," Claire answered. "Let's just go to the house and get our little welcome home finger foods on the table, and you can watch for them out the window. Hopefully, this is just a little blow-over storm and it'll pass in a few minutes."

There was a difference in a shower and a winter storm. This had the feel of the latter—a cold rain that could turn to sleet any second. Levi parked as close to the porch as he possibly could and turned toward Claire. "I'm going to take Zaylie inside, and then I'll come back for you."

She nodded, but as soon as he had Zaylie in his arms, she made a beeline for the house right behind him. Icy rain ran down his neck, and he shivered all the way to his toenails when he set the child down in the foyer.

"See there." He turned to face her. "You couldn't even wait and let me come back for you."

With dripping hair, she bowed up to him. "I was trying to do something nice for you so that you didn't have to go back out in that. We were both going to get wet either way. I wouldn't fuss if you'd bring me a towel though."

"I guess that's a step in the right direction." He managed a smile as he picked up two towels from the laundry basket.

"Retta!" Zaylie squealed, and pointed.

"Surprise! We got home about half an hour ago," Retta said.

"Well, praise the Lord!" Justin came in the back door and removed his cowboy hat. "You didn't have to drive in this rain, did you?"

Cade stepped out of the kitchen carrying two bottles of root beer. "Amen, brother. It's good to be home, and, no, we beat the rain home by a few minutes."

"Root beer?" Levi asked. "Did you get the wrong thing from the fridge?"

"Nope, if Retta can't drink, then I'm not going to either," Cade answered.

Zaylie stomped her foot. "We had a surprise party."

"Well, let's get out all the fixin's, and we'll have our party anyway." Cade put a bottle in Retta's hand.

"I hear you've got a new calf since we've been gone." Retta sat down beside Zaylie and pulled her close for a hug.

Zaylie grinned. "Nomie is the new baby cow's name, and I told her about you today."

"Hey, guys." Levi took the towel from Claire's hand and dried her hair for her. "Let's pull out all that stuff Claire has made while these ladies talk about Nomie."

"Sounds good to me." Justin nodded. "I've been waitin' all day to get into those brownies and that chocolate dessert thing that Claire has been holding back."

Justin threw an arm around Cade's shoulder, and the three of them disappeared toward the kitchen. "Levi's got something to tell you."

"That he and Claire are a couple?" Cade grinned.

"How'd you know?" Levi opened the fridge and brought out a tray of finger sandwiches.

"The look on both your faces as you dried her hair," Cade said. "God, I'm glad to be home. I got worse homesick that last day than Retta did. We had an amazing honeymoon, but I swear being away just made me love this ranch more than ever."

"So is that the lingo. We aren't dating. We are a couple?" Levi asked.

"I think it is. What did Mavis say?" Cade asked.

"She's fine with it," Levi answered.

"She's probably already making baby quilts for y'all as well as for me and Retta." Cade carried a dessert to the table.

"It's something big in my world to think about a relationship that involves more than friendship. You're talkin' permanent, and that's way ahead of me," Levi said.

"You'll get there if she's the one," Cade told him, and then pointed at Justin. "And you are next."

Justin threw up both palms defensively. "Whoa! How'd I get involved in this conversation? Levi is in the spotlight, not me. I'm not finished sowing oats, and it could be that I never will."

"I said that six months ago, remember. Never say never," Levi reminded him.

Justin lowered his hands. "I didn't say never. I said a long, long time if ever."

"Pretty close to the same thing. Let's get all this stuff on the table. Retta's hungry." Cade picked up two plates of food. "And, Levi, I'm happy for you. Congratulations."

"Thank you." Levi got a flash picture of Claire in a wedding gown, and it didn't scare him. It might be a year or two down the road, but if things worked out, at least he wasn't afraid.

* *|* *

"What's happened while I was gone?" Retta sipped at the root beer Cade had given her. "It's plain that you and Levi…"

"Levi can walk on water," Zaylie blurted out before she wiggled free of Retta's embrace and hurried to the fireplace to hug Beau.

"What does she mean by that?" Retta took a long sip of the root beer. "This is my new craving. It seems to help the morning sickness."

"She heard that song by Randy Travis yesterday and decided that if his grandpa could walk on water, then Levi could," Claire explained. "And Levi and I only decided half an hour ago that we are dating."

"Mavis?" Retta asked.

"Levi says she's okay with it."

"I bet she is. She's wanted a daughter-in-law for years. She will spoil you, Claire, but not as much as Levi."

"I'm not sure I know how to take spoilin'," Claire whispered.

"You'll learn." Retta patted her arm.

"Hey, we got the party on the table," Cade called out.

"Thanks." Claire covered Retta's hand with hers and gave it a squeeze.

"Anytime. I've already walked down the path you're treading, so anytime you need to talk, I'm here. Now let's go eat. Those peanuts on the plane didn't last long."

"Forgot to ask in all the excitement. How's the mornin' sickness?"

"Pretty much gone. I talked to Mavis the whole way home from the airport. She told me about the Harris house and how she's asked you to stay a while longer. Are you going to? I would love it if you could..." Retta's voice dropped to a whisper. "And you could figure out if you could stand that spoilin' business from Levi and Mavis. Besides you're going to be living down here anyway, so why uproot Zaylie until her dad comes home? Then the transition won't be so traumatic for her."

Claire wasn't aware she was holding her breath until it came out in a whoosh. "It does make things a lot easier, so yes, and thank you, and there's more to tell you about the surprise story there."

"Is he going to let her have kittens?" Retta asked.

"More than that." Claire looked around and saw Zaylie in the dining room chattering away with Levi about Nomie. "He's resigning and coming home for good, and he's probably getting married soon."

"Wow!" Retta's brown eyes twinkled. "Now that's a Christmas present she'll never forget."

"What's a present?" Zaylie whipped around to face them.

"We can't tell," Retta said. "We promised Santa."

"When did you see him?" Zaylie skipped across the room.

"In Florida. I had to know what he was bringing you so I'd know what I could get that would be different," Retta answered.

Levi met Claire's gaze, and their eyes locked. Could she really learn to let someone else help her without feeling like she was losing her independence? She was willing to try, but that didn't mean it would be easy.

Chapter Twenty

Claire loved the smell of the land after a hard rain. Add in a brisk breeze and it made for a pleasant walk from the house to the barn that Tuesday evening. When she was only a few yards from the barn and ready to turn around and go back to the bunkhouse, Beau ran out to meet her. Putting his big paws on her chest, he licked her up across the face and then ran back inside.

Levi startled her when he stepped out of the shadows. "Where's Zaylie?"

"Retta took her to church. Her little girls' Sunday school class is making cookies to take to the nursing home tomorrow evening. She wants Zaylie to go with her to that too. They'll sing Christmas carols for the old folks and pass out treat bags with cookies."

Levi opened his arms and she walked into them. He pulled her close to his body and rested his chin on the top of her head. "You were made for me, Claire Mason."

"Why's that?"

"Because I feel complete when I'm with you," he said.

"Me too." She shivered in spite of the warmth spreading through her body.

"You're cold, darlin'. Let's get you inside to the tack room." He tucked her hand into his, and she followed him into the barn. Beau yipped from his bed in a pile of hay, and his tail thumped a couple of times, but then he closed his eyes and went back to sleep.

Warmth rushed out of the tack room when he opened the door. Then they were inside with the smell of leather and the remnants of his woodsy shaving lotion from that morning— all blending together. He took her hand in his and laid it on his broad, work-hardened chest, and she could feel his heart racing.

"This is what just being near you does to me, Claire. I've never experienced anything like this, and I'm afraid I'm going to mess it up," he drawled.

"Me too," she admitted honestly as she picked up his hand and laid it over her heart. "This is scary on more than one level for both of us."

He removed her hand and kissed the palm. "We've got at least two hours all to ourselves. Justin and Cade went to Bowie to buy more Christmas lights."

"Then we'd better make the best of it." She tugged at the top of his coat and unfastened all the snaps in one fell swoop. Then she started at the top button of his chambray work shirt and slowly undid enough that she could slip hands inside and run them over his bare skin.

He groaned. "You are killin' me, woman."

"But what a way to die," she said as she grinned up at him.

His lips found hers, and the sparks ignited the dimly lit

room. "One more of those and you won't have to undress me. All my clothes will go up in flames."

"Are you sure about this, Claire?" His voice was hoarse and his eyes searched hers.

"I'm not sure about anything, but I know that I want this with you, Levi. It's a rare opportunity that we're on this ranch alone, so let's make the most of it."

He gently removed her jacket and then tugged her sweatshirt up over her head. Static electricity made her hair fly out like she'd stuck her finger in a light socket. He smoothed it down with his fingertips, and she shivered again.

"Your touch," she started.

"I know." He threw his shirt off to the side and undid her bra. Then it was skin against skin, her breasts against the brown hair on his chest. "My God, that feels good."

She could feel the hardness behind his zipper begging to be freed, so she slipped her hand between them and undid his belt buckle, the button on his jeans, and pulled the zipper down.

"Oh my!" she gasped when she realized he was commando.

"Never been one much for underwear." He grinned.

"I see," she whispered.

He kicked off his boots and took off his socks and jeans, then tossed them over toward the end of the sofa. Standing there before her with only the fire from the heater to light the room, he looked like a Greek statue of a perfect man, only this one was flesh and blood. She wanted him to make love to her, ached to feel him inside her.

"Oh no!" he said when he'd finished undressing her and laid her on the sofa.

"What? What's wrong?" she asked.

"I don't have protection," he groaned.

"I'm on the pill," she whispered.

"Great." He smiled as he reached for his jeans and pulled his phone from the hip pocket, touched a few icons, and "Good Morning, Beautiful," by Steve Holy started to play.

"Someday I'll wake up with you by my side, but right now the words say the way I feel about you, Claire, and I want you to hear it as we make love," he whispered.

His kisses turned loose desire and emotions that she'd never felt before. When she thought that she'd surely melt from the inside out, she reached down and guided him inside her, and they began a rhythm together as the song played all the way to the end. He brought her right up to the edge of an amazing climax. She wrapped her legs around his middle and raked her nails across his back as she nipped his ear. "I need you. I want you. Please, right now."

He picked up the pace and smothered her with steaming-hot kisses, and together they reached a height where the air was so thin they had trouble breathing. Then with a final hard thrust, they fell all the way back to earth with her in his arms.

"My God. That was a first," he gasped.

"Surely not," she panted.

"It was, darlin', my first time to make love rather than have sex." He rolled to one side, but the sofa was so narrow that they were still plastered against each other.

"It's a good thing we don't have all night. We'd burn down the ranch," she said.

"Amen and there'd be nothing left of us but a pile of ashes. This was..." He stopped as if he couldn't think of the right word.

"Amazin'?" she asked.

"Oh, honey, I don't think there's enough words in the dictionary to describe what this really was." He kissed her again and shut his eyes.

"Don't you fall asleep, cowboy. We've only got a few more minutes before the family comes home."

Family.

Home.

The two words branded themselves on Claire's heart as she snuggled up next to him to make the most of every single second they had left.

Chapter Twenty-One

Claire awoke the next morning with doubts. Had she gone too fast? She'd known Levi less than a month. Even with her first boyfriend in college, she'd known him a whole semester before they'd had sex.

But what you had last night went beyond plain old sex; Levi made love to you, a soft voice in her head reminded her.

Even that couldn't erase the niggling uncertainty of her actions. She'd only been a notch above the bar bunnies that he'd taken home for a weekend. She'd instigated the whole thing just like they'd do. Now what? Would he have as many second thoughts as she had and avoid her like the plague?

Zaylie rubbed the sleep from her eyes with her knuckles as she crawled up in bed with Claire and flopped back on the spare pillow. "Are you goin' to come see me sing tonight at the nursing home?"

"Of course I am," Claire answered.

"And Levi?"

Claire's cheeks burned at just hearing his name. "You'll have to ask him."

"'Kay." She yawned and then sat up with eyes wide open. "I have to call Teresa and see if she can come too."

Claire patted her on the arm. "Teresa lives too far away to come to the singing, but I'll video it and you can send it to her. How would that work?"

Zaylie's lower lip rolled out. "I miss her."

Claire picked her up and held her close. "I know you do. I miss your dad and Angela and Teresa and even Franny. But Christmas isn't far away, and we'll see them all then."

"Is that when we're leavin'?" Zaylie asked.

"Maybe," Claire answered.

"But I don't want to leave my kitties and Retta and Levi," Zaylie whined. "Daddy can come home and we can live in this house happy ever after."

If only things were as simple as they are seen through the eyes of a five-year-old, Claire thought as she set Zaylie on the floor and got out of bed herself. "We'll see what happens when the time comes," she said. "But for right now, we'll think about the ranch party. It's coming up real soon. What are you going to wear?"

"My pretty Christmas dress." Zaylie's tone changed to excited as she raced off to the living room. "We can send Daddy a picture of me and the kitties on party day."

"Yes, we will," Claire agreed.

She picked up the shirt that she'd tossed on the dresser the night before and buried her face in it. Inhaling deeply, she could still smell Levi's aftershave mixed with the scent of the tack room. She was definitely going to miss seeing him every day when she moved away from the ranch.

*   *   *

Levi had been dreaming about Claire and was reaching out to touch her face when he awoke to find that he was caressing a pillow. He picked it up and threw it against the wall.

That's no way to treat the woman you are seeing. Skip's laughter rang out in his head so clearly that he looked across the room to see if he was sitting in the rocking chair by the window.

"It wasn't Claire. If it had been, I wouldn't be in this mood." He threw the covers back and jerked a shirt over his head. The one he'd worn the night before still smelled faintly of her perfume, so it didn't go into the hamper but was left draped over the rocking chair.

"Mornin'." He nodded to Mavis, Skip, and Retta when he made it to the kitchen.

"What's got you all grumpy? You usually get up in a good mood," Mavis asked.

"Nothin'," he muttered. "And what makes you think I'm grumpy. I said good mornin' to all y'all."

"The look on your face," Mavis told him.

Retta laid a hand on his shoulder. "Must be a male thing. Cade and Justin neither one are real perky this morning either. They're in the livin' room if you want to join them."

"I'm good right here." He took a sip of his coffee and turned toward Mavis. "Why did you and Skip come so early? Didn't you have to take Benjy to school?"

"The FFA is giving the 4-H club a breakfast this mornin'. And we got us a little miracle this holiday season. Benjy made a friend. He goes to a special class a couple of hours a day, and there's a little girl in there who's also high-functioning autistic, and they've been talkin' on the phone. She remembers numbers like he does details."

"That's fabulous. Do we get to meet her?" Levi perked up.

"Maybe. I've asked her mother to come to our church,"

Mavis answered. "She said that she'd be happy to attend. They only moved here a few weeks ago."

"Levi! Levi! Where are you?" Zaylie's voice echoed off the walls.

"In the kitchen, princess." He raised his voice.

She bounced into the room dragging her jacket behind her and stopped abruptly when she saw Skip and Mavis. "Where's Benjy?"

Mavis told her about the FFA breakfast and then nudged Levi when Claire entered the room right behind the child. "Well, that sure enough put a smile on your face," she whispered.

"Guess it did." His grin got bigger.

"Hello, everyone. It looks like it's goin' to be a sunny day." Claire's eyes locked with Levi's and held for a few seconds.

"Yep, and we can use some good days to get decorated up for this party." Skip tucked his hands into the bib of his overalls. "Me and the boys are goin' to do that today. Cade just thought he'd get out of helping."

"Can I help?" Zaylie asked.

"You can help me," Mavis told her. "I'm going to bake cookies all day, and I could use someone to help decorate them."

"Santa cookies?" Zaylie whispered.

"Iced sugar cookies," Claire interpreted.

"Yes, Santa cookies. We'll make reindeer and Santa and maybe if we have time even some gingerbread men," Mavis told her.

"Yes, yes, yes!" Zaylie did a couple of twirls.

"But first breakfast. I could eat a dozen biscuits with sausage gravy this mornin'," Retta said. "It's great to be over mornin' sickness."

"I think I'll refill my cup and go on in the living room with the guys after all," Levi said. As he passed by Claire he bumped her on the shoulder and whispered, "Good mornin', beautiful."

*   *   *

Heat crawled up from her neck to her cheeks. The song that had been playing while they made love the night before played through her head as her face went from red to crimson.

"Little warm there?" Retta asked.

"Nope, downright hot," Claire answered.

"You're too young for hot flashes." Mavis put a large pan of biscuits in the oven.

"Depends on who's makin' you hot," Retta said. "Mavis, I don't think you've ever told me about when you met Skip. Did you ever get a hot flash when you first met him'?"

Mavis chuckled. "Oh, honey, you might not know it now, but Skip was the sexiest cowboy in the whole state of Texas at one time, and I was one lucky girl that he fell in love with me."

"How old were you?" Retta winked at Claire.

"Sixteen. We married when I was seventeen. That was fifty years ago. We ran off to Wichita Falls, got married at the county clerk's, and spent a night in a motel. Then we came home to face the music." Mavis crumbled sausage into a big cast iron skillet and handed a wooden spoon to Claire. "You can keep this stirred while it browns."

"Face the music?" Retta asked.

"My daddy thought Skip wasn't good enough for his little girl," Mavis answered.

"Ever have any regrets?" Claire asked.

Mavis whipped around to stare at her. "Not a single one."

"I love that story," Claire said. "It reminds me of the

one that Franny told me when I was..." She started to say home, but if it was true that home was where the heart is, she wasn't sure where it was that morning. She cleared her throat and went on. "When Zaylie and I went to Randlett."

Retta got down the plates to set the table. "Changing the subject. Are you and Skip coming to the nursing home to see my Sunday school girls sing to the old folks tonight?"

"Wouldn't miss it for the world. Got lots of friends in the home," Mavis said.

"Are you like Cinderella?" Zaylie asked Mavis. "Did you live happy ever after?"

Mavis touched Zaylie on the cheek. "I was at one time. Now I'm the fairy godmother."

"Oh!" Zaylie's blue eyes widened. "Do you have a magic wand? Can you turn a pumpkin into a coach?"

"I'm sure Mavis can do anything." Claire smiled.

"Then she can do her wand like this." Zaylie picked up a spoon and waved it around. "And my daddy will come home forever."

"I bet she can." Claire's smile turned to laughter. "But right now we've got breakfast to think about, so put the spoon down and come help."

"Let's talk about them Santa cookies," Zaylie said as she returned the spoon to the table.

"I agree," Mavis said. "One more question. What is your brother going to say?"

"I run my own life, not my parents or my brother. They've lived the way they wanted all their lives, so they don't have any room to be tellin' me how or what to do with my heart," Claire answered.

Retta bumped her hip against Mavis's. "Who does that remind you of?"

"You," Mavis answered.

"I was thinkin' someone a little shorter, older, and with kinky hair." Retta laughed.

"Like Mavis?" Zaylie asked.

"Out of the mouths of babes," Retta said. "Zaylie, would you go tell the guys that by the time they get washed up, we'll have breakfast on the table."

Because there were too many for the kitchen table, the one in the dining room had been set up for breakfast. Levi usually sat across from Claire in the kitchen, but that morning he chose the chair right next to her. When Cade asked Skip to say grace, Levi laid his hand on Claire's knee. She tucked her hand into his, and he squeezed it gently. That simple gesture meant more to her than a room full of expensive roses or a dinner at a five-star restaurant.

Chapter Twenty-Two

Claire dressed four times that evening before she finally settled on a straight denim skirt that skimmed her knees and a bright red Christmas sweater with crossed candy canes on the front. She put a few bouncy curls in her long, dark hair and applied a little more makeup than usual.

"When can I have makeup?" Zaylie asked as she watched her put on mascara.

"That's between you and your daddy, but I'm thinkin' maybe when you are twenty-one," Claire answered.

"That's forever," she groaned.

"Yes it is, and I hope it goes slow. I like you as a little girl," Claire said.

A hard rap on the door sent Zaylie out of the room, her ponytail flying behind her like a frayed flag of victory.

Levi's deep drawl floated into the bedroom. "Well, now, you sure do look just like a princess tonight."

Claire checked her reflection one more time. She'd give

a year's salary to be at least six inches taller and ten pounds thinner, but that wasn't happening. She slipped her feet into a pair of red high heels and went out into the living room.

"Well, good evening, beautiful." His eyes started at her feet and traveled up to her hair, made a trip back down—stopping at her chest for an extra second—and then making one more sweep back up to her eyes.

"Is she a princess too?" Zaylie asked.

"No, darlin', she's the queen," Levi answered.

"Thank you, but I'm really just Claire." She smiled at him.

He picked up her coat and held it out. "To the rest of the world, maybe, but to me you are the queen of my heart."

Zaylie handed him her jacket. "And I'm the princess, right?"

"You got it." Levi buttoned her coat and pulled the hood up over her hair. "I'm takin' the two prettiest girls in Montague County to the singing tonight." He straightened up and escorted Claire outside.

Warmth penetrated all the way to her insides, and yet a shiver danced up her spine. Would Levi's touch always affect her like that, or would it someday get to be old hat and she wouldn't feel a thing?

The nursing home was only a fifteen-minute drive from the house, but Zaylie wiggled and asked how much farther it was at least a dozen times. When they arrived, Retta and Cade parked right beside them, and she could hardly wait to get out and put her hand in Retta's.

"Looks like I'm losin' my place," Claire said.

Levi laced his fingers in hers. "Darlin', you'll always be number one with me."

"Is that a pickup line?" she asked.

"No, ma'am, it's the gospel truth," he answered. "But if it was, would it work?"

"Maybe," she said. "I don't think I've ever been number one with anyone. I kind of like the feelin'."

The lobby of the nursing home was filled with old folks on sofas, chairs, and even in wheelchairs. The glee in their wrinkled faces said that they were as excited to have children in the house as the kids were to be there. Claire and Levi found two empty chairs at the back of the room and settled into them. He helped her remove her coat and then took her hand in his again, resting it on his knee.

She tried to take in the whole, huge room with one glance, but it was impossible. Decorations were everywhere—from coloring sheets from the local school kids taped to the walls to bright-colored garland looped around the windows. A tree that had to be eight feet tall was placed in one corner and had every kind of ornament imaginable adorning it, from cartoon characters to plain red and green bulbs.

Someone from the nursing home staff tapped on the microphone and introduced Retta and the kids. Then the piano player sat down behind the old upright piano and hit a few keys. The little girls gathered up around the microphone, and Retta sat down on a chair in front of them.

"I understand that the lady playing the piano could have been your wife if you'd played your cards right," Claire whispered to Levi.

"Glad I didn't. Something better came along," he said.

"And if something better than me comes along in a few weeks?" she asked.

"Impossible. You can't get no better than perfection." He gave her a quick kiss on the cheek.

"Silent night, holy night," the little girls started. One of the elderly ladies joined in and then several more. Before long they were singing louder than the girls.

When that finished, the older four girls started singing

"Jingle Bells." The younger ones like Zaylie shook ribbons with jingle bells attached to them every time they sang the words. She was in her element up there with all those kids.

"I'm just glad that she's not substituting the words to 'Tennessee Whiskey' to any of the carols," Claire told Levi.

"Might liven this crowd up even more," he said, and chuckled.

"Could give them all heart attacks," she said out the corner of her mouth.

"You ever think about a place like this when you get old?" he asked.

She shook her head. No, she didn't want to be tucked away in a nursing home. She wanted to make her quilts and have so many kids that they'd fight over who got to have her in their home when she was old. She wanted a close-knit family, not one like she'd grown up in, but one like Levi had known.

"Me either. When I'm old and gray, I want to sit on the porch in a rocking chair and laugh at my great-grandkids playin' in the yard."

She nodded. "Or sit on a quilt under a shade tree and reminisce about a night in the tack room?"

"Yes, ma'am," he said.

"And that's all of our program," Retta said. "But we've got cookies and punch in the dining room for everyone. Our girls made the treats special for you folks, and they'll be serving y'all."

The old folks applauded loudly, and Zaylie bowed twice before she ran back to Claire and Levi. "Did I do good?"

"Yes, you did, and now you've got to go with Retta and help give out cookies and carry punch," Claire told her. "Want me to go with you?"

"No, I want Levi. I don't know them people, and he'll rescue me, 'cause he can walk on water," Zaylie answered.

"Wow!" Levi barely got out one word.

"Don't let your head get too big for your hat. She got that from that song about a grandpa walkin' on water," Claire informed him.

"Ouch!" he said.

Zaylie grabbed his free hand and tugged. "Come on. We gots to help Retta now."

"Yes, ma'am. Can Claire come with us?"

"Okay," Zaylie said. "Did you take pictures for Teresa?"

"Retta had a camera set up at the front, and she's going to let me have a copy. It'll be better than what I could do." Claire followed her and Levi down the hallway to the dining room, where Christmas carols were playing on a CD player and a table had been laid out with cookies, punch, and finger foods.

She wasn't surprised that Zaylie intermingled with the elderly strangers. The child had, after all, been raised close to a grandmother and with Franny right next door. But she did notice as she helped take small plates to the folks in wheelchairs that Zaylie made sure Levi was close enough that she could see him at all times.

In that moment, Claire was glad that Grant was coming home. Zaylie needed a daddy in her life on a permanent basis. Keeping her had been a delight, and Claire would miss her so much, but she'd be able to drive up to Randlett any evening or Sunday afternoon that she wanted.

Her phone rang, and she pulled it out of her skirt pocket. "Hello, Franny. What's going on?"

"Just makin' sure that you're comin' to Randlett in time for church this next Sunday. You bringin' that cowboy with you?"

"Plannin' on it." She told her where they were right then.

"That's great. But I hear something sad in your voice. What's wrong?"

"Even though I'm happy for my brother and the new little family, I'll still miss Zaylie. She'll have a new mama and a sister, and there's even a possibility she'll have more siblings later on down the road. I'll just be her aunt from now on. How can a person be sad when there's so much happiness about to happen?" Claire asked.

"Honey, she's always going to love you, you'll see. But right now I want to hear more about Levi. How are things going?" Franny asked.

"Going well. We're dating or in a relationship or we're a couple. I never really know what to call it," Claire answered.

"Well, holy smoke, girl. Don't stand there talkin' to me. Go on over to wherever he is and stand next to him. I been in them nursing homes, and the girls who work there is goin' to flirt with him if they don't know he's a marked man," Franny said. "I'll look to see you on Sunday, and bring pictures of Zaylie singing so I can see them. Good-bye."

She didn't even have time to say good-bye back to Franny when the call ended.

"Grant?" Levi asked.

"No, Franny checkin' to see if we were comin' to church with her on Sunday."

"It'll mean gettin' up a little early after the ranch party. Maybe I should have a sleepover at your bunkhouse so we won't oversleep," he teased.

"Oh, honey, we wouldn't sleep at all if we did that," she said.

"That's what I was countin' on. I haven't had time to talk to you alone since last night," he said.

With a wave of her hand, she took in the whole room. "You call this alone?"

"The best place in the world to be alone is in a crowd of people who aren't a bit interested in what you are sayin'.

I dreamed about you last night and woke up frustrated because you weren't in bed with me," he said.

"I woke up afraid that you'd have second thoughts about things," she admitted.

"Not me. You?" he asked.

"Not a single one. Do you really think we can make this work? I won't be right here on the ranch and we won't see each other every single day."

"Anything, darlin' "—he brought her fingertips to his lips and kissed each one of them—"is possible with a little work."

"I believe you. After all, you can walk on water." Her fingers could sure use a little dousing in ice water about then.

"Not until I'm a grandpa, but don't tell Zaylie." He grinned.

Chapter Twenty-Three

For the next two days everyone had a job to do on the ranch. Mavis, Retta, and Claire kept the oven going from daylight until after supper making dozens and dozens of cookies. The guys worked outside getting decorations all put up and ready for the party on Saturday night. Mavis was the ultimate boss about everything. She'd organized the parties for so long that she knew exactly what to get done and how to tell everyone how to do their jobs including Claire and Retta.

Claire had managed to get a lot of quilting done during the previous days, but that evening she'd put aside the throw to talk to a supplier about buying bolts of fabric wholesale. While she was on her cell, one of the kittens got stuck under the sofa and set up a howl that sounded like it was dying. Gussie was running back and forth from basket to sofa. The supplier was talking fast, and Claire was trying to take notes. Then the house phone rang, and Zaylie was throwing such a fit about her cat, which she was sure was dying, that she couldn't answer it for the sobs. As if that wasn't enough, the electricity blinked off for five seconds. Claire didn't know whether the cat or Zaylie was crying the hardest.

Just as the lights came back on, Levi rapped on the door, but he didn't wait to be invited in. "What is going on?"

"My kitty cat is hurtin', and Aunt Claire won't get off the phone, and I miss my daddy and..."

"Help me, please," Claire begged.

Levi picked Zaylie up and dried her tears. Then he turned the sofa over and rescued the kitten. "I believe that Grumpy is hungry. Let's put him in the basket with Gussie. And we'll get your coat on and take a ride out to the barn to see Nomie."

Thank you, Claire mouthed.

Levi's head bobbed in a brief nod, and just like that the bunkhouse was quiet enough that she could give the supplier her business number and make a huge order for the quilt shop. She ended the call and put her head in her hands.

Did that hurt? Her grandmother popped into her head.

"Yes, it did. My poor nerves were so frazzled, I wanted to scream," she answered out loud.

Not that. Did it hurt to ask for help?

Claire pushed back her chair and paced around the table a couple of times. Levi had come to her rescue, and it felt right. Maybe she'd shed some of those porcupine quills without even knowing it.

"And he'll always be here for me. I know it because that's the kind of man he is." A smile spread across her face as she picked up small pieces of fabric and sewed them together. "I'm beginning to believe that maybe he can walk on water."

Half an hour later, Zaylie bounced into the house with Levi right behind her. She went straight to the basket of kittens. She was in the process of kissing Grumpy on the nose when the phone rang.

Claire was never so glad in her life to see a picture of her brother pop up on the screen. "Hello! I'm going to put you on speaker, and you talk to your daughter for thirty minutes."

"With pleasure," Grant said.

"Daddy, Daddy," Zaylie squealed. "We made cookies for three days and I put Santa's hat on them and I ate six today. And Levi came and took me to the barn because Aunt Claire wouldn't get off the phone and help me."

"What was your aunt doing?" he asked.

"Just talkin' on the phone. I'm mad at her. I'm going to take the phone to my kitties so you can see how scared Grumpy still is," Zaylie said.

"You should go take a long soaking bath while she's on the phone." Levi kissed Claire on the forehead.

"I'd rather spend time with you," she said.

"Who says you can't have both?" Levi waggled his eyebrows.

She shot a look toward Zaylie.

"Just go take a bath. You need it to relax." After a sweet kiss brushed across her lips, he left.

Claire ran a tub of water, shook some bath salts into it, and stripped out of her clothing. She'd just gotten into the tub and hadn't even sat down yet when she heard gravel hitting the bathroom window. She peeked through the curtains to find Levi with his nose pressed against the glass.

"What are you doin' out there?" she asked.

"You said you wanted to spend time with me. Unlock the window."

She slid it up, and he slung a long leg over into the bathroom. His eyes scanned her body before he took her in his arms and kissed her, his tongue mating with hers and leaving her panting when he pulled away.

"Sit down and I'll wash your hair for you." He dropped down on his knees and adjusted the flow of the water.

She eased down into the tub. "Are you kiddin' me?"

"No, ma'am. You've been workin' hard for three days. You need some pampering. Lean back a little." He filled a plastic cup and poured warm water through her hair three times. When it was all wet, he lathered it, massaging her scalp with his fingertips.

"That is amazing." Surely all the heat in her body would make the bathwater begin to boil any minute.

When he finished rinsing it, he brushed her wet hair to the side and kissed her on the soft, tender spot right under her ear. "Now sit up and I'll work on those tight neck muscles a little before I have to leave."

Wet skin. His big hands. Kisses strung across her bare shoulders and neck. Pulse racing. She felt relaxed, and yet every nerve in her body begged for more. Then he changed positions, tipped her chin up, and his lips found hers in another series of searing-hot kisses.

"Time's up. Good night, darlin'," he whispered, and then in an instant he was gone.

Had she dreamed the whole thing? *No I didn't, because the air coming through that open window and cooling me down says that he was here.* She stood up and closed the window, turned off the water, and sank down to her neck in the bathwater.

"Aunt Claire, are you about done in there? Daddy wants to talk to you now," Zaylie yelled from the living area.

"Tell him five minutes." She rose up out of the water and

shivered from the instant chill. It would take at least ten minutes to warm up the room with the door open before she could let Zaylie have her bath.

Wrapping a towel around her wet hair and slipping on a floor-length terry-cloth robe, she visualized a world where no little girl was in the house—one where Levi could strip out of his jeans and boots and join her in a shower or a bathtub.

Zaylie handed off the phone to her when she reached the living room, gathered up her kittens, and carried them to her room. Claire curled up on the end of the sofa and saw that her brother was laughing.

"What?" she asked.

"You're flushed like you used to be as a little girl when you'd done something you shouldn't. Zaylie has that same look in her face sometimes," he said.

She took him off FaceTime and put the phone to her ear. "It was steamy in the bathroom. What's going on?"

"Angela and I got married today," he blurted out.

"Sweet Lord!" she gasped. "I thought you were waiting until you got home to see how the family blended together."

"We are home. Our mission was accomplished early, so they flew us back. We're going to spend a week here in California, and then we'll be at the ranch to get Zaylie. We wanted all of us to be together before Christmas, and we want to decorate our first tree together in Randlett," he explained.

"Congratulations, brother. I'm happy for both of you and for Zaylie and Teresa. She's going to be over the moon. I've got news too. Levi and I are getting a little more serious," she said.

"Whoa! You've only known him a few weeks," Grant fussed. "Just how far has this relationship gone?"

"Well, neither of us is going to be dating anyone else,

though we're not planning a wedding or anything. Right now, we just want to see where it goes. He's invited me to the ranch Christmas party," she told him.

"I trust you'll use your good sense with this." Grant's happy tone changed to concerned in an instant.

"Maybe I'll throw common sense out the bathroom window and just let my heart lead me," she said.

"I'd like to see that in you." Grant chuckled.

"Are you saying that I'm too serious and don't know how to have a good time?"

"Something like that. If Levi makes you happy and a lot less staid, then I'll be the first one to shake his hand."

"Staid!" Her voice went high and squeaky. "That's a word you use for an old maid."

"Yep, it is. And now I'm changing the subject before that squeaky voice deafens me. Think you could stay at the ranch until I get there? Zaylie's going to pitch a fit if you make her leave."

"I think that might be doable," she said. "I can't wait to see you. One week from today?"

"From tomorrow. We'll be there the fifteenth before supper time. Can you have Zaylie's things packed, and will those kittens be ready to go? I'll bring a carrier if they are."

"It'll take some work to get her ready without her nosiness getting in the way, but I'll do my best, and, yes, the kittens are ready now. They're eating real food and they're litter trained," she said.

"Okay, then. I'll call again tomorrow evening," he said.

"Make it early. The party starts at six."

"Got it. Thanks for all you've done, sis." His tone softened.

"It was all out of love." Tears ran down her cheeks.

"Love you." His voice cracked, and the call ended.

Her mind went into high gear as she paced the floor. It

would be easy to get the rest of her personal things out of the master bedroom at the house in Randlett the next time she went back there. Zaylie wouldn't think a thing of that since she'd taken a suitcase full back to the ranch the two times they'd gone there. But the room she'd used as a quilting room needed to be ready for Teresa, and she couldn't figure out a way to take care of that before Grant arrived.

She'd always been super organized. When they moved from one state or country to another, she'd been the one who'd made lists, marked boxes, and gotten everything put together for the moves. But she needed help, even if it was tough to admit it.

She whipped the towel from her head and got dressed in a worn sweat suit. And then she called Levi. Surely, if he could walk on water, he could help with a plan that wouldn't spoil the surprise for Zaylic.

"Do you have a few minutes to talk?" she said the minute he answered.

"I'll be there soon as I can get my boots on," he told her.

She hit the end button and yelled at Zaylie. "Time for your bath, sweetheart. Kiss the kitties good night, and toss your clothes by the washer."

Zaylie tiptoed out of her bedroom with her finger over her lips. "Shhh. They're sleepin'. I read a book to them." She dropped her things on the tiny kitchen floor and beat Claire to the bathroom. She got her bath time Barbie out of a basket along with some ABC blocks that stuck to the side of the tub, and then she crawled right into the bathwater. The poor doll's blond hair looked like a mop that had been hung upside down in a windstorm, but Zaylie loved her as much as her other dolls.

When Claire got back to the living area, Levi was sitting on the sofa. He handed her a cold bottle of beer and nodded toward the place right next to him. "Are we in trouble? Are you having second thoughts about us?"

"No, nothing like that. I need help, and this is me asking for it." She tipped up the beer and swallowed several times before she told him the news.

He set his beer on the coffee table and drew her into his arms. "It's simple, darlin'. We'll get the bedroom all ready for the newlyweds while we're there on Sunday. Then on Monday I'll take the truck back up there and bring all those boxes and your sewing stuff to the boys' bunkhouse. It'll be out of Zaylie's sight and will be right here if you need it."

"Zaylie's right. You are able to walk on water." Claire pulled his face to hers and kissed him.

"Don't know about that, but as the foreman, sometimes I have to get things organized around here." He wrapped her up into his arms, tipped up her chin, and followed her single kiss with a dozen more, each hotter than the last. His thumb made lazy circles right below her ear as his other hand found its way under her sweatshirt to cup a breast.

"Aunt Claire!" Zaylie yelled from the bathroom.

She jumped, and instantly her cheeks were scarlet and burning like fire. Levi let go of her and scooted a few inches away.

"Aunt Claire, I'm ready to get out now!" Zaylie hollered again.

"I'm on my way," she called out.

"Need a cold rag for your face?" Levi asked.

"No, I need a cup of ice to eat to cool my insides," she answered.

"I'm going to sneak out and go home to take my second cold shower of the evening," he whispered. "See you at breakfast." He brushed a sweet kiss across her lips and let himself out the door.

*   *   *

By the time Levi walked back to the house in the cold night air, he didn't need that second cold shower, and it had dawned on him that Claire had asked for his help.

"You look like the cat that just found a way to open the canary cage door," Retta said.

"Maybe so." He hung up his coat and sank down on the sofa. "I need a big favor on Monday." He told her about the plan.

"Yes." She nodded. "If it'll help Claire out I'll do it."

"Why are you so determined to keep her around?" Cade asked from across the room.

"Your parents are coming for the week of Christmas. I'm nervous about that, and Claire and I've become really good friends in this short time. Besides I'll babysit Zaylie anytime I get the chance."

Levi yawned. "I'm going to bed now. Lots of last-minute stuff to get ready for the party tomorrow."

"Good night," Cade and Retta said at the same time.

Levi flipped on the light in his bedroom and took stock of the room that had been his for the past ten years. A queen-size bed, dresser, chest of drawers, and a recliner. And even those things weren't really his. They were part of the ranch and the house. He had a pretty good chunk of money in the bank, maybe enough for a small down payment on five or ten acres if Justin and Cade would sell him a little parcel to get a start.

Serious meant that he'd have to live up to the cowboy honor code and be faithful to one woman for the rest of his life. He'd never be able to walk into the Rusty Spur and hit on a woman with hopes of sweet talking a tall blonde into spending the night with him. The excitement of discovering all the things that made a woman scream his name—gone. He snapped his fingers and stretched out on his bed.

"Gone!" he said aloud. "But the tradeoff would be that I could come home every evening to Claire, that we could grow old together and raise a family."

Is that enough?

He thought about it for a few seconds and then nodded.

If it doesn't work out and she breaks it off?

He remembered a story that Skip told him years ago about an old Indian who talked about two spirits in a man. One only wanted to be free and wild. The other wanted to put down roots.

"Which one won?" he asked Skip.

"The one that the man fed," Skip answered.

It made a hell of a lot more sense that cold winter night in December than it had when Skip told him the story in the heat of summer between his junior and senior year. Levi just had to be absolutely sure which one he wanted to feed because he didn't want to ever cause Claire even a tiny bit of pain.

Chapter Twenty-Four

Claire worried that she'd be underdressed for the ranch party when she took a simple little dark green dress from the closet, but it was the fanciest thing that she'd brought with her from Randlett so it would have to do. It skimmed her knees and had a scooped neckline, so she added a necklace with red and green stones. Then she slipped on a pair of red high heels and took a final look in the mirror. It looked like Christmas, but she would have far rather worn her jeans and a sweatshirt with Rudolph on the front.

Zaylie was already dressed in the red dress that Claire had designed and sewn for her to wear to the church Christmas dinner. She twirled around several times to show off how the full skirt swirled out to show the gathered tulle petticoat underneath.

"We look like Christmas," she declared when she stopped and plopped down on the sofa and watched Claire put on red stud earrings. "I love parties. When can I have pierced ears like you do?"

"When your daddy says you can. Maybe when you are thirteen or maybe thirty," Claire told her.

"That's forever and ever." Zaylie sighed.

"Yes it is, but time goes by fast." Claire didn't know if she was talking to Zaylie or to herself. She wondered where she'd be and if she'd have children of her own when Zaylie was thirteen. That was eight years down the road, and a lot could change in the course of a single day. She'd proven that when she lost control of the car and wound up on the Longhorn Canyon Ranch for the past few weeks.

She thought that she was early, but the house was already full when she arrived. The caterers had charge of the kitchen, and the dining room table was full of finger foods, eggnog—both with and without rum—and platters of homemade cookies. Zaylie zeroed in on a gaggle of little girls that she'd sung with at the nursing home and joined them.

Claire recognized a few of the hired hands she'd seen on the ranch and some of the folks she'd met at church. Then she saw Levi standing over by the Christmas tree, and everyone else disappeared. His green western shirt hugged his broad chest, and his jeans had been pressed and creased. Black boots were almost as shiny as his silver belt buckle. His eyes drew her to him like a magnet, and she wasn't aware of anyone as she made her way around the perimeter of the living room to stand beside him.

He slipped her hand into his and said, "You are gorgeous."

"You clean up pretty good yourself, cowboy," she told him.

"I do the best I can with the little I have to work with." He kissed her on the forehead.

"Don't give me that line. Modesty doesn't fit you," she told him.

"Well, beautiful sure does fit you, darlin'. Shall we go get some eggnog?"

"Love some," she said.

He led her to the table. "Spiked or plain?"

"You better give me some with high octane. With all these people around me, I need a little liquid courage," she answered.

"Don't give me that line." He poured two cups and handed one to her. "You'd take on a crowd twice this size and never break a nervous sweat."

"How did you figure me out so quickly in only a few weeks?" The eggnog had just the right amount of kick for her taste.

"Honey, I figured you out the first five minutes I was in the cabin. You had a pistol pointed at my heart, and I've never doubted you for a second since then," he said. "I'd rather spend this evening in the tack room with just you as around all these people."

"You don't share well with others?" she teased.

"Not when it comes to you." He led her by the hand across the foyer into the office. He kicked the door shut and set their cups on the end of the desk. Then he picked her up and set her on the other end. She wrapped her legs around his waist, and his lips found hers in a series of searing-hot kisses. His fingertips trailed up the inside of her leg to the rim of her lacy bikinis.

Her hands splayed out on his chest to feel his heart go from first to second gear and then kick it right up to third. They were both panting when they heard a knock on the office door. She hurriedly slid off onto the floor.

"Who is it?" Levi called out.

"Me," Zaylie's little voice said. "Is Aunt Claire in there? I can't find her."

Claire covered the distance from the desk to the door in a split second. "What's the matter, baby girl?"

"Benjy is going to the barn to see Little Bit. Can me and the girls go?" she asked.

"I don't think so. Not in your fancy dress. You can go see him tomorrow." Claire slipped through the door, leaving it ajar. "Does Mavis know that Benjy is going to the barn?"

Zaylie folded her arms over her chest. "Skip is goin' with him."

"And you are wearing your pretty dress that has to be nice for the Christmas program in Randlett. The answer is no."

Zaylie stomped her foot.

Levi's soft whisper came through the open space. "What if I went with her? I can't stand to see her disappointed."

"What does no mean, Miss Priss?" Claire asked.

"When you say no it means no, but sometimes Daddy changes his mind." She grinned. "Can I have some chocolate milk? I don't like that stuff in the punch bowl."

Levi stepped out into the light. "I'd kind of like some chocolate milk too. I could mix us both up one if it's all right with Claire."

"That will be fine," Claire said. "Mix three and I'll have one too. Nothing like chocolate milk with Christmas cookies. You think your little friends would like some too?"

"I'll ask them." She took off for the living room.

Levi slipped his arms around Claire's waist from behind and kissed the top of her head. "You're going to make a wonderful mother."

"You're goin' to make a horrible father, especially if you have daughters." She put her hands on his.

"Probably so." He chuckled.

*   *   *

Levi brought out a pitcher of chocolate milk, and immediately Zaylie and her little friends surrounded him, holding up empty cups. He poured for all of them and then filled a plate with a variety of cookies. Five cute little girls of varying looks and sizes were all lined up against the wall in the foyer, pretending to have a tea party when he left them.

Justin caught up with him and pulled him to the side. "You'd better get in there and protect your interests. Buddy is about to make off with your woman." He nodded toward the other side of the room where Buddy had a hand on a wall and the other one on Claire's shoulder.

She caught his gaze, said something to Buddy, and then crossed the room to tiptoe and kiss Levi briefly on the lips.

He slipped an arm around her shoulders. "Someone tryin' to steal my girlfriend?"

"Strange, isn't it? When no one wants a person, then she's a wallflower. But let someone show a little interest and suddenly she's a whole lot more desirable."

"Darlin', you were never a wallflower." He planted a quick kiss on the top of her head. "What did you say to him?"

"Nothing much. Actions speak louder than words, and I just kissed you," she answered. "Where's Zaylie?"

"Havin' a chocolate milk tea party with her friends in the foyer," he answered. "Let's start makin' the rounds. Should've done that first and then Buddy wouldn't have hit on you, but I just had to kiss you."

He started at the edge of the room and introduced her to everyone that was there. Pretty soon that bunch cleared out and was replaced by a second round, and he repeated the introductions, leaving no room for doubt that he was with Claire that evening and they were an item.

The third group of people had arrived when Retta stole Claire with the excuse that she needed her help with replenishing the cookies. Suddenly Levi felt alone, as if part of him was gone.

"Hey, where's your arm candy?" Buddy elbowed him in the side.

"She's a little more than that," Levi answered.

"I can tell and I'm jealous as hell." Buddy chuckled. "You're one lucky cowboy." Buddy walked away, shaking his head.

"Don't I know it," Levi whispered.

* * *

Retta led Claire into the spare bedroom and turned on the light. She sank down on the edge of the bed and rolled her eyes. "I needed to get somewhere quiet for a few minutes. Hope you don't mind me stealing you from Levi."

Claire kicked off her high heels and crawled up into the middle of the bed. "How long does the party last?"

"Until midnight or after. It's come and go and there's several parties going on in the area, so folks kind of hop from one to the other. My face hurts from smiling." She fell back on the pillow. "It's my first ranch party, and I knew it would be a big thing. I just didn't realize how many people would arrive. I miss the beach where it was just me and Cade."

"I'd rather be out in the barn with Little Bit and Nomie," Claire admitted.

"Couple of fine ranchin' women we are." Retta closed her eyes. "Can't even make it through the first party." She laid a hand on Claire's knee. "Thanks for stickin' around, my friend."

Claire patted her hand. "We can get through this together."

"Amen, sister!" Retta managed a grin. "But for five minutes let's hide out in here to gossip. Did you see that woman who's been hanging all over Justin?"

"I sure did. I asked Levi about her, if she was Justin's date. He said that she'd come with one of the other ranchers and zeroed in on Justin," Claire said.

"Well, at the rate of sounding bitchy, her dress is way too tight, and she's wearin' too much makeup," Retta said.

"And she's not used to wearing heels that high. She can barely walk in them." Claire nodded.

Retta giggled. "I bet she's really a hardworkin' ranch woman, used to wearin' jeans and boots, and here we are judging her."

"Probably so." Claire put her shoes back on. "But we should get back out there before Cade misses you and comes lookin' to make sure you're not sick."

"Or Levi misses you," Retta said.

When they went back out, it was with smiles pasted on their faces. Cade met Retta in the doorway and led her toward a new couple. She shook hands with them and was her old cordial self.

"So where've you been?" Levi whispered right behind her.

"We had to have a few minutes to recharge," she answered honestly. "This is all a little overwhelming."

"I thought you'd tackle a forest fire with a cup of water," he said with a laugh.

"Maybe if it was going to burn up my family or loved ones. But I'm basically a hermit. I like one-on-one better than big crowds," she told him. "I can drag out my social skills for an evening, but if I had my way, I'd be sitting in the bunkhouse having a beer with you."

"Then if I was to ask you to go dancin' with me at the Rusty Spur after Grant picks up Zaylie, you'd say no?" he asked.

She rolled up on her toes and pulled his ear down to her lips. "I'd rather play some music out in the barn or in the bunkhouse and dance naked with you."

"If we did that, there wouldn't be much dancin' goin' on," he said.

"Now you're beginning to understand me." She smiled. "Shall we have some more eggnog and then meet some of the people who've just arrived? I thought this was a small rural community."

"It is and a lot of them work for the Longhorn Ranch. They look forward to this party all year and the bonus they'll all take home tonight. That's why we have the party early in the month. The bonus gives them extra money for their Christmas shopping," he told her.

"That's really kind and generous," she said.

"It's the Longhorn way."

"As in the ranch or the football team?" she asked.

"Both." He grinned.

The rest of the evening went by in a blur, and Claire decided that the most beautiful sight in the world was the taillights as the last of the folks left the party. Zaylie had curled up on the end of the sofa an hour before and was sleeping soundly, so Levi draped a throw over her and carried her back to the bunkhouse. Together, he and Claire changed her from her fancy little dress into pajamas and put her to bed.

Then they collapsed on the sofa together. Claire kicked off her shoes and put her feet in Levi's lap. He massaged the right one for five minutes and then the left one an equal amount of time.

"It's time to kiss the most beautiful woman in Texas good night now." He covered a yawn with his hand. "Or else I'm going to fall asleep right here and your brother will insist that I make an honest woman of you."

"Or Mavis will bring a shotgun and haul us to the preacher for me to make an honest man of you," she told him.

He cupped her cheek in his hand. "I loved having you beside me tonight, Claire. It felt right."

"It really did. Good night, Levi." The touch of his rough, callused hand on her bare skin sent another shiver down her spine.

"Night, darlin'. Want one naked dance before I go?" His green eyes twinkled even if they did look tired.

"I'll take a rain check." She walked him to the door and got one more good night kiss before he left. "But I will cash it someday," she called out as he left.

"I'm lookin' forward to it."

She didn't even take time for a shower but slipped out of her dress and into a nightshirt that came halfway to her ankles and fell into bed. In six hours she had to be up to help get breakfast ready, and then they were going to Randlett for church.

Levi was in her dreams all night, and she awoke feeling worse than when she'd gone to bed. She took a shower and remembered every detail of the recurring dream. Levi was walking away from her, and she was angry about something. She knew if she didn't go after him she'd lose him forever, and she also knew that she'd caused the argument. But pride kept her from saying a word.

You've got to fight for what you want. Franny's voice was clear in her head.

"I know," she said out loud. "And I will. Levi is worth it."

Chapter Twenty-Five

Claire wiggled in church that morning, as much to stay awake as out of boredom. Zaylie had curled up with her head resting in Claire's lap five minutes into the sermon. She gently brushed the child's hair back out of her face, and tears welled up in her eyes when she realized that next Sunday she wouldn't be there.

Angela and Zaylie needed to bond, but Claire felt like she was giving up her child for adoption. Angela was going to be a stay-at-home mom to the girls, and that was wonderful. Grant would be home in time for supper every evening, and they'd soon find a place in the small community.

And I'll be right there in Sunset. Levi and I can see each other as often as we want. It is what it is, so I might as well stop dwelling on the part that makes me sad, she thought.

The preacher ended the sermon by saying, "We're having a Christmas potluck dinner in the fellowship hall, and everyone is welcome to stay. I went through there between Sunday school and church, and I think there's enough food to feed the whole state of Oklahoma. So if you forgot and didn't bring anything, stay anyway. There's plenty."

"I brought two pies and a slow cooker full of chicken and dressin'. That'll cover us," Franny whispered.

"We brought leftover cookies from the ranch party," Claire said.

"Is it over? Can we eat?" Zaylie opened her eyes.

"Yes, we can, sweetheart." Franny stood up. "Let's get on into the fellowship hall before all the chocolate pie is gone. Mary Sue makes a good one."

Zaylie tugged on Claire's hand. "There's my friend Riley. Can I go with her?"

"Long as you wait right inside the door for me. I'll need to help you with your plate," Claire said.

Zaylie scampered through the pews to where Riley was waving. She grabbed her little friend's hand and the two of them wound through the people toward the fellowship hall.

Franny lowered her voice. "Riley's mama, Mindy, is going to ask if Zaylie can go home with them for a playdate as soon as we get through eating. That will give y'all enough time to get things done at the house. I'll even keep an eye out and call when Mindy brings Zaylie home."

"Why would you do that?" Claire asked.

Franny rolled her eyes toward the ceiling and then rested them on Levi. "I can think of one almighty sexy reason."

"Franny!" Claire blushed.

"Don't you Franny me. I might be old, but my eyesight is fine, and the way he fills out them jeans would put any woman's under-britches in a knot."

"Did you say something to me? I was watching Zaylie to be sure she didn't get lost in the crowd," Levi said.

"Franny has arranged for a playdate for Zaylie so we can

get things out of the house without her underfoot." Claire tucked her arm into his.

Franny moved to the other side and looped her arm into his other one. "I never pass up the opportunity to make a grand entrance with a handsome cowboy."

*   *   *

Levi knew exactly how Claire must've felt the night before at the ranch party. He knew only one old guy at the potluck dinner, and that was because he'd bought a bull from the man a while back. He was introduced to what seemed like the whole town of Randlett, and although he tried to keep all the names and faces together, it was an impossible task.

He wound up sitting between Franny and Claire and listening to everyone around him talk about what was going on in town. It wasn't a bit different from the church dinners in Sunset, except that he didn't know the people or the events they were discussing.

"If it was summertime, I'd suggest that we sneak out of here and go dance barefoot and naked by the creek at the backside of the Longhorn Canyon," he whispered to Claire.

The visual of that turned her face crimson. She glanced up, but no lightning came zipping down through the ceiling.

"What's up there?" he asked.

"Lightning bolts that God will send down if he hears you talking about gettin' naked by the creek," she answered.

"I'm thinkin' that maybe God's too busy to listen to us today?"

"We could dance naked in the bunkhouse and go skinny-dippin' in that big tub." She slipped her hand on his thigh and squeezed. No way was she letting him get ahead of her on her own stomping grounds.

"I bet after a few kisses that the water would boil." He lowered his voice even more.

Her face burned. "You're pushin' your luck. Any minute now we're both going to get zapped."

A little lady that was sitting across the table from them giggled. "I remember back when my husband, God rest his soul, used to make me blush."

"He's not my husband, Miz Letha," Claire said.

"Neither was my feller then, but he was a few months later," Letha said. "It's good to see you so happy, Claire. We've been tryin' to fix you up with someone ever since you moved here to take care of Pauline. Guess God had other plans."

Claire wasn't sure that God had anything to do with it, but she nodded and changed the subject. "So when are y'all havin' the ladies' gift exchange?"

"Next Sunday but I understand that there's going to be some changes at Pauline's place and you won't be here," Letha said with a sideways glance toward Zaylie.

"But we drew names, and I don't want the person I got to be left out so I've got my present all wrapped and ready. I'll send it with Franny," Claire said. "And next year my new sister-in-law will be with y'all for the fun."

"We'll gladly take her right in." Letha nodded.

And I'd gladly take you right in if you'd stay at the ranch forever, Levi thought. He jerked his head up and looked around to be sure he hadn't said the words out loud and then went back to eating his chocolate pie. Franny was right...he did love the pie...but not as much as he loved Claire.

When had that happened? When exactly had he fallen in love with her? He'd liked her from the first with her independence, her mothering instinct, and sass. But somehow over the course of time, admiring her had developed into something more. His eyes cut around to really look at her. She hadn't changed in that moment when he'd figured out that he was in love. There was no halo over her head or wings on her back. She was still the same Claire Mason who'd pointed a gun at him, but something was definitely different and it all had to do with him.

*   *   *

After the dinner, they hurried back to the house to get things taken care of while Zaylie was gone. He took out several boxes of quilts while she packed bolts of fabric into big black garbage bags for travel. She was on the other side of the room, when she felt his presence. She turned slowly to see him standing in the doorway, light coming in from behind him creating nothing more than a silhouette. This time he didn't look like the abominable snowman, and his arms were wide open, so she walked right into them and laid her head on his chest.

"Tell me that you're never going to leave me?" she said.

"Only if God has other plans. I'm in this for the long haul." He cupped her cheeks in his big hands and lowered his lips to hers.

With her eyes shut and heat flooding her body, her soul found its peace right there in the cold, empty house. So it was true...home wasn't a place, it really was a feeling. Home was Levi—being with him, sharing life's experiences with him.

He kissed her once more and said, "Let's get this room cleared out. Zaylie will be home at three Franny said, and if we leave right then, we can be home by dark."

Home.

The word kept popping up, and every time it did she go

a visual of the ranch, not Nanny's house or the new Harris property or even Grant's place on the base in San Antonio.

"I'll get the new battery installed while you get the rest of the fabric ready," he said. "And I don't work for free, darlin'. You have to pay me with a kiss every time I take a load of stuff to the truck."

"Then maybe I'll hire you to tote all my personal stuff out to the car." Her eyes twinkled in merriment.

"I'm available for as many kisses as you are willing to pay out." His eyes twinkled.

"Think you can stand that many?" She pulled another bag from the box.

"It might set me plumb on fire, but sweetheart, I'm willin' to go out in a blaze of glory if you are," he teased.

"Better wait a week so poor little Zaylie doesn't have to live with Franny until her daddy gets home."

"That's right." Levi stopped long enough to help her tie off the bag.

They'd had some hot and heavy makeout sessions, and they'd had sex, but his touch still sent ripples racing through her body—every single time.

With a little hop, Claire wrapped her legs around his waist and her arms around his neck. "Here's a bonus kiss to get you started."

He carried her to the sofa where he sat down with her in his lap. "We could use the next hour to . . ."

She put her fingers on his lips to shush him. "Darlin', don't even say the words. My body is already beggin' for that, and we don't have the time. But next week, my bedroom window will always be open."

"Honey, after Grant gets Zaylie, I'm coming right in the front door. I don't care who knows that we're seeing each other or sleeping together."

"You plannin' on sleepin'? I had something else in mind." She hopped up from his lap. "And it didn't involve snoring."

"I can live with that plan," he said. "But right now I've got a truck to load, Miz Mason."

An hour and many kisses later, she stood on the porch and waved at him until the truck was completely out of sight. Her grandmother's car was parked out on the curb, leaving the garage empty for Grant and Angela. The trunk was full, as well as the passenger seat and half the backseat, leaving only room for Zaylie. Everything she owned could be put into a truck and a car. That didn't say a lot for a woman her age.

She walked through the house one last time, letting the memories flood her mind. She and Grant had lived there for a year. There were arguments between them, but then there were good times during that time. Nanny had still been lucid and very outspoken. She'd given them room to make their own decisions, but if they got too far out of line with it, she didn't hesitate to draw them right back in. And there was always, always the smell of something cooking in the house. Claire missed that when she went to her parents' next duty station—Florida, she remembered. It had been one of her favorite spots, but they'd only been there six months when her father went on deployment to Kuwait. Her mother was transferred to California, so they'd been jerked out of school and put into a brand-new environment—again.

Then there was the past three years when she'd taken care of Nanny and watched her mind slowly leave her body. Role reversal was what it had been. She'd become the adult and Nanny was the child. She shut her eyes and leaned against the wall, remembering all the times when Zaylie and Nanny played together like two little girls. Those days were sad but happy at the same time. Nanny had reverted back to her childhood, and Zaylie loved having a playmate when she visited them.

"Aunt Claire!" Zaylie's voice brought her back to the present day. She opened the door and two little girls burst in, ponytails flipping from one side to the other.

Zaylie looked around the room and frowned. "Where's Levi and the truck? How are we goin' to get home?"

"We're going to drive Nanny's car so we can have our own vehicle at the ranch. Levi put a new battery in it for us. He left a few minutes ago, but he'll be there when we get there. Why?"

"Because Riley has a bunny and I wanted to tell him about it," she said. "It don't look like Hopalong. It's white."

"Hey." Riley's mother waved at the door. "Just makin' sure she got inside safely. We've got to run, but when y'all get back up here permanently, we need to have lunch and discuss that cowboy you had stayin' close to you all during the dinner."

"Thanks for letting her go play with Riley and yes, ma'am, we will have lunch." Claire waved back, not letting on that Grant would be the one staying here permanently.

Riley gave Zaylie a hug, and then they were gone, leaving Claire and Zaylie alone in the house. She glanced around one more time, said a silent good-bye to the best place that she'd ever lived, and took Zaylie by the hand.

"You ready, sweetie?"

"Yep. I'm ready to go home."

"Me too," Claire said.

Chapter Twenty-Six

Justin came from around the back side of the boys' bunkhouse and waved when Levi parked his loaded truck out front. While he stepped out and stretched the kinks from his back, Justin picked up two boxes. "Prop that door open so we can go back and forth easier," he said.

"Appreciate the help." Levi nodded.

"I'm bored so it gives me something to do. Took a walk out to the barn and back," Justin told him.

"Make you feel better?" Levi asked.

"Nope." He carried the boxes inside and came back for more.

"What's your problem?" Levi stacked three lightweight ones up and headed toward the porch with them.

"It's Retta and Cade. They're so damned happy, and now you've got Claire, and I . . . well hell, Levi, I'm beginning to think about a permanent-type relationship. But I don't even know where to begin," he admitted.

"I'm in love with Claire," Levi blurted. "I want to spend the rest of my life with her, and I'm scared to death to tell her. It's too soon, and I'm afraid I'll scare her off."

"And that leaves me as the fifth wheel for sure." Justin sighed.

"Hey, just when you give up ever finding someone, she'll fall right in your lap. Trust me because I'm speaking from experience. Look at what happened with Cade and Retta and"—he crossed his fingers like a little boy—"I'm hopin' for me and Claire."

Levi and Justin had finished unloading and were on their way back to the ranch house when Claire drove up in her vintage car. She honked, and they both turned around and headed right back toward the girls' bunkhouse.

"I will marry you tomorrow if you'll give me that car," Justin teased as he opened the door for her.

"What have you been drinkin'?" she shot right back at him.

"I'm sober as a judge, darlin'. I want to ask first because when Buddy and some of the other cowboys see this car, they'll be lined up outside your door with engagement rings in hand. We can go pick out whatever kind of ring you want tomorrow," Justin joked. "This is a beauty of a car, worthy of any man's proposal."

"Thank you." She giggled. "But when I accept a proposal, it will be for me, not my car."

"You've broken my heart. I may never get over this." Justin threw a hand up to his chest.

"You'll forget me and the Lincoln when a tall blonde offers to make breakfast for you," Claire told him.

Levi eased the back door open and picked up Zaylie. "Shhh, don't wake the baby," he told them.

"Levi!" Her blue eyes popped open. "Riley has a bunny."

"Is that right?" He carried her toward the bunkhouse.

"Yep and it's white. I'm hungry. Is it time for a snack?"

"No, sweetheart, it's supper time. Soon as me and Justin get things unloaded, we'll go up to the ranch house and eat," he said. "But while we get that job done, there's three little kittens who want to see you."

Zaylie squirmed out of his arms and ran across the porch and into the house. "My poor babies. They missed me."

Levi kissed Claire on the cheek and whispered, "Not as much as I'm going to miss her when Grant takes her away from us."

Claire leaned into his shoulder. "I don't even want to think about it. I always get sad when I have to give her up, but this time it's permanent."

"Put your worries in my pocket," he said.

"I can't thank you enough for everything," she told him.

"Don't thank me, darlin'. Just love me as much as I do you," he said.

"I do," she said simply.

*   *   *

Retta and Claire were sitting at the table having a cup of hot tea when Mavis arrived that Monday morning. As usual she talked the whole time she hung up her coat and poured a cup of coffee. "I thought maybe us girls could go to Bowie today and do a little Christmas shopping. I've only just gotten started. I need to hit the western wear store for sure."

"I was about to ask Retta if I could sneak away for an hour to sign the papers on the house," Claire said.

"And I know how much you value your time with Zaylie since this is the last week before her daddy comes home, but

I was going to ask if I could have her this morning. I need to do some shopping also," Retta said.

"Looks like you girls are on the same wave. Retta and Zaylie can come with me, and you can go do your legal business. Let me finish this cup of coffee and we'll all get this show on the road," Mavis said.

"I can call you and pick her up when I'm done," Claire said.

"Good friends share their toys," Retta said. "Let us keep her for a few hours. We'll have her home by lunchtime."

"Thank you," Claire said. "I can use the time to finish up a few little dolly outfits I'm sewing for her and Teresa's Christmas. It's been a chore to get them done without her realizing what I'm doing. But a word of warning. She tells everything, so if you're getting presents for the guys you better hide them well."

"I'm buying a few things for the guys on my list, so thanks for the heads-up," Mavis said. "You'll have to distract her for me, Retta."

"I'm shopping today for my in-laws. They're arriving right before Christmas Eve and staying through New Year's. Thank God you'll be here to help me get through those days," Retta said.

"First time they've been here since you became the lady of the house?" Claire asked.

Retta nodded.

"I'll be here to support you. We're friends," Claire said.

Retta smiled. "I knew the minute that you came into the house that we'd get along like a house on fire."

"You were right. Do they stay in the guest room?" she said.

"No need," Mavis said. "They always bring their big old motor home and park it in the backyard."

Retta started out of the room. "Will that make it easier? Will Gloria still want to take over like the ranch is still hers?"

"Honey, Gloria is a force," Mavis said. "But she's got a good heart and her family comes first, so don't worry about it."

Claire patted Retta on the back. "Hey, it doesn't matter. Together we'll show her that we've got everything runnin' smooth."

Zaylie was so excited to get to go shopping with Mavis and Retta that she didn't even ask why Claire wasn't going with them.

Claire waited until they were completely out of sight before she left driving her grandmother's old Lincoln. When she arrived at the lawyer's office the receptionist pointed toward an open door. "If you are Claire, they're waiting for you. They got here a little early."

"Thank you." Claire squared her shoulders and went in with a smile on her face. "Hello, I hope you didn't have a long wait."

"Not at all. We've already done our part of the signing. So now it's your turn," Delores said. "The insurance on the house is paid up until January first. That will give you time to take care of that." She told her the name of the company they'd used. "They'll have all the information about the place."

"Thank you. I'll go talk to them when we get done here," Claire said.

"It's right next door. This won't take long, but please have a seat." The lawyer slid papers across the table. "Your signature goes where the orange tabs are."

She read through each paper carefully before she signed at the bottom. "Will a personal check do, or should I go get a cashier's check at the bank?"

"Personal is fine," Delores said.

Their trust amazed Claire, but she carefully wrote out a check for the most money she'd ever spent at one time.

When she handed it over, the lawyer separated the pages and handed Delores and Claire each a copy.

"That's it?" Claire asked.

"Yes, ma'am. Cash sales don't require nearly as much work as when you have to go through the bank. You are now the proud owner of a house in Sunset, Texas."

"And we wish you happiness and good luck with your store," Delores said. "Got time for an ice cream to celebrate?"

"Thank you, but I'd better go on to the insurance company, and then I've got a full morning ahead of me," Claire answered.

Delores stood up and opened her arms. "A hug from someone who had good days in that house and hopes that you prosper there?"

Claire moved around the desk and hugged the lady. "I just know I'm going to be happy in Sunset. You come see me when you're in town."

"Oh, honey, I will. Quilting is what keeps my mind active and my fingers nimble. First thing I did when I moved was start a quilting bee at my church. I miss Mavis and the old group, but this new one is pretty lively," Delores said.

"Well, then I'll look to see you at my store before too many months pass," Claire said.

"I'll bring cookies." Delores moved toward the door with Joe and Frank behind her.

Thirty minutes later Claire had written a check to cover insurance for a year. And she was on her way back home to the ranch. When she went through Sunset, she pulled into the driveway of her house and sat there for a few minutes staring at it. Something was missing. It looked the same, and it was empty so there was no way anything had been stolen.

Then she realized what was wrong. She didn't want to go

inside alone for the first time as the owner. She wanted to share the experience with Levi. She fished her phone from her purse and sent a text.

Are you busy?

Immediately her phone rang.

She answered, "That was fast. I'm sitting in front of my house."

"Papers signed then?" Levi asked.

"No problems there, but I know you are busy..." She paused.

"I'm never too busy to take a few minutes or even longer for you."

"This is going to sound silly, but I want you to share the experience of going inside the first time that I own it with you," she said.

"I'll be there in ten minutes," he said.

The call ended and she turned on the radio. Ten minutes wasn't so long—it was only three songs.

Before the second one ended, Levi had pulled his truck in behind her. He opened the door for her and placed his hands on her waist. But when she was on the ground, he didn't let go like usual. He pulled her tightly to his chest.

"This makes me so happy," he said.

"I was afraid that I'd be interfering with your work."

"Darlin', don't you understand? There's a priority in a cowboy's life—God, his woman, and then his work."

Tears welled up in her eyes. She'd always wanted to have first place with someone—anyone—but taking second place behind God? Well, it didn't get any better than that.

She expected a kiss, but instead he took her by the hand and led her to the porch. He waited patiently for her to find the key in her purse and unlock the door. Then he scooped her up in his arms like a bride and carried her over the threshold. Once inside he shut the door with the heel of his boot, set her down, and claimed her lips in a scorching kiss.

"Welcome to the quiltin' house," he whispered softly in her ear when the kiss ended.

"That will be the name of the business," she said. "The Quiltin' House. I love it even more since you said it."

A grin spread across his face. "You're going to do great here. I just know it."

Two blessings in one day. But the most important one was from Levi. He supported her, and that meant the world to Claire.

*   *   *

On Tuesday it rained all day, and Zaylie was cranky. She whined because she had to leave her kittens in the bunkhouse and then because Beau didn't show up to follow them to the ranch house. Not even talking to her dad helped that afternoon. It was like a kid the day after Christmas or their birthday when all the excitement was over. She'd had the fun of the ranch party and then seeing her little friend on Sunday, followed up by a day with Retta. And now it was just a normal day, until Levi popped his head in the back door in the middle of the afternoon.

"Hey, anyone here want to go out to the barn and see Nomie and Little Bit? Poor little things are beggin' for some little girl company," he hollered.

"Me, me, me!" Zaylie came alive and danced on her tiptoes all the way across the room.

"And me, me, me!" Claire giggled.

"Great!" Levi winked. "Get your coats on, and we'll race

to the truck. If we run between the raindrops we might not get wet."

"Silly Levi, you can't do that," Zaylie said.

"I thought he could walk on water." Claire zipped up her coat and pulled a stocking hat down over her hair.

"He can when he's a grandpa, but he's too big to run between raindrops," Zaylie declared, and took off in a flash across the yard.

Levi took a moment to brush a brief kiss across Claire's lips, then grabbed her hand, and they ran like kids through the rain to the truck. "I don't feel like a grandpa," he said as he got Zaylie into the backseat.

"You ain't one yet." Zaylie sighed. "You gots to have kids first."

"I see, and that makes me a grandpa?"

"No, silly!" Zaylie giggled. "That makes you a daddy."

"When do I get to be a grandpa?"

"When them kids has babies," she told him.

He shut the door and hurried around the back end of the truck, crawled inside, and shivered. "How did you get to be so smart, Zaylie?"

She sucked in a lung full of air and let it out in a whoosh. "Aunt Claire tells me stuff and I 'member. If she tells you stuff, then you can be smart."

He'd brought the calf and the miniature donkey both into the barn, but he hadn't put them in stalls, so they were romping around playfully when they arrived. Zaylie ran right to Little Bit and threw her arms around his neck. After she'd given the little donkey kisses and hugs, she went over to the calf to hug her.

Levi sat down on a bale of hay and pulled Claire into his lap. "I wouldn't be surprised if she grows up to be a vet or do something with animals."

"Me either," she said. "I could kiss you for rescuing her

today. She's had so much excitement these past three days that it's tough just having a normal day."

"No day with you in it could ever be normal," he whispered. "And I'll take that kiss whenever you want to deliver it."

She brought his lips to hers in a sweet kiss but ended it quickly when Zaylie tugged on her hand.

"Why are you kissin' Levi? Is he still your boyfriend?"

"What do you know about boyfriends?" Claire asked.

"Me and Riley both like Jason. He's our boyfriend. I wanted Justin to be my boyfriend, but he said he's too old, but Jason is only six so he's not too old. When can I kiss him?" she asked.

"When you are twenty-one," Claire answered.

"Okay, I'll tell Riley and Teresa." She ran off to play with the animals again.

"Well, that was easy enough, and you sure know how to sidestep questions," Levi said. "Am I your boyfriend?"

"Do you want to be?" she asked.

"Yes, ma'am, I sure do. I may be old fashioned, but I like sayin' that you're my girlfriend more than sayin' that we're in a relationship." He nodded.

"Me too." She nudged him with her shoulder. "It just sounds more personal, doesn't it?"

"Yes, darlin', it does."

*   *   *

In the next three days there were hours the clock refused to move and then others when the day sped by so fast that Claire wondered how time could pass so quickly. Suddenly it was the last night that she'd have Zaylie. She was thinking about maybe a movie and a trip to Zaylie's favorite burger shop, when Levi came up with a better plan.

"Let's drive over to McKinney and take her to see the festival of lights. We can leave early enough to have burgers, see the lights, go let her see Santa Claus—I checked and he's at one of the department stores tonight—and then have ice cream at Culvers," Levi suggested.

"I like that idea," Claire said. "You want to take the car or your truck?"

"You'd trust me to drive the car?" Levi asked as if he was stunned.

"Sure I would. It's just a car."

"Naw, let's take the truck. That'll let Zaylie sit up higher so she can see everything better."

"You're a good man, Levi Jackson," she said.

He muttered something that sounded a lot like, "I hope I'm good enough."

*   *   *

When they got home from the light show, Grant called, and Zaylie talked the whole time about seeing Cinderella's pumpkin coach and Rudolph and Mickey Mouse and "Oh!" she gasped. "We got ice cream and I went to sleep on the way home and Levi carried me in the house."

When she finally wound down, Grant asked if he could talk to Claire.

"I'm jealous of Levi tonight, and I've never even met him," Grant said.

"He adores her." Claire yawned. "But tomorrow she's all yours."

"Go to bed, sis. You sound tired."

"I've got less than one ounce of energy left, for sure. See you tomorrow."

"Yes, ma'am," he said, and the call ended.

On Saturday morning Claire awoke with a settled heart. Her brother was on his way home, and she'd never have to worry about getting a knock on the door from two uniformed airmen sent to deliver the most devastating news possible.

Grant called in the middle of the morning to tell her that they were an hour away and would be there soon. She started to pace the floor of the ranch house. Everything was packed and ready. Levi had bought a carrier for the kittens so the girls could take them home with them. She was so anxious to see Grant but even more so to see Zaylie's reaction when she heard that her daddy was home for good.

Levi came through the house, and without a word, he took her in his arms and held her tightly. "I'm here for you always. Where is Zaylie?"

"In the living room. She's been cranky all morning. I'm glad you're here, Levi. You give me strength," she told him.

"Just lean on me, and we'll get through this together," he said.

"I will," she said simply.

"Aunt Claire, there's a red car outside. Oh! Oh!" Zaylie clamped a hand over her mouth. "That's Teresa and my daddy." Every word got higher as she ran toward the door to sling it open and throw herself into Grant's arms.

"It's selfish to be sad when I look at that happiness." Claire watched Grant hug her so tight that she squealed and then twirl her around until they were both dizzy. To begrudge him a single moment of being a full-time father would be downright hateful.

"Keep that picture in your mind while you go out there and do some hugging of your own." Levi led her to the door with his hand in hers.

Grant rushed up on the porch, picked her up in a fierce bear hug, and said, "I owe you so much."

"Just be happy," she said, and laughed.

Angela followed him onto the porch. "Thank you for keeping this a secret. We haven't told Teresa yet."

"Then it's time, and I'm glad that we're sisters." Claire wrapped her arms around Angela. "See that second little house down there. Y'all put the girls in your van and take them in there and tell them. Her things are all packed up, and there's a carrier for the kittens. When you come back we'll have lunch ready."

"Thank you for everything," Angela said.

She was a beautiful woman—almost as tall as Grant, with her dark hair and skin the color of coffee with lots of cream.

"You could come with us," Grant offered.

"I'll stay right here with Levi." She slapped a hand over her mouth. "My manners just escaped in all the excitement. This is Levi Jackson. Levi, meet my bother, Grant, and Angela and that little dark-haired girl out there talkin' a mile a minute with Zaylie is Teresa."

Levi stuck out a hand. "Pleased to meet you. Claire has talked a lot about you."

"And you as well." Grant shook with him and then took a step back. "You look happy, sis."

"I am," she told him.

"I'm glad. That makes this easier for me. So you sure you don't want to join us?"

"Positive. Go make a family, and then come back and eat with us before you go home," she said around the lump forming in her throat.

"Would it be terribly rude if we just grabbed a to-go burger at the next town? We want to get unpacked and get our tree up tonight," Angela asked. "There's so much to do and so many decisions to make."

"Not a bit," Claire answered. "I understand."

"We're anxious to settle in. Do you think you and Levi could visit some evening this next week? I grill a mean steak, and we could get to know each other a little better," Grant asked.

"Of course we can. You just name the day and we'll be there," Levi answered. "I'll bring the beer."

"Sounds good." Grant slipped an arm around Angela's waist and yelled out across the lawn, "Hey, you two beautiful ladies. Get in the van. Claire says that Zaylie needs to show us some kittens down in the bunkhouse."

The girls scrambled into the backseat.

But I wanted just a little more time. Not all day. Just one more meal with her. One more hour to listen to her and Teresa giggle together.

Levi drew her close to his side, and suddenly it was all right. A clean break would be better for everyone, including Zaylie. Claire would see the whole new little family in a week or so when she went to Randlett for Christmas.

Chapter Twenty-Seven

Zaylie was the first one out of the van when it stopped in front of the ranch house thirty minutes later. She barreled into Claire's arms and hugged her. "Guess what, Aunt Claire, I got the bestest mommy in the whole world for Christmas, and Teresa got the bestest daddy, and we get to take the kittens home with us and put up our own Christmas tree tonight and..." She stopped for a breath and went on, "and Teresa likes our kitties' names and Angela says if I want to I can call her mommy, but I don't have to. Do you think my mommy in heaven will be sad if I do?"

"I think your mommy in heaven would be happy that you have someone to love you, so if you feel comfortable calling Angela mommy, then that's okay," Claire answered. "Will you send me a picture of your tree when you get it finished?"

"Yep." Zaylie nodded seriously, and her expression changed to worry. "You're comin' to Christmas Day, right?"

"Sure I am, darlin'," Claire answered. "Can I bring Levi?"

Zaylie giggled. "Yes, yes, yes! And Little Bit and Hopalong and Nomie."

Levi picked Zaylie up to hug her and then set her back on the porch. "I don't think they'd be happy in the truck, but you can come back and see them anytime you want. Maybe you and Teresa can spend the weekend with us sometime after Christmas so we can get to know her better."

"Yes!" Teresa pumped her fist in the air. "And if there's more kittens..."

"Whoa!" Angela shook her head. "Three cats in one house is enough."

"Can we have a donkey then?" Zaylie asked.

"Only if you want to leave all three kittens here," Grant said.

Zaylie hung her head for a moment and then said, "I'll keep my kittens. They'd be sad without me."

"Okay, girls, let's get moving. We've got lots to do before the end of the day." Grant drew Claire close to him. "Remember when we used to say we wanted a normal family like other kids had, where we lived in a town long enough to get to know everyone? Well, I think I'm about to have that for me and for Zaylie. I hope you and this cowboy find the same thing that I have with Angela."

"Me too, brother," she whispered. "Now get out of here before I cry."

"Yes, ma'am." He stepped back and nodded toward Levi. "Take care of her. The first days after she gives Zaylie back to me are rough on everyone."

"Do my best, and y'all come back anytime—for supper, for Sunday afternoon, or for a week. We've got lots of room, and we'd love to have you." Levi slipped his arm around Claire.

"Road goes both ways, and our home is always open to y'all," Angela said.

"Next time I want to meet the rest of the family," Grant said.

"They're all off to do the last of their shopping today, but I'd love for you to meet them," Claire said. "Now go. The girls are waiting in the van and I'll be fine."

"Promise?" Grant asked.

"I don't make promises I can't keep." She managed a weak smile.

She and Levi both waved as the van pulled away from the ranch. When it was completely out of sight, he gently scooped her up into his arms and carried her into the house. Without a word, he took her down the hallway to his bedroom, kicked the door shut with his boot heel, and laid her on the bed. Then he took off his boots and work coat and stretched out beside her.

"I'm here for you if you want to cry, throw a fit, or take a nap." He gathered her into his arms, and she rested her head on his chest.

"I love you," she said. "But I'm not going to weep or pitch a hissy. There's no way I can sleep, but I can think of something we might do since we have the house to ourselves for the next few hours."

*   *   *

Levi propped up on an elbow and got lost in her green eyes for several moments. "I could stay right here forever, just drowning in your eyes," he said.

"That's a beautiful pickup line," she teased as she sat up, removed her jacket and shoes, and tossed them over to the side. "Ever see *Top Gun*?"

"I'm not sure a boy can truly grow up without seeing it. It almost put me in the Air Force rather than ranchin'. Why?"

"I'm thinkin' of a line in it that says, 'Take me to bed or lose me forever.'"

"Well, darlin'"—he stroked her cheek with his fingertips—"I don't want to lose you for a single day, much less forever."

She put her hand on his and held it on her face. "I love the way your touch makes me feel."

"How's that?" He kissed her knuckles one at a time.

"Like I'm special."

"Oh, honey, you are beyond special to me," Levi whispered as he removed his hand and began to unbutton her shirt. "When you touch me or even glance my way, I feel like I'm sittin' on a king's throne."

He removed her shirt and her bra and tossed both toward the end of the bed. Then he took off his shirt and threw it in the pile with her things.

"I love your curves." He ran his hands down her sides and then brought her to his chest so he could feel her breasts against his bare skin. "Truth is, I love everything about you, Claire Mason. Your eyes, your lips, your hair that always smells like vanilla, and your body—you flat out turn me on just lookin' at you."

She leaned back enough and ran her fingers through the soft hair on his chest.

Just like the last time, they made love so passionately and so hot that when it was over, they were still floating somewhere above the clouds with their fingers entwined and their hearts beating as one. When they finally drifted back to earth, he rolled off to one side and brought her to his side with an arm around her, while they struggled for breath.

"We belong together," he said.

"I believe we do," she muttered.

*   *   *

Claire was starving when she awoke with one leg thrown over Levi's naked body and tangled sheets around them both. She peeked over the top of his broad chest so she could see the clock on the nightstand. Two o'clock! Retta, Cade, and Justin could be returning any minute.

She got out of bed, scooped up her clothing, and hurried to the bathroom. She turned on the water in the shower and waited impatiently for it to warm up. She'd barely stepped under the spray when Levi pulled back the curtain and joined her.

"What's the hurry?"

"Two things. I'm hungry, and the family will be home soon," she answered.

"We're consenting adults." He lathered up his hands and starting at her neck, worked his way to her ankles.

Her hormones raced, and new desire flooded her whole body. "You're making me so hot..." She turned around, and with a little hop, her legs were around his waist. "Ever had shower sex?"

"No, but I've got a feeling we're about to," he answered.

She wiggled her hand between them, and he pressed her up against the shower wall. With water spraying on them like a warm rain, they rocked together until they both reached the climax at the same time, and then they sank down to the floor, breathless again.

After a few moments, he stood up and extended a hand to help her.

She put hers in it and took the fastest shower she'd ever

taken in her life. When she finished she dried off and got dressed, then headed for the kitchen. She was only there a few minutes when Levi arrived with water droplets hanging on his gorgeous brown hair.

His arms circled around her from behind, and he buried his face in her wet hair. "You are beautiful."

"And you are sexy as hell," she said. "You want cold fried chicken or lasagna heated up in the microwave for lunch."

"Both." He kissed her on the neck. "Or maybe a third round on the kitchen table?"

The sound of pickup doors slamming made them step away from each other, and seconds later Retta rushed in the back door with gift bags in her hands. "Cade and Justin are bringing in more presents to go under the tree, so don't shut the door. It's cold out there. Did your brother get Zaylie yet?"

"They're probably in Randlett by now," Levi answered for Claire.

"Did you cry?" Retta's eyes went to Claire.

"Almost, but it took a lot of willpower not to." Claire fixed a plate of lasagna and heated it in the microwave. "Always before, I knew that Grant would call on me before long to come get her, or it would be a holiday or sometime when I was needed. This time was different. I'll see her probably more often, but I'm not needed anymore."

"You'll always be a part of her life." Levi draped an arm around Claire's shoulders. "It's just in a different way now."

"He's right." Retta set the bags on the table and removed her coat. "And besides, we need you here on the ranch. I'll hire you after New Year's if you want to stay. I'm going to need help after the baby comes for sure, and I understand that you know your way around bookkeeping as well as the kitchen."

"That's sweet but…" Claire couldn't think of a single *but*. Retta had just offered her the opportunity to live right there on the ranch where she felt at home. If Levi would offer her the same thing, she just might take them up on it.

Chapter Twenty-Eight

Claire found a sock under the edge of Zaylie's bed and one of her hair bows on the dresser that evening, and she clutched both to her chest and let the tears flow. She wanted a child, preferably a daughter, but she wouldn't complain for a single moment if she had a whole house full of sons just like Levi.

She didn't even hear the knock on the door, but suddenly Levi was sitting on the floor beside the bed with her, his arm around her shoulders as she sobbed. "I thought I was okay, and then I found these. It's just a crumpled hair bow and a dirty sock, but I feel like I gave away my own child today."

"Let's just throw away your birth control pills and have one a year until we get a dozen," Levi said.

"I'm not that sad, but I wouldn't fuss about four in the next ten years." She wiped at her cheek.

He pulled a handkerchief from his pocket and dabbed the tears away. "Shall we start on the first one tonight? I'm not leaving you alone, Claire. I brought my toothbrush."

"And jammies?"

"I don't like those any better than underwear. They bind me up. I want to wake up with you next to me, but I can always take my bag right back to the ranch house if you aren't comfortable with us spending the night together," he answered.

For the first time in her life, she was only responsible for herself. During her growing-up years she had to be careful not to do anything that would bring shame to her mother's and father's careers. The year she lived with her grandmother, she felt that she had to do what her grandmother wanted so that she wouldn't disgrace her in the small town of Randlett. After that she was busy with college, teaching, and then taking care of Zaylie and her Nanny, often at the same time.

Make sure you're not substituting all of them with Levi, Nanny's voice whispered softly in her head.

Oh, Nanny, I can't imagine living without him.

"Well?" Levi asked.

"I want you to stay," she whispered. "When I reach for you tomorrow morning I don't want to get an arm full of nothing but air."

"Or a pillow," he said. "I brought a couple of beers. Want one?"

She nodded, and he stood to his feet. In only a few minutes he was back with a plate of cookies and two longneck bottles of Coors. He set the cookies on the floor, handed her a beer, and took his place again right beside her.

"Folks usually eat pretzels with beer for the salt, but I've always liked cookies better. These arc leftovers from the party, but they're still good."

She picked up a pecan sandy and bit off a piece and then took a sip of beer. He was right—it was so much better than pretzels. "We should buy us a honky-tonk and put out cookies instead of nuts and pretzels on the bar. Bet we'd make a fortune."

"If you were drawin' up the beer and makin' drinks, we'd get rich real quick." He nodded. "But I really like it right here on the ranch. Which reminds me, we're going to be super busy tryin' to get everything caught up this next week. That way when Justin and Cade's folks are here, they can spend time with them."

"And I imagine Retta and I'll be pretty busy in the house." This time she chose a peanut butter cookie. "But we'll have the nights together, right?"

"Yes, darlin'. A million times, yes."

*　　*　　*

Claire awoke the next morning to see Levi propped up on an elbow staring at her. The way his eyes twinkled told her that he'd enjoyed sharing her bed as much as she'd liked him being there. But now it was time to get dressed and go to the ranch house, to face Justin, Cade, and Retta. She wasn't a child but hoped that it wasn't awkward like that morning when Justin's one-night stand had been cooking breakfast.

"Good mornin'," he drawled. "I could sure enough get used to this. Just thinkin' about it comin' to an end when you move into your house makes this old cowboy want to weep."

"But you can still come spend nights with me, right?" Claire said.

Levi sat up so fast that he jerked all the covers off her. "Every single one that you want me to."

"That will be all of them." She rolled out of bed and opened up her dresser drawer to find underpants and a clean bra. She'd never done it before, but there was something downright exhilarating and free about sleeping in the raw.

Levi got out of bed and pulled on his jeans. "Then I'll be there as soon as I get the evening chores done every day."

Beau and Gussie met them that morning as they went hand in hand from the bunkhouse to the ranch house. Beau romped on ahead to send a squirrel up the dormant pecan tree, but with her tail high like a regal queen, Gussie stayed right beside Claire and darted into the house when the door was opened.

"I wonder where Hopalong is this mornin'," Claire said.

"Probably holed up in a mesquite thicket with his girl-friend," Retta answered.

"It's warmer in a bunkhouse under a nice quilt," Claire said.

"It's a good thing those bunkhouse walls can't talk." Retta giggled.

"Amen to that," Claire said.

Cade and Justin yelled at Levi from the living room, and Claire followed Retta on into the kitchen. She got out a cast iron skillet and started frying slabs of ham while Retta made biscuits.

"Claire, you are welcome to stay here as long as you want. You can live in the bunkhouse until you get your new house all ready. We don't need it until summer when the kids arrive," Retta said.

"Thank you, but I'm hoping to get things set up to move in right after Christmas. I thought signing the papers would be a big thing, but it wasn't. I think the day that I move into the bedroom, it'll seem real," Claire said.

Retta pointed toward a cabinet door. "Would you hand me a pan? My hands have dough on them. I see a future in which you are part of the family."

Claire jerked her head around so quickly that it made her dizzy. "Did Levi say something?"

"Nope, but I can see it in his eyes and the way he is when you are around. That cowboy is in love. It just takes him a while to say the words." Retta rolled the dough out.

"Seems like everything has happened in a whirlwind, and at the same time it seems like I've lived on the ranch forever and ever," Claire admitted.

"I know the feeling. I arrived the first of June and by July fourth, I was so in love with Cade that it hurt to think of ever being away from him. You've heard that old saying that God works in mysterious ways. Well, I believe it now," Retta said.

"Did you ever feel like something bad was going to happen?" Claire asked.

"At first." Retta nodded. "It seemed like when things were going good for me that something always happened, so I expected things with Cade to go sideways at any time, but..." She paused. "Maybe that's the mysterious part because here we are. That don't mean we don't disagree and get angry with each other." She lowered her voice. "But the makeup sex is amazing."

Claire slapped at her with a dish towel. "I'd miss this and you."

Retta laughed. "Me too. God might've sent you to Levi, but he also sent me a friend."

"Well, thank you for the offer to stay, and I'll take you up on it. After all, one should not try to argue with God's plan, should they?"

*   *   *

Levi parked the four-wheeler in front of the cabin and just sat there looking at it. If he could buy any five acres on the ranch it would be this little corner, because it was where he first met Claire. He wished he'd thought to take a picture of her with that pistol in her hands to hang above the mantel. But there was no way he would have reached inside his pocket for his phone at that moment for fear she'd pull the trigger.

Beau ran past him, up onto the porch, and put his paws on the doorknob. Then he ran back to Levi and barked before he ran back to the door a second time.

"Okay, old boy, what's the problem? Is there another damsel in distress in the cabin this mornin'?" He followed Beau and opened the door. No one was there, but he took a long, hard look at the cabin. If he took those bunk beds out and put in a queen-size bed and maybe built a few more cabinets, it would be livable until he could build a real house.

Beau flopped down in front of the cold fireplace and put a paw over his nose.

"I know it's crazy thinking. Claire deserves more than a rundown hunter's cabin way back here in the sticks."

As if Beau understood, he yipped once and hopped up on the sofa. Levi sat down beside him and scratched his ears. The dog laid his head over on Levi's lap and whined.

"If someone had told me two months ago that marriage would be on my mind in the next ten years, I'd have asked them what they'd been smokin'. But I can't imagine life without her, Beau. It's just happened too fast. She's had wings, not roots, and what if the fire goes out and she doesn't want roots? Kind of like what happened with Julie and Cade?" Levi recalled how Julie had been engaged to Cade, but she broke it off on their wedding day. Thank God he had found Retta, who turns out was his soul mate after all.

Beau shut his eyes and went to sleep. "Some help you

are. Wake up." Levi shook him. "It's almost noon and Retta and Claire will have our dinner on the table."

Beau bounded off the sofa and ran to the door. Levi let him out and rode the four-wheeler back to the barn where the hired hands were sitting around with their lunch buckets, sack lunches, and thermos bottles. Some of them had already finished and were laid back on hay bales taking a power nap with their cowboy hats over their eyes.

Skip pushed his back with his finger. "I got an extra sandwich over there in my lunch pail if you want it."

"What are you doin' out here?" Levi frowned.

"Don't want to stay home by myself and ain't about to stay in the house with three women—no sir," Skip whispered.

"Thanks, but I'm on my way inside."

"Ah, the ways of young love." Skip pulled his hat back over his eyes.

"Wonderful, ain't it?" Levi said.

Chapter Twenty-Nine

There was no doubt that Vernon Maguire was Justin and Cade's father. They all had the same angular face structure and blue eyes. Vernon wasn't quite as tall as Cade but more the height of Justin. But Gloria wasn't anything like what Claire had imagined. Not even the family picture above the mantel prepared her for Gloria's size. The woman was about Claire's height and was at least twenty pounds lighter. She had blond hair and clear blue eyes, and when she entered the room that Sunday afternoon, it was like a force had arrived. No wonder Retta was intimidated by her.

"I'd like you to meet Claire," Levi said after the hugs were given.

Gloria took a step forward and sized Claire up from head to toe and then grabbed her in an embrace. "I believe in Texas-size hugs, especially when someone is part of our family." Then she whispered, "Levi is like a son to me."

"I'm glad to meet and hug you," Claire said. "And I understand that Levi spent a lot of time on the ranch."

"You guys get on outside and help Vernon get the RV all hooked up. Retta, let's have a glass of sweet tea and talk about this baby. Have y'all picked out names? There's no use in choosing a girl's name. Maguires have sons, not daughters." She led the way to the kitchen, talking the whole time.

Man alive, that woman had clout because all four of those grown cowboys got their coats and headed out the back door without a single argument. Claire poured three glasses of tea and put a variety of cookies on a platter.

When they were all three seated around the table, Gloria shook her head slowly. "You both failed the test."

"What test?" Claire asked.

"Retta, this is your house now, not mine. You shouldn't have let me boss Cade like that. And Claire, whether you break Levi's heart or elope with him tomorrow is your business," Gloria said.

"You scare me a little," Retta said.

"Don't ever let anyone do that. Walk into a room like you own the whole damn place and haven't decided whether to keep it or burn it down. According to Mavis, you are both full of spit and vinegar. I expect to see more of that and less of this yes, ma'am, shit. That's what it takes to run the Longhorn Canyon." Gloria picked up a cookie. "Now about this baby. If you're already over morning sickness, then I reckon it's one of those jet airplane babies."

"What?" Claire asked.

"One that arrives on a jet airplane rather than takin' nine months. I want grandkids, and I'm going to claim Levi's too, so both of you better get busy," Gloria said.

"Baby is due at the end of May. I was pregnant when we got married, but I didn't know it at the time," Retta admitted.

"So was I. Cade is one of them fast babies, born eight

months after we were married. I really, really wanted a daughter, so you could give me a granddaughter. And if she doesn't, then . . . " She turned to Claire.

Claire threw up both hands. "Levi hasn't even asked me to live with him much less marry him."

"He will," Gloria said. "Now let's talk about Christmas dinner. Retta, what have you got planned?"

Retta inhaled and let it out very slowly. "I thought maybe we'd do something different for Christmas dinner this year—like maybe steaks."

Gloria slapped the table. "I love it and so will Vernon. We've had enough turkey and dressin' to do us for a year."

"We still have some frozen leftovers from Thanksgiving," Claire said. "If anyone disagrees with steak, then they can heat up that."

"Them boys won't ever turn down a good juicy T-bone. I vote that we make them grill them, and we'll just make the sides," Gloria said.

"Is this another test?" Claire asked.

"No, but if you've got another idea, I'm willin' to listen," she answered.

Retta laid her hand on Gloria's arm. "I think we're going to get along just fine."

Claire got up to get more tea and peeked out the kitchen window at the four guys standing in front of the enormous RV. Was Vernon telling them that they'd failed the test too?

*   *   *

Vernon tapped Levi on the shoulder. "So tell me, son, what's this spark I see between you and Claire? She's sure not what I expected to come home and find you ridin' the river with."

"What did you expect?" Levi asked.

Vernon rubbed a hand across his chin. "Tall, blond, blue eyed, hangin' on your arm all the time instead of havin' some independence and sass."

"So you think Claire is sassy?" Justin asked. "You only met her for a few minutes. How did you come to that conclusion?"

"It's in her eyes. Dynamite comes in small packages." Vernon chuckled. "And I know that because I've been livin' with your mother for more than thirty years."

Levi nodded and changed the subject. "You want to take a tour of the ranch now or wait until later this afternoon?"

"I'm not through talkin' about women." Vernon poked Justin on the arm. "I was wonderin' if maybe there's one more of them sassy girls out there who'll fall out of the trees for Justin here. I'd like to see him settlin' down too."

"Who says I'm even thinkin' about settlin' down?" Levi asked.

"Nobody has to say it, son. It's written all over you."

"And why would I want a woman who is dumb enough to fall out of a tree?" Justin teased.

Vernon chuckled. "Never look a gift horse in the mouth, son. Now let's get this RV hooked up, and then we'll take a drive around the place. Looks to me like you boys are doin' a fine job of carryin' on without me. I wouldn't expect anything less, but I always like seein' all the progress you've made."

Cade drove with Vernon riding shotgun and Levi and Justin in the backseat. The conversation went to cows, hay, winter wheat, and the feed bill, and Levi nodded when he should and said a few words when asked for an opinion. But Levi's thoughts went to what Vernon had said about Claire. Was it really that obvious that he'd fallen in love with her?

*   *   *

All the quilts were wrapped in pretty paper, ready to take up to the ranch house and put under the tree. Claire stacked them up on one of the recliners that evening while she waited on Levi—one each for all her new friends. And a queen-size wedding ring design for Grant and Angela's Christmas, plus a couple of doll-size ones for Teresa and Zaylie along with half a dozen outfits she'd made for their dolls.

And nothing for Gloria and Vernon? The voice in her head asked.

"Oh!" she gasped as she grabbed her coat and shoved her feet into her shoes. Mentally, she went through the boxes in the boys' bunkhouse. There was a patchwork quilt over there that she hadn't listed on Etsy yet. She hoped she had enough paper left to wrap it.

She was digging through the boxes when she felt Levi's presence. Turning slowly she found him with a shoulder braced on a doorjamb and a grin on his face.

"It's a little late to be mailin' something if you want it to get there by Christmas," he said.

"Don't need to mail it. Just need to wrap it up. There it is." She pointed over his shoulder. "I almost forgot to get something ready for Gloria and Vernon."

"I'm sure they aren't expecting anything, but if this is one of your quilts, I'm equally sure they'll love it." He pulled her to his chest. "We didn't get to spend hardly any time together today. I missed you."

"When I open up shop, Levi, there will be days and days when we scarcely see each other. You'll go to work in the morning and be out all day. It's life," she said.

"But let the sun go down and the nights will belong to

us. Is it too soon to ask for a drawer in your dresser and a place to put my toothbrush in the bathroom?" He tipped up her chin.

"Not at all. You can have a whole chest of drawers of your own and a shelf in the medicine cabinet." She got lost in his dark green eyes before they closed slowly and his lips found hers in a searing kiss.

He took a step back. "Where's your mind?"

"On the future," she answered honestly as she picked up the box. "Let's go get this wrapped up. I hope I've got enough paper left."

"If you don't there's probably a dozen rolls up at the house. I'll go get you some. What about the future? I'll carry that for you. You can switch off the lights and make sure the door is closed," he said.

A cold wind blasted down from the north and whipped her ponytail around in her face as she covered the distance from one bunkhouse to the other. Dry leaves crunched under her feet as she decided that maybe she'd wait to go over to Grant and Angela's place until after the girls had gotten up on Christmas morning. They'd need to have that time to bond as a family.

"Are you going to answer me?" Levi asked.

"About what? I didn't hear a question." She slung the door open and stood to the side to let him get through the door with the big box.

"The future as in not so far away. Aren't we going to get up early and drive up to Randlett on Christmas morning?" He set the box on the table.

She took a deep breath and then spit it out. "Yes, we are. My mind was just whipping around in circles about the new shop and us. Everything's happened so fast that I feel like I'm living in a whirlwind."

He scooped her up in his arms and carried her to a recliner where he sat down with her in his lap. "This is going wherever you want and at the speed you want. I've fallen in love with you, Claire. I want a future with you, but I don't want to rush you into anything."

She searched his face. They'd just told each other that they were in love, and the wind was still howling outside; time didn't stop, and neither of their hearts stopped beating. Levi Jackson was the most honest person she'd ever known in her whole life, so she believed him but...

No! There are no buts this time, she fussed with the pesky inner voice trying to trip her up and give her doubts.

"Let's leave after the gift opening, find us a hotel in Wichita Falls, and then drive on up to Randlett in time for Christmas dinner," she said.

His eyes twinkled. "I've got a better idea. Will you trust me with your life for one night? We'll be in Randlett for Christmas dinner, I promise," he said.

"My heart and my life are in your hands," she told him.

Chapter Thirty

Oh. My. Goodness!" Gloria squealed when she and Vernon opened their gift from Claire. "This is priceless and way too pretty to be using every day."

"No, no!" Claire threw up both hands. "You are supposed to use it, not put it on a shelf. That's what quilts are for."

"Well, I'm going to use mine. It's going to lay right over there on my chair, and I'm going to cover up with it while I watch television." Cade's eyes twinkled as he looked over at Retta. "You can cuddle under it with me."

She finished opening her gift and said, "I'll be glad to, cowboy, but I've got one of my own, and would you look at this, there's a matching one for the baby. I'm taking this to the hospital to use when we bring her home."

"Her?" Vernon raised an eyebrow.

"Or him," Retta answered.

"We can pray, honey." Gloria patted her on the arm. "I would love to have a granddaughter to spoil."

"And I get one too!" Justin pulled his throw from the box and held it up. "And look at this, Cade, it's long enough to go from chin to toes. You can't buy one this long in the store."

"No, you can't," Skip said from the corner of the room. "My mama used to make quilts, and we all loved them so much more than blankets. What do you think, Benjy?"

The young boy wrapped his quilt around his shoulders and smiled at Claire. "Quilts go back to the Egyptian times. The word comes from *culcita*, which means padded and tied mattress. I looked it up when Levi told me that you liked to make quilts. This is very nice, and I will be careful with it. Thank you, Claire."

"You are so welcome." Claire wanted to hug him. Maybe someday he'd be comfortable enough around her to make that possible. For now, she'd have to be satisfied with that cute little grin.

"The colors remind me of all the seasons on the ranch. Green for spring, yellow for summer, orange for fall, and blue for now. I draw pictures with paper and your art is quilts," Benjy said.

"That's the sweetest thing you could say," Claire said. "I'm glad that you could see the reason for the colors. You told me at Thanksgiving that you loved every season on the ranch."

"But I like this one best of all 'cause we get presents," Benjy said.

The floor was covered with brightly colored paper, and the gifts were all opened when Cade cocked his head to one side. "I hope this isn't rude, but didn't you two get presents for each other?"

Levi smiled and nodded. "We'll be opening ours later.

And speaking of that, we hate to open and run, but we have an appointment to keep. We'll be going up to Randlett tomorrow morning real early, so we won't see y'all until evening. So here's wishin' everyone a Merry Christmas. And thank you for everything. This has been the best Christmas ever."

"Awww, shucks," Benjy said. "I thought we was all goin' to have Christmas dinner together."

"How about Christmas supper?" Levi said. "We can be back in time for that, can't we, Claire?"

"We sure can." She nodded. "You won't leave until we get here, will you?"

"Of course not." Mavis crossed the room to hug Claire. "And this was a lot of work that you've done for us. Handmade gifts are priceless." She whispered softly in her ear, "I wouldn't mind having a granddaughter either."

Claire felt the heat rising from her neck to her cheeks. "What did you say?"

"I can see how happy you make him, and that brings me peace," Mavis said.

"What are you whisperin' about?" Levi stood up and offered a hand to Claire.

"That, son, is between us womenfolks. Merry Christmas, and we'll look to see you tomorrow evening. I ain't never spent a Christmas without seein' you, and I ain't startin' this year." She gave him a quick hug.

Claire put her hand in Levi's and took time to look around at the newfound family she'd become a part of. "That's a beautiful sight."

"Yes, it is, and I take it for granted too often." Levi held her coat for her and then pulled her stocking cap down over her hair, taking time to tuck all the errant strands up under it. "We've got to get you a cowboy hat."

"Is that my Christmas present?"

"No, darlin', that's a necessity. A present should be something special." He quickly got into his coat and ushered her out the back door with his hand on her lower back.

"Where are we going?" she asked when she was settled into the passenger's seat of his truck.

"Back to the future." He leaned across the console and planted a steamy kiss on her lips.

"That sounds pretty cryptic," she said.

"It's the only way to describe it, but you'll figure it out before we ever arrive at the end destination, I'm sure." He started the engine and drove past the barn.

"To the cabin?" Her heart beat faster and her pulse raced. Of all the places that she'd choose to exchange gifts with him, the cabin would top the list.

"Disappointed? It's not a five-star hotel."

"Not a bit. I remember a cold winter evening when it looked like a five-star to me." She could hardly sit still. Did he mean that their future was in the cabin?

Warm yellow lights flowed out from the two windows, giving the place a Thomas Kinkade look. That was candlelight, not electricity, she was seeing, and it looked so romantic as Levi grabbed her bags and they walked hand in hand from the truck to the porch.

"Close your eyes," he said.

She shut them tightly. Funny, she didn't remember the door making that screeching sound when she opened it or when he first appeared looking like a snow-covered grizzly bear either.

"Keep them shut." He led her inside.

Warm air, the kind that comes from a real fire, wrapped itself around her body. He'd started a blaze in the fireplace. She could smell it and hear the crackle.

"Okay, now open them," he said.

She tried to take it all in at once, but it was impossible. The bunk beds were gone, and there was a queen-size four-poster in their place. Two nightstands with burning hurricane lamps flanked the bed, which was covered with a colorful, worn quilt. A small real Christmas tree stood on one side of the fireplace with only one pretty red ornament on it. She looked closely to read the writing that said, "Our First Christmas."

She retrieved something from her bag—her gift to him—and placed it under the tree, noticing there was already a small box there. Her gaze traveled to the mantel to find half a dozen new photos. Most of them were of her, taken when she didn't even know it. One with Gussie in her lap, another of her and Zaylie, and one of her with Little Bit.

"This is amazing," she said. "I can't think of a better present, Levi."

He drew her into his arms. "You haven't opened the one under the tree yet."

"Can we always have a little tree like this and add an ornament every year?" she asked as she sat down on the floor in front of the fireplace. "And not turn on the lights but only have hurricane lamps?"

He sat down beside her. "Whatever you want, darlin'. It sounds like we're making our own traditions, and I love it."

She handed him her gift and watched his face as he tore the paper from the box. It seemed like so little after a present like the cabin for a whole evening and night. She glanced at the bed again, and a sweet little shiver danced down her spine.

He pulled the quilt out of the box, and his eyes brimmed with tears. He quickly wiped them away, and she wanted to throw the damn quilt into the fire. He was disappointed.

"Darlin', this is the one you designed right here. I can't believe you've given me something this..." He stammered, trying to find the right word. "It's priceless. A cowboy doesn't cry, but this is our life right here. It started in the cold snow, and it's gotten warmer and warmer until this moment. I can't think of anything I'd like better. I'm glad it's not a big one that would cover a whole bed. I want it to be small enough that you have to snuggle up next to me until the first baby comes along, and then you can make us one big enough for three."

"Baby?" She thought of what Mavis had said.

"Back to the future," he reminded her. "That's what I see in our future. What do you see?" He reached under the tree and retrieved the small, long box.

"You. That's what I see in my future." She threw her arms around him and brought his lips to hers.

"Okay, sweetheart, it's time for you to open your present or else we're going to skip the rest of our tradition and wind up under my new quilt on that bed over there," he said.

She sat up straight. "Sounds good to me, but I do want to open my present."

He put the box in her hands. "It's sure not as amazing as what you've done, but it's the best this old cowboy could think to do. Remember now, I got it when we weren't nearly as serious as we are tonight."

She opened it carefully and popped open the long velvet box to find the necklace with the three charms—a snowflake, a tiny set of longhorns, and an open heart. "Levi, it's beautiful, and it means more knowing that you got it even before."

"A cowboy can always hope." He took the necklace from the box and fastened it around her neck. "A snowflake for the time when we met, longhorns to remind you of the ranch, and an open heart that says my heart is always open for you—anytime, anyplace."

Tears rolled down her cheeks. "I love you, Levi Jackson."

He kissed away the tears one by one and then led her to the bed. "I'm glad to hear you say those words, just like that. I don't have much to offer a woman, Claire. And you deserve more than I'll ever be, but..." He paused as he sat down on the bed and patted the place beside him.

She eased down, not knowing what to expect next. "Levi, if you know me at all, you know that..."

"I know but it doesn't change the fact that you could do better than an old ranch foreman or that I love you so much I want the best for you. But this is what I am, and, well, yesterday I asked Cade and Justin to sell me this cabin and the five acres around it."

"You did what?" she squealed. "Did they say yes?"

"They said no," he answered.

Her heart fell. If they wouldn't sell it to Levi, then they sure wouldn't consider selling it to her.

"They gave it to me and told me to use the money I've saved up to build on to it someday or else build a new house somewhere back here. Justin is a pretty good draftsman. He's designed a couple of barns for us. Thought I'd ask him to help us draw up house plans, and we'd start building real soon," he told her.

She jumped into his arms. "For real? Are you askin' me to live with you?"

"No," he said. "I can't do that."

Once again her heart dropped all the way to the floor.

He got down on one knee and took both her hands in his. "I want more than for us to move in together, Claire. I love you. Will you marry me? I thought maybe we could live together in your new house until..." He paused.

"Yes, darlin', yes a thousand times, yes to everything." She covered his face with kisses. "What a wonderful way to start a new year."

"Beginning right now." He grinned as he flipped her back on the bed.

Keep reading for a peek
at Justin's story in

COWBOY BRAVE

Coming in early 2019

Emily Baker wore a dress and high heels and had even shaved her legs. She felt a little like a homecoming queen as she made her way from the break room where she'd changed out of her scrubs to the front door of the retirement center. Five octogenarians followed along behind her, clapping their hands and singing an old Etta James tune, "At Last."

Otis ran ahead of her and held the door. "Go get 'em, and don't take no for an answer."

"We'll take up a collection and pay the big bucks. Tell 'em that." Bess waved a lace hanky at her as she stepped out into the brisk Texas air.

"Ready, okay!" Patsy did a few snap movements like a cheerleader and led the rest in a cheer. "Two bits, four bits, six bits, a dollar. All for Emily, stand up and holler."

All five of them shouted like they were at a football pep rally. Then Sarah put a key chain with a rabbit's foot in her hand. "For good luck."

"Okay," Larry said. "We got to let her go. Let's go to my room and play a game of cards while we wait for her to come back with the good news."

Twenty minutes later, she was pulling through the gates of the Longhorn Canyon Ranch, still humming Etta James. With a smile on her face, she parked her bright red Mustang and stepped out of the car. But one wobbly step forward on her four-inch spike heels and her smile dropped right off.

Shit. Literally. She'd stepped her way right into a big ole pile of cow manure.

So much for making a great first impression. But there was no way she could disappoint the Fab Five, so Emily squared her shoulders and continued forward to the front door, hoping she might find something to wipe her shoe with along the way.

Before she even had a chance to knock, a tall, blue-eyed cowboy swung the door open.

"Can I help you?" His eyes started at her strawberry-blond hair, traveled over her size 16 curves, all the way to her soiled shoes. That put her right at his height.

"Hi there. I'm Emily Baker, and I was hopin' I could talk to you about renting your bunkhouses for a week." She spit it all out at once without taking a breath.

He opened the door for her. "Come on in. I'm Justin Maguire."

She kicked off her shoes on the porch, glanced down at her chipped toenail polish, and wished that she'd taken time to redo her pedicure.

"Should've been a little more careful about where I was steppin'," she said.

"Evidently you haven't lived on a ranch." Justin chuckled. "Can I get you a cup of coffee, glass of tea, water?"

Oh, honey, you are so wrong about me living on a ranch, but I appreciate the compliment. Evidently, I've come far enough that folks don't see my past, she thought.

"I'm good, thank you," she said.

"Okay then." He led her to the doorway and motioned for her to enter first. "We can talk in here. Have a seat anywhere. Sorry about the mess."

She glanced down at all the papers strewn about his coffee table. "You're building a house? Are you an architect?"

"Not really, but I've always been interested in this kind of thing. I'm trying my hand at drawing up the plans for our foreman and his new wife," he said.

Emily sat down on the end of the sofa. "It looks so cute and cozy."

His eyes sparkled as he smiled. "Thanks. I wanted to start small and make it easy for them to add on later."

He was one fine-looking cowboy with those steely blue eyes and that strong, squared-off chin. He raked his fingers through light brown hair that matched the light scruff on his face. The black western-cut shirt fit his body like a glove, and judging from the silver belt buckle, he'd probably ridden a few bulls.

He eased down into a chair on the other side of the sofa. "So tell me, Miz Emily, why do you want to rent our bunkhouses?"

"I'm the senior recreation director at the Oakview Retirement Home, and we try to have an outing for our residents a couple of times a year. One elderly gentleman asked if we could visit a ranch for a week this spring. He had a big spread up near the Red River when he was younger. He's been with us for about a year now, and I can tell he gets homesick," she said.

"For the smell of fresh cow manure?" Justin glanced down at her feet.

A slow burn crept from her neck to her face. "And hay and baby calves and all that goes with ranchin'. Anyway, there are five of them who are interested, and the youngest two are seventy-nine years old. Otis was the rancher and his buddy, Larry, owned a construction business. Then there's Sarah, Patsy, and Bess, who want to get away for a while. Sarah was a schoolteacher, and Patsy and Bess are eighty-year-old twins who were raised on a ranch back in the forties and fifties."

"I'll have to run it by the rest of the family. When were you hoping to have this outing?"

"Maybe in a week or two, if that's possible. We're flexible."

"We're pretty busy with the ranch work this time of year. Were you thinking of any special activities for them?" he asked.

"Oh, that's okay. You don't have to do much extra. And I'm sure they'd be glad to help out with whatever they can."

"Sounds like they won't be a bit of trouble then," Justin said.

Famous last words. "Thank you, Mr. Maguire. I'll be lookin' forward to hearing from you. Here's my card. I've written my cell phone number on the back."

Well, crap! Now he's going to think he can call for something other than business.

He quickly laid the card on the table and then shook hands with her. "I'll let you know as soon as I can."

Growing up, Emily had never been a petite girl. She topped out at five feet eight inches, and shopped in the plus-size section. But her hand felt tiny in Justin's big, callused palm.

Like a gentleman, he walked her to the door and waited until she got her shoes back on before he closed it. Thank God he'd already gone back inside, because as she was walking from the porch to the car, she stepped in that same cow patty—again.

About the Author

Carolyn Brown is a *New York Times* and *USA Today* bestselling romance author and RITA® Finalist who has sold more than 3 million books. She presently writes both women's fiction and cowboy romance. She has also written historical single title, historical series, contemporary single title, and contemporary series. She lives in southern Oklahoma with her husband, a former English teacher and mystery author. They have three children and enough grandchildren and great-grandchildren to keep them young. For a complete listing of her books (series in order) and to sign up for her newsletter, check out her website at CarolynBrownBooks.com or visit her on Facebook at CarolynBrownBooks.

O Little Town of Bramble

Katie Lane

All Ethan Miller wants for Christmas is to celebrate in Bramble, Texas, with family and friends. But when his childhood neighbor, Samantha Henderson, comes home for the holiday, Ethan realizes that the girl next door could be the girl of his drcams.

Keep reading for a bonus holiday story from *USA Today* bestselling author Katie Lane, in print for the first time!

Chapter One

The folks of Bramble, Texas, believed in doing things up big. And the holidays were no exception. Every building along Main Street was decorated with garland, balls, and bows. A giant, ornament-filled Douglas fir stood in front of the town hall, fake poinsettias spouted from storefront flower boxes, and ropes of evergreen encircled each light post.

Having lived in Bramble for all of his life, the excess was nothing new to Ethan Miller. In fact, he had to admit he liked the town all spiffed up. It put him more in the mood for Christmas—which was only a day away.

As Ethan ambled along the street, he looked up at the blue west Texas skies. It was clear now, but the weather was about to change. He could feel it in his bones.

"Nice ass."

The words caused Ethan to stop so fast that Buckwheat ran into him from behind. And being run into by a four-hundred-pound donkey could bring even a big man down in a hurry. One knee hit the cement, and he had to grab on to the back of the bench in front of Sutter's Pharmacy to keep from landing on his face. Old Moses Tate, who was sleeping on the bench, didn't even break-snore. Of course, without his hearing aids, the man was as deaf as a stone.

With pain shooting up his thigh, Ethan turned to get after Buckwheat for tailgating when his gaze got snagged by the woman who had just spoken. Words dried up in his mouth. Of course, words always dried up in Ethan's mouth when he was around a woman he found attractive. And this woman he found much more than attractive. She was downright breathtaking.

Hair as thick and black as a bay horse's tail fell around a face with high cheekbones, a button nose, and lips painted the pink of the sky right before sunrise. She wore big movie-star sunglasses that concealed her eyes and city clothes that would be useless on a farm—but were damned nice to look at. A long, red sweater hugged breasts the size of plump September peaches and curved down over slim hips that would sit real pretty in a saddle. Of course, the painted-on jeans and knee-high boots with their tall, skinny heels wouldn't work for riding.

Leastways, not horses.

A tingling of sexual awareness settled in Ethan's stomach. But it wasn't the first time he'd ignored the feeling, and it wouldn't be the last. Farm life left little time for giving in to one's desires.

"Uhh...excuse me, ma'am?" The slow, awkward words that came out of his mouth had his face heating, and his embarrassment only grew when her pretty lips tipped up in a soft smile.

She moved away from the pharmacy window with its display of a tiny tinsel Christmas tree surrounded by brightly wrapped packages and came to stand directly in front of him. Seeing as Ethan was still kneeling, it brought those sweet peaches mere inches from his mouth. And there was no ignoring the heat that slammed into him much harder than Buckwheat.

"Are you plannin' on makin' a declaration, Ethan?" she said. "Or are you just takin' a mornin' prayer break?"

The country twang that had been missing when she'd commented on his ass was now thick and familiar. His head came up, and he squinted at her mouth, trying to visualize it without paint. But it wasn't until she reached up and removed the sunglasses that he recognized the face. Eyes the deep blue of Morning Glories stared back at him, and Ethan's voice rang out as clear as one of Hope Scrogg's hog calls.

"Sam?" With only a small cringe, he climbed to his feet and within two steps had the woman in his arms. He swung her around once before he realized what he was doing. Then he quickly set her back on her feet and stepped away, more than a little embarrassed by his uncharacteristic behavior. If it had been any other woman, he would've been stammering his apologies like a bashful idiot.

But this was Sam.

He grinned back at her, not quite believing his eyes. "Would you look at you? I thought you'd gone and left Bramble for good."

"I thought so too," she said rather breathlessly. Her gaze wandered over his face as if taking in all the changes. He figured there had to be plenty. The last couple years had been hard—what with his daddy's accident and the majority of the farm work falling to him. To a young woman five years his junior, he must look as old and weathered as a leather harness left out in the sun.

While she, on the other hand, looked as fresh as a new spring daffodil. She even smelled like flowers. He filled his lungs with the subtle, sweet scent, realizing too late the effect it would have on a man who hadn't been this close to a woman, other than his mama, in a while. Suddenly, he felt like he had the time he'd gotten sandwiched between a couple linebackers during a high school football game—kinda dazed and loopy.

Confused by his reactions, he dropped his head and ran a hand over the back of his neck. What was the matter with him? Sure, it had been a while since he'd been around a pretty woman. But this was little Sam Henderson, who used to sneak out to the farm every chance she got. Sam, who Ethan had taught to swim and fish and ride a horse. Sam, who, up until she graduated and went off to college, was the closest thing Ethan had to a sibling—or a best friend.

In an effort to get his bodily reactions back on the right track, he reached out and ruffled her hair. "So what brings you back, little Sammy?" He glanced down at the boots. "Besides playin' dress up?"

The soft smile slipped, and her entire body stiffened. Ethan didn't know a lot about women, but he knew a lot about animals. And Sam suddenly seemed as pissed as Clara the barn cat when his hound dog, Hooper, got a little frisky. Those pretty eyes narrowed at him right before she placed her sunglasses back on.

"People call me Samantha now," she said in a citified voice. "Dr. Samantha Henderson."

He'd heard the rumor going around town about Sam becoming a doctor. But since "doctor" just didn't seem to go with the image he'd held in his head of a skinny girl in a lopsided ponytail, he couldn't help but laugh. Which he figured out soon enough wasn't a good thing to do when a woman was upset already.

"Is something funny, Ethan Michael Miller?" The words came out between her even, white teeth. Her hands tightened into fists. And for a second, he wondered if she was going to haul off and slug him like she had Joe Riley when he'd teased Ethan about his size. The thought made Ethan laugh even more.

She crossed her arms over her chest. "You haven't changed a lick in the last seven years, have you, Ethan?"

He sobered. "Seven years? No kiddin'?" He shook his head. "I guess time flies when you're havin' fun."

She glared back at him. "And is your life fun, Ethan?"

The question took him by surprise. No one in town ever asked him questions like that. They asked him about his daddy and mama. Asked about his opinions on crops, animals, and weather. But never about his personal feelings. Which was probably why it took him so long to come up with an answer. Fun? No, he wouldn't say his life was fun. It was familiar and comfortable. And that was about all a person could ask for.

Wasn't it?

A munching noise pulled him away from his thoughts, and he turned to find Buckwheat helping himself to a mid-morning snack. Although Ethan didn't think the fake poinsettias in front of the pharmacy were a good choice. And obviously, Sam didn't think so either.

"No!" she yelled, and those skinny heels clicked against the sidewalk as she hurried over to where Buckwheat was grazing. "Get away from there!" She waved her arms, but Buckwheat ignored her completely and continued to munch on the bright red flowers. Still, Sam had always been tenacious, and Ethan had to grin when she hooked an arm around the donkey's neck and tried to pull him away. Too bad Buckwheat had a thing about people touching him. With one flick of his head, he threw her off balance, and she tittered on those silly heels for a second or two before landing hard on her butt.

This time Ethan was smart enough to control his laughter.

"You okay?" He ambled over and stretched out a hand. But she completely ignored it and climbed to her feet.

"I expected more from you, Ethan Miller." She pointed a finger at Buckwheat, who'd gone back to munching the flowers. "Do you realize the kind of stomach and intestinal problems the dyes and synthetic materials could cause that poor animal?"

Figuring she had a point, Ethan made a distinct clicking noise with his tongue, and the donkey turned from the flowers and trotted over. For his reward, Ethan pulled out a carrot from his overall pocket and stroked the donkey's soft, long ears while he ate the treat.

"I wouldn't worry too much," he said. "Buckwheat's eaten worse and survived."

Sam plucked a poinsettia leaf from the corner of the donkey's mouth. "Obviously, he has dietary needs you're not meeting. What are you feeding him? I hope it's not the same thing you're giving your horses. Donkeys need more protein and fiber." She glanced down. "And when was the last time you trimmed his hooves? You need to do that every twelve weeks or his joints and tendons will get deformed."

Ethan squinted at her, suddenly feeling as annoyed as she looked. He might not have a doctorate, but he knew animals. And he sure didn't need a sassy woman in crazy shoes telling him how to take care of his donkey. Especially a woman who used to think he hung the moon.

He pulled off his straw cowboy hat and scratched his head. "You know a lot about donkeys, do ya, Samantha Louise? Because I seem to remember a young skinny girl who was terrified to get on a horse." He lifted an eyebrow. "And it took a good three months to convince her otherwise. 'Course, that girl didn't look nothin' like the one standin' before me. So maybe I'm wrong."

Before Sam could do more than sputter, Rachel Dean's voice rang out.

"Why, Samantha Henderson, I thought that was you!" She hurried across the street, wiping her large hands on her waitressing apron. She grabbed Sam up and gave her a big bear hug. "I didn't realize you was comin' in for the holidays. Last I heard, you was goin' to some fancy college back East to become a doctor."

Since Sam's face was squashed against Rachel Dean's holiday corsage, she had to wait to be released before she could answer. "I graduated just last week."

Rachel beamed. "Why, ain't that somethin'? Little Sam Henderson a doctor. Maybe later I can get you to take a look at my bunions. The medicine Doc Mathers prescribed don't work a lick."

"I'd love to help you, Rachel," Sam said. "But I'm not that kind of a doctor." She looked over at Ethan and tipped her cute little nose in the air. "I'm a doctor of veterinary medicine."

Ethan felt like he'd been kicked in the stomach by Buckwheat. Ever since he was old enough to help his father with the livestock, Ethan had wanted to become a veterinarian. But besides not having enough money, his parents had needed his help on the farm. So he'd put his dream on the shelf. In fact, the only person who knew about his secret desire was the same woman rubbing his nose in it. It was enough to make a grown man want to toss down his hat and cuss a blue streak. But farm folk weren't ones to show their emotions. So instead, he plopped his hat back on his head and nodded to both ladies.

"I best be gettin' Buckwheat over to Lowell's barn."

"We sure appreciate you takin' care of all the animals for the live nativity over at The First Baptist, Ethan," Rachel Dean said. "Nobody handles animals better than you do. Why, it's almost like you speak their language. Sorta like that Doctor Doolittle feller—without the singin', of course."

Ethan had to fight down the strong urge to snort a "hah" at Sam. Still, Rachel Dean's praise didn't change the jealousy that ate at his insides. A gift was one thing, a diploma something else entirely. While most of his knowledge came from what he could scrounge up on the Internet or in library books, Sam had been taught by the top experts in the field.

"Why don't you come on over to the diner, Sam?" Rachel Dean said. "If anything will put meat back on those skinny bones of yours, it's Josephine's chicken fried steak. And while you eat, I'll fill you in on all the juicy gossip. Things have sure been excitin' while you've been gone."

Sam hesitated, as if there was something else she wanted to say to Ethan. But as far as he was concerned, they'd said everything they needed to. The little Sam Henderson he once knew was long gone. And he had no use for an uppity vet who didn't understand the first thing about a man's pride.

"Goodbye, Ethan," Sam said in a voice that didn't sound all that uppity. A gust of cool December wind blew her hair over her face. She pushed it back and sent Ethan one last look before Rachel tugged her across the street toward the bright pink caboose that served as Josephine's Diner.

Ethan stood on the sidewalk and watched as they walked

away, his gaze trailing down the length of ebony hair to the curvy behind covered in the painted-on jeans. He was still as mad as a dog on bath day, but that didn't seem to stop two words from popping into his head.

Nice ass.

Chapter Two

...So Faith Aldridge ended up being Hope Scroggs's long-lost twin sister." Rachel kept right on talking as she filled Sam's cup with steaming, black coffee. "And I'll tell you what. Those two look so much alike that the entire town was fooled. All except for Slate. He knew after just one kiss that Faith wasn't Hope. 'Course, he figured out some other things as well—like he couldn't live without our little Faith."

The news surprised Sam. Slate Calhoun had been the hometown football hero while Hope Scroggs had been the homecoming queen. It just made sense that they would end up getting married. Of course, love had never made sense.

Sam glanced out the front windows, but Ethan had long since returned to his old truck and driven away.

"I bet Hope was brokenhearted," she said.

"We all figured as much." Mayor Harley Sutter swiveled around on the barstool next to Sam's, his big belly brushing the counter, and his handlebar mustache wiggling as he talked. "But as it turned out, Hope has always been in love with Colt Lomax."

"Which surprised the heck out of me," Sheriff Winslow said. "Colt spent more time in my jail than Elmer Tate."

"And maybe that's why Hope fell in love with him. It's hard to resist a bad boy." Rachel winked at Sam. "Ain't it, girl?"

Sam smiled in agreement, even though she'd never had a thing for bad boys with bad attitudes. Just soft-spoken farm boys. And it seemed that time hadn't diminished her feelings. The moment she looked into Ethan's green eyes, she'd been lost all over again. And when he'd pulled her into his arms, for one brief second, she'd thought he'd felt it too. But it turned out his greeting had been no different than Rachel Dean's.

"So how long do you get to stay, Sam?"

Sam glanced down the counter to the cowboy with the contagious grin. "Only until the day after Christmas, Kenny Gene. If I'm going to pay back all my student loans, I need to find a job and quick."

"Well, I don't know why you couldn't just set up shop right here in Bramble," the mayor said. "Folks in Bramble have to go all the way to Odessa to find a vet. 'Course, most folks don't mess with that and just take their animals to Ethan. That boy has a real gift."

"So I've heard," Sam said dryly. Of course she knew Ethan had a gift and had known it long before anyone else. It was Ethan who opened up the world of animals to her. Ethan who showed her the comfort found in the soft cuddle of fur or the warm nuzzle of a cold nose. And maybe that was her problem. She'd gotten her love of animals confused with her feelings for the young man who had offered a haven from her dysfunctional family.

As if reading her thoughts, Mayor Sutter asked, "So how's your mama doin'? She still livin' in Austin?"

Sam didn't have a clue. The last time Sam had spoken to her mama had been on her fourteenth birthday—the day her mother had left town. She wanted to blame her mother for the rift in their relationship, but Sam was the one who hadn't returned her letters or phone calls. Still, the town didn't need to know that.

"So tell me more about this live nativity scene," she said in an attempt to change the subject.

Fortunately, Mayor Sutter latched on to the new topic like a bass to live bait. "It was Pastor Robbins's idea. I guess the church he worked at before us used to have one every Christmas Eve—supposedly it gets everyone's thoughts back on the reason for the season."

"Animal poop?" Kenny Gene piped up. "Because I gotta tell you, puttin' all those animals in that little stable the pastor had me build is just askin' for trouble."

"Which is why we put you on poop patrol," Rachel Dean said.

Kenny Gene's eyes narrowed. "But I thought I got to be the Angel of the Lord."

"You do, son." Mayor Sutter patted him on the back. "But when you ain't spreadin' tidin's of great joy to all people, you'll be spreadin' manure in the church flower beds."

Kenny's eyes lit up. "Well, I guess that ain't so bad."

"I just wish our hunt for baby Jesuses was goin' so well," Rachel said as she poured the mayor more coffee.

"Jesuses?" Sam said. "You need more than one?"

Rachel's smile got even bigger. "Since we couldn't decide on who should get to be Mary and Joseph—Faith and Slate or Hope and Colt—we decided to have two shifts. 'Course, now we need two Jesuses. And we've had tryouts for the last week and a half, and not a Jesus have we found. Dusty Ray don't fit in the manger. Rufus Miles throws fits like he's possessed. And Titus Smith is allergic to hay." She released her breath in a long sigh. "Which means we might have to settle for the porcelain doll Darla made. And I gotta tell you that Chucky-lookin' thing scares me to death."

Sam muffled her laugh behind a cough. She had missed the craziness of Bramble. Missed it more than she'd realized. In the last seven years, she'd tried to become a cosmopolitan girl. But all it had taken was five minutes in Josephine's to realize she was small town through and through.

"Not to say that Darla ain't gifted," Rachel continued. "Why, her manger-decoratin' skills are gonna surprise the pants right off of Pastor Robbins when he gets back from that preacher convention in Dallas."

Mayor Sutter nodded. "The pastor might've had a nice enough live nativity at his last church, but it's not gonna hold a candle to ours."

There was a chorus of "shore ain'ts" before the conversation moved on to Hope and Faith's pregnancies and what they should name their babies. After a good hour of listening to children's names weirder than Hollywood movie stars', Sam decided she had delayed seeing her family long enough and got up from the stool.

"If you stop by the church a little before six, Sam, I'll fix you up with a costume," Rachel Dean said as she handed Sam her change. "We don't got any more heavenly hosts' wings or shepherd sheets, but I'll find you somethin'."

Sam smiled. It was so like the people of Bramble to include everyone.

"I'll try to be there," she said as she made her way to the door.

The weather had turned while Sam had been in the diner. Gray clouds blocked out the blue west Texas sky, and a cold wind pressed against her as she hurried to her rental car. She probably could've called her sister, Marcy, to pick her up from the airport in Lubbock. But she wasn't willing to be stuck at her father's house without a means of escape.

The one-story stucco house she'd grown up in hadn't changed all that much over the last seven years. The lawn and flower beds were better cared for, and the yellow trim looked freshly painted, but other than that, it looked the same. It wasn't a big house—no more than six rooms total—but it had been a comfortable home.

At least physically.

Emotionally was another story.

Ever since Sam could remember, there had been underlying tension in the house. When her mother and father weren't arguing, they weren't speaking. And their discontentment had filtered down to their children. By the time her mother had left, Sam felt almost relieved. Until she realized she was stuck with a father who didn't know the first thing about showing love to his two teenage daughters.

As Sam got out of the car, a black Lab and a Yorkshire terrier came running up. But since her father had never particularly cared for animals, she figured they belonged to a neighbor. She gave each dog a good scratch before heading up the steps of the porch.

Rather than just walk in, she tapped softly on the screen door. But when the sound of Christmas music drifted from the closed windows, she pressed hard on the doorbell.

The door was pulled open by a woman Sam recognized immediately from the wedding pictures she'd sent. A puff of orange hair surrounded a round face with laugh crinkles at the eyes. Those eyes widened for only a second before the screen door was pushed open. The dogs squeezed past Sam's legs just as she was pulled against a bright red sweatshirt with reindeer appliqués and a soft body that smelled of gingerbread.

"You came," Laverne said against her hair. "I worried myself sick that you wouldn't." The back door slammed, and before Sam could utter a word, Laverne was herding her over to the large Christmas tree set up in the corner.

"I know I shouldn't have kept it a secret," Laverne whispered under her breath. "But I just didn't want him to be disappointed if you didn't show up." She grabbed a big gold bow off a package beneath the tree and slapped it on Sam's head. "There." She grinned so brightly, her eyes disappeared. "You're going to be the best Christmas present he'll ever get."

"Laverne!"

Sam's father's voice boomed from the kitchen, and Sam jumped. But Laverne didn't seem to be too intimidated by the gruffness.

"Would you keep it down, Phillip!" she hollered back as she hurried toward the kitchen, the dogs on her heels. "I swear you're goin' as deaf as Moses Tate."

"I'm not deaf, woman," her father said, "I'm starvin'. When will that turkey be done?" There was a creak of the oven door, followed by a sharp slap.

"Oh, no you don't, Phillip James Henderson," Laverne scolded. "You're not gettin' a taste until it's finished."

"Blame ornery woman," her father huffed, but with more humor than anger. "Well, if I'm not gonna get any turkey, I might as well get me some sugar."

In the silence that followed, Sam stared at the doorway and tried to reconcile the happy, loving man in the kitchen with the angry, bitter father of her youth.

It proved impossible.

Pulling off the bow, she tossed it to the coffee table and was halfway to the door when her father's voice stopped her.

"Samantha?"

She turned. Unlike the house, Phillip Henderson had changed a great deal. His hair was completely gray, and he was almost as chubby as his wife. Sam had to admit that the added weight looked good on him. It softened his features and made him seem more approachable. Or maybe it was the smile on his face. A smile that had been missing for much of her childhood.

Not knowing what to do, Sam held up her hands. "Merry Christmas, Daddy."

They stared at each other for a few moments until Laverne prodded.

"Well, go on, Phillip. Hug the girl."

Her father hesitated only a moment before taking the three steps necessary to pull her into his arms. It was awkward. Sam didn't pull away; nor did she sink into the broad chest that smelled like Old Spice and chewing tobacco. She just stiffened up and waited for it to be over so things could go back to normal. But when her father finally pulled back, he didn't appear normal. He appeared to be crying.

And Laverne wasn't far behind him.

"I'll just let you two chat," she sniffed before heading back to the kitchen.

Once she was gone, Sam moved over to the partially decorated tree so she wouldn't have to look at the man she no longer recognized. She had just leaned closer to examine a clay horse ornament when he finally spoke.

"I wrote you some letters."

Her hand stilled on the bumpy horse's mane. "I didn't get them."

"Because I never mailed them. I never could get the words right."

Sam turned to find him standing close behind her. His eyes still glittered with tears, but his voice was strong.

"You made that one in fifth grade." He nodded at the horse ornament. "I always refer to that year as the year of the horse. Every drawing, every library book, and every gift you asked for—or gave—always had to do with horses." He reached down and lifted another ornament from the box on the table. His callused fingers gently removed the cotton before lifting a red-glitter pinecone. "Now, this one you made in first grade. It started losing its glitter the second year, which was why your mama wrapped it in cotton from then on."

Sam hadn't remembered that, and she wondered how he had. He went on to describe every ornament she'd ever made, recounting the year and details that she'd long forgotten.

"This one you and Marcy made." He pulled out a colorful beaded wreath. "First time you'd ever worked on something together without fightin'."

Sam couldn't help the words that spilled from her mouth. "Unlike you and mama, who could never do anything without fighting."

A sad smile played around his mouth as he hung the ornament on the tree. When he didn't say anything, she continued with the questions that had eaten her up over the years.

"I realize people get divorced when they discover they don't love each other anymore, but what I don't understand is why you waited so long. Why did you continue to put your children through that?"

A long sigh escaped his lips, and he walked to the recliner and sat down. The Lab came wandering back in, and her father ran a hand over the dog's shiny coat. "Because, believe it or not, I love your mama. And will love her until the day I die. It just took us a while to figure out that sometimes you can love someone and still not be able to live with them."

"Geez, Daddy." Sam couldn't keep the sarcasm, or pain, from her voice. "I wish you'd figured that out before you had kids."

Her father's gaze snapped up, and he pointed a finger. "Don't you even think it, Sam Louise. I'm sorry for a lot of things, but havin' you and Marcy aren't among them. Now, I realize you aren't goin' to forgive me anytime soon, and I guess I'll have to live with that. But remember that forgiveness is like a gift—the receiver's not the only one who benefits. And if you can't see fit to forgive me, I wish you'd forgive your mama. She's been real upset about you not replyin' to her letters."

Sam stared at him. "You talk to Mama?"

"About every week."

"Without fighting?"

He laughed. "As strange as it may seem, your mama and I are better friends than we ever were husband and wife."

"Hey, you two." Laverne came back into the room carrying a tray filled with eggnog and gingerbread cookies. She set it on the coffee table and handed Sam the Santa mug she'd used as a child. "Marcy should be here any minute. So let's turn up the music and finish decoratin' that tree. But first I thought we'd have ourselves a little toast." After handing Sam's daddy a mug, she lifted her own. "Here's to new beginnin's."

A part of Sam didn't want to toast, or decorate a tree, or eat turkey dinner in a house filled with memories of her dysfunctional family. But there was another part of her—the part that had been so lonely the last seven years—that wanted to believe that people could change. That no one was perfect. And time might actually heal all wounds. And maybe those were the truths she needed to embrace this Christmas Eve while standing next to a father she'd yet to forgive and a stepmother who looked like a redheaded Mrs. Claus.

Sam lifted her Santa mug. "To new beginnings."

Chapter Three

You want to what?" Ethan stared at his parents as if they had lost their minds. It was a possibility. Winter on a farm could make people a little stir-crazy. Ever since returning from town, Ethan had felt like he'd swallowed a bucket of bees. Of course, that had more to do with Sam Henderson than two hundred acres of farmland.

His mother reached out and patted his hand, which rested on the linen tablecloth his great-great-grandmother had brought over from Germany. "I know this is a shock, Ethan, but it's not like we're fallin' off the face of the earth. We're just moving to South Padre Island."

"Just?" Ethan pulled his hand out from under hers and got up from the table, pacing back and forth. "What about the farm? The animals? The folks of Bramble?" He turned and stared at his parents. "Me?"

The weathered skin around his father's green eyes scrunched up. "You're thirty years old, boy. You still scared of the dark?"

His mother jumped back in. "Of course he's not scared of the dark." She shot Ethan a skeptical look before addressing her husband. "I told you we shouldn't just drop the news on him, Jeb—especially on Christmas Eve."

"Hell." His father got up from his chair. "I thought the boy would be excited to finally get rid of us. I figured that was why he'd never married or brought a girl home besides that cute little Sam Henderson." He studied Ethan again. "You ain't one of them…"

"No!" The word came out louder than Ethan intended, and he quickly tacked on a "sir."

"Then what's your problem?" his father asked. "You ain't worried about being able to handle the farm, are you? 'Cause you've been doin' most of the work ever since I fell off that danged ladder and screwed up my back."

"I just think it's crazy, is all," Ethan said. "Why would you and Mama want to live on a beach when you've spent your entire life on a farm?"

"Maybe that's why," his mother said in the soft voice that had always soothed Ethan. She patted the table. "Come sit down, Ethan, and quit pacing like an expectant cat."

Begrudgingly, he sat back down in the chair, but couldn't help crossing his arms and staring belligerently at the toes of his work boots.

"In case you haven't noticed," his mother said, "your father and I aren't exactly spring chickens. We were in our late thirties when God finally blessed us with you." Since Ethan's hands were tucked under his armpits, she reached out and patted his knee. "And we couldn't be more proud of the man you've grown into. But I agree with your father. There comes a time in every man's life when he needs some space. And since you don't seem to be in any hurry to fly the coop—we are."

"Fly the coop?" Ethan's jaw dropped as he stared at his mother. "I stayed for you—for you and Daddy because I didn't think you two could make a go of the farm without me."

"Now, don't lie, boy," his father said. "You get flustered just walkin' into Josephine's Diner."

Ethan jumped back up from the chair and sputtered out the words. "F-flustered or not, if I'd known how you felt, I would've left a long time ago to pursue my own dreams."

"Now, don't be gettin' all upset, Ethan." His mother stood up and sent his father a stern look. "What your father means is that anyone can see that you were born to be a farmer. It's obvious in the way you love animals and get so darned excited during harvest. But if you want to sell the farm, your father and I will support that." She shrugged. "Maybe it's time for all of us to leave the hard work behind and have us a little fun."

Fun? First Sam and now his parents. Ethan was really starting to hate that word. Fun was something kids had, not grown adults who had responsibilities. He ignored the fact that he wasn't exactly acting like an adult either.

"We're not selling the farm," he said. "I'll figure out a way to buy you out so you can race off to South Padre and have some fun on the beach."

His parents exchanged bright smiles.

"That won't be necessary," his daddy said. "Back when you was born, we put a little money aside, and since you never used it for college..."

*   *   *

The tires of the truck hit another pothole, but Ethan still didn't slow down. He had never been the violent type, but he couldn't help thumping the steering wheel with his fist as he turned onto the highway that led into Bramble.

A college fund? His parents had put money in a college fund and never mentioned a word? Okay, so maybe at eighteen he hadn't exactly acted like he wanted to go to college. And maybe some of that had to do with being a little scared. But what good were parents if they couldn't force a shy, backward kid out the door?

Of course, it had worked out real well for them. They had gotten years of free labor and now had a nice, fat nest egg to buy a motor home so they could "have fun" in some South Padre retirement village. Well, maybe it was time for Ethan to have a little fun too. He pressed harder on the accelerator and watched the skinny gauge of the speedometer inch up the miles per hour. Except when it got to seventy-five, the old truck started to shake so badly that he had to ease back down to sixty.

Ethan still made it to Bramble in record time. He'd planned on heading over to Lowell's barn to check on the animals people had brought in for the nativity scene, but instead he pulled into Bootlegger's Bar. He'd been to the bar before—every person over eighteen years of age had been in Bootlegger's at one time or another. Ethan just wasn't what you would call a regular, which explained the surprised faces when he ambled in the door.

Of course, Ethan was a little surprised himself when he looked at the bar and saw who was sitting there. The beginning line of a joke popped into his head: *An angel, a beer-bellied wiseman, Joseph, and a pig walked into a bar...*

"Well, hey, Ethan!" Kenny Gene waved him over so exuberantly that his wing clipped Mayor Harley Sutter's wiseman crown and knocked it to the floor.

Harley sent him an annoyed look before leaning down to pick it up. "So what brings you to Boot's, Ethan?" He readjusted the plastic crown on his balding head. "I thought you were supposed to be gettin' the animals over to the church."

"I am. But I thought I'd have me a beer first." *Or six,* Ethan thought as he slipped onto the stool next to Joseph. Even in his sour mood, Ethan couldn't help grinning at the floral sheets draped around his friend Colt Lomax—especially when the man had once been the biggest bad boy in Bramble. But before Ethan could do a little friendly teasing, the baby pig sitting on Colt's lap released a squeal of delight and launched himself at Ethan.

Ethan laughed as his face was covered in wet pig kisses. "I've missed you too, Sherman. But it looks like you've been well taken care of."

"That's putting it lightly," Colt said. He took another drink from his long-necked bottle, the pink-flowered sheet sliding up his tattooed arm. "Hope and my sister, Shirlene, spoil that pig rotten."

Ethan was glad to hear it. Ever since he'd given the pig to Hope as a gift, he'd had second thoughts. Sherman was special—the runt of the litter that Ethan hadn't expected to live. But the tiny piglet had surprised him. And what Sherman lacked in physical size and strength, he'd made up for in brains. And not just brains, but a sixth sense about people. Even now, he studied Ethan with his intense beady eyes, almost as if he could feel Ethan's emotional turmoil.

"I'm okay, boy," Ethan whispered close to his ear. Still, Sherman continued to stare at him until Manny, the bartender, brought over the beer and a bowl of mixed nuts. And food could distract Sherman from just about anything.

While the pig devoured the nuts, Ethan turned back to Colt. "So I guess Darla is responsible for your Joseph's outfit?"

"I wish," Colt grumbled. "If Darla had made it, I

could've gotten out of it. But how do you tell your wife of two weeks—your pregnant wife, no less—that you aren't going to wear the costume that she went to all the trouble to make for you?"

"Well, I have to admit that the purple yarn belt is a little flashy," Ethan teased. "But other than that, it's not so bad."

Colt grumbled something under his breath about annoying farmers before Mayor Sutter spoke up.

"Well, I think you should be honored, son. It's not every day that a man gets to be Joseph to our little Hope's Mary. It just doesn't get much better than that." The look on Colt's face said that he could think of a lot of things that were better.

"Unless you're Slate and get to be Faith's Joseph." Kenny Gene shook his head, causing the halo that was attached to his cowboy hat to wobble. "Man, Pastor Robbins ain't gonna know what hit him when he sees our nativity scene."

Ethan figured that was an understatement. The pastor had been in Bramble for only a year and was still trying to adjust to west Texas life. Tonight might just send him straight back to California—or over the edge.

Colt downed the rest of his beer and slipped off the stool. Standing, the floor-length floral robes looked even more amusing.

"Come on, Sherman." Colt jerked the sheet from under the toe of his biker boots and picked up the staff that leaned against the bar. "Let's get this over with."

But the pig refused to budge from Ethan's lap. Even when Colt reached for him, he grunted out a refusal and continued to lick the nut bowl.

"Smart pig." Colt patted Sherman's head. "I wish I could get out of it so easily."

Ethan laughed. "I'll watch out for him, Colt. You just watch out for that lightnin' bolt when God notices who's playin' Joseph."

"Real funny, Ethan," Colt said before he headed for the door.

"We better get goin' too, Kenny," Mayor Sutter said. "Cindy Lynn will have our hides if we're not there for the big dress rehearsal." He glanced at Ethan. "You comin', son?"

Ethan held up his beer. "After I finish this."

Once they were gone, Ethan sipped his beer and tried to have fun. He failed miserably. Manny was busy closing up the bar for the night, which left Ethan no choice but to watch the Christmas movie on the television over the bar. It was the one where Jimmy Stewart gets to see how the world would change if he'd never been born. And it depressed the hell out of Ethan. Since he didn't have a brother to save from a frozen pond, wasn't married, and didn't have children, he figured the world would do nicely without him.

"Every time a bell rings, an angel gets its wings."

Instead of coming from the television, the words came from just over his shoulder. And Ethan turned to find Sam's sister, Marcy, standing there. She wasn't wearing a sheet or wings, just a red dress that revealed more of her large breasts than it covered. She reached up and flicked one of the jingle bells that hung from her earlobes, and the tinkling noise had her laughing.

"What do you know, Marcy Henderson is handin' out wings to angels," she said as she slung an arm over Ethan's shoulders.

"Hey, Marcy," he said. Since he'd never found Marcy attractive, Ethan had no problem talking to her. Too bad they'd never had anything to talk about. While Sam loved animals, football, the farm, and a multitude of other things that Ethan liked as well, Marcy seemed to like only two things—herself and men. And Ethan didn't care to talk about either subject. He glanced at the door and wondered how long it would take him to get to it. But before he could even gather Sherman up in his arms, Marcy took the seat next to him.

"Buy a girl a drink?"

Figuring a drink might get her arm off him, he motioned to Manny, who came over to take her order for "Sex on the Beach." Manny didn't even blink at the word, but Ethan's face burned with heat. Or maybe his embarrassment had more to do with the image that flashed into his brain. An image of his parents having sex on the beach in South Padre.

Geez, I really am losing it. He shook the image away, disrupting a sleeping Sherman and causing him to grunt in disapproval. But the sound achieved what Ethan wanted. Marcy removed her arm as she jumped off her stool.

She held a hand to her chest and waved one long red nail at Sherman. "Who let that thing in?"

"Marcy, you know animals have always been welcome in Boot's," Manny said as he placed her drink on one of those little napkins. "Especially if they know how to mind their manners." He reached out and patted the pig's head. "And Sherman always minds his manners." He arched a brow at Marcy. "Unlike some people I know."

Marcy ignored the comment and turned back to Ethan. "It figures that you would have some kind of animal with you. You and that sister of mine can't seem to stay away from them." Casting a wary look at Sherman, she eased back onto the stool. "I just had to suffer through two hours of Laverne and Daddy gushing over my sister becomin' a doctor. Not a real doctor, mind you, but an animal doctor. Geez, what was she thinkin'?"

Ethan wondered the same thing. What had Sam been thinking when she stole his profession? And why hadn't she ever mentioned the fact to him? Of course, she had written him a few times, and he'd never written her back. He had justified it by telling himself he was too busy with the farm, but in reality he'd been mad at her for leaving in the first place. Hell, he was still mad at her.

As he took another drink of beer, Marcy stuck out a leg and pointed to her red shoe. "Although I got me a pair of New York designer shoes out of the deal. 'Course, now I have to come up with a gift for Sam. Somethin' that's never been easy, considerin' she has the worse taste in clothes of any human I know. Unlike me, who happens to have unlimited fashion sense."

Ethan glanced over at Marcy. Fashion sense wasn't the only difference between her and Sam. Marcy didn't have a cute little button nose. Or a mouth shaped like a rosebud. Or a slim body with breasts that were...perfect. Two perfect swells that looked great in a red sweater. Or a snug Western shirt. Or a tiny, white drill team uniform.

Ethan's brow crinkled. What the hell? Where had all those images come from? He could understand the red sweater—he'd just seen her in that today—but the other clothes she hadn't worn since high school. And while he was puzzling over this, some locked chamber in his brain opened up and a wellspring of images flooded his mind. Images of Sam horseback riding, her cute butt nestled against the saddle and her breasts jiggling in a tight T-shirt. Leaning over the corral fence in a pair of tattered cutoffs. Stretched out in a pile of fresh-cut hay in faded jeans and a snap-down Western shirt that showed just a hint of cleavage.

And once those images ended, his mind filled with others. Sam helping him with the birth of a calf and laughing as the wobbly baby cow took its first steps. Sam eating water-melon and spitting the seeds at him. Sam catching her first fish. Sam helping his mother can pickles. Sam sending his father get-well cards when he'd fallen off the ladder.

Sam.

"See anything you like?"

Marcy's words made Ethan realize too late that, while he'd been thinking about Sam, he'd been staring at her sister's abundant breasts. As his face heated, she leaned closer.

"It's a shame, you know." She tapped his bottom lip with one long fingernail. "You really are cute, Ethan Miller. And I've often wondered about those big feet of yours. But as much as I love men, I can't bring myself to poach on my sister's property." She shook her head. "You would think that with all them good-lookin' college boys, she'd get over you and move on. But nooo, every time she calls she asks a million and one questions. Is he married? Does he have a girlfriend? Is his hair still as blond? His eyes still as green? Even when I mentioned that there was a distinct possibility that you were gay, she wouldn't shut up."

Suddenly Ethan couldn't get his mouth to work. All he could do was stare at Marcy as his heart thundered in his ears. Sam wasn't over him?

Completely unaware of his stunned confusion, Marcy took another sip of her drink and continued, "I figure it has to do with all those reruns of *Little House on the Prairie* she used to watch. She was obsessed with the episodes that featured that awkward, blond farmer dude. She specially liked the one where Half-pint finally gets him to notice she's a woman by wearing a pair of high-heeled—"

"Boots." The word slipped out of Ethan's mouth without much thought, especially considering he'd never watched that particular television show in his life.

Marcy shot a glance over at him. "I was going to say shoes." Her eyes crinkled like two squashed spiders. "You actually noticed what my sister was wearin'? What color was her sweater?"

If Marcy's plan was to confuse the hell out of him, she was doing a pretty damned good job. Between the things she'd said about Sam, *Little House on the Prairie*, and shoes, he didn't know what they were talking about. Still, he answered the question.

"Macintosh-apple red."

"And her eyes?" She leaned closer, her face starting to look intense and scary.

He swallowed. "Deep blue like the sky at twilight just after the last rays of the sun flicker out."

Marcy plopped back on her stool as if she couldn't quite believe his words. Ethan knew how she felt. He was pretty stunned himself. Which was why he almost fell off the stool when Marcy reached over and grabbed the front of his Western shirt.

"Now, I realize you like to do things nice and slow, Ethan," she said. "And I'll be the first to tell you that, on certain occasions, nice and slow works out real good. But this ain't one of those times. Sam plans on flyin' out day after tomorrow." She smiled slyly. "And if Half-pint is going to get her awkward farmer for Christmas, we have no time to lose."

Chapter Four

Y'all!" Cindy Lynn's high-pitched voice came through the bullhorn she held to her mouth, causing most of the costumed folks of Bramble to cover their ears. "Would you stop yammerin' and get in your positions? And, shepherds, remember, I said 'sore' afraid—that means you're so scared your muscles hurt. So look hurt!"

Sam didn't have to worry about looking "sore afraid." Instead, she had to worry about looking like a complete idiot in the sheep costume Rachel Dean had given her. At least she wasn't the only one. Being that Bramble was a cattle town, the shepherd's herd was made up of a good twenty townsfolk and a billy goat that was eating the hem of Moses Tate's wiseman robe as Moses slept in one corner of the stable.

"Good Lord." Shirlene Dalton sashayed up in a pretty white dress and huge wings, looking more like a voluptuous Victoria's Secret model than a member of the heavenly host.

"If Cindy Lynn doesn't put a sock in it, this angel is going to deliver something more than good tidin's." She winked at Sam. "Hey, honey, I heard you were back in town and pretty as ever." She reached out and adjusted the sheep ears on Sam's white hoodie. "Which is saying something in that getup."

Sam grinned. She had always liked Shirlene. Of course, everyone liked Shirlene. The woman was not only beautiful. She was sweet and fun-loving. Not to mention filthy rich. At the thought of all her oil money, Sam's grin faded.

"I was sure sorry to hear about Lyle's death, Shirlene," she said.

Shirlene's smile never even drooped, but her pretty green eyes held a sadness that spoke volumes. "Weren't we all, honey. Weren't we all." She flapped a hand that glittered with diamonds. "But let's not talk about me. How have you been? I can't tell you how proud your daddy is of you graduating with honors from that big, fancy school. And I know he's hoping—as we all are—that you'll start up your practice right here in Bramble."

For Sam, opening a practice in Bramble would be like a dream come true. Or half a dream. Her gaze swept over to the stable.

Ethan was there comforting the animals that had been tied to the rails of the wooden structure. He usually wore overalls, but tonight he was dressed in pressed jeans, a Western shirt, and a blue jean jacket. With the black felt hat pulled low on his head, he looked more like a cowboy than a farmer. At least he did until the baby pig popped his head out of the top of the jean jacket. Then Ethan just looked heartbreakingly perfect.

"If you feel that way about Ethan, honey, why'd you stay away so long?"

Sam looked back at Shirlene. Either Shirlene was extremely observant or Sam wasn't as good as she thought she was at hiding her feelings. Of course, it made no difference now. Tomorrow Sam would be on her way back to New York. The thought caused a lump to form in her throat that not even a hard swallow could remove.

"Maybe because Ethan doesn't feel the same way," Sam said as she plucked at the lumpy cotton batting that covered her sweatshirt.

"Then change his mind."

Sam shook her head. "You don't know Ethan. He might be sweet, but he's as stubborn as they come."

Shirlene snorted. "Believe me, honey. There was no one more stubborn than Lyle Dalton. The man was convinced I was too young for him. And if I'd waited around for him to make the first move, I'd still be waitin'." Her perfectly plucked eyebrows lifted. "Men don't know what they want until you show them."

That was easy for a woman who looked like Shirlene Dalton to say. One little twitch of her hips made men go wild. Sam, on the other hand, wasn't quite as well endowed. Besides, she'd thrown herself at Ethan more times than she could count without a reaction, and her self-esteem couldn't take any more rejection.

"Shirlene!" Cindy Lynn's voice echoed across the front lawn of the church. "I realize you think you deserve special treatment because you're hostin' the big Christmas party tomorrow night. But tonight I am in charge, and you need to be with the other angels on the bleachers instead of ca-vortin' with the sheep."

Shirlene's eyes narrowed. "If her husband doesn't wise up and slip that woman a Xanax, I'm going to do it for him.

Because if anyone should be tranquilized, it's Cindy Lynn."
She sashayed off just as Rye Pickett came hustling around
the corner of the church.

"Pastor Robbins is comin'!" he yelled. "He just pulled up
into the back parkin' lot and should be here any second."

"Places, y'all!" Cindy Lynn's voice screeched even
higher.

Not wanting to bring on Cindy Lynn's wrath, Sam hurried to get to her flock on the other side of the stable.
Unfortunately, as she came around the corner of the wooden
structure, she ran smack dab into Ethan. His hands slipped
around her waist, and she was lifted clean off her boots. As
always, the closeness of his large body sucked all the wind
right out of her.

Usually, he released her as soon as he touched her. But
this time, his hands tightened on her waist as he continued
to hold her inches from the ground. Beneath the brim of his
cowboy hat, his deep green eyes stared at her as if it was the
first time he'd seen her.

"Sam." The word hung in the cold night air between
them, not quite a question and not quite an answer.

"It looks like Ethan was just a late bloomer." Rye
Pickett's voice cut through Sam's daze. "First, I saw
him at Bootlegger's with Marcy, and now he's hittin' on
her sister."

Her eyes narrowed. Ethan had been at Bootlegger's with
Marcy?

Anger replaced desire, and she shoved against his
chest until he released her. She might've given him a
piece of her mind if the outside lights hadn't clicked
off, throwing the front lawn of the church into darkness.
The darkness worked much better than Cindy Lynn's
screeches. Before Sam could utter a word, she was being

pushed along with the crowd as people hurried to get to their spots.

Sam no longer felt like being part of the Christmas celebration. But just as she started to make her way through the flock, the doors of the church opened.

"Hit it, Darla!" Cindy Lynn yelled through the bullhorn.

The outside lights came back on along with about a zillion others. Twinkle lights covered all the bushes and trees. Multicolored lights lined the windows of the church. And a bunch of Japanese lanterns hung from the eaves of the stable Kenny Gene had built. A stable that was painted bright Bramble High purple and framed by fake palm trees covered in more lights.

" 'And there were in the same country,' " Cindy Lynn's voice rang out. "A country no doubt very similar to the great state of Texas." There was a mutter of "amens." " 'Shepherds abiding in the field, keepin' watch over their sheep by night.' "

The townsfolk sheep all started to baa, except for the goat who continued to munch on sleeping Moses' robe. " 'And, lo, the angel of the Lord came upon them.' " When nothing happened, Cindy yelled louder. "And an angel of the Lord came upon them!"

A spotlight suddenly shone on the stable. And with a creak of rope, Kenny Gene rose above the huge star on the very peak. He might've looked pretty authentic if not for the cowboy hat and the shovel of poop in his hand.

"I ain't ready," he said. But when Cindy Lynn hissed at him through the bullhorn, he stopped looking for a place to drop the pooper scooper and spoke his lines.

"Don't be scared, for I bring y'all tidin's of great joy that will be to all folks. For unto yew is born this day in the city of David, a Savior, which is Christ the Lord. And this will be a sign onto y'all: Yew shall find the babe wrapped in swallowin' clothes and lyin' in a manger."

On cue, Mary leaned over the tiny wooden manger. Since Faith and Hope looked identical in their costumes, Sam wasn't sure which Mary it was until Slate Calhoun stepped up. He looked down at Faith with so much love that tears welled up in Sam's eyes. But they evaporated quickly enough when Faith lifted the baby Jesus from the manger.

It had to be the scariest-looking doll Sam had ever seen in her life. With its vacant glass eyes and sneering expression, the porcelain face could only be described as demonic. And Rufus Miles, who was perched on Hope's hip waiting for his turn at baby Jesus, must've thought so too. Rufus took one look at the doll and let out a bloodcurdling howl that sent shivers up Sam's spine.

The howl frightened Lowell's cow so much that he jerked back on his lead rope and pulled a two-by-four loose. The board slapped Ethan's donkey, Buckwheat, in the butt, causing him to kick the back wall of the stable in self-defense. Japanese lanterns wobbled as the entire stable fell backward, the top point of the star of Bethlehem catching Kenny's arm and sending animal poop showering down. But it wasn't the poop that had the people scurrying for cover as much as the icy rain that suddenly fell from the sky. Josephs scooped up Marys, and along with wisemen, shepherds, sheep, and the heavenly host, made a mad dash for the church while Cindy Lynn screamed through the bullhorn.

"Come back here! We ain't finished!"

But a freezing rainstorm beat out a live nativity scene any day.

Instead of heading inside, Sam chased after the goat that was following Moses Tate into the church, still munching on his robes. And once she had the goat by his halter, she turned back to the collapsed stable to help Ethan with the other animals.

Lowell's barn was only a block and a half away from Main Street. But by the time she finished helping Ethan get the animals safely inside, she was soaked to the skin and freezing. She would've headed home for a hot bath if Ethan hadn't been blocking the only exit.

He held his hat in his hand, his wheat-colored hair wet and in need of a good trim. Droplets of water dripped down his cheeks and a square jaw that was as stubble-free as it had been earlier that morning. He opened his mouth to speak, but then closed it again.

"What, Ethan?" Sam propped a hand on her hip, squeezing water from her jeans. "Don't tell me you've suddenly lost the ability to talk to me. Especially since it's only women you're interested in that seem to make you stammer." She lifted her eyebrows, but the effect was lost beneath the soaked, sagging hood. She shoved it off her head. "Of course, I guess you didn't worry about talkin' when you were at Bootlegger's with my sister."

A baffled look spread across his face, and he rubbed the back of his neck. At one time, the gesture had been endearing. But now it just annoyed her.

"I guess not," he said. "Seein' as how me and your sister didn't do much talkin'."

Could blood vessels pop from mere anger? Sam thought it might be possible as she stared at Ethan and tried to keep from racing over and slapping him upside the head.

"Now, you and me, on the other hand," he continued, completely unaware of her anger, "we've always been able to talk up a storm. Something I've missed more than I was willing to admit." He glanced up at her, and his eyes crinkled at the corners. "Are you gonna hit me, Sammy?"

It took a real effort to unclench her fists.

"No, Ethan," she said. "I'm not going to hit you. I'm going to leave." She walked around him. But before she could get through the huge opening, the wide wooden doors slammed shut. At first she thought it was the wind. Except when she tried to push them open, neither would budge. She pressed an eye to a knothole just in time to see a devil in a red dress race off in the sleety night.

"Marcy!" she yelled as she rattled the doors. "This isn't funny." But her only answer was a shriek of laughter, followed by a "Merry Christmas, baby sister." Sam turned to find Ethan smiling. "You think it's funny, do you?"

"A little," he said. "And the Sam I used to know would've thought it was funny too. Did you lose all your humor?"

"No. I just acquired some taste."

Ethan's eyes ran over her soaked sheep sweatshirt, and his smile got even bigger. "I can see that."

She ignored the comment and turned back to the doors, but no matter how much she shoved, pulled, and kicked, they refused to open. Finally, she gave up and slumped down to the dirt floor. The baby pig came trotting over and sat down only inches away, staring at her with eyes that seemed a little too human. She might've questioned Ethan about the animal if the wind hadn't blown through the cracks in the door, causing her to shiver until her teeth chattered.

"We'd best get you out of those clothes," Ethan said. And when her gaze snapped up to him, he blushed. "Uhh . . . I mean you'd better get out of those clothes before you catch a chill."

"Are you proposing that I run around buck naked, Ethan?"

His face got even redder, but the look that entered his eyes wasn't what Sam would call embarrassment. More heat with a whole lot of sizzle. "Didn't you once ask me to do the same thing?"

"I did not," she protested as she climbed to her feet.

His blond eyebrows hiked up. "Sutter Springs. Your senior year."

The memory snapped back and hit her square between the eyes. "Oh. That time." She turned away and walked over to Buckwheat's stall. She held out her hand and waited for the donkey to nuzzle it before she stroked his big, soft ears. "That doesn't count. I was only a stupid kid who thought that skinny-dippin' might be fun."

The popping noise of snaps coming undone had her looking back at Ethan. Her breath got hung up in her chest. She had seen Ethan without a shirt many times over the years—farm work could be hot and sweaty. But that didn't prepare her for the sight that greeted her now. The skinny body of a boy had been replaced with the hard body of a man, and it took every ounce of willpower Sam had to keep her mouth from dropping open—or her body from melting into a puddle. Ethan had muscles. Lots and lots of tanned muscles.

"Fun." Ethan tossed the shirt into the corner with a flex of bicep. "I've been hearing that word a lot lately." He sat down on a milking stool and tugged off his boots before he removed first one sock and then the other. His big feet had her thinking about what Marcy had once told her, which in turn had a question popping out of her mouth.

"Is that what you were doing with Marcy at Bootlegger's, having a little fun?"

His gaze moved back over to her, and his head cocked to

one side. "Me and Marcy? I wouldn't call it fun—" A grin split his face. And Ethan's smiles had always made Sam's stomach feel all light and airy.

"Are you jealous, Sam?"

"Yeah, right." She turned back around to pet Buckwheat. "Why would I be jealous of you and my sister, Ethan?" Suddenly, Ethan was standing right behind her, his body radiating heat like a thoroughbred after a long, hard ride.

"I've never had fun with your sister, Sam," he said in his soft, soothing voice. "In fact, the only woman I've ever really had fun with is you."

Sam tried to remember how to breathe. "Me?"

He reached over her shoulder and stroked a hand down Buckwheat's forehead, and she found herself transfixed by the gentleness of his long fingers. "You don't think we had fun together?"

It was hard to think when surrounded by hard muscle and the scent of damp male. "N-no, it's not that. It's just that I didn't think you . . . noticed."

His hand slipped from Buckwheat and curled over the edge of the stall door. "I noticed. It seems I noticed a lot more than I thought I had." His breath fell warm against the top of her head. "I came by your house the night you left."

She turned around to find him much too close. "You came by my house?"

He nodded. "I wanted to say goodbye."

"But we'd said goodbye earlier that day."

He swallowed hard, and she watched his Adam's apple slide up and down his tanned throat. "Not the way I wanted to."

Her stomach did a crazy, little quivery thing that had nothing to do with her soaked sweatshirt. "And what way was that, Ethan?"

Heartbeats ticked off what seemed like a year's time before he lifted his hand and stroked a trail of heat down the chilled skin of her cheek. Using just one callused finger, he traced over her lips, pressing the bottom one down gently before letting it spring back up. She sucked in a breath and tried to steady her suddenly tipsy world, but then those long, golden-tipped lashes lifted, and she was lost all over again in the deep green of his eyes.

"Did you miss me, Sam?" His words came out rough and hushed. "Did you miss me as much as I missed you?" He dipped his head and replaced his finger with his lips. He was hesitant at first, taking small sweet sips that had Sam swaying on her boot heels. His large hand cradled her chin as his other dropped from the railing and settled on her hip to steady her.

"You're soaked," he whispered against her mouth. "Lift your arms."

She obeyed without the slightest hesitation. Numerous questions nibbled at the edges of her mind. But for now, she was exactly where she'd always wanted to be: in Ethan's arms. Although, once he pulled the hoodie over her head, she couldn't help but feel a slight twinge of embarrassment. Especially when his gaze settled on her simple white bra. She couldn't see his eyes beneath the thick fringe of his lashes, but it wasn't hard to figure out what he was thinking when his nostrils flared and his hands tightened in fists on her wet sweatshirt.

Only seconds later, the sweatshirt was tossed aside, and she found herself in the heated embrace of a man who was through with sweet kisses. His lips settled over hers in a hot, hungry assault that held not a trace of shy farm boy. While his tongue brushed against hers, his large hands encircled her waist just above the low rise of her jeans and tugged her closer to the heat of his wide chest. The kiss seemed to last for hours, yet ended much too soon.

He pulled back and rested his forehead against hers as their heartbeats echoed each other's. "Now, that was fun."

Chapter Five

Ethan planned on having a lot more fun. But then Sam shivered. He might've thought it had to do with his kisses if goose bumps hadn't covered the arms looped around his neck. Figuring his fun could wait, he pulled back. He glanced down at the soft flesh that swelled above her bra, and it took closing his eyes before he could finally step away. A stack of horse blankets sat on the seat of an old tractor, and he lifted a couple off the top.

"Here," he said as he handed her one of the blankets.

She took it slowly, her eyes wide and confused. He couldn't blame her. After Marcy had left the bar, he'd felt pretty dazed and confused himself. But surprisingly, it hadn't taken that long for things to fall into place. It seemed his hesitant heart just needed a little nudge.

Whistling, Ethan headed to the back of the barn to look for Lowell's space heater. He was on his second round of "Jingle Bells" when he finally located the heater behind an old bike and some farming tools. He quickly found an outlet and plugged it in, and then stretched out the extension cord as he walked back toward the front stalls.

Sam had wrapped a blanket around her and was hanging his wet shirt on the railing, right next to her sweatshirt, jeans, the white bra, and a teeny-tiny pair of flowered panties.

Ethan's whistling stopped mid "dashing through the snow" as his gaze flickered over her body. The blanket was tucked up under her arms and covered her from breastbone to calves. Still, all it would take was one yank to have her as nekked as the day she was born.

"Are you going to turn that on?"

The question brought his eyes back up to her pretty blue ones, and he thanked God for the cold, wet denim that kept embarrassment at bay. As it was, his voice still broke like a fourteen-year-old boy's when he spoke. "Y-yes, ma'am."

To hide his blush, he stepped into the only empty stall. It turned out to be not as empty as he thought. Sherman was stretched out in a pile of fresh hay. His gaze followed Ethan as he set the heater in one corner and clicked it on.

Sam peeked into the stall. "Why are you putting it in there?"

"It will conserve heat if we stay in a more confined space," he said as he walked back out and grabbed the rest of the blankets.

She clutched the blanket and looked around. "You don't think we'll have to spend the night here, do you? I mean, surely someone will come looking for us once the storm dies down."

"Probably." He tried not to look at her as he shooed Sherman over and spread the blanket out on the hay. "But just in case, we should be prepared."

Sherman snorted, and Ethan glanced over at the pig to

find those beady eyes pinned on him with something that could only be described as condemnation. Ethan tried to ignore the look and continue making the bed, but it wasn't easy. Especially when Ethan was lying through his teeth. Not lying exactly, more like failing to mention the fact that in the corner behind that tall stack of baled hay was a door. A door that Sam would have no problem walking through if she knew it was there. And Ethan wasn't ready to let her go. At least, not yet. Not until he got some answers.

And a few more kisses.

Unfortunately, when Sam stepped into the stall, she didn't look like she was in that big of a hurry to get back to the kissing portion of things.

"I'm not sleeping with you, Ethan Miller." Her arms were folded tightly over her chest.

Just the thought of sleeping with Sam had Ethan's face flaming. He cleared his throat and rubbed the back of his neck. "I was thinking that we would do more talking than...uhh...sleeping. But first I need to get out of these wet jeans. They're starting to itch worse than a bad case of fleas."

Her big blue eyes wandered down to the fly of his jeans. And figuring even wet denim wasn't going to keep him from embarrassing himself, he hurried out of the stall. It didn't take him long to get his jeans off and spread them out on the rail with the rest of their clothing. He left his boxers on and tucked a blanket around his waist, then went about shutting off all the lights. By the time he returned, Sam was sitting on the blanket he'd spread on the hay with Sherman's head in her lap, the orange coils of the space heater reflecting off her dark hair.

"It's almost like he can talk to you with his eyes," she said as she scratched between the pig's ears.

"He likes you," Ethan said as he took a seat across from

her. He hesitated only a moment before adding, "You'll make a good vet, Dr. Samantha Henderson."

Her gaze lifted to his. "Not better than you."

"I'm not a vet."

"Tell that to half the people in Haskins County." Her serious look filled his heart with pride. She glanced down at Sherman. "He is a pet, right?"

Ethan smiled. "You think I'm fattening him up for slaughter? You should know that I've never much cared for pork."

"Or beef, mutton, or venison."

"Shhh." He held a finger to his mouth. "Don't tell anyone. Josephine will have my hide if she ever found out I didn't like her chicken fried steak." He squinted at her. "How did you get out of eating it this morning?"

"I hid most of it in my napkin."

He laughed. "I bet we're the only two vegetarians in the entire state of Texas."

"No doubt." She smiled. It was a smile he hadn't seen enough of since she'd been back, and he basked in the glow like a cat in the sun.

"We know each other pretty well, don't we?" he said.

She looked down and ran her hand over Sherman's back. "I thought I knew you, but the Ethan I remember never hung out at Bootlegger's—or tried to kiss me."

"My mistake."

Her gaze snapped back over to him, but he continued before he lost his nerve. "Do you have a crush on me, Samantha Louise?"

Her mouth dropped open, right before her eyes scrunched up. "Marcy."

He felt like jumping up and punching the air like a ten-year-old. Instead he kept it together. "So you do have a crush on me."

"Did."

The word deflated him like an overfilled balloon. "So you don't now?"

"Kids have crushes, Ethan. In case you haven't figured it out by now, I'm a woman."

His gaze drifted down to the blanket that had inched low enough to reveal two soft swells of perfection. "Believe me, I've figured that one out." He lifted his eyes. "So how does the woman feel about me?"

Even in the dim light, he could tell that her face turned as red as an August tomato. "I-I . . . well, I think I . . ."

He smiled. "I'm the one who stammers, Sam. Don't you start." He scooted closer until their knees touched, and took her hand. It was much smaller and softer than his with smooth close-clipped nails. And he couldn't help lifting it and brushing his lips over the tiny blue veins that pulsed in her wrist. "How about if we take it slower, sort of like we did when you were learning to ride? Do you like me?"

"Of course I like you, Ethan."

The quick reply had him grinning like a fool. "What do you like about me?"

She stared down at their clasped hands for what seemed like forever before answering. "I like that you don't take anything for granted. Not the sun, or the rain, or a friendship. I like the way you treat animals and people, with love and understanding. And I like that you rarely lose your temper. Even when I couldn't do something, you never got mad and started screaming. You just showed me again until I got it right." Her gaze lifted. Her deep blue eyes uncertain. "Do you like me?"

Like wasn't really the word, but he also didn't want to scare her off.

"Yes," he said as he caressed her palm with his thumb.

"I like you, Sam Henderson. I like that you never made me feel stupid because I do things slower than most folks. And I liked that no matter what I was doing—mucking out a stall or weeding a garden—you joined right in and helped me. And I like the way you treat animals. And the way you don't like to hurt people's feelings. But mostly, I liked the way you looked in your drill team uniform."

She sat up, dislodging Sherman's head. "My what?"

He waved his hand at her body. "That tiny little skirt and white top that you wore when you were on the drill team."

"When I was seventeen, Ethan Miller?" A smile eased over her face. "Why, you pervert."

"I was, you know. As hard as I tried, I couldn't get the thought of those can-can kicks out of my mind."

She shook her head. "Now you tell me. Do you realize how hard I worked to get you to notice me? How many excuses I came up with to try to get you to touch me—to kiss me?"

"You're five years younger than I am," he said. "I guess I was waiting until you grew up."

"I was eighteen for six months before I left. Why didn't you do anything then?"

The hurt in her eyes was like a swift kick to his stomach, and it brought with it all the pain he'd felt when she left. A pain he'd tried to ignore by pretending that what he felt for Sam had been nothing more than friendship.

"I guess I was scared. Since I had never had a girlfriend before, I didn't understand my emotions. All I knew was that I didn't want you to go. But once I was standing on your front porch, staring at your doorbell, it seemed like a pretty selfish reason to keep you in Bramble."

"I would've stayed, Ethan," she whispered. "For you, I would do just about anything."

He released her hand and rose to his knees, pulling her up with him. "Then don't go, Sam." He pulled her into his arms and spoke against her damp hair. "Stay here in Bramble."

"Why?" The word came out muffled against his throat, and she pulled back and repeated it. "Why do you want me to stay, Ethan?"

For a man who had trouble talking to women, the words slipped out without a hitch. "Because I love you, Sam Louise. And if you leave, I'll be forced to follow you to New York, where I'll be a fish out of water if ever there was one."

She smiled up at him. "I don't want to go back to New York. I want to live on a farm in my hometown with the man I love."

He kissed her then, and her mouth opened up for him like a flower to a bee. Her hands slipped around his neck, and she pulled him closer, close enough to realize that scratchy wool blankets no longer stood between them. The shock of skin against skin had them both pulling back. Sam's eyes were wide and innocent, while Ethan's couldn't help dropping down to sweet raspberry-topped peaches that trembled from her quickened breath.

"I've never been with a man," she said.

Her words had his heartbeat tripling, and his gaze sliding back up to her eyes. A smile broke out on his face, a smile he felt all the way down to his toes.

"And I've never been with a woman," he said. Her eyes widened even more, but before the questions could start, he kissed her. Not a hungry kiss that would lead to hours of unbridled passion, just a sweet kiss that tasted of springtime and promises yet to keep. Pulling back from that kiss was one of the hardest things Ethan had ever done. He reached down and lifted the blanket around her and, after a brief, heated slide of knuckles against soft breast, tucked it neatly into place.

"You're not going to make love to me, Ethan?" She looked so disappointed and hurt that he almost gave in. But if he'd learned anything on the farm, it was that time and patience always produced the best harvests.

"Oh, I'm going to make love to you, Sam. I'm going to love you like no man has ever loved a woman. But since this is our first go-around, I figure we shouldn't put the cart before the horse."

Her brow knotted. "And just what does that mean, Ethan Michael?"

"I want to court you. I want to bring you flowers, and sit on your porch swing, and see how many kisses I can swipe before your daddy comes out and tells me to leave. I want to take you to the movies, and football games, and maybe just into town to show off my girl."

If it wasn't for her big smile, Ethan might've been worried about the tears that trickled down Sam's cheeks. But since his own eyes brimmed, he figured he understood and merely cradled her chin and kissed them away.

"And after I've made up for all the missed opportunities of my youth—including taking a few college courses, I'm going to make you my wife. In name. Soul. And body."

"Oh, Ethan." She threw herself into his arms, knocking him back to the hay as she covered his face with kisses.

"Enough." He laughed. "If you keep this up, I won't be responsible for what happens."

She gave him one last kiss on the very tip of his nose before settling down in the hay next to him. Ethan probably should tell her about the door so they could get dressed and get back to the church. And in a few minutes, he would. But for now he just wanted to savor the moment. To lie there in the sweet-smelling hay with the girl he'd always loved, and the woman he'd never expected.

Sherman trotted over and nosed his way between them. When he had snuffled around until he was comfortable, he looked up at Ethan.

And damned if that baby pig didn't wink.

*   *   *

"Shhh." Pastor Robbins held a finger to his mouth. "I've found them."

Most of the town crowded in through the big barn doors, taking turns peeking at the two sleeping forms curled together in the stall.

"Poor things are out cold," Rachel Dean said. " 'Course, I can't say as I blame them. Live nativity scenes are more exhaustin' than a person thinks."

"Too bad all the hard work was for nothin'." Cindy Lynn glared at Rye Pickett. "Pastor Robbins didn't even get to see our performance."

"Well, it ain't my fault," Rye defended himself. "He did pull up in the back. I can't help it if Rachel Dean had to go inside to the bathroom and chose that moment to come out the front door of the church."

"When a girl's gotta go, a girl's gotta go," Rachel said.

Kenny Gene pushed his way through the group, smacking everyone with his large wings as he went. "Except now that the stable's all busted to smithereens, the pastor ain't gonna get his live nativity scene."

The entire town looked forlorn until the young pastor spoke.

"I don't know about that, Kenny." He glanced down in the stall at Ethan and Sam. "I think I'm looking at one right now."

"What do you mean, pastor?" Rachel Dean craned her

neck to get a better look in the stall. "You mean Ethan and Sam? But then that would mean that Sherman is..."

Harley Sutter took off his wiseman crown and scratched his head. "Well, that pig does have a pure heart."

"As pure as they come." Moses Tate rubbed the sleep from his eyes. "And he sure ain't as loud as that Rufus Miles."

"Well, I'm not buyin' it," Cindy Lynn said. "Joseph and Mary weren't cuddled together like a couple of spoons in a drawer. They were kneelin' over the baby Jesus, givin' him his due respect."

"You're right, Cindy Lynn," Pastor Robbins said. "But doesn't it also make sense that Joseph and Mary were tired? They had traveled a long way, and Mary had just given birth. So it seems reasonable that they would lie down in the hay to sleep that first Christmas night so long ago. And that Joseph, being filled with love for his new family, would've placed a protective arm around them and pulled them close—just like Ethan has done with Sam and Sherman. Because isn't that what Christmas is all about—love and family?"

Kenny Gene looked at Pastor Robbins. "And the folks of Bramble are family, ain't we, Pastor?"

"We sure are, Kenny. Everyone on the face of the earth is part of God's family."

Kenny smiled, and his shoulders lifted, causing his wings to expand. The storm had passed, and the clear night sky filled the opened barn doors, casting Kenny in soft starlight.

"'And suddenly there was with the angel a multitude of the heavenly host praisin' God, and sayin', Glory to God in the highest, and on earth peace, and goodwill toward men.'"

Read more about Bramble, Texas, in Katie's
Deep in the Heart of Texas series:

Going Cowboy Crazy
Make Mine a Bad Boy
Catch Me a Cowboy
Trouble in Texas
Flirting with Texas
A Match Made in Texas
The Last Cowboy in Texas

About the Author

Katie Lane is the *USA Today* bestselling author of the Deep in the Heart of Texas, Hunk for the Holidays, Overnight Billionaire, and Tender Heart Texas series. Katie lives in Albuquerque, New Mexico, and when she isn't writing, enjoys reading, going to the gym, golfing, traveling, or just snuggling next to her high school sweetheart and a cairn terrier named Roo. Katie loves to hear from her readers and can be found at www.katielanebooks.com, Twitter @ktlane3, and Facebook.com/katielaneauthor.

Looking for more Cowboys?
Forever brings the heat with these sexy studs.

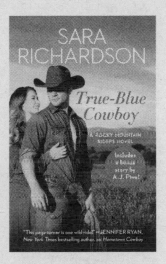

True-Blue Cowboy
By Sara Richardson

Everly Brooks wants nothing to do with her sexy new landlord, but when he comes to her with a deal she can't refuse, staying away from him is not as easy as it seems.

Tough Luck Cowboy
By A.J. Pine

Rugged and reckless, Luke Everett has always lived life on the dangerous side—until a rodeo accident leaves his career in shambles. But life for Luke isn't as bad as it seems when he gets the chance to spend time with the woman he's always wanted but could never have.

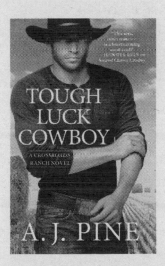

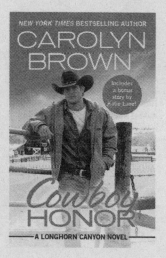

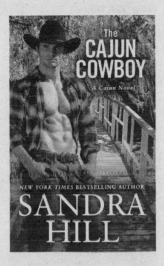
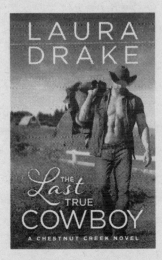

Look for more at: forever-romance.com

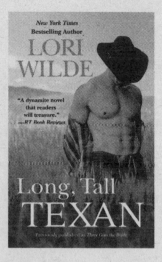

Long, Tall Texan
By Lori Wilde

With an altar to avoid and a cop to dream of, Delany Cartwright is a runaway bride who hopes a little magic will unveil the true destiny of her heart. But be careful what you wish for... (Previously published as *There Goes the Bride*)

Cowboy Brave
By Carolyn Brown

After meeting a handsome cowboy who literally sweeps her off her feet, Emily Thompson starts to wonder if the way to fix her broken heart is to fall in love.

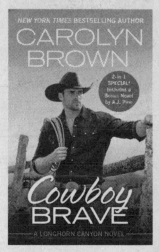